The Coming Conquest of England

August Niemann

Contents

THE COMING CONQUEST
OF ENGLAND

BY

August Niemann

AUTHOR'S PREFACE

I recall to mind a British colonel, who said to me in Calcutta: "This is the third time that I have been sent to India. Twenty-five years ago, as lieutenant, and then the Russians were some fifteen hundred miles from the Indian frontier; then, six years since, as captain, and the Russians were then only five hundred miles away. A year ago I came here as lieutenant-colonel, and the Russians are right up to the passes leading to India."

The map of the world unfolds itself before me. All seas are ploughed by the keels of English vessels, all coasts dotted with the coaling stations and fortresses of the British world-power. In England is vested the dominion of the globe, and England will retain it; she cannot permit the Russian monster to drink life and mobility from the sea.

"Without England's permission no shot can be fired on the ocean," once said William Pitt, England's greatest statesman. For many, many years England has increased her lead, owing to dissensions among the continental Powers. Almost all wars have, for centuries past, been waged in the interests of England, and almost all have been incited by England. Only when Bismarck's genius presided over Germany did the German Michael become conscious of his own strength, and wage his own wars.

Are things to come to this pass, that Germany is to crave of England's bounty--her air and light, and her very daily bread? or does their ancient vigour no longer animate Michael's arms?

Shall the three Powers who, after Japan's victory over China, joined hands in the treaty of Shimonoseki, in order to thwart England's aims, shall they--Germany, France, and Russia--still fold their hands, or shall they not rather mutually join them in a common cause?

In my mind's eye I see the armies and the fleets of Germany, France, and Russia moving together against the common enemy, who with his polypus arms enfolds the globe. The iron onslaught of the three allied Powers will free the whole of Europe from England's tight embrace. The great war lies in the lap of the future.

The story that I shall portray in the following pages is not a chapter of the world's past history; it is the picture as it clearly developed itself to my mind's eye, on the publication of the first despatch of the Viceroy Alexieff to the Tsar of Russia. And, simultaneously like a flash of lightning, the telegram which the Emperor William sent to the Boers after Jameson's Raid crosses my memory--that telegram which aroused in the heart of the German nation such an abiding echo. I gaze into the picture, and am mindful of the duties and aims of our German nation. My dreams, the dreams of a German, show me the war that is to be, and the victory of the three great allied nations. Germany, France, and Russia--and a new division of the possessions of the earth as the final aim and object of this gigantic universal war.

THE AUTHOR.

TRANSLATOR'S NOTE

This volume is the authorised translation of Der Weltkrieg deutsche Traume (F. W. Vobach and Co., Leipsic). The translator offers no comment on the day-dream which he reproduces in the English language for English readers. The meaning and the moral should be obvious and valuable.

LONDON, September, 1904.

I
THE COUNCIL OF STATE

It was a brilliant assemblage of high dignitaries and military officers that had gathered in the Imperial Winter Palace at St. Petersburg. Of the influential personages, who, by reason of their official position or their personal relations to the ruling house, were summoned to advise and determine the destiny of the Tsar's Empire, scarcely one was absent. But it was no festal occasion that had called them here; for all faces wore an expression of deep seriousness, amounting in certain cases to one of grave anxiety. The conversation, carried on in undertones, was of matters of the gravest import.

The broad folding-doors facing the lifesize portrait of the reigning Tsar were thrown wide open, and amid the breathless silence of all assembled, the grey-headed President of the Imperial Council, Grand Duke Michael, entered the hall. Two other members of the Imperial house, the Grand Dukes Vladimir Alexandrovitch and Alexis Alexandrovitch, brothers of the late Tsar, accompanied him.

The princes graciously acknowledged the deep obeisances of all present. At a sign from the Grand Duke Michael, the whole company took their places at the long conference table, covered with green cloth, which stood in the centre of the pillared hall. Deep, respectful silence still continued, until, at a sign from the President, State Secretary Witte, the chief of the ministerial council, turned to the Grand Dukes and began thus:--

"Your Imperial Highnesses and Gentlemen! Your Imperial Highness has summoned us to an urgent meeting, and has commissioned me to lay before you the reasons for, and the purpose of, our deliberations. We are all aware that His Majesty the Emperor, our gracious Lord and Master, has declared the preservation of the peace of the world to be the highest aim of his policy. The Christian idea that mankind should be 'ONE fold under ONE shepherd' has, in the person of our il-lustrious ruler, found its first and principal representative here on earth. The league of universal peace is solely due to His Majesty, and if we are called upon to present to our gracious Lord and Master our humble proposals for combating the danger which immediately menaces our country, all our deliberations should be inspired by that spirit which animates the Christian law of brotherly love."

Grand Duke Michael raised his hand in interruption. "Alexander Nicolaievitch," he said, turning to the Secretary, "do not omit to write down this last sentence WORD FOR WORD."

The Secretary of State made a short pause, only to continue with a somewhat louder voice and in a more emphatic tone--

"No especial assurance is required that, in view of this, our noble liege lord's exalted frame of mind, a breach of the world's peace could not possibly come from our side. But our national honour is a sacred possession, which we can never per-mit others to assail, and the attack which Japan has made upon us in the Far East forced us to defend it sword in hand. There is not a single right-minded man in the whole world who could level a reproach at us for this war, which has been forced upon us. But in our present danger a law of self-preservation impels us to inquire whether Japan is, after all, the only and the real enemy against whom we have to defend ourselves; and there are substantial reasons for believing that this question should be answered in the negative. His Majesty's Government is convinced that we are indebted for this attack on the part of Japan solely to the constant enmity of England, who never ceases her secret machinations against us. It has been Eng-land's eternal policy to damage us for her own aggrandisement. All our endeavours to promote the welfare of this Empire and make the peoples happy have ever met with resistance on the part of England. From the China Seas, throughout all Asia to the Baltic, England has ever thrown obstacles in our way, in order to deprive us of the fruits of our civilising policy. No one of us doubts for a moment that Japan is, in reality, doing England's work. Moreover, in every part of the globe where our in-terests are at stake, we encounter either the open or covert hostility of England. The complications in the Balkans and in Turkey, which England has incited and fos-tered by the most despicable methods, have simply the one object in view--to bring us into mortal conflict with Austria and Germany. Yet nowhere are Great Britain's real aims clearer seen than in Central Asia. With indescribable toil and with untold sacrifice of treasure and blood our rulers have entered the barren tracts of country lying between the Black Sea and the Caspian, once inhabited by semibarbarous tribes, and, further east again, the lands stretching away to the Chinese frontier and the Himalayas, and have rendered them accessible to Russian civilisation. But we have never taken a step, either east or south, without meeting with English opposition or English intrigues. To-day our frontiers march with the frontier of British East India, and impinge upon the frontier of Persia and Afghanistan. We have opened up friendly relations with both these states, entertain close commercial intercourse with their peoples, support their industrial undertakings, and shun no sacrifice to make them amenable to the blessings of civilisation. Yet, step by step, England endeavours to hamper our activity. British gold and British intrigues have succeeded in making Afghanistan adopt a hostile attitude towards us. We must at last ask ourselves this question: How long do we intend to look on quietly at these undertakings? Russia must push her way down to the sea. Millions of strong arms till the soil of our country. We have at our own command inexhaustible treasures of corn, wood, and all products of agriculture; yet we are unable to reach the markets of the world with even an insignificant fraction of these fruits of the earth that Providence has bestowed, because we are hemmed in, and hampered on every side, so long as our way to the sea is blocked. Our mid-Asiatic possessions are suffocated from want of sea air. England knows this but too well, and therefore she devotes all her energies towards cutting us off from the sea. With an insolence, for which there is no justification, she declares the Persian Gulf to be her own domain, and would like to claim the whole of the Indian Ocean, as she already claims India itself, as her own exclusive property. This aggression must at last be met with a firm 'Hands off,' unless our dear country is to run the risk of suffering incalculable damage. It is not we who seek war; war is being forced upon us. As to the means at our disposal for waging it, supposing England will not spontaneously agree to our just demands, His Excellency the Minister of War will be best able to give us particulars."

He bowed once more to the Grand Dukes and resumed his seat. The tall, stately figure of the War Minister, Kuropatkin, next rose, at a sign from the President, and said--

"For twenty years I served in Central Asia and I am able to judge, from my own experience, of our position on the south frontier. In case of a war with England, Afghanistan is the battle-ground of primary importance. Three strategic passes lead from Afghanistan into India: the Khyber Pass, the Bolan Pass, and the Kuram Valley. When, in 1878, the English marched into Afghanistan they proceeded in three columns from Peshawar, Kohat, and Quetta to Cabul, Ghazni, and Kandahar respectively. These three roads have also been laid down as our lines of march. Public opinion considers them the only possible routes. It would carry me too far into detail were I to propound in this place my views as to the 'pros and cons' of this accepted view. In short, we SHALL find our way into India. Hahibullah Khan would join us with his army, 60,000 strong, as soon as we enter his territory. Of course, he is an ally of doubtful integrity, for he would probably quite as readily join the English, were they to anticipate us and make their appearance in his country with a sufficiently imposing force. But nothing prevents our being first. Our railway goes as far as Merv, seventy-five miles from Herat, and from this central station to the Afghan frontier. With our trans-Caspian railway we can bring the Caucasian army corps and the troops of Turkestan to the Afghan frontier. I would undertake, within four weeks of the outbreak of war, to mass a sufficient field army in Afghanistan round Herat. Our first army can then be followed by a ceaseless stream of regiments and batteries. The reserves of the Russian army are inexhaustible, and we could place, if needs be, four million soldiers and more than half a million of horses in the field. However, I am more than doubtful whether England would meet us in Afghanistan. The English generals would not, in any case, be well advised to leave India. Were they defeated in Afghanistan only small fragments of their army at most would escape back to India. The Afghans would show no mercy to a fleeing English army and would destroy it, as has happened on a previous occasion. If, on the other hand, which God forbid! the fortune of war should turn against us, we should always find a line of retreat to Turkestan open and be able to renew the attack at pleasure. If the English army is defeated, then India is lost to Great Britain; for the English are, in India, in the enemy's country; as a defeated people they will find no support in the Indian people. They would be attacked on all sides by the Indian native chieftains, whose independence they have so brutally destroyed, at the very moment that their power is broken. We, on the other hand, should be received with open arms, as rescuers of the Indian people from their intolerable yoke. The Anglo-Indian army looks on paper much more formidable than it really is; its strength is put at 200,000 men, yet only one-third of this number are English soldiers, the rest being composed of natives. This army, moreover, consists of four divisions, which are scattered over the whole great territory of India. A field army, for employment on the frontier or across it, cannot possibly consist of more than 60,000 men; for, considering the untrustworthiness of the population, the land cannot be denuded of its garrisons. As a result of what I have said, I record my conviction that the war will have to be waged in India itself, and that God will give us the victory."

The words of the General, spoken in an energetic and confident tone, made a deep impression upon his hearers; only respect for the presence of the Grand Dukes prevented applause. The greyhaired President gave the Minister of War his hand, and invited the Minister for Foreign Affairs to address them.

"In my opinion," said the diplomatist, "there is no doubt that the strategical opinions just delivered by His Excellency the Minister for War are based upon an expert's sound and correct estimate of the circumstances, and I also am certain that the troops of His Majesty the Tsar, accustomed as they are to victory, will, in the event of war, soon be standing upon the plain of the Indus. It is also my firm conviction that Russia would be best advised to take the offensive as soon as ever the impossibility of our present relations to England has been demonstrated. But whoever goes to war with England must not look to one battleground alone. On the contrary, we must be prepared for attacks of the most varied kinds, for an attack upon our finances, to begin with, and upon our credit, as to which His Excellency Witte could give better information than I could. The Bank of England, and the great banking firms allied with it, would at once open this financial campaign. Moreover, a ship sailing under the Russian flag would hardly dare show itself on the open seas, and our international trade would, until our enemy had been crushed, be absolutely at a standstill. Moreover, more vital for us than considerations of this sort would be the question: What of the attitude of the other great Powers? England's political art has, since the days of Oliver Cromwell, displayed itself chiefly in adroitly making use of the continental Powers. It is no exaggeration to say that England's wars have been chiefly waged with continental armies. This is not said in depreciation of England's military powers. Wherever the English fleet and English armies have been seen on the field of battle, the energy, endurance, and intrepidity of their officers, sailors, and soldiers have ever been brilliantly noticeable. The traditions of the English troops who, under the Black Prince and Henry V., marched in days of yore victorious through France, were again green in the wars in the eighteenth century against France and against Napoleon. Yet infinitely greater than her own military record has been England's success in persuading foreign countries to fight for her, and in leading the troops of Austria, France, Germany, and Russia against each other on the Continent. For the last two hundred years very few wars have ever been waged without England's co-operation, and without her reaping the advantage. These few exceptions were the wars of Bismarck, waged for the advantage and for the glory of his own country, by which he earned the hatred of every good Englishman. While the continent of Europe was racked by internal wars, which English diplomacy had incited, Great Britain acquired her vast colonial possessions. England has implicated us too in wars which redounded to her sole advantage. I need only refer to the bloody, exhausting war of 1877-8, and to the disastrous peace of San Stefano, where England's intrigues deprived us of the price of our victory over the Crescent. I refer, further, to the Crimean War, in which a small English and a large French army defeated us to the profit and advantage of England. That England, and England alone, is again behind this attack upon us by Japan has been dwelt upon by those who have already addressed you. Our enemies do not see themselves called upon to depart in the slightest degree from a policy that has so long stood them in such good stead, and it must, therefore, be our policy to assure ourselves of the alliance, or at least, where an alliance is unattainable, of the benevolent neutrality of the other continental Powers in view of a war with England. To begin with, as regards our ally, the French Republic, a satisfactory solution of our task in this direction is already assured by the existing treaties. Yet these treaties do not bind the French Government to afford us military support in the case of a war which, in the eyes of shortsighted observers, might perhaps be regarded as one which we had ourselves provoked. We have accordingly opened negotiations through our Ambassador with M. Delcasse, the French Minister for Foreign Affairs, and with the President of the Republic himself. I have the supreme satisfaction of being in a position to lay before you the result of these negotiations in the form of a despatch just received from our Ambassador in Paris. It runs, in the main, as follows: 'I hasten to inform Your Excellency that, in the name of the French Republic, M. Delcasse has given me the solemn assurance that France will declare war upon England at the moment His Majesty the Tsar has directed his armies to march upon India. The considerations which have prompted the French Government to take this step have been further explained to me by M. Delcasse in our conference of this day, when he expressed himself somewhat as follows: 'Napoleon, a hundred years ago, perceived with rare discernment that England was the real enemy of all continental nations, and that the European continent could not pursue any other policy but to combine in resisting that great pirate. The magnificent plan of Napoleon was the alliance of France with Spain, Italy, Austria, Germany, and Russia, in order to combat the rapacity of England. And he would, in all probability, have carried his scheme through had it not been that considerations of domestic policy determined the Tsar Alexander I., in spite of his admiration for Napoleon's ability, to run counter to the latter's intentions. The consequences of Napoleon's defeat have shown themselves sufficiently clearly during the past hundred years in the enormous growth of the English power. The present political constellation, which in many respects is very similar to that of the year 1804, should be utilised to revive Napoleon's plan once more. Russia has, of course, the first and most vital interest in the downfall of England, for, so long as Great Britain controls all the seas and all the important coastlines, it is like a giant whose hands and feet are fettered. Yet France is also checked in her natural development. Her flourishing colonies in America and the Atlantic Ocean were wrested from her in the eighteenth century. She was ousted by this overpowering adversary from her settlements in the East Indies and--what the French nation feels perhaps most acutely--Egypt, purchased for France by the great Napoleon with the blood of his soldiers, was weaned away by English gold and English intrigues. The Suez Canal, built by a Frenchman, Lesseps, is in the possession of the English, facilitating their communications with India, and securing them the sovereignty of the world. France will accordingly make certain stipulations as the price of its alliance--stipulations which are so loyal and equitable that there is no question whatever of their not being agreed to on the part of her ally, Russia. France demands that her possessions in Tonking, Cochin China, Cambodia, Annam, and Laos shall be guaranteed; that Russia be instrumental in assisting her to acquire Egypt, and that it pledge itself to support the French policy in Tunis and the rest of Africa." In accordance with my instructions, I felt myself empowered to assure M. Delcasse that his conditions were accepted on our side. In answer to my question, whether a war with England would be popular in France, the Minister said: "The French people will be ready for any sacrifice if we make Fashoda our war-cry. British insolence never showed itself more brutal and insulting than over this affair. Our brave Marchand was on the spot with a superior force, and France was within her rights. The simple demand of an English officer, who possessed no other force but the moral one of the English flag, compelled us, however, under the political circumstances which then obtained, to abandon our righteous claims, and to recall our brave leader. How the French people viewed this defeat has been plainly seen. The Parisians gave Marchand a splendid ovation as a national hero, and the French Government seriously contemplated the possibility of a revolution. We are now in a position to take revenge for the humiliation which we then endured, probably out of excessive prudence. If we inscribe the word FASHODA on the tricolour there will not be in the whole of France a man capable of bearing arms who will not follow our lead with enthusiasm." It appeared to me to be politic to assure myself whether the Government or the inspired press would not perhaps promise the people the recovery of Alsace-Lorraine as the price of a victorious issue of the war. But the Minister replied decidedly, "No. The question of Alsace-Lorraine," he declared, "must remain outside our view as soon as we make up our minds to go in for practical politics. Nothing could possibly be more fatal than to rouse bad blood in Germany. For the German Emperor is the tongue of the balance in which the destinies of the world are weighed. England in her own esteem has nothing to fear from him. She regards him more as an Englishman than a German. Her confidence in this respect must not be disturbed; it forms one of the props on which British arrogance supports itself. The everlasting assurances of the German Emperor, that he intends peace and nothing but peace, appear, of course, to confirm the correctness of this view. But I am certain that the Emperor William's love of peace has its limits where the welfare and the security of Germany are seriously jeopardised. In spite of his impulsive temperament, he is not the ruler to allow himself to be influenced by every expression of popular clamour, and to be driven by every ebullition of public feeling, to embark on a decisive course of action. But he is far-seeing enough to discern at the right moment a real danger, and to meet it with the whole force of his personality. I do not, therefore, look upon the hope of gaining him for an ally as a Utopian dream, and I trust that Russian diplomacy will join with ours in bringing this alliance about. A war with England without Germany's support would always be a hazardous enterprise. Of course we are prepared to embark upon such a war, alike for our friendship with Russia and for the sake of our national honour, but we could only promise ourselves a successful issue if all the continental great Powers join hands in this momentous undertaking."

Although the fact of an offensive and defensive alliance with France in view of a war with England could not have been unknown to the majority of the assembled company, yet the reading of this despatch, which was followed with breathless attention, evidently produced a deep impression. Its publication left no room for doubt that this war had been resolved on in the highest quarters, and although no loud manifestation of applause followed its reading, the illustrious assemblage now breathed freely, and almost all faces wore an expression of joyous satisfaction.

Only one man, with knitted brows, regarded the scene with serious disapproval. For decades past he had been regarded as the most influential man in Russia--as a power, in fact, who had constantly thwarted the plans of the leading statesmen and had carried his opinions through with unswerving energy.

This solitary malcontent was Pobiedonostsev, the Chief Procurator of the Holy Synod, who, despite his grey hairs, was detested only less than he was feared.

His gloomy mien and his shake of the head had not escaped the presiding Grand Duke, and the latter evidently considered it to be his duty to give this man who had enjoyed the confidence of three successive Tsars an opportunity of recording his divergent opinion.

At his summons the Chief Procurator arose, and, amid complete silence, said--

"It cannot be my duty to deliver an opinion as to the possibility or on the prospects of an alliance with Germany, for I am as little acquainted as any here present with the intentions and plans of the German Emperor. William II. is the greatest sphinx of our age. He talks much, and his speeches give the impression of complete sincerity; but who can guess what is really behind them? That he has formulated a fixed programme as his life's work, and that he is the man to carry it out, regardless whether public opinion is on his side or not, thus much appears to me to be certain. If the subjection of England is a part of his programme, then the hopes of the French Minister would, in fact, be no Utopia, only supposing that the Emperor William considers the present the most suitable time for disclosing to the world his ultimate aims. It would be the task of our diplomatic representative at the Court of Berlin to assure himself on this point. But it is quite another question whether Russia really needs an alliance either with Germany or with the Western Power just referred to, and my view of the case leads me to answer this question in the negative. Russia is, at the present time, the last and sole bulwark of absolutism in Europe, and if a ruler called by God's grace to the highest and most responsible of all earthly offices is to remain strong enough to crush the spirit of rebellion and immorality which here and there, under the influence of foreign elements, has shown itself in our beloved country, we must, before all things, take heed to keep far away from our people the poison of the so-called liberal ideas, infidelity, and atheism with which it seems likely to be contaminated from the West. In like manner, as we, a century ago, crushed the powerful leader of the revolution, so also shall we to-day triumph over our foe--we single-handed! Let our armies march into Persia, Afghanistan, and India, and lead throughout all Asia the dominion of the true faith to victory. But keep our holy Russia uncontaminated by the poison of that heretical spirit, which would be a worse foe than any foreign power can be."

He sat down, and for a moment absolute silence reigned. The Grand Duke made a serious face, and exchanged a few whispered words with both his nephews.

Then he said: "All the gentlemen who have here given us their views on the situation are agreed that a declaration of war upon England is an exceedingly lamentable but, under the circumstances, unavoidable necessity; yet before I communicate to His Majesty, our gracious Lord, this view, which is that of us all, I put to you, gentlemen, the question whether there is anyone here who is of a contrary opinion. In this case, I would beg of him to address us."

He waited a short while, but as no one wished to be allowed to speak, he rose from his chair, and with a few words of thanks and a gentle bow to the dignitaries, who had also risen in their places, notified that he regarded the sitting, fraught with momentous consequences for the destiny of the world, as closed.

II
THE OFFICERS' MESS

The place was Chanidigot, in British East India. The blinding brightness of the hot day had been immediately followed, almost without the transition to twilight, by the darkness of evening, which brought with it a refreshing coolness, allowing all living things to breathe again freely. In the wide plain, which served as the encampment ground for the English regiment of lancers, all was alive again with the setting of the sun. The soldiers, freed from the toil of duty, enjoyed themselves, according to their ideas and dispositions, either in playing cards, singing, or merrily drinking. The large tent, used as a messroom by the officers, also showed signs of life. Dinner was over, and a number of gentlemen sat down to a game of cards, as was their daily custom. But here the amusement was of a less harmless character than in the case of the private soldiers. For not innocent bridge, but "poker" was the order of the day, a game much affected in America and also in some parts of England, a game which is solely determined by chance together with a certain histrionic bluffing on the part of the players, and the stakes were rather high. It was mostly played by the younger gentlemen, who could not do without their nerve-tonic in the evenings, in the monotony of camp life. The older men sat apart at tables, talking and drinking whisky-and-soda, and smoking their short pipes. Amongst them there was also a gentleman in civilian dress. The hospitality with which he was treated showed that he was not one of the officers of the regiment, but their guest. The sound of his name--he was addressed as Mr. Heideck--would have betrayed his German origin, even had his appearance not proclaimed it. He was of but medium height, but athletic in build. His erect, soldiery bearing and the elasticity of his movements plainly betokened his excellent health and considerable bodily strength. A foreigner can hardly present better credentials to an Englishman than these qualities. Perhaps, more than anything else, it was his distinguished appearance, in conjunction with his amiable and thoroughly gentlemanly bearing, that had so quickly opened the usually very exclusive officers' circle to the young German, with his clever, energetic features, and his honest blue eyes.

Judged by his profession he did not, perhaps, belong to their society, according to the ideas of some of these gentlemen. It was known that he was travelling for a large commercial house in Hamburg. His uncle, the head of the house, imported indigo. And since the Maharajah of Chanidigot was the owner of very extensive indigo fields, young Heideck had been detained here a whole fortnight by commercial negotiations with the prince. He had succeeded, during this time, in gaining the lively sympathies of all, but particularly of the older British officers. In Indian garrisons every European is welcome. Heideck was also invited to those social functions at which the ladies of the regiment were present.

He had always refused an invitation to cards with polite firmness, and to-day also he was at most an uninterested and unconcerned spectator.

Presently the door of the tent opened and a tall, but extremely slim officer joined the circle of his comrades, jingling his spurs with a self-conscious, almost haughty attitude. He was in undress uniform and talked to one of the gentlemen, who addressed him as Captain Irwin, about just returning from a fatiguing ride for the inspection of an outpost. He demanded from one of the orderlies in attendance a refreshing drink, the favourite whisky-and-soda, then he drew close to the gaming-table.

"Room for a little one?" he asked. And place was readily made for him.

For a little while the game of poker went on in the same quiet way as before. But suddenly something extraordinary must have happened. All the gentlemen, except Captain Irwin and one of the players, laid down their cards, and the unpleasantly penetrating voice of Captain Irwin was heard.

"You are an old fox, Captain McGregor! But I am aware of your tricks and cannot be taken in by them. Therefore, once more, six hundred rupees!"

Every poker-player knows that, so far from being considered dishonourable, it is a chief sign of skill in the game, where each man plays for his own hand, for one to deceive the rest as to the value of the cards he holds. The name of "bluff," which has been given to this game, is itself sufficient to show that everyone has to try his best to puzzle his adversaries.

But this time Irwin appeared to have met his match in McGregor. For the Captain replied calmly: "Six hundred and fifty. But I advise you not to see me, Irwin."

"Seven hundred."

"Seven hundred and fifty."

"Thousand!" shouted Irwin with resounding voice, and leant back in his chair smiling, as if certain of victory.

"You had better consider what you are about," said McGregor. "I have given you warning."

"A convenient way to haul in seven hundred and fifty rupees. I repeat: A thousand rupees."

"One thousand and fifty!"

"Two thousand!"

All the gentlemen present in the tent had risen and stood round the two players, who, their cards concealed in their hands, watched each other with sharp glances. Hermann Heideck, who had stepped behind Irwin, noticed on the right hand of the Captain a magnificent diamond ring. But he also perceived, by the way the bright sparkle of the stone quivered, how the gambler's fingers trembled.

Captain McGregor turned to his companions. "I take the gentlemen to witness that I have advised my comrade Irwin not to see me at six hundred."

"To the devil with your advice!" Irwin interrupted almost furiously. "Am I a boy? Will you see me at two thousand, McGregor, or will you not?"

"Very well, since you insist upon it--three thousand."

"Five thousand."

"Five thousand five hundred."

"Ten thousand."

One of the higher officers, Major Robertson, laid his hand lightly upon the shoulder of the rash gambler.

"That is too much, Irwin. I do not care to interfere in these things, and since you do not belong to my regiment, I can only speak to you as a comrade, not as a superior. But I am afraid you will be in difficulties if you lose."

Angrily the Captain fired up--

"What do you mean by that, sir? If your words are intended to express a doubt as to my solvency--"

"Well! well--I did not mean to offend you. After all, you must know best yourself what you are justified in doing."

Irwin repeated with a defiant air--

"Ten thousand! I am waiting for your answer, McGregor."

The adversary remained as calm as before.

"Ten thousand five hundred."

"Twenty thousand!"

"Are you drunk, Irwin?" whispered the young Lieutenant Temple into the Captain's ear, from the other side. But he only glanced round with a furious look.

"Not more than you. Leave me alone, if you please."

"Twenty-one thousand," came the calm response from the other side of the table.

A short, awkward pause followed. Captain Irwin nervously gnawed his small dark moustache. Then he raised his slim figure and called out--

"Fifty thousand!"

Once more the Major considered it his duty to endeavour to stop the game.

"I object," he said. "It has been always a rule that the pool cannot be raised by more than a thousand rupees at a time. This limit has long since been passed."

A rude, hoarse laugh escaped Irwin's lips.

"It appears you want to save me, Major. But I am not in need of any saviour. If I lose I pay, and I don't understand why the gentlemen are so concerned on my behalf."

The Major, who at last saw that all his good endeavours were misplaced, shrugged his shoulders. Lieutenant Temple, however, thought he had a good idea, and with an apparently unintentional, though violent, movement pushed against the light camp-table, and sent ashtrays, bottles, glasses, and cards flying on the ground. But he did not gain anything by this, for the two players held their cards firmly in their hands, and did not allow this contretemps to disturb their sangfroid for a single moment.

"Fifty-one," said McGregor.

"Sixty."

"Sixty-one."

"Seventy."

"Seventy-one."

"Eighty."

"Eighty-one."

"A lakh!" cried Irwin, who was now pale from excitement.

"Really?" asked McGregor calmly, "that is a fine bid. A lakh--that is, reckoned at the present rate of exchange, 6,500 pounds sterling. You will be a wealthy man, Irwin, if you win. Now, then, I see you."

With trembling fingers, but with a triumphant look, the Captain laid down his cards.

"Straight flush," he said hoarsely.

"Yes, a strong hand," replied the other, smiling. "But which is your highest card?"

"The king, as you see for yourself."

"That's a pity, for I have also, as it happens, a straight flush, but mine is up to the ace."

Slowly, one after the other, he laid down his cards--ace of hearts, king of hearts, queen of hearts, knave of hearts, ten of hearts. One single exclamation of surprise came from the lips of the bystanders. None of them had ever seen the coincidence of such an extraordinary sequence.

Captain Irwin sat motionless for a moment, fixing his unsteady eyes straight upon his adversary's cards. Then he suddenly sprang up with a wild laugh, and left the tent with jingling steps.

"This loss spells ruin for Irwin," said the Major gravely. "He is not in a position to pay such a sum."

"With his wife's assistance he could," chimed in another; "but it would eat up pretty well the rest of her fortune."

"I call you, gentlemen, to witness that it is not my fault," said McGregor, who thought he perceived a certain degree of reproach in the faces of the bystanders; but all agreed with him.

Lieutenant Temple, who alone of all those present kept up a certain superficial friendship with Irwin, remarked, "Somebody must go after him to see that he does not do something foolish in his first excitement."

He turned as if to leave the room, but a call from McGregor stopped him.

"It will be no use, Temple, unless you are able to calm him in some way or other. In my opinion there is only one thing to do. He must be persuaded that the whole affair is only a joke, and that the cards had been shuffled beforehand."

The Lieutenant went back to the table.

"The suggestion of this way of putting it does you honour, Captain; only I have my doubts if any of us would have the courage to go to him with this manifest lie."

The silence of the others appeared to confirm this doubt, when the decisive voice of the German guest interrupted with--

"Will you entrust me, gentlemen, with this mission? I know Captain Irwin only slightly, it is true, and should have no reason to interfere with his private concerns; but I hear that it is his wife's property which has been at stake here, and as I consider Mrs. Irwin a very honourable lady I would gladly do my best to save her from such a heavy pecuniary loss."

McGregor held out his hand.

"You would place me under a great obligation, Mr. Heideck, if you could succeed in this matter, but I warn you that there is no time to lose."

Heideck quickly left the tent, but when he had come out into the delicious moonlight night the first thing that met his eye was Captain Irwin, some twenty yards distant, standing by his horse. The servant held the animal by the bridle, and Captain Irwin was about to mount. On coming nearer he saw the servant move off and perceived that Irwin held a revolver in his hand. With a quick motion he seized the officer's wrist.

"One moment, Captain Irwin."

Irwin started, turned round, and looked with fury at Heideck.

"I beg your pardon," said the German, "but you are labouring under a mistake, Captain. The game was all a jest; they were playing a trick upon you. The cards were arranged beforehand."

Irwin made no reply, but whistled to his servant and went back into the tent, revolver still in hand, without a single word to Heideck. Heideck followed. Both gentlemen stepped up to the card-table, and Irwin turned to McGregor.

"You tell me the game was all a got-up thing, do you?" he asked.

"As a lesson to you, Irwin--you who always plunge as a madman, and imagine yourself a good player, when you have not the necessary cold blood for gambling."

"Well," said Irwin, "that is a story that I will take care goes the round of all the garrisons in India, as an instance of kind comrade-like feeling, so that everyone may be warned against coming along here and being induced to take a hand. I never in my life came across a more despicable story; but it certainly is a lesson for me, that only honourable persons should be--"

"No, Captain Irwin," said McGregor, standing bolt upright, levelling at his in-sulter a withering look from his great blue eyes, "you should rather think of your poor wife, whom you would have made a pauper if this game had not been all a hoax."

Irwin reeled back; the revolver fell from his grasp.

"What," he gasped--"what do you mean? It was, then, no joke, after all. I, then, really lost the money? Oh, you--you--But what do you take me for? Be quite certain that I will pay. But," he cried, collecting himself, "I should like to know what the real truth is, after all. I ask this question of you all, and call you rogues and liars if you do not tell me the truth. Have I only really been played with, or has the game been a straightforward one?"

"Captain Irwin," replied the Major, advancing towards him, "I, as the senior, tell you, in the name of our comrades, that your behaviour would have been unpar-donable unless a sort of madness had seized you. The game was a straightforward one, and only the generosity of Captain McGregor--"

Irwin did not wait for the conclusion of the sentence, but, with a bound, was again outside the tent.

III

A RUSSIAN COMRADE

Hermann Heideck lived in a dak bungalow, one of those hotels kept going by the Government, which afford travellers shelter, but neither bed nor food. On returning home from the camp he found his servant, Morar Gopal, standing at the door ready to receive his master, and was informed that a newcomer had arrived with two attendants. As this dak bungalow was more roomy than most of the others, the new arrivals were able to find accommodation, and Heideck was not obliged, as is usual, to make way as the earlier guest for a later arrival.

"What countryman is the gentleman?" he inquired.

"An Englishman, sahib!"

Heideck entered his room and sat down at the table, upon which, besides the two dim candles, stood a bottle of whisky, a few bottles of soda-water and the inevitable box of cigarettes. He was moody and in a bad humour. The exciting scene in the officers' mess had affected him greatly, not on account of Captain Irwin, who, from the first moment of their acquaintance, was quite unsympathetic to him, but solely on account of the beautiful young wife of the frivolous officer, of whom he had a lively recollection from their repeated meetings in social circles. None of the other officers' wives--and there were many beautiful and amiable women among them--had made such a deep and abiding impression upon him as Edith Irwin, whose personal charms had fascinated him as much as her extraordinary intellectual powers had astonished him. The reflection that this graceful creature was fettered with indissoluble bonds to a brutal and dissolute fellow of Irwin's stamp, and that her husband would perhaps one day drag her down with him into inevitable ruin, awoke in him most painful feelings. He would so gladly have done something for the unhappy wife. But he was obliged to admit that there was no possibility for him, a stranger, who was nothing to her but a superficial acquaintance, to achieve anything in the way he most desired. The Captain would be completely justified in rejecting every uncalled-for interference with his affairs as a piece of monstrous impudence; and then, too, in what way could he hope to be of any assistance?

A sudden noise in the next room aroused Heideck from his sad reverie. He heard loud scolding and a clapping sound, as if blows from a whip were falling upon a bare human body. A minute later and the door between the rooms flew open and an Indian, dressed only in cummerbund and turban, burst into the room, as if intending to seek here protection from his tormentor. A tall European, dressed entirely in white flannel, followed at the man's heels and brought his riding-whip down mercilessly upon the naked back of the howling wretch. Heideck's presence did not, evidently, disturb him in the least.

At the first glance the young German perceived that his neighbour could not be an Englishman, as his servant had told him he was. His strikingly thin, finely-cut features, and his peculiarly oval, black eyes and soft, dark beard betrayed much more the Sarmatic than the characteristic Anglo-Saxon type.

The man's appearance did not make an unfavourable impression, but he could not possibly overlook his behaviour. Stepping between him and his victim he demanded, energetically, what this scene meant. The other, laughing, let drop the arm which had been again raised to strike.

"I beg your pardon, sir," he said with a foreign accent, "a very good boy, but he steals like a crow, and must have the whip occasionally. I am sure that he has concealed somewhere about him the five rupees which have been stolen from me again to-day." On saying this, as if he considered this information quite sufficient explanation, he again caught hold of the black fellow, and with a single wrench tore the turban from his head. From the white, red-bordered cloth a few pieces of silver fell and rolled jingling over the tiles; and at the same time a larger object fell at Heideck's feet. He picked it up and held in his hand a gold cigarette-case, the lid of which was engraved with a prince's coronet. On handing it to the stranger, the latter bowed his thanks and made his apologies like a man of good breeding. The Indian the while took the opportunity, in a few monkey-like bounds, to make good his escape. The sight of the coat-of-arms on the cigarette-case aroused in Heideck the desire to make nearer acquaintance with his impetuous neighbour. As though he had quite forgotten the extraordinary manner of his entrance into the room, he asked, blandly, if he might invite his neighbour, whom accident had thus thrust upon him, to a cigar and a "nightcap."

The other accepted the invitation with amiable alacrity. "You are also a commercial traveller, sir?" inquired Heideck; and on receiving an affirmative answer, continued, "we are then colleagues. Are you satisfied with your results here?"

"Oh, things might be better. There is too much competition."

"Cotton?"

"No. Bronze goods and silk. Have brought some marvellous gold ornaments from Delhi."

"Then probably your cigarette-case comes from Delhi also?" The oval eyes of the other shot over him in an inquiring glance.

"My cigarette-case? No--are you travelling perhaps in skins, colleague? Do you deal in Cashmir goats?"

"I have everything. My house trades in everything."

"You do not come from Calcutta?"

"No! not from Calcutta."

"Bad weather down there. All my leather is spoilt."

"Is it so damp there?"

"Vapour bath, I tell you; a real vapour bath!"

Heideck had long since made up his mind that he had a Russian before him. But, in order to be quite on the safe side, he made a jocular remark in Russian. His new acquaintance looked up astonished.

"You speak Russian, sir?"

"A little."

"But you are no Russian?"

"No; I am a German, who, during a temporary stay in Russia, have picked up a little knowledge of languages. We merchants go about a lot."

The gentleman who, according to his statement, travelled in bronze and silk was evidently delighted to hear in a place where he had least expected it the familiar tones of his mother tongue, and Heideck did his utmost, with almost an excess of zeal, to keep him in good humour. He called his servant and bade him get some hot water.

"It's quite chilly to-night," he said, turning to his guest. "A hot brandy-and-water is not to be despised."

"Ah," said the Russian, "stop a moment; better chuck the water away and let something more palatable take its place."

He went into his room and returned immediately with a bottle of sherry and two bottles of champagne.

"I will, with your permission, brew in this kettle a bowl in Russian fashion. Sugar must go in too; for this champagne, prepared for English taste, is too dry, and must be sweetened to make it palatable for us." He poured the bottle of cognac, which the servant had brought, together with the sherry into the champagne and filled the glasses.

In German fashion the two gentlemen touched glasses. As they did so, Heideck once more attentively observed his new acquaintance. The lurking expression with which he felt that the eyes of the other were fixed upon him made him start for a moment. What if the Russian perhaps only had the same intention as himself, and only wanted to make his tongue wag with the champagne? At all events, he was now on his guard.

"May I ask you to try one of my Havannah cigars?" asked the Russian in passing his cigar-case. "The Indian cigars are not bad and very cheap. The Beaconsfield is my favourite brand. But now and then one must smoke something else for a change."

Heideck accepted with thanks, and now began a fairly good booze, in which the Russian set the example. He was, however, evidently not so proof against the effects of the tasty and strong drink as was the German. With each minute he became more loquacious, and soon began to address his new friend as "Dear old chap," and to narrate all manner of more or less compromising stories. He also, induced by several adroit questions on the part of Heideck, began to prate of his family affairs. He mocked at an old aunt of his, who was wont to cover her hair with roses the better to conceal bald spots, and added that this aunt was a great favourite at the Court of the Tsar, on account of her incomparable gossiping stories. It apparently never occurred to him that such intimate family relations were a rather strange subject for conversation in a commercial traveller.

In the course of his conversation he mentioned that not long before he had been in China.

"We are too slow, dear chap, much too slow," he declared; "with fifty thousand men we could take all that we want, and we ought to have attacked those Japanese long since."

"Tell me, then," said Heideck, with apparent indifference, "how strong really is the army of the Governor-General of Turkestan?"

The Russian looked up, but it was not because he was thinking what answer to give; for, after having tossed off a glass of soda-water, he replied--

"If you want to live well, my dear fellow, you must go to Manchuria. Salmon, I tell you--ah! and they cost next to nothing--and pretty girls in abundance! You can buy furs, too, for next to nothing at all. What costs in St. Petersburg ten thousand rubles, you can get in China, up there in the north, for a hundred."

"Then of course you have brought some beautiful furs with you?"

"Furs in India? they would be eaten by the ants in a second. For my own personal use, I have certainly brought one with me, which in St. Petersburg would be worth, at the least, five thousand rubles. I shall have use enough for it later on, in the mountains. You can smell it a mile away, it has been pickled so well."

Again there was a short pause, and then after gazing intently at his vis-a-vis, Heideck suddenly said--

"You are an officer?"

Without being able to collect himself the Russian stared into his face.

"Let us be candid with each other," he rejoined, after long reflection. "You are also a soldier, sir?"

"I need not deny it in reply to a comrade. My name is Captain Hermann Heideck of the Prussian General Staff."

The Russian rose and made a correct bow. "And my name is Prince Fedor Andreievitch Tchajawadse, Captain in the Preobraschensky regiment of the Guards."

They then once more touched glasses: "To ourselves as good comrades" rang their mutual toast.

"Comrade, I will tell you something," said the Russian. "General Ivanov is on the march towards the Indian frontier. The Tsar has given up his theosophy; he intends to declare war upon England."

Heideck would have wished to learn more, but the Prince had addressed himself to the good liquor somewhat more than his head could stand, and he began to sing indecent French chansons, only to pass of a sudden to melancholy Russian popular songs. In his present condition it was impossible to think of continuing a sensible conversation with him further.

Heideck already found himself somewhat perplexed what to do with his intoxicated guest, when a new surprise was sprung upon him. The door to the next room opened and a tall, handsome young fellow, of at most eighteen years, appeared on the threshold.

He was garbed in a sort of fantastic page's dress, which in any other country but that of rainbow-hued picturesque India would have looked like that of a masquerader. The blue gold-embroidered jacket was girded with a red silk scarf, and the loose red trousers disappeared at the knees in patent leather topboots, the elegant shape of which showed the contour of the smallest of feet. Thick golden locks fell like waves almost down to the shoulders of the boyish youth. The handsome oval face had the complexion of a blushing rose; the great, blue eyes, however, showed the energy of a strong will.

As soon as the Prince had set eyes on the young visitor, he stopped singing.

"Ah! Georgi?" he stammered.

Without uttering a syllable, the page had advanced towards him, and had quickly raised the intoxicated man from the chair. Prince Tchajawadse flung his arm round the boy's shoulders, and without bidding his German comrade as much as "good night," allowed himself to be led away.

Heideck did not doubt for a moment that this slender page was a girl in disguise. The splendid build and the strange expression of untamed energy in the admirably regular features were the unmistakable characteristics of the Circassian type. This so-called Georgi could be none other but a child of the Caucasian Mountains; and Tchajawadse also, as his name showed, was a scion of those old Caucasian dynastic houses which in days of yore had played a role in that mountain land, which Russia had so slowly, and with such difficulty, finally subjugated.

IV
THE CIRCASSIAN BEAUTY

Captain Heideck's statement that he travelled for a Hamburg firm was not really an untruth. As a matter of fact he was engaged in commercial undertakings, which served as a cloak for the real object of his travels.

He had been commissioned by the chief of the General Staff to study the Indian military organisation, and, in particular, the strategic importance of the North-west frontier, and for this purpose unlimited leave had been granted him.

But the General had expressly stated to him--

"You travel as a private gentleman, and should you come into conflict with the English, we shall in no manner accept responsibility for your actions and adventures. We furnish you with a passport in your own name, but, of course, without denoting your military rank. It is also a matter of course that we should not fail to disclose it in case inquiries are addressed to us in this regard. In a certain sense you may be said to travel at your own risk. Your own tact must be your safest guide."

Hereupon Heideck entered into correspondence with his uncle, and received from him the necessary letters of introduction to his Indian agents. He reached the northern provinces by way of Bombay and Allahabad, visiting on the way all the more important garrison towns--Cawnpore, Lucknow, Delhi, and Lahore. After finishing his business in Chanidigot, his intention was to proceed further north, making his way to Afghanistan by way of the Khyber Pass. It was purely with a view to this journey that he had wished to become more intimate with the Russian. He was absolutely certain that the Russian had received a commission from his Government similar to his own, and certain hints that the Prince had let drop strengthened his opinion that the latter intended to take the same route as himself. Accordingly, it could only redound to the advantage of the German officer if he joined his Russian comrade, who would be in a position to procure him valuable introductions when once on Russian territory.

When Heideck woke early the next morning the Prince's potent bowl of the evening before made itself perceptible in various disagreeable after effects; but the cold bath that Morar Gopal got ready for him, added to a cup of tea, put him on his legs again.

It was an Indian morning of dazzling beauty into which he stepped. February in the Indus Valley in 29 degrees longitude has a temperature like that of May in Rome. In the hours of midday the thermometer usually rises to 100 degrees Fahr.; but the evenings are refreshingly cool, and the nights, with their damp fogs, even appreciably chilly.

Heideck made his toilet on this morning with special care, for he had been invited to a conference with the Minister of the Maharajah, in order to negotiate with him about some indigo business.

The Minister lived in a house on the outskirts of the town. It was a one-story building, with broad airy verandahs, situate in the middle of a large garden. When Heideck arrived, the staircase of the entrance hall was occupied by a crowd of divers people waiting to be received. But he, as a representative of the white race, was saved the tiresome annoyance of waiting his turn. The porter, dressed in white muslin, and adorned, as a sign of his office, with a broad red scarf, conducted him at once into the Minister's study, a room furnished in European style.

It was only in his outward appearance, namely, his colour and his features, that the Minister looked like an Indian. Both dress and manners were those of a Western diplomatist. Giving Heideck his hand, he told him that His Highness himself wished to negotiate with him about the indigo business.

"The price you intend to pay is exceedingly low," he whispered in a tone of disapproval.

Heideck was evidently prepared for this objection.

"Your Excellency may be right in saying that the price offered is lower than in former years; but it is still very high, if the changes which have since occurred in the market values are taken into consideration. In Germany a substitute has been found in aniline, which is so cheap that within a measurable distance of time no indigo whatever will be bought. If I may be permitted to give His Highness any advice, I would recommend him in the future to establish an industry instead of planting indigo."

"And which, may I ask, are you thinking of?"

"Oil mills and cotton mills would appear to me to be the most profitable. You could with them meet both European and Japanese competition."

An Indian servant came with a message, and the Minister invited Heideck to drive with him to the Maharajah. They entered an open carriage horsed by two quick Turkestan horses. The yellow uniformed coachman, who had an extraordinary likeness to a dressed-up monkey, clicked his tongue, and away they went through spacious grounds to the palace, whose white marble walls soon gleamed through the foliage of the palms and tamarinds.

During the short drive Heideck pondered on the innumerable battles that had seethed over this ground, before English sovereignty had, as it seemed, stopped for ever all religious struggles, all bloody insurrections, and all the incursions of foreign conquerors. Here, on this place, where Alexander the Great's invincible hosts had fought and died, where Mohammedans and Hindoos, Afghans and worshippers of the sun had fought their sanguinary conflicts, works of peace had been established which would endure for generations to come. It was a triumph of civilisation; and a student of India's historical past could scarcely fail to be impressed by it.

The Maharajah of Chanidigot was, like the majority of his fellow-countrymen, a believer in Islam, and the exterior view of his palace at once betrayed the Mohammedan prince. Away from the main building, but connected with it by a covered gallery, was a small wing--the harem, the interior of which was sufficiently guarded from prying eyes. Here, as in the adornment of the palace, the most splendid lavishness had been employed. Heideck thought the while with pity on the poor subjects of the Maharajah whose slavery had to provide the means for all this meretricious luxury. The Minister and his companion were not conducted into the large audience hall, which was set apart for special functions, but into a loggia on the first floor. Between the graceful marble pillars, which supported it, one looked out into an inner court, which, with exotic plants, afforded an enchanting spectacle. A gently splashing fountain, springing from a marble basin in the centre, cast up a fine spray as high as the loggia and dispersed a refreshing coolness.

The Minister left him waiting for a considerable time, but then returned and gave him a mute sign to accompany him to the Prince.

The room in which the Maharajah received them was strangely furnished, presenting to the eyes of a European a not altogether happy combination of Eastern luxury and English style. Among splendid carpets and precious weapons, with which the walls were adorned, there hung glaring pictures of truly barbaric taste--such as in Germany would hardly be met with in the house of a fairly well-to-do citizen. Similar incongruities there were many, and perhaps the appearance of the Prince himself was the most incongruous of them all. For this stalwart man with the soft black beard and penetrating eyes, who in the picturesque attire of his country would doubtless have been a handsome and imposing figure, made an inharmonious impression in his grey English suit and with the red turban on his head.

He sat in an English club chair, covered with red Russia leather and gently inclined his head in response to Heideck's deep bow.

It did not escape the notice of the German officer that the Maharajah looked extremely annoyed, and Heideck concluded that it was the low price he had offered for his indigo which had made him so. But the first words of the Prince reassured him. "As I learn," he said in somewhat broken English, "you are in fact a European, but no Englishman, and so I hope to hear the truth from you. I am quite ready to reward you for your information."

"I am accustomed to speak the truth, even without reward, Highness!"

The Maharajah measured him with a mistrustful look. "I am a true friend of England," he continued after a short hesitation, "and am on the best of terms with the Viceroy; but things are now happening which I cannot possibly understand. This very morning I received a message from Calcutta, which absolutely astonished me. The Indian Government intends to mass an army corps at Quetta, and calls upon me to despatch thither a contingent of a thousand infantry, five hundred cavalry, a battery, and two thousand camels. Can you tell me, sir, what makes England mass such a large force at Quetta?"

"It will only be a precautionary measure, Highness! perhaps disturbances have broken out again in Afghanistan."

"Disturbances in Afghanistan, do you say? Then Russia must have a hand in it. Can you perhaps give me more definite information?"

Heideck had to express his inability to do so, and the Maharajah, who did not conceal his vexation, began to open his heart to the stranger in a rather imprudent way.

"I am a faithful friend of the English, but the burden they lay upon us is becoming every day more intolerable. If England is bent upon war, why should we sacrifice our blood and treasure upon it? Do we not know full well what powerful foes England has? You do not belong to this nation, as my Minister informed me; you are in a position, therefore, to instruct me about these matters. It is true I have been in Europe, but I was not permitted to go beyond London, whither I had proceeded to congratulate the late Queen on her birthday. I have seen nothing but many, many ships and a gigantic dirty town. Are there not in Europe strong and powerful states hostile to England?"

Such questions were disagreeable for Heideck to answer, and he therefore preferred to avoid giving a definite reply.

"I have been in India for nearly a year," he replied, "and know about such political matters only what the India Times and other English newspapers report. Of course, there is always a certain rivalry among the European great Powers, and England has, during the past few decades, become so great that she cannot fail to have enemies; but on this point, as also on that of the present political situation, I do not venture to express an opinion."

The Maharajah gloomily shook his head.

"Transact the business with this gentleman in the way you think best," he said, turning abruptly to his Minister, a wave of the hand at the same time denoting to the young German that the audience was at an end.

As Heideck again stepped into the loggia he saw Captain Irwin appear at the entrance door in company with an official of the Court. The British officer started on perceiving the man who passed for a commercial traveller. He cast at him a malicious look, and an almost inimical reserve lay in the manner with which he returned Heideck's salutation. The latter took little notice, and slowly wended his way through the extensive park, in whose magnificent old trees monkeys were disporting themselves. The Maharajah's communication to him as to the English orders which he had received, taken in conjunction with General Ivanov's advance, entirely preoccupied him. After this he was no longer in doubt that serious military events were impending, or were even then in full swing. Quetta, in Beluchistan, lying directly on the Afghan frontier, was the gate of the line of march towards Kandahar; and if England was summoning the Indian princes to its aid the situation could be none other than critical. War had certainly not yet been declared, but Heideck's mission might, under the circumstances, suddenly acquire a peculiar importance, and it was, at all events, impossible to make at this moment any definite plans for the immediate future.

The walk to his bungalow in the immediate vicinity of the English camp took perhaps an hour, and was sufficient to give him a keen appetite. He was not, therefore, at all disappointed to find his Russian comrade sitting at breakfast in a shady spot before the door of the hotel, and, heartily returning his salutation, he lost no time in seating himself at the table. Prince Tchajawadse looked pale, and applied himself to soda-water, which, contrary to all established usage, he drank without the slightest admixture of whisky. The appetising dish of eggs and bacon was standing untouched before him, and he smiled rather sadly when he saw what an inroad his guest made upon it.

They had hardly exchanged a few commonplace words when two Indian girls made their appearance, offering all sorts of nicknacks for sale. The younger, whose bare breast glowed like bronze, was of marvellous beauty, even the paint on her face could not destroy the natural grace of her fine features. Yet, beautiful as she was, she was as great a coquette. She had evidently determined to make an impression on the Russian. Stepping behind his chair, she held her glittering little wares before his face. Her manner became more and more intimate. At length she slipped a golden bracelet on her slender brown wrist and bent, in order that he should notice it, so far over his shoulder that her glowing young breast touched his cheek.

Prince Tchajawadse was of too passionate a temperament to long resist such a temptation. His eyes flashed, and with a rapid movement he turned round and embraced the girl's lithe body with his arm.

A stop was put to further familiarities, however, for this little adventure, which was very distasteful to Heideck, was suddenly interrupted.

Without being perceived by those sitting at the table, the handsome young page of the Prince had stepped from the door of the bungalow with a plate of bananas and mangoes in his hand. For a few seconds he regarded with flashing eyes the scene just described, and then, stealing nearer with noiseless steps, flung, without saying a word, the plate with the fruit with such vigour and unerring aim at the dark beauty, that the girl, with a loud cry, clasped her hand upon her wounded shoulder, while the fragments of china fell clattering to the ground.

The next moment she and her companion had disappeared in hurried flight. The Prince's face was livid with rage; he sprang up and seized the riding-whip which lay near him.

Heideck was on the point of intervening in order to save the disguised girl from a similar punishment to that which his new friend had meted out the day before to his Indian "boy," but he soon saw that his intervention was unnecessary.

Standing bolt upright and with an almost disdainful quiver of his fair lips, the young page stepped straight up to the Prince. A half-loud hissing word, the meaning of which Heideck did not understand, must have suddenly pacified the wrath of the Russian, for he let his upraised arm fall and threw the whip on to the table.

"Go and fetch us another plate of dessert, Georgi," he said quietly, as if nothing had happened. "It's a confounded nuisance, that these Indian vagabonds don't allow one a moment's peace."

A triumphant smile played across the face of the Circassian beauty. She threw a friendly glance at Heideck and silently returned to the bungalow. Full of admiration and not without a slight emotion of envy for the happy possessor of such an entrancing female beauty, Heideck followed her with his eyes, as she tripped gracefully away with her lithe graceful figure. A remark was just on the point of passing his lips, acquainting the Prince that he had discovered the certainly very transparent secret of his disguised lady companion, when he was prevented doing so by a fresh incident.

An English soldier in orderly's uniform stepped up to the table and handed Heideck, whom he must have known by sight, with a military salute, a letter.

"From the Colonel," he said, "and I am ordered to say that the matter is urgent."

With surprise, Heideck took the missive. It contained in polite, but yet somewhat decided terms, a request that Herr Hermann Heideck would favour him with a visit as soon as possible. This, considering the high official position that Colonel Baird occupied in Chanidigot, was tantamount to a command, which he was bound to obey without delay or further excuse.

Baird was the commander-in-chief of the detachment stationed in Chanidigot, consisting of an infantry regiment, about six hundred strong, a lancer regiment of two hundred and forty sabres, and a battery of field artillery. As in all the other residences of the great Indian chiefs, the British Government had stationed here also a military force, strong enough to keep the Maharajah in respect and to nip all seeds of insurrection in the bud. As Colonel Baird, moreover, occupied the position of Resident at the Court of the Prince, and thus combined all the military and diplomatic power in his own person, he had come to be regarded as the real lord and master in Chanidigot.

His bungalow was in the centre of the camp, which lay in the middle of a broad grassy plain. It consisted of a group of buildings which surrounded a quadrangular courtyard, adorned with exotics and a splashing fountain.

As it appeared, he had given orders that Heideck was to be admitted immediately on arrival; for the adjutant, to whom he had announced himself, conducted him at once into the study of his superior officer.

Quite politely, though with a frigidity that contrasted with his former behaviour towards the popular guest of the officers' mess, the fine man, with his martial carriage, thanked him for his prompt visit.

"Please be seated, Mr. Heideck," he began. "I have been very unwilling to disturb you, but I could not spare you this trouble. I have received the intelligence that you were received by the Maharajah this morning."

"It is true. I had to talk to him about some business; I am on the point of purchasing from him a large consignment of indigo for my Hamburg firm."

"I have, of course, nothing to do with your business; but I must inform you that we do not approve of direct communication between Europeans and the native princes. You will, therefore, for the future, be best advised to communicate with me when you are summoned to the Maharajah, so that we may arrive at an understanding as to what you may, or may not, say to him. We cannot, unfortunately, trust all the Indian princes, and this one here is, perhaps, the most unreliable of them all. You must not, however, regard what I say to you as an expression of any want of confidence in yourself. The responsibility of my position imposes upon me, as you see, the greatest possible prudence."

"I understand that completely, Colonel!"

"At this very moment the situation appears to be more than ever complicated. I shall be very much surprised, if we are not on the eve of very disquieting times. The Governor-General of Turkestan is marching this way, and his advance guard has already passed the Afghan frontier."

Heideck had difficulty in concealing the excitement, which this confirmation of Tchajawadse's story aroused in him.

"Is that certain, Colonel? What do the Russians want in Afghanistan?"

"What do the Russians want there? Now, my dear Mr. Heideck, I think that is plain enough. Their advance means war with us. Russia will, of course, not openly allow this at present. They treat their advance as a matter which only concerns the Emir and with which we have nothing to do. But one must be very simple not to discern their real intentions."

"And may I ask, Colonel, what you are thinking of doing?"

Colonel Baird must really have held the young German for a very trustworthy or, at least, for a very harmless personage, for he replied to his question at once--

"The Russian advance guard has crossed the Amu Darya and is marching up the Murghab Valley upon Herat. We shall take our measures accordingly. The Muscovites will have been deceived in us. We are not, after all, so patient and long-suffering as to let our dear neighbours slip in by the open door. I think the Russian generals will pull long faces when they suddenly find themselves confronted in Afghanistan by our battalions, by our Sikhs and Gourkas."

The adjutant made his appearance with what was evidently an important message, and as Heideck perceived that the Colonel wished to speak privately to his orderly officer, he considered that politeness required him to retire.

The words of the Colonel, "The Russian advance into Afghanistan means war," rung unceasingly in his ears. He thanked his good fortune for having brought him at the right moment to the theatre of the great events in the world's history, and all his thoughts were now solely directed as to the "where and how" of his being able, on the outbreak of hostilities, to be present both as spectator and observer.

That his Russian friend was animated by the same desire he could all the easier surmise, owing to the fact that Prince Tchajawadse belonged, of course, to one of the nations immediately concerned. He hastened, therefore, to acquaint him with the results of his interview with Colonel Baird. The effect of his communications upon the Prince was quite as he had anticipated.

"So, really! The advance guard is already across the Amu Darya. War will, then, break out just in the proper quarter," exclaimed the Russian in a loud outburst of joy. "In our army the fear prevailed that the Tsar would never brace himself up to the decision to make war. Powerful and irresistible influences must have been at work to have finally conquered his love of peace."

"You will, of course, get to the army as soon as possible?" inquired Heideck; and as the Prince answered in the affirmative, he continued: "I should be grateful to you if you would allow me to join you. But how shall we get across the frontier? It is to be hoped that we shall be allowed to pass quietly as unsuspected merchants."

"That is not quite so certain; we shall probably not be able to leave India quite as readily as we entered it; but, at any rate, we must try our best. We can reach Peshawar by rail in twelve hours and Quetta in fifteen. Both these lines of railway are not likely at present to be blocked by military trains, but we shall do well to hasten our departure. In all probability we shall, either by way of Peshawar or Quetta, soon meet with Russian troops, for I have no doubt that a Russian army corps is also on the march upon Cabul, although the Colonel, as you say, only spoke of an advance guard moving on Herat."

"I would suggest that we go by way of Peshawar and the Khyber Pass, because we should thus reach Cabul most speedily and with the greater security."

"We will talk more of this anon, comrade! At all events, it is settled that we travel together. I hope most fervently that in the great theatre of the world your nation is at this present moment standing shoulder to shoulder with mine against England."

V
THE CAPTAIN'S WIFE

As a married man, Captain Irwin was not quartered in one of the wooden barracks of the English camp, but had his own bungalow in the suburbs.

It was a house of one story with a broad verandah, was surrounded by a large well-kept garden, and formerly served a high official of the Maharajah as a residence. Apart from it lay two smaller buildings used as servants' quarters, of which, however, only one was at present in use.

The sun of that same day, that had brought Hermann Heideck face to face with such momentous matters affecting his future for his final decision, was sinking rapidly into the heavens as he passed through the cactus hedge and bamboo thicket of the garden surrounding Irwin's bungalow.

He was attired in an evening dress of the lightest black cloth, such as is prescribed by English custom for a visit paid at the dinner-hour in those climes.

He did not come that evening of his own initiative, for Irwin's morning salutation did not promise anything in the way of an invitation. A letter from Mrs. Irwin had, to his surprise, begged his company at this hour. He had gathered from the tone of the letter that something especially urgent required his presence, and he was not slow in supposing that the reason was the unfortunate party at poker in which the Captain had taken part.

What, however, could have induced Mrs. Irwin to appeal to him was still an enigma, for his relations to the beautiful young wife had until then not been of a confidential nature. He had met her on several occasions in big society functions, at the officers' polo-parties, and at similar gatherings, and if, attracted by her grace and intellect, he had perhaps paid more attention to the Captain's wife than to any of the other ladies of the party, their relations had been strictly confined within conventional limits, and it would never have occurred to him to imagine himself specially favoured by Mrs. Irwin.

The dainty Indian handmaid of the lady received him and conducted him to the verandah. Mrs. Irwin, who, dressed in red silk, had been seated in a rocking-chair, advanced a few steps to meet him. Once more Irwin felt himself enchanted by the charm of her appearance.

She was a genuine English beauty of tall and splendid proportions, finely chiselled features, and that white transparent skin which lends to Albion's daughters their distinctive charm. Abundant dark brown hair clustered in thick, natural folds round the broad forehead, and her blue eyes had the clear, calm gaze of a personality at once intelligent and strong-minded.

At this moment the young wife, whom Heideck had hitherto only known as the placid and unemotional lady of the world, certainly seemed to labour under some excitement, which she could not completely conceal. There was something of embarrassment in the manner with which she received her visitor.

"I am exceedingly obliged to you for coming, Mr. Heideck. My invitation will have surprised you, but I did not know what else to do. Please let us go into the drawing-room; it is getting very chilly outside."

Heideck did not notice anything of the chilliness of which she complained, but he thought he understood that it was only the fear of eavesdropping that prompted the wish of the young wife. As a matter of fact, she closed the glass door behind him, and motioned him to be seated in one of the large cane chairs before her.

"Captain Irwin is not at home," she began, evidently struggling with severe embarrassment. "He has ridden off to inspect his squadron, and will not be home, as he told me, before daybreak."

Heideck did not quite understand why she told him this. Had he been a flirt, convinced of his own irresistibility, he would perhaps have found in her words a very transparent encouragement; but he was far from discerning any such meaning in Edith's words. The respect in which he had held this beautiful young wife, since the first moment of their acquaintance, sufficiently protected her from any such dishonourable suspicions. That she had bidden him there at a time when she must know that their conversation would not be disturbed by the presence of her husband, must assuredly have had other reasons than the mere desire for an adventure.

And as he saw her sitting before him, with a look of deep distress on her face, there arose in his heart no other than the honest wish to be able to do this poor creature, who was evidently most unhappy, some chivalrous service.

But he had not the courage to suggest anything of the sort before she had given him in an unequivocal way a right to do so. Hence it was that he waited in silence for anything further that she might wish to say. And there was a fairly long and somewhat painful pause before Mrs. Irwin, evidently collecting all her courage, went on: "You witnessed the scene that took place last evening in the officers' mess between my husband and Captain McGregor? If I have been rightly informed, I owe it solely to you that my husband did not, in the excitement of the moment, lay hand on himself."

Heideck turned modestly away.

"I did absolutely nothing to give me any claim to your gratitude, Mrs. Irwin, and I do not really believe that your husband would have so far forgot himself as to commit such a silly and desperate deed. At the last moment, a thought of you would certainly have restrained him from taking such a step."

He was surprised at the expression of disdain which the face of the young wife assumed as he said this, and at the hard ring in her voice, when she replied--

"Thoughts of me? No! how little you know my husband. He is not wont to make the smallest sacrifice for me, and, maybe, his voluntary death would not, after all, be the worst misery he is capable of inflicting on me."

She saw the look of utter surprise in his eyes, and therefore quickly added--

"You will, I know, consider me the most heartless woman in the world because I can talk to a stranger like this; but is not in your country loss of honour regarded as worse than death?"

"Under certain circumstances--yes; but your husband's position is not, I hope, to be viewed in this tragic light. Judging from the impression that Captain McGregor's personality has made upon me, I should say that he is not the man to drive Mr. Irwin to take an extreme course on account of a recklessly incurred debt at cards."

"Oh no! you judge of that honourable man quite correctly. He would be best pleased to forego the whole amount, and with the intention of bringing about such an arrangement he called here this afternoon. But the foolish pride and unbounded vanity of Irwin brought all his good intentions to naught. The result of McGregor's well-meant endeavours was only a violent scene, which made matters a thousand times worse. My husband is determined to pay his debt at any price."

"And--pardon me the indiscreet question--is he capable of doing so?"

"If he uses my fortune for the purpose--certainly! and I have at once placed it at his disposal; and I further told him that he could take everything, even the last penny, if this sacrifice on my part would suffice to get rid of him for ever."

Heideck could scarcely believe his ears. He was prepared for anything on earth except to hear such confessions. He began to doubt this woman, who hitherto had seemed to him to be the paragon of all feminine virtues, and he sought an opportunity of escaping from further confessions of the kind, which, as he told himself, she would repent of in the course of an hour or so.

"Nobody can expect of you, Mrs. Irwin, that for a criminal recklessness, a hasty action on the part of your husband, who was probably deep in his cups, you should make such a tremendous sacrifice; but, as you have now done me the honour to consult me on these matters, it is perhaps not unbecoming on my part if I tell you that your husband should, in my opinion, be forced to bear the consequences of his action. You need not be at all apprehensive that these consequences will be very serious. McGregor will certainly not press him; and as we seem to be on the threshold of a war, his superior officers are not likely to be too severe upon him in this matter. He will, perhaps, either find an opportunity to rehabilitate his compromised honour or will find his death on the battlefield. Within a few weeks, or months, all these matters which at present cause you so much trouble will present quite a different aspect."

"You are very kind, Mr. Heideck, and I thank you for your friendly intentions; but I would not have invited you here at this unusual hour had it been solely my intention to enlist your kind sympathy. I am in a most deplorable plight--doubly so, because there is no one here to whom I can turn for advice and assistance. That in my despair I thought of you has, no doubt, greatly surprised you; and now I can myself hardly understand how I could have presumed to trouble you with my worries."

"If you would only, Mrs. Irwin, show me how I can be of service to you, I would pray you to make any use you will of me. I am absolutely and entirely at your disposal, and your confidence would make me exceedingly happy."

"As a gentleman, you could not, of course, give any other answer. But, in your heart of hearts, you probably consider my conduct both unwomanly and unbecoming, for it is true that we hardly know each other. Over in England, and certainly in your German fatherland quite as well, such casual meetings as ours have been could not possibly give me the right to treat you as a friend, and I do not really know how far you are influenced by these European considerations."

"In Germany, as in England, every defenceless and unhappy woman would have an immediate claim upon my assistance," he seriously replied. "If you give me the preference over your friends here, I, on my part, have only to be grateful, and need not inquire further into your motives."

"But, of course, I will tell you what my motives are. My friends in this place are naturally my husband's comrades, and I cannot turn to them if I do not intend to sign Irwin's death warrant. Not a single man amongst them would allow that a man of my husband's stamp should remain an hour longer a member of the corps of officers in the British Army."

"I do not quite understand you, Mrs. Irwin. The gambling debt of your husband is, after all, no longer a secret to his comrades."

"That is not the point. How do you judge of a man who would sell his wife to pay his gambling debts?"

This last sentence struck Heideck like a blow. With dilated eyes he stared at the young wife who had launched such a terrible indictment against her husband. Never had she looked to him so charming as in this moment, when a sensation of womanly shame had suffused her pale cheeks with a crimson blush. Never had he felt with such clearness what a precious treasure this charming creature would be to a man to whom she gave herself in love for his very own; and the less he doubted that she had just spoken the simple truth, the more did his heart rise in passionate wrath at the miserable reptile who was abandoned enough to drag this precious pearl in the mire.

"I do not presume to connect your question with Captain Irwin," said Heideck, in a perceptibly tremulous voice, "for if he were really capable of doing so--"

Edith interrupted him, pointing to a small case that lay on the little table beside her.

"Would you kindly just look at this ring, Mr. Heideck?"

He did as he was asked, and thought he recognised the beautiful diamond ring that he had yesterday seen sparkling on Irwin's finger. He asked whether it was so, and the young wife nodded assent.

"I gave it to my husband on our wedding-day. The ring is an heirloom in my family. Jewellers value it at more than a thousand pounds."

"And why, may I ask, does your husband no longer wear it?"

"Because he intends to sell it. Of course, the Maharajah is the only person who can afford the luxury of such articles, and my husband wishes me to conclude the bargain with the Prince."

"You, Mrs. Irwin? And why, pray, does he not do it himself?"

"Because the Maharajah will not pay him the price he demands. My husband will not let the ring go under two lakhs."

"But that is a tremendous sum! That would be paying for it twelve times over!"

"My husband is, all the same, certain that the bargain would come off quite easily, provided I personally negotiated it."

It was impossible to misunderstand the meaning of these words, and so great was the indignation they awoke in Heideck, that he sprang up in a bound from his chair.

"No! that is impossible--it cannot be! He cannot possibly have suggested that! You must have misunderstood him. No man, no officer, no gentleman, could ever be guilty of such a low, mean action!"

"You would be less surprised if you had had the opportunity to know him, as I have had, during the short time of our wedded life. There is practically no act or deed of his that would surprise me now. He has long since ceased to love me; and a wife, whose person has become indifferent to him, has, in his eyes, only a market-able value. It may be that some excuse can even be found for his way of regarding things. It is, possibly, an atavistic relapse into the views of his ancestors, who, when they were sick of their wives, led them with a halter round their necks into the marketplace and sold them to the highest bidder. They say it is not so long ago that this pretty custom has gone out of vogue."

"No more, Mrs. Irwin," Heideck broke in; "I cannot bear to hear you speak like that. I must say that I still consider the Captain to have been out of his mind when he dared to expect such a thing of you."

The young wife shook her head with a severe quiver of the lips. "Oh no! he was neither intoxicated nor especially excited when he asked me to do him this 'LITTLE' kindness; he probably considered that I ought to feel myself intensely flattered that His Indian Highness thought my insignificant person worth such a large price. I have certainly for some time past been quite conscious of the fact that, quite unwittingly, I have attracted the notice of the Maharajah. Immediately after our first meeting he began to annoy me with his attentions. I never took any notice, and never, for one moment, dreamt of the possibility that his--his--what shall I call it--his admiration could rise to criminal desires; but, after what I have experienced to-day, I cannot help believing that it is the case."

"But this monstrosity, Mrs. Irwin, will be past and gone as soon as you indignantly repudiate the suggestion of your abandoned husband?"

"Between him and me--yes, that is true. But I am not at all certain if the Maharajah's infatuation will then have really ceased to exist. My Indian handmaid has been told by one of her countrymen to warn me of a danger that threatens me. The man did not tell her wherein this danger consists, but I am at a loss to know from what quarter it should threaten, if not from the Maharajah."

Heideck shook his head incredulously.

"You have certainly nothing to fear in that quarter; he knows full well that he would have the whole of the British power against him dared he only--be it with one word--attempt to wrong the wife of an English officer. He would be a sheer madman to allow things to come to that pass."

"Well, after all, he may have some despotic insanity in him. We must not forget that the time is not so far distant when all these tyrants disposed absolutely of the life and death and body and soul of their subjects. Who knows, too, what my husband--But perhaps you are right. It may only be a foolish suspicion that has upset me; and it is just for this reason that I did not wish to speak about it to any of my husband's messmates. I have opened my heart to you alone. I know that you are an honourable man, and that nobody will learn from your mouth what we have spoken about during this past hour."

"I am very much indebted to you, Mrs. Irwin, for your confidence, and should be only too willing to do what I could to relieve your anxiety and trouble. You are apprehensive of some unknown danger, and you are this night, in your husband's absence, without any other protection but that of your Indian servants. Would you permit me to remain close by, until tomorrow daybreak?"

With a blush that made her heart beat faster, Edith Irwin shook her head.

"No! no! that is impossible; and I do not think that here, in the protection of my house and among my own servants, any mishap could befall me. Only in case that something should happen to me at another time and at another place, I would beg of you to acquaint Colonel Baird with the subject of our conversation this evening; people will then perhaps better understand the connexion of things."

And now Heideck perfectly understood why she had chosen to make him, a stranger, her confidant; and he thought that he understood also that it was not so much of an attempt on the part of the Maharajah as of her own husband's villainy that the unhappy young wife was afraid. But his delicate feelings restrained him from saying in outspoken language that he had comprehended what she wished to convey. It was after all enough that she knew she could rely upon him; and of this she must have been already sufficiently convinced, although it was only the fire of his eyes that told her so, and the long, warm kiss that his lips impressed upon the small, icy-cold hand which the poor young lady presented to him at parting.

"You will permit me to pay you another call tomorrow, will you not?"

"I will send you word when I expect you. I should not care for you to meet my husband; perhaps he has some idea that you are friendly inclined towards me; and that would be sufficient to fill him with suspicion and aversion towards you."

She clapped her hands, and as the Indian handmaid entered the room to escort the visitor to the door, Heideck had to leave her last remark unanswered. But, as on the threshold he again turned to bow his farewell, his eyes met hers, and though their lips were dumb, they had perhaps told one another more in this single second than during the whole time of their long tete-a-tete.

VI
THE OUTRAGE

When Heideck stepped into the garden he was scarcely able to find his way, but having taken a few steps his eyes had become accustomed to the gloom, and the pale light of the stars showed him his path. The garden was surrounded by an impenetrable hedge of cactus plants, low enough to allow a tall man to look over. On having closed the wooden gate behind him, Heideck stood and gazed back at the brightly illuminated windows of the house. In the presence of the charming woman he had manfully suppressed his feelings. No rash word, betraying the tempest that this nocturnal conversation had left surging in his bosom, had escaped his lips. He had not for a moment forgotten that she was the wife of another, and it would be an infamy to covet her for his wife so long as she was tied to that other. But he could not disguise from himself the fact that he yearned towards her with a passionate love. He was to-day, for the first time, conscious that he loved this woman with a passion that he had never before felt for another; but there was nothing intoxicating or pleasurable in this self-confession. It was rather a feeling of apprehension of coming difficulties and struggles that would beset him in his passion for this charming creature. Had she not needed his protection, and had he not promised to remain on the spot to assist her, he would have escaped in rapid flight from this struggle within him. Yet, under the existing circumstances, there could be no question of his doing this. He had only himself to blame for having given her the right to count upon his friendship; and it was a behest of chivalry to deserve her confidence. Incapable of tearing himself from the place, where he knew his loved one remained, Heideck must have stayed a quarter of an hour rooted to the spot, and just when he had resolved--on becoming conscious of the folly of his behaviour--on turning homewards, he perceived something unusual enough to cause him to stay his steps.

He saw the house-door, which the Indian maid had a short time before closed behind him, open, and in the flood of light which streamed out into the darkness, perceived that several men dressed in white garments hurried, closely following each other, up the steps.

Remembering Mrs. Irwin's enigmatical references to a danger which possibly threatened her, and seized by a horrible dread of something about to happen, he pushed open the garden gate and rushed towards the house.

He had not yet reached it, when the shrill cry of a woman in distress fell upon his ear. Heideck drew the revolver he always carried from his pocket and sprang up the steps at a bound. The door of the drawing-room, where he had shortly before been in conversation with the Captain's wife, was wide open, and from it rang the cries for help, whose desperate tones brought home to the Captain the certainty that Edith Irwin was in the gravest peril. Only a few steps, and he saw the young English lady defending herself heroically against three white-dressed natives, who were evidently about to carry her off. Her light silk dress was torn to shreds in this unequal struggle, and so great was Heideck's indignation at the monstrous brutality of the assailants that he did not for a moment hesitate to turn his weapon upon the tall, wild-looking fellow, whose brown hands were roughly clutching the bare arms of the young lady.

He fired, and with a short, dull cry of pain the fellow reeled to the ground. The other two, horror-stricken, let go their victim. One of them drew his sabre from the sheath and rushed upon the German. Heideck could not fire a second time, being afraid of harming Edith, and so he threw the revolver down, and with a rapid motion, for which his adversary was fully unprepared, caught the arm of the Indian which was raised to strike. Being much more than his match in physical strength, he wrested the sabre with a quick jerk from his grasp. The man, now defenceless, gave up the struggle and like his companion, who had already in silent, cat-like bounds made his escape, hurried off as fast as his legs would carry him.

Heideck did not pursue him. His only thoughts were for Edith, and his fears were that she had perhaps received some hurt at the hands of these bandits. In the same moment that the violent hands of the Indians had let her loose, she had fallen down on the carpet, and her marble-pale face looked to Heideck as that of a dead person. Whilst, curiously enough, neither Edith's screams for help nor the crack of the shot had had the effect of summoning any one of her servants to her aid, now, when the danger was over, all of a sudden a few scared brown faces peered in through the open door; and the peremptory order that Heideck addressed in English to the terrified maid brought her back to her sense of duty to her mistress.

With her assistance, Heideck carried the fainting woman to a couch, and perceiving one of the little green flasks of lavender water, which are never wanting in an English house, on the table, he employed the strong perfume as well as he was able, whilst the Indian maid rubbed the soles of her young mistress' feet, and adopted divers other methods, well known among the natives, of resuscitating her.

Under their joint attentions, Edith soon opened her eyes, and gazed with bewildered looks around her. But on seeing lying on the floor the corpse of the Indian whom Heideck had shot, her consciousness returned with perfect clearness.

Shaking off the last traces of faintness with a firm will, she got up.

"It was you who saved me, Mr. Heideck! You risked your life for me! How can I thank you enough?"

"Solely, madam, by allowing me to conduct you at once to the Colonel's house, whose protection you must necessarily claim until your husband's return. Whoever may have been the instigator of this hellish plot--whether these rogues were common thieves or whether they acted on orders, I do not feel myself strong enough, single-handed, to accept the responsibility for your security."

"You are right," Edith replied gently. "I will get ready at once and go with you--but this man here," she added, shivering, "is he dead, or can something be done for him?"

Heideck stooped down and regarded the motionless figure. A single look into the sallow, drawn face, with the dilated, glassy eyes, sufficed to assure him that any further examination was useless.

"He has got his reward," he said, "and he has no further claim upon your generous compassion; but is there no one to help me get the body away?"

"They are all out," said the maid; "the butler invited them to spend a jolly evening with him in the town."

Edith and Heideck exchanged a significant look; neither of them now doubted in the least that the audacious attack had been the result of a plot to which the

Indian servants were parties, and each guessed that the other entertained the same suspicion as to who was the instigator of the shameful outrage.

But they did not utter a syllable about it. It was just because they had been brought as near to each other by the events of this night as fate can possibly bring two young beings of different sex, that each felt almost instinctively the fear of that first word which probably would have broken down the last barrier between them. And Captain Irwin's name was not mentioned by either.

VII
THE MAHARAJAH

It was noon the next day when Captain Irwin stepped out of the Colonel's bungalow and turned towards home. The interview with his superior officer appeared to have been serious and far from pleasant for him, for he was very pale. Red spots were burning on his cheeks, and his deep-set eyes flashed darkly, as though with suppressed wrath. A few minutes later the Colonel's horse was led to the door, and a company of lancers under the command of a sergeant rode into the courtyard.

The commander came out in full uniform, and, placing himself at the head of the company, galloped towards the Maharajah's palace.

The cavalry drew up before the palace gates, and Colonel Baird shouted out in a loud commanding voice to the servants lounging at the door that he wished to speak to the Maharajah.

A few minutes passed, and a gorgeously attired palace official made his appearance with the answer that His Highness could not receive at present; the Colonel would be informed as soon as the audience could be granted.

The commander leapt from the saddle, and with jingling spurs walked firmly into the palace, trailing his sword noisily over the marble floor.

"Tell the Prince I desire to see him at once," he called out in a threatening voice to the palace officials and servants who followed him in evident embarrassment. It was evident that no one dare disobey such a peremptory command. All gates flew open before the Englishman, and he had hardly to wait a minute in the anteroom before the Prince consented to receive him. On a small high-raised terrace of the ground floor the Maharajah sat at luncheon. He purposely did not change his easy attitude when the English resident approached, and the glaring look which his dark eyes cast at the incomer was obviously intended to intimidate.

With his helmet on his head and his hand resting on his sword the Colonel stood straight before the Prince.

"I desire to have a few words with you, Maharajah!"

"And I have instructed my servants to inform you that I am not at your service. You see I am at luncheon!"

"That, in your case, is no reason for refusing to receive the representative of His Britannic Majesty. The message you sent me was an insult, which, if repeated, will have to be punished."

In a transport of rage the Prince sprang up from his chair. He hurled an abusive epithet into the Colonel's face, and his right hand sought the dagger in his belt. The attendant, who was about to serve up to his master a ruddy lobster on a silver dish, recoiled in alarm. But the Colonel, without moving an inch from his place, placed the silver hunting whistle that hung from his shoulder to his mouth. Two shrill calls, and at once the trotting of horses and the rattle of arms was audible. The high, blue-striped turbans of the cavalry and the pennons of their lances made their appearance under the terrace.

"Call my bodyguard!" cried the Prince, with a voice hoarse with rage.

But in a voice of icy calm the Colonel retorted, "If you summon your bodyguard, Maharajah, you are a dead man. That would be rebellion; and with rebels we make short shrift."

The Prince pressed his lips together; the rage he had with the greatest difficulty suppressed caused his body to quiver as in a paroxysm of fever, but he had to realise that he was here the weaker, and without a word more he fell back again into his chair.

The Colonel stepped to the balcony of the terrace.

"Sergeant Thomson!" he called down into the park.

Heavy steps were heard on the marble stairs, and the man summoned, followed by two soldiers, stood at attention before his superior officer.

"Sergeant, do you know the gentleman sitting at that table?"

"Yes, sir! It is His Highness the Maharajah."

"If I gave you orders to arrest this gentleman and bring him to camp, would you hesitate to obey?"

The sergeant regarded his superior officer as if the doubt of his loyal military obedience astonished him. He at once gave the two soldiers who were with him a nod and advanced a step further towards the Prince, as though at once to carry out the order.

"Stop, sergeant!" cried the Colonel. "I hope that His Highness will not let matters go as far as that. You are perhaps ready now, Maharajah, to receive me?"

The Indian silently pointed to the golden chair at the other end of the table. At a sign from the Colonel the sergeant and the two soldiers withdrew.

"I have a very serious question to put to you, Maharajah."

"Speak!"

"Last evening, during Captain Irwin's absence, several rascals entered his house with the intention of committing an act of violence on the person of the Captain's wife. What do you know about the matter, Maharajah?"

"I do not understand, Colonel. What should I know?"

"Perhaps you would be well advised to try and remember. Do you mean to tell me that you now hear of this business for the first time?"

"Certainly! I have not heard a word about it until now."

"And you have not been told that one of the assailants who was killed on the spot was one of your servants?"

"No. I have a great many servants, and I am not responsible for their actions, if they are not done by my orders."

"But this is exactly what I believe to have been the case. You will hardly expect me to believe that one of your servants would have dared to make such an attack on his own initiative. Unfortunately, the other villains have escaped, but one of them left behind him a sabre belonging to a man in your bodyguard."

It was evident that the Maharajah had a hard struggle to keep his composure. Endeavouring to conceal his rage behind a supercilious smile, he answered--

"It is beneath my dignity, Colonel, to answer you."

"There can be no question of dignity justifying you in a refusal to answer the British resident, when he demands it. You are dealing not with an ordinary British officer, but with the representative of His Majesty the Emperor of India. It is your duty to answer, as it is mine to question you. A refusal might have the most serious consequences for Your Highness; for the Government Commissioners that would be despatched from Calcutta to Chanidigot on my report might be but little impressed by your dignity."

The Indian set his teeth and a wild passionate hate flashed from his eyes, but, at the same time, he probably reflected that he would not have been the first of the Indian princes to be deprived of the last remnant of sham sovereignty for a paltry indiscretion.

"If you consider it necessary to make a report to Calcutta, I cannot prevent your doing so; but I should think that the Viceroy would hesitate before giving offence to a faithful ally of England, and at the very moment when he has to ask him to despatch his contingent of auxiliary forces."

"Since you refer to this matter--whom have you appointed to command your force?"

"My cousin, Tasatat Maharajah."

"And when will he start?"

"In about four weeks, I hope."

The officer shook his head.

"That would be much longer than we can allow. Your force is to join my detachment, and I am starting at latest in a fortnight from now."

"You are asking what is impossible. At present we have not a sufficient number of horses, and I do not know where to procure two thousand camels in such a short time; and I have not nearly enough ammunition for the infantry."

"The requisite ammunition can be provided by the arsenal at Mooltan and debited to your account, Highness. As for the horses and camels, you will, no doubt, be able to furnish them in time, if you take the trouble. I repeat that in a fortnight all must be ready. Do not forget that the punctual execution of these orders is in a way an earnest of your fidelity and zeal. Every unwarranted delay and all equivocation on your part will be fatal to you."

The emphasis with which these words were spoken showed how seriously they were meant, and the Maharajah, whose yellow skin had for a moment become darker, silently inclined his head.

Colonel Baird rose from his seat.

"As to the affair touching Mrs. Irwin, I demand that a thorough investigation shall be immediately set on foot, and require that it shall be conducted with unsparing rigour, without any underhand tricks and quibbles. The insult that has been offered by some of your subjects to an officer of His Majesty and a British lady is so heinous that not only the criminals themselves, but also the instigators of the crime, must be delivered up to suffer their well-merited punishment. I allow you twenty-four hours. If I do not receive a satisfactory report from you before the expiry of this time, I shall myself conduct the inquiry. You may rest assured that the information required will then be obtained within the shortest space of time."

He made a military bow and descended the steps of the terrace, this time taking the shortest way. The cavalry dashed off amid a jingling of swords and accoutrements. The Maharajah followed their departure with lowering, flashing eyes. He then ordered his servant to fetch his body physician, Mohammed Bhawon. And when, a few minutes later, the lean, shrivelled little man, with his wrinkled brown face and penetrating black eyes, dressed entirely in white muslin, was ushered into his presence, he beckoned to him graciously, inviting him to be seated by him on the gold-embroidered cushion.

A second imperious wave of the hand dismissed the attendant. Placing his arm confidentially round the neck of the physician, the Maharajah talked long and intimately to him in carefully hushed tones--but in a friendly and coaxing manner, as one talks to someone from whom one demands something out of the way, his eyes flashing the while with passionate rage and deadly hate.

VIII
THE PAMIRS

In vain did Heideck, on the day following the night-attack, wait for a message from Edith, giving him an opportunity of seeing her again. He was prepared to be taken to task by Irwin on account of his evening visit at the villa. But the Captain did not show himself.

In the early morning Heideck had been summoned to the Colonel to report on the incident of the preceding night. The conversation had been short, and Heideck gained the impression that the Colonel observed a studied reserve in his questions.

He evidently desired the German to believe that in his own conviction they had only to deal with bold burglars, who had acted on their own responsibility. He mentioned quite incidentally that the dead man had been recognised as one of the Maharajah's bodyguard. To Heideck's inquiry whether the killing of the man could involve him in difficulties with the civil authorities, the Colonel answered with a decisive--

"No. You acted in justifiable self-defence in shooting the fellow down. I give you my word, you will neither be troubled about it by the authorities nor by the Maharajah."

His inquiry after Mrs. Irwin's health was also satisfactorily answered.

"The lady, I am glad to say, is in the best of health," said the Colonel. "She has admirable courage."

The next morning again, Captain Irwin neither made his appearance nor sent any message. Heideck and Prince Tchajawadse were sitting in their bungalow at breakfast discussing the important intelligence brought by the morning papers.

The India Times declared that Russia had infringed the treaties of London by her invasion of Afghanistan, and that England was thus justified, nay compelled, to send an army to Afghanistan. It was earnestly to be hoped that peaceful negotiations would succeed in averting the threatened conflict. But should the Russian army not return to Turkestan, England also would be obliged to have recourse to strong measures. An English force would occupy Afghanistan, and compel the Ameer, as an ally of the Indian Government, to fulfil his obligations. To provide for all contingencies, a strong fleet was being fitted out in the harbours of Portsmouth and Plymouth to proceed to the Baltic at the right moment.

"Still more significant than this," said Heideck, "is the fact that the two and a half per cent. Consols were quoted at ninety yesterday on the London Exchange, while a week ago they stood at ninety-six. The English are reluctant to declare openly that war has already commenced."

"War without a declaration of war," the Prince agreed. "In any case we must hurry, if we are to get over the frontier. I should be sorry to miss the moment when fighting begins in Afghanistan."

"I can feel with you there. But there really is no time to lose."

"If you agree, we will start this very day. At midnight we shall arrive at Mooltan, and at noon to-morrow in Attock. To-morrow night we can be in Peshawar. There we must get our permits to cross the Khyber Pass. The sooner we get through the Pass the better, for later we might have difficulties in obtaining permission."

"I hope you are carrying nothing suspicious about you--charts, drawings, or things of that sort."

The Russian smilingly shook his head. "Nothing but Murray's Guide, the indispensable companion of all travellers; I should take good care not to take anything else. As for you, of course you need not be so careful."

"Why?"

"Because you are a German. There is no war with Germany, but I should at once be in danger of being arrested as a spy."

"I really believe that neither of us need fear anything, even if we were recognised as officers. I should think that there are quite as many English officers on Russian territory at this very moment as Russian officers here in India."

"As long as war has not been actually declared, it is customary to be civil to the officers of foreign Powers, but, under the circumstances, I would not rely upon this. The possibility of being drumhead court-martialled and shot might not be remote.

Luckily, not even Roentgen rays could discover what a store of drawings, charts, and fortress plans I keep in my memory. But you have not answered my question yet, comrade!--are you prepared to start to-day?"

"I am sorry, but I must ask you not to count upon me; I should prefer to stay here for the present."

On noting the surprise of the Russian he continued: "You yourself said just now that I, as a German, am in a less precarious position. Even if I am recognised as an officer, it is hardly probable that I should find myself in serious difficulties. At least, not here, where there is nothing to spy into."

He did not betray that it was solely the thought of Mrs. Irwin that had suddenly made him change his plans. And the Russian evidently did not trouble further about his motives.

"Do you know what my whole anxiety is, at this moment?" he asked. "I am afraid of Germany seizing the convenient opportunity, and attacking us in our rear. Your nation does not love ours; let us make no mistake about it. There was a time when Teutonism played a great role in our national life. But all that has changed since the days of Alexander the Third. We also cannot forget that at the Berlin Congress Master Bismarck cheated us of the prize of our victory over the Turks."

"Pardon me, Prince, for contradicting you on this point. The fault was solely Gortchakow's in not understanding how to follow up his opportunity. The English took advantage of that. No doubt Bismarck would have agreed to every Russian demand. But I can assure you that there is no question of national German enmity against Russia, in educated circles especially."

"It is possible, but Russia will always consider this aversion as a factor to be taken into account at critical moments, otherwise the treaty with France would probably never have been made. I, for one, can hardly blame your nation for entertaining a certain degree of hostility towards us. We possess diverse territories geographically belonging more naturally to Germany. If your country could take eight million peasants from your superfluous population and settle them in Poland it would be a grand thing for her. Were I at the head of your Government I should, first, with Austria's consent, seize Russian Poland, and then crush Austria, annex Bohemia, Moravia, Carinthia, Styria and the Tyrol as German territory, and limit the Austrian dynasty to Transleithania."

Heideck could not help smiling.

"Those are bold fancies, Prince! Rest assured that nobody in Germany seriously entertains such plans."

"Strange, if that is so. I should think it would seem the most natural thing for you. What, then, do you mean by a German Empire, if the most German countries do not belong to it? Do you not consider the population of Austria's German provinces is more closely related to you than that of North-East Prussia? But possibly you are too conscientious and too treaty-abiding to carry out a policy of such dimensions."

Heideck, not unintentionally, turned the conversation back to the original subject of discussion.

"Which route do you intend taking? Have you decided for Peshawar, or are you also taking Quetta into your consideration?"

"I have not as yet quite made up my mind. In any case, I mean to take the shortest way back to our army."

"If that is so, I would suggest Quetta. Most probably the Russian main army will turn southwards. Their first objective will probably be Herat. The best roads from the north and north-west converge on that point. It is the meeting-place of the caravan roads from India, Persia, and Turkestan. In Herat a large army can be concentrated, for it is situated in fertile country. Once your advance guard is firmly established, 60,000 men can be conveyed there in a relatively short time. If the English advance to Kandahar the collision between the forces will take place at that point. But the Russians will outnumber the English so greatly that the latter will hardly venture the march upon Kandahar. Reinforced by the Afghan forces, General Ivanov, with 100,000 men, can push on without hindrance to the Bolan Pass."

"If he should succeed," said the Prince, "the way would then be open for him to the valley of the Indus. For England would be unable to hold the Pass against such a force."

"Is it really so difficult to cross the Pass, as it is said to be?" inquired Heideck.

"The Pass is about fifty versts in length. In 1839 the Bengal corps of the Indus army advanced through it against the Afghan army, and managed without difficulty to take with them twenty-four-pound howitzers as well as eighteen-pound field guns."

"If I remember rightly they arrived, without having met with any opposition worth mentioning, at Kandahar, and occupied the whole of Afghanistan. But, in spite of this, they finally suffered a disastrous defeat. Of their 15,000 men only 4,500 succeeded in returning in precipitate flight through the Khyber Pass back to India."

Prince Tchajawadse laughed ironically.

"Fifteen thousand? Yes, if one can trust English sources of information! But I can assure you, according to better information, that the English in 1839 advanced upon Afghanistan with no less than 21,000 combatants and a transport of 70,000 men and 60,000 camels. They marched through the Bolan Pass, took Kandahar and Ghazni, entered Cabul, and placed Shah Shuja upon the throne. They did not suffer any decisive defeat in battle, but a general insurrection of the Afghans drove them from their positions and entirely wiped out their force."

"I admire your memory, Prince!"

"Oh! all this we are obliged to have off by heart in the General Staff College, if we are not to be miserably ploughed in examination. In November, 1878, we were rather weak in Central Asia through having to devote all our resources to bringing the war with Turkey to a close, and so the English again entered Afghanistan. They meant to take advantage of our embarrassments to bring the country entirely under their suzerainty. They advanced in three columns by way of the Bolan Pass, the Kuram Valley, and the Khyber Pass. But on this occasion too they were unable to stand their ground, and had to retire with great loss. No Power will ever be able to establish itself in Afghanistan without the sympathies of the natives on its side. And the sympathies of the Afghans are on our side. We understand how to manage these people; the English are solely infidels in their eyes."

"Do you believe that Russia merely covets the buffer-state Afghanistan, or do its intentions go further?"

"Oh, my dear comrade, at present we mean India. For more than a hundred years past we have had our eye on this rich country. The final aim of all our conquests in Central Asia has been India. As early as 1801 the Emperor Paul commanded the Hetman of the army of the Don, Orlov, to march upon the Ganges with 22,000 Cossacks. It is true that the campaign at that time was considered a far simpler matter than it really is. The Emperor died, and his venturesome plan was not proceeded with. During the Crimea General Kauffmann offered to conquer India with 25,000 men. But nothing came of this project. Since then ideas have changed. We have seen that only a gradual advance can lead us to our objective. And we have not lost time. In the west we have approached Herat, until now we are only about sixty miles away, and in the east, in the Pamirs, we have pushed much nearer still to India."

"It is most interesting to hear all this. I have done my best to get at the lie of the land, but till now the Pamir frontiers have always been a mystery to me."

"They mystify most people, you will find. Only a person who has been there can understand the situation. And he who has been there does not know the frontier line either, for there is, in fact, no exact boundary. The Pamir plateau lies to the north of Peshawar, and is bounded in the south by the Hindu-Kush range. The territorial spheres of government are extremely complicated. The Ameer of the neighbouring country of Afghanistan claims the sovereignty over the khanates Shugnan and Roshan, which form the larger portion of the Pamirs. Moreover, he likewise raises pretensions to the province of Seistan, which is also claimed by Persia. Now this province is of peculiar importance, because the English could seize it from Baluchistan without much difficulty, and, if so, they would obtain a strong flank position to the south of our line of march, Merv-Herat, by way of Kandahar-Quetta."

"The conditions are, certainly, very complicated."

"So complicated, indeed, that for many years past we have had differences with the English touching the frontier question. Our British friends have over and over again forced the Ameer of Afghanistan to send troops thither; an English expedition for the purpose of frontier delimitation has been frequently camped on the Pamir Mountains. Of course, in this respect, we have not been behindhand either. I myself have before now taken part in such a scientific expedition."

"And it really was merely a scientific expedition?"

"Let us call it a military scientific excursion!" replied the Prince, smiling. "We had 2,000 Cossacks with us, and got as far as the Hindu-Kush--the Baragil Pass and another, unnamed, which we called, in honour of our colonel, the Yonov Pass. There we were confronted by Afghan troops, and defeated them at Somatash. By order of the English, who were paying him subsidies, Ameer Abdur-Rahman was obliged to resent this and petition their assistance. An English envoy arrived in

Cabul, and negotiations were entered into, which we contrived to spin out sufficiently to gain time for the erection of small forts in the Pamirs. Finally an arrangement was arrived at in London to the effect that the Pench should be the boundary
between Russia and Afghanistan in the Pamir territory. A few months later we
were met by an English expedition on the Sarykul; we were to determine the exact
boundary-line together. It was great fun; our English comrades tried hard not to let
us see that they had orders to be complacent. We had soon discovered it, and drew
the line just as we pleased. The upshot was that only a very narrow strip of land
between Bukhara and the Indian border remained to the Ameer, and that he had
to undertake neither to station troops there nor to erect fortifications. Our territory
had been pushed forward up to within about twelve miles of English territory. It
is there that we are closest to India, and we can, if we choose, at any time descend
from the passes of the Hindu-Kush to the Chitral Valley, within the British sphere
of influence."

A servant, bringing an invitation to Heideck from Mrs. Baird to dine with them
that evening, interrupted the conversation. The Captain was scarcely able to disguise his pleasure; he had no doubt that this invitation was due to Edith, and was
happy in the prospect of seeing her again.

"You are on good terms with the Colonel," said the Prince, as soon as the servant had left with Heideck's letter of acceptance. "This can be of the greatest assistance to you under present circumstances. Do make him give you a passport and
come with me."

"I am sorry, Prince! I should be delighted to travel in such pleasant company,
but business keeps me here a little longer for the present."

"Well--as you please--I must not try to over-persuade you; but I will not abandon the hope that we shall meet again, and it is unnecessary to assure you that you
can count upon me in any situation in which you may find yourself."

IX
THE GERMAN EMPEROR

The German Emperor was paying his annual visit to the moors at Springe. But this year he had little time to spare for the noble sport which usually brought him fresh vigour and recreation in the refreshing solitude of the forest. The telegraph was busy without interruption, and statesmen, diplomats, and high officers arrived daily at the hunting-box, and held long conferences with the Emperor. The windows of his study were lit up till late at night, and the early morning generally found the monarch again at his writing-desk.

After a night half spent at work, to-day the yearning for a breath of fresh air had taken the Emperor at early dawn into the silent pine-woods.

A light hoar-frost had fallen during the night, covering the ground with fine white crystals. The shadows of dawn still lingered between the tree-trunks. But in the east a glowing light suffused the pale, greyish-blue sky.

The Emperor directed his gaze in that direction. He halted under a tall, ancient fir-tree, and his lips moved in silent prayer. He asked for counsel and strength from Him who decides the fate of nations, to enable him to arrive at his weighty and difficult decision at this grave crisis. Suddenly, the sound of human voices struck his ear. He perceived two men, evidently unaware of his presence, coming towards him hard by, on the small huntsman's track in the wood, engaged in lively conversation. The Emperor's keen huntsman's eye recognised in one of the two tall gentlemen his Master of Horse, Count Wedel. The other was a stranger to him.

It was the stranger who now said--

"It is a great pleasure to me, at last, to be able to talk to you face to face. I have deeply mourned the rift in our old friendship and fellowship. On my side, the irritation is long since past. I did not wish to enter the Prussian service at that time, because I could not bear the thought of our old, brave Hanoverian army having ceased to exist, and I was angry with you, my dear Ernest, because you, an old Hanoverian Garde du Corps officer, appeared to have forgotten the honour due to your narrower Fatherland. But the generous resolution of the Emperor to revive Hanoverian traditions, to open a new home to our old corps of officers, and to inscribe our glorious emblems upon the flags and standards of these new regiments, has made everything right. I hope the time is not far distant when also those Hanoverians, who still hold aloof in anger, will allow that a war lord of such noble disposition is the chosen shepherd and leader of the universal Fatherland."

"Well, I have never misjudged you and your iron will. Meanwhile, you have thoroughly made acquaintance with the world, and since you are a merchant prince of Hamburg, I suppose you are the possessor of a large fortune."

"My life has been both interesting and successful, but I have not got what is best after all. I long for a sphere of activity in keeping with my disposition. I am a soldier, as my forbears have been for centuries before me. Had I entered the Prussian army in 1866, I might to-day be in command, and might perhaps in a short time have the honour to lead my corps into the field under the eyes of our Emperor himself."

"You believe Germany will be brought into this war? Against whom should we fight?"

"If our Emperor is really the sharp-sighted and energetic spirit for which I take him--"

The monarch did not care to let the gentlemen talk on longer in ignorance of his presence.

"Hallo! gentlemen!" he called out merrily. "Do not betray your secrets without knowing who is listening!"

"His Majesty!" the Count said under his breath, taking off his hat and bowing low. His companion followed his example, and as the Emperor looked at him with a questioning glance, said--

"At your Majesty's command; Grubenhagen, of Hamburg."

The monarch's eyes travelled over the tall, broad-shouldered figure of the fine man, and he asked smilingly--

"You have been in the service?"

"Yes, your Majesty--as lieutenant in the Royal Hanoverian Garde du Corps."

"There were then commoners as officers in that regiment."

"May it please your Majesty, my name is Baron von Grubenhagen, but the 'Baron' was in the way of the merchant."

The open and manly bearing of the Baron, combined with the deference due to his sovereign, appeared to please the Emperor. He gazed long into the clear-cut, energetic face, with its bold and intelligent eyes.

"You have seen much of the world?"

"Your Majesty, I was in America, and for many years in England, before entering business."

"A good merchant often sees more than a diplomatist, for his view is unbiassed, and freer. I love your Hamburg; it is a loyal city, full of intelligence and enterprise."

"The Alster people would reckon themselves happy to hear your Majesty say so."

"Do not the Hamburgers suffer great losses from the war?"

"Many people in Hamburg think as I do, your Majesty."

"And what is your opinion?"

"That, under the glorious reign of your Majesty, all Germans on the Continent will be united to one whole grand nation, to which all Germanic races of the north will be attracted by the law of gravitation--Danes, Swedes, and Norwegians."

"You have the courage of your opinions."

"Your Majesty, we live in an age, the characteristic of which is the formation of great empires."

The monarch interrupted him with a friendly movement of his hand.

"Let us go in to breakfast, gentlemen. Baron von Grubenhagen, you are my guest. I shall be interested to hear more of your bold ideas."

Immediately after his return to the hunting-box, the Imperial Chancellor, who had arrived from Berlin by a night train, had been announced to the Emperor. With the monarch's suite he also was present at the breakfast-table, probably not a little surprised to find a strange guest in the company of the Emperor, who was evidently very kindly disposed to him.

After breakfast, when the company were seated around the table in the smoke-room, and when, upon a sign from the Emperor, the aide-de-camp du jour had ordered the servants to withdraw, the Emperor William turned with a grave face to Baron von Grubenhagen.

"And now let us hear, openly and without reserve, how, according to your observation, the German nation regards the possibility of a war."

The Baron raised his fine, characteristic head. Looking openly and naturally into the Emperor's eyes, he replied--

"Your Majesty, no one is in doubt that it would, on the one hand, be a fatal step to declare war. By it many thousands will be sent to an early grave, lands devastated, and commerce perhaps ruined for many long years to come; and countless tears are the inevitable concomitants of war. But there is a supreme law, to which all others must yield--the commandment to preserve honour unsullied. A nation has its honour, like the individual. Where this honour is at stake, it must not shrink from war. For the conservation of all other of this world's goods is dependent upon the conservation of the national honour; where peace has to be preserved at any price, even at the price of national honour, all the benefits and blessings of peace will by degrees be lost, and the nation falls a prey to its neighbours. Iron is more precious than gold, for it is to iron we owe all our possessions. What use would be our army and navy? They are the outward sign of the political truth, that only courage and power are guarantees for the continuance and prosperity of a nation. Russia and France have joined hands to fight England. And the German nation feels it is time to take its share in these struggles. But nowhere is there any uncertainty as to which side Germany ought to join. Our nation has for a long time past been exasperated by English intrigues and encroachments. The human heart knows no other feeling so profound and powerful as the sense of justice, and the sense of justice has constantly been wounded by England's policy. Only one word from the Emperor is needed to strike the deepest chords in the German soul, and to raise a flame of enthusiasm that will swallow up all internal dissension and all party quarrels. We must not ask what might possibly happen; we must obey the dictates of the hour. If Germany fights with the whole of her strength, she must be victorious. And victory is always its own justification."

X
FIVE LAKHS OF RUPEES

At noon Prince Tchajawadse departed northwards accompanied by his page Georgi and his Indian servant. Heideck had observed great reserve during the short time he had known the beautiful Circassian, and had never betrayed that he had guessed the secret of her disguise. She seemed to be grateful, for although they never had exchanged words, she smiled at him and gave him very friendly glances at their chance meetings. There could be no doubt concerning the relation of the beautiful page and his master. Heideck may have felt some jealousy--he hardly ever had seen a more charming girl than this Circassian beauty in her picturesque dress; but all his thoughts were with Edith. The Russian was indeed a lucky fellow to have found such a charming travelling companion. She never forgot her assumed part of the page, when strangers were near, and yet it was clear to Heideck that she in truth was master. A single glance of her flashing eyes was sufficient to keep the Prince in order, when under the influence of intoxicants he would have otherwise given way to his brutal instincts. In her presence he never dared to use ambiguous and frivolous language.

With sincere regret Heideck saw the Prince depart. He did not share the hope, which the latter expressed to him, that they would meet again. But he remembered him as one of his most interesting acquaintances and a very charming comrade notwithstanding those little foibles he had noticed.

. . . .

It struck seven o'clock when Heideck in full evening dress entered the Colonel's drawing-room. He felt a wave of keen joy surging through him when he noticed that it was empty, except for Edith Irwin. The horrible events she had passed through had left her a little pale. To him she seemed more beautiful than ever. She met him with a smile and gave him her hand, which he kissed with great emotion.

"Mrs. Baird and the Colonel beg to be excused for a quarter of an hour," said she. "The Colonel has still much to do with the preparations for the mobilisation. Mrs. Baird is suffering from one of her bad attacks of headache and has had to lie down for a short time."

Heideck's face told Edith clearly enough that he gladly forgave his host and hostess this little impoliteness. After having taken a chair opposite hers, he began--

"I hope most sincerely, Mrs. Irwin, that you have had no annoyance on account of my late call. All day long yesterday this was on my mind."

With a sad smile she replied, "No, no. On the contrary, my husband has asked me to tell you that he is very sorry not to be able to thank you personally for your heroic behaviour. He hopes to be able to do so later on. He has been ordered to go to Lahore in great haste and for an indefinite period. There was not time for him to see you, in order to thank you."

Heideck imagined that he knew what this order meant. But he only asked: "And are you going to stay on here under the protection of the Colonel?"

"Nothing definite has been arranged as yet. Nobody knows what may happen to-morrow. It is certain that extraordinary events are in preparation. In case of war, we poor women have to do as we are told, you know."

"And the Maharajah? You have not heard about him?"

"Colonel Baird saw the Prince officially yesterday; but I do not know anything more; I had not the courage to ask. It seems to me quite certain that the Maharajah is hostilely disposed towards the Colonel. The event which happened here to-day is, I think, immediately to be connected with the Maharajah. I know the ways of these Indian despots!"

"May I venture to ask what has happened?"

"An attempt to poison the Colonel at his own table."

"To poison the Colonel?" asked Heideck surprised.

"Yes. Colonel Baird's habit is to drink a tumbler of ice-water before each meal. To-day, at tiffin, the Indian butler gave it him as usual. The water appeared to him rather cloudy. He did not drink it at once, and after a few minutes he noticed distinctly a white sediment at the bottom of the tumbler. When he called for the Indian butler, the man had disappeared, and has not been found yet. That increased our suspicion that an attempt at poisoning had been made. A small quantity of the fluid had been put into a dish which contained the food for the dogs. It was then placed into a rat-trap which contained five or six of these ravenous beasts. Ten minutes later they were dead. The remains of the water have been given to Doctor Hopkins. He is going to make a chemical analysis, and to tell us about it at dinner-time."

Before Heideck could find the time again to resume the discussion of Edith's personal affairs, Mrs. Baird came in, accompanied by the Colonel and his adjutant. They all shook hands with him in the most charming way, and after Doctor Hopkins had also arrived, a small man with a very vivacious manner, they went in to dinner.

Perhaps the Colonel would have preferred that nothing should be said in Heideck's presence about the poisoning attempt. His wife's impatience and excitement, however, could not be restrained.

"Well, Doctor Hopkins," she asked, "and what have you found?"

The Doctor evidently had been waiting for this.

"One of the most deadly poisons the Indians know," he answered. "The diamond powder. There is no antidote for it, and it is impossible to trace it in the body of the poisoned person, because it is of vegetable nature, and gets absorbed in the tissues."

A cry of horror escaped Mrs. Baird. She covered her eyes with her hand.

Mr. Hopkins continued: "I have never before come across the diamond powder, notwithstanding its use is said not to be uncommon. The preparation of it is a secret, anxiously guarded by the Indian physicians. It seems to play the same part at the Courts of the Indian princes that the celebrated 'aqua tuffana' did in the Middle Ages amongst the Italian despots."

These learned explanations of Doctor Hopkins were not adapted to raise the spirits of the company. Everyone remembered that this horrible attempt had only been frustrated by a lucky chance. The Colonel, who seemed to feel very uncomfortable on listening to the Doctor's conversation, gave a sign to his wife to rise, rather sooner than usual.

Tea and drinks cooled in ice were served in the verandah, charmingly illuminated by coloured lamps. Heideck had only had eyes for Edith all the evening. But he had avoided anxiously everything which might have betrayed his feelings. And, even now, he would not have dared to join her in the half-dark corner of the verandah, where she had seated herself, unless she had called out to him asking him to take the empty seat at her side.

"Mr. Heideck, here is another chair," she said, in a perfectly natural voice, drawing aside the pleats of her foulard skirt in order to let him pass. Again their eyes met unnoticed by the others. The violent beating of his heart would have told him that he was entirely in the thraldom of this beautiful young woman had he not known it already.

Suddenly the well-known shouts and cries of Indian drivers were heard. The conversation stopped and everybody looked and observed with astonishment the curious procession of waggons which they could see approaching, as the night was pretty clear. The Colonel excepted, no one understood the meaning of this spectacle. There were five waggons drawn by richly harnessed bullocks and escorted by a bodyguard of the Maharajah on horseback. Their captain rode till close to the verandah, then dismounted, and went up the steps. His mien was distinguished, and at the same time dignified. He was young and handsome, with Greek features and big, melancholy eyes. He wore a blouse of yellow silk, held around the waist by a shawl of violet silk, English riding-breeches, and high, yellow boots. A string of pearls was laid round his turban of violet-striped silk, and diamonds, large as hazel-nuts, sparkled on his breast as they caught the light of the lamp.

"That is Tasatat Rajah, the cousin and favourite of the Prince," whispered Edith, in answer to a question which she read in Heideck's face. "No doubt the Maharajah is sending him with a special mission."

The Colonel had risen and gone to meet his visitor, but he neither shook hands with him nor asked him to be seated.

"Greetings, long life and happiness, sahib, to you in the name of His Highness," he began with that noble air peculiar to the high-born Indian. "In token of his friendship and his respect he is sending you a small gift. He hopes you will accept it as a proof that you have forgotten the conversation which you had yesterday with His Highness in consequence of an unfortunate misunderstanding."

"His Highness is very kind," was the Colonel's answer, in a voice rather formal, "may I ask in what consists the present he is sending me?"

"Every one of these five waggons, sahib, contains a hundred thousand rupees."

"That is as much as five lakhs?"

"It is so. And I ask you once more kindly to favour His Highness with a reply."

The Colonel considered a moment, and then answered with the same quiet demeanour and impenetrable expression, "Thanks to you, Prince. Have the contents of these waggons carried into the hall. The Viceroy will decide what is to be done with it later on."

The Prince's face clearly showed his disappointment. For a little while he remained there standing as if considering what to do. But recognising that the Englishman wished to end the conversation, he touched the middle of his forehead with his right hand and descended the steps of the verandah. With the assistance of English soldiers a great many small casks were carried into the hall. The procession moved on again with the same cries and shouts which had accompanied its approach and soon disappeared.

A smile flitted across the Colonel's face, erstwhile so unemotional, as he turned towards his guests, probably feeling that some sort of explanation for his attitude was due to them.

"I consider this half-million a very desirable acquisition towards the war expenses of my detachment. But these Orientals never can understand our way of thinking, and our ideas of honour will always remain an insoluble riddle to them. With a present, that he, of course, has meant for me personally, this despot believes he has smoothed over everything that could possibly spell trouble for him--the plot against Mrs. Irwin as well as the diamond powder business. For, of course, he has already been informed by the butler who has disappeared of the failure of his plot, and he is well aware of what is in store for him if I report the scandalous story to Calcutta."

It was the first time the Colonel had openly declared his conviction that the Maharajah was the author of both plots. No doubt he had especial reasons for this, and Heideck fancied he had fathomed them, when, in reply to the question of the regimental surgeon as to his intention of sending in such a report, the Colonel replied--

"I do not know--I really do not know yet. According to the principle, fiat justitia, pereat mundus, I ought to do so, no doubt. But the pereat mundus is, after all, a debatable point. Probably war is imminent, and I am afraid the Viceroy would not be grateful to me were I to add fresh cares to all his other anxieties. At present these Indian princes are indispensable to us. They have to place their troops at our disposal, and we must not have any enemies in the rear when our army is engaged in Afghanistan. A harsh procedure against one of them, and all these princes might revolt. And a single defeat, or even only the false report of one, might entail incalculable consequences."

Doctor Hopkins assented without further discussion, and also the other officers present shared the opinion of their chief. As usual, during these last days a lively discussion had arisen as to the probabilities of war, and as to the probable course events would take. Heideck, certain of learning nothing new from the mouths of these gentlemen, all so confident of victory, utilised the opportunity afforded by the noisy conversation to ask Edith, in a low voice--

"Not only political considerations, but also your wishes, have prevented the Colonel from reporting the outrage of the other night to Calcutta--is it not so?"

"Yes, I begged him not to do so," she answered in the same low whisper. "But to-day, after the abominable plot upon his life, I told him that I do not ask any longer for any consideration to be shown me, or my--husband."

"You seriously think it possible that Captain Irwin--"

"Pray do not let us talk about it now, and not here, Mr. Heideck," she begged, raising her eyes to him imploringly. "You cannot have any idea how terribly I suffer from these dreadful thoughts. I feel as if before me lay only dark, impenetrable night. And when I reflect that some day I may be again forced--"

She did not finish her sentence, but Heideck knew well enough what she had omitted to say. An irresistible impulse made him answer--

"You must not allow yourself to be driven to take any course repugnant to your heart, Mrs. Irwin. And who is there who would dare to attempt to force you?"

"Oh, Mr. Heideck, you have no idea what regard for so-called 'GOOD FORM' means for us English people. No scandal--for Heaven's sake, no scandal! That is the first and prime law of our Society. Kind as the Colonel and his wife have been to me until now, I am very much afraid they would drop me, without question of my guilt or innocence, if I should allow anything to take place which they consider a scandal."

"And yet you must obey solely your own feeling--only the commands of your heart and conscience, Mrs. Irwin; not the narrow views of the Colonel or any other person. You must not become a martyr to a prejudice--I simply cannot hear the idea. And you must promise me--"

He stopped short. A sudden lull in the general conversation caused him to be silent also. And he fancied he saw the intelligent and penetrating eyes of Mrs. Baird directed upon himself with an expression of mistrust. He was displeased with himself. Displeased, because the intoxicating proximity of the adored being, and his aversion for her husband, that had almost increased to passionate hatred, had led him into the danger of compromising her. But when, soon afterwards, he took his leave, together with the other guests, a soft pressure of Edith's hand gave him the delightful assurance that she was far from being angry with him.

XI
THE MOBILISATION

Every day now brought fresh news, and the threatening spectre of war drew nearer and nearer. The order for mobilisation had been given. The field-troops were separated from the depot, destined to remain in Chanidigot. The infantry were provided with ammunition, and were daily exercised in firing and bayonet drill. Horses were bought up and a transport organised, which comprised an enormous number of camels. The commissariat stores were replenished, and the officers eagerly studied the maps of Afghanistan.

According to Heideck's ideas of mobilisation progress was much too slow, and the Maharajah appeared still less in a hurry with the equipment of his auxiliary troops.

Military trains from the South passed without cessation through Chanidigot, carrying horses and troops further north. Their immediate goal was Peshawar, where Lieutenant-General Sir Bindon Blood, Commander-in-Chief of the Punjab Army Corps, had concentrated a large field-army. Heideck noticed with surprise that the regiments which were being hurried up had been drafted from the most heterogeneous corps, so that, therefore, the tactical union of these corps, as well as their organisation, had been destroyed. No doubt the Government wished, at any cost, to mass large bodies of troops as rapidly as possible on the frontier, and to this end left all calculation of later events out of consideration. Viscount Kitchener, the Commander-in-Chief of India, as well as the Viceroy and the Cabinet Ministers in London, seemed to entertain no doubt that the English army would be victorious from the very beginning, and could not possibly be forced to retire to the fortresses of the North-west provinces. The contempt with which the officers in Chanidigot talked about the Russian army and the Afghans sufficiently confirmed this general belief.

At last it was clear that war had become a fait accompli. On the tenth day after the announcement of the Russian invasion of Afghanistan uncertainty was at an end.

The Cabinet in London had inquired in St. Petersburg as to the meaning of that invasion, and it received the answer that Russia felt compelled to come to the rescue of the Ameer at his request, for the Afghan ruler was anxious for his independence, in view of the measures which were taken by England. Nothing was further removed from the intention of the Russian Government than to challenge England, but she felt it impossible to look on at the embarrassment of the Ameer with equanimity, and so determined to fight for the independence of Afghanistan.

Thereupon England declared war, and Lieutenant-General Blood received the order immediately to advance through the Khyber Pass into Afghanistan. Further, Lieutenant-General Hunter, the Commander-in-Chief of the Bombay Army Corps, was ordered to march with an army from Quetta towards Kandahar. At the same time an English fleet was to leave Portsmouth.

Although the English papers published in India had evidently been instructed to maintain silence about matters which might place England in an unfavourable light, they furnished a good deal of news which gave the intelligent reader all manner of clues as to the present warlike situation. It could be seen that England was also arming against France. Only as to the attitude of Germany in the universal war that threatened every clue was wanting.

The intention of removing the families of the military and civil officers, stationed in Chanidigot, south to Bombay, or to Calcutta in the east, had soon been dropped. The spreading of the plague in both cities and the difficulties of the journey were against it; for the railways were completely given over to the transport of troops. It was determined that the women and children should, for the time being, remain with the depot in Chanidigot. Captain Irwin, who had returned from Lahore and who, apart from his duty, in which he displayed an almost feverish zeal, led the life of a hermit, was appointed to command this depot. But his wife, whom he had not yet once met since his arrival, was not to be placed with the others under his charge. Colonel Baird, who had given way to his wife's urgent entreaties to be allowed with her children to accompany him to Quetta, had asked Edith Irwin to join them.

Orders had been given that the detachment should start in conjunction with the forces of the Maharajah of Chanidigot. Heideck had obtained permission to accompany it. The Colonel was well disposed towards him, and it was evidently pleasant for the former to have about him, as protector to the ladies, such a chivalrous man, upon whom he could always implicitly rely when his military duties prevented him from looking after them. On the day preceding the start Heideck was at tiffin with the Colonel, and coming events were being discussed in a serious manner, when from outside the dull screech of an automobile's horn caught their ears. Two minutes later, covered with dust and with his face a dark red from the heat, an officer appeared on the verandah who introduced himself as Captain Elliot, General Blood's adjutant.

"The General," he said, adopting the proper military attitude, "has sent me to report that all the plans have been altered. Your orders are not to march to Quetta, but to hasten your preparations and start as soon as possible for Mooltan."

"And what is the reason for this change of orders?" asked the Colonel.

"The Russians are coming down from the Hindu-Kush, and are marching down the valley of the Indus, thus taking our army in the rear. General Blood is marching south, so as not to be cut off. I am sent round to direct all detachments upon Mooltan."

"No! is that possible? Is there not perhaps some mistake? How can the Russians cross the Hindu-Kush?"

"I have myself seen Russian infantry in the gorges of the Indus Valley, Colonel. The march upon Herat and the occupation of Cabul under General Ivanov were mainly blinds. Ivanov, with twenty thousand men under his command, and reinforced by a like number of Afghans, is advancing from Cabul upon the Khyber Pass. But the main attack will be made from the Pamirs in the direction of Rawal-Pindi and Lahore."

"Rawal-Pindi?" exclaimed the Colonel. "If the Russians come down the Indus, they will first of all arrive at Attock, and this strong fortress will check their advance long enough."

"Let us hope so, but we must not absolutely reckon upon it. The strength of the Russian army is not at present known to us; but their advance has evidently been magnificently planned. Their engineers must have done perfect wonders in the difficult passes of the Hindu-Kush; and these Russian soldiers are like iron."

"Well," said the Colonel, "we will soon show them that we are of steel."

The adjutant handed over the written instructions, and after having read them, the Colonel replied--

"To-morrow morning early I start for Mooltan, and expect to arrive there with my detachment by tomorrow evening. The commissariat and ammunition columns will, of course, not be able to get there until a few days later, and then only in part. What in all the world can have possessed the General not to meet the enemy in Rawal-Pindi? That town is fortified and surrounded by strong forts; it is one of the greatest depots in India. Why must the General retire so far back, so far as Mooltan?"

"The General is expecting a decisive battle, and intends for the purpose to co-operate with the army of General Hunter. But both armies are, at present, equidistant from Mooltan, and the Russians would, the General thinks, hesitate to advance so far, from fear of having their left flank attacked from Lahore. In Lahore there is at present a force of ten thousand men, which is being reinforced every day from Delhi."

With the departure of the adjutant, who, owing to the exigencies of duty, was obliged to decline the Colonel's offer of a seat at table, the luncheon-party broke up, and the Colonel made apologies to his guest for being unable, under existing circumstances, to devote more time to him. His officers accompanied him, and soon after Mrs. Baird was also called away. Quite unexpectedly Heideck and Edith Irwin found themselves alone.

For a few moments neither spoke, as though neither wished to give expression to the feelings that filled their hearts. The young wife first broke silence.

"You were intending to go with us into the field, Mr. Heideck, and I know that your decision was prompted by a desire to assist us women with your protection. But now all the arrangements are altered, and I beg of you to abandon your intention."

He looked at her surprisedly. "What, Mrs. Irwin? do you intend to deprive me of the pleasure I had looked forward to of accompanying you, and being your protector? And why?"

"You also have just heard that all the arrangements are altered. Had we gone to Quetta, then, as soon as our army had crossed the frontier, you would have been easily able to find another place; but if the battle takes place on Indian soil you will find yourself in constant danger."

"In my quality as foreigner? Certainly. I should, under the circumstances, be exposed to much unpleasantness, but before I change my plans, I should like to hear from you if you, too, intend to remain with the troops under these altered conditions?"

"Since Mrs. Baird has given me permission to accompany her, yes."

"And you believe that I shall show less courage than you, who will also certainly be exposed to serious risks?"

"How could I doubt your courage, Mr. Heideck? But that is, after all, something quite different. The place of us soldiers' wives is at the side of our husbands, whom we have followed to India. And, moreover, we are, perhaps, nowhere safer than with the army. But you have no concern with this war and with our army. If you, now, were to leave here to take up your quarters in one of the hill stations far from the seat of war, and where you were not exposed to the risks of battle and the plague, you would be certainly allowed, as a German merchant, to remain there unmolested."

"And why do you not yourself go to such a hill station, Mrs. Irwin? I should suggest Simla, if it were not so near to the seat of war. But do, pray, go to Poona, or into one of the other mountain stations in the south."

The young lady shook her head.

"I expect that that would be going straight to destruction."

"And what, may I ask, makes you think this?"

"I have already told you that in case of war English women are, here in India, only tolerably safe when in the immediate neighbourhood of soldiers. If we were to be defeated, the revenge the people would take on its oppressors would be terrible. Are you aware of the cruel instincts which slumber in these men, apparently so polite and submissive? The defenceless women and children would, without doubt, be their first victims. It was so in the Mutiny of 1857, and so it will be again under similar conditions. Nana Sahib and his crew wallowed at that time in the fiendish tortures of white women and children, and shed streams of innocent blood. And the civilisation of the lower classes has certainly since then not improved."

"You speak as if you considered a defeat of your army probable."

"I cannot get rid of my melancholy forebodings. And you, yourself, Mr. Heideck--please be straightforward with me! When the adjutant was standing there a little while ago, and when every one of his words showed the want of circumspection in our generals, I watched your face, and I read more from its expression than you have any idea of. I will not try to enter into your secrets, but I should be grateful if you would be candid with me. You are not the person for whom you here give yourself out."

He did not hesitate for a moment to confess to her the truth.

"No, I am a German officer, and have been sent here by my superiors to study the Anglo-Indian army."

Edith's surprise was evidently not great.

"I had an inkling of it. And now please answer my question quite as straightforwardly. Do you believe that the British army will be victorious?"

"I would not permit myself to give an opinion on this point, Mrs. Irwin."

"But you must have an idea. And I would give a great deal to know what it is."

"Well, then--I believe in English bravery, but not in English victory."

She heaved a deep sigh, but she nodded her head in assent, as if he had only expressed her own conviction. Then she gave him her hand and said softly--

"I thank you for your confidence, and as a matter of course no one shall ever learn from me who you are. But now I must insist more than ever that you leave us for your own safety's sake."

"And if I were to refuse? Supposing that in my position as soldier I were to consider it to be my duty not to leave you in the lurch? Would you be angry with me? Would you no longer permit me to enjoy the happiness of your society?"

Her breast heaved, but she bowed her head and was silent. Heideck plainly saw the glistening tears which stole from under her eyelids, and slowly rolled down her delicate cheek.

That was answer enough for him. He bowed, and kissing both her hands, whispered--

"I knew that you would not be so cruel as to drive me from you. Wherever fate may lead me, it will find me at your side as long as you require my protection."

For a few seconds she let him keep her hand. She then gently withdrew it from his grasp.

"I know that I ought to forbid you for your own safety to follow me; but I have not the strength to do so. Heaven grant that you may never reproach me for having acted as I have done."

XII
THE CAMP OF LAHORE

An unusually beautiful and dry spring favoured the advance of the Russian army through the mountains. In the north of India the temperature kept at an average of 68 degrees F., and day after day the sun streamed down from a cloudless blue sky upon the broad plains of the Punjab, through the bright green of which the Russian troops, in their white summer uniforms, pushed on like long streaks of silver.

Everything pointed to the fortune of war being on their side, for they had overcome the difficult and dreaded passage at Attock with unexpected ease.

The commander of this lofty fortress received orders not to break down the bridge across the Indus until General Blood's army, which was directed to hold Peshawar and the Khyber Pass, had effected its retreat and had to the last man passed the river.

The bridge at Attock, which is a high structure built across the narrow bed of the Indus, which here foams down with swirling swiftness, is considered a masterpiece of engineering. It is built in two tiers, the upper of which carries the railway, while the lower forms a road for carriages, beasts of burden, and foot-passengers. On either side of the river is a fortified gate. The English commander of Attock trusted to the strength of the forts standing some 800 feet above the river, and imagined the Russians to be still far away.

The Russian vanguard had crossed the river Cabul, which joins the Indus at Attock, at a point a few miles above the city, and thus appeared simultaneously with General Blood's troops before the fortress.

Blood's troops were passing the bridge in endless long columns. Their movement was often checked by blocks, caused by the dislocation of the several units, and so it came about that, in the early morning, a superior Russian force had, un-perceived by the English, reached the northern end of the bridge just as a gap had been caused in the English columns.

The thick fog of the morning had hidden the approach of the Russians from the English outposts. The Russians at once occupied the bridge, and so cut off the remainder of the English that were on the northern bank from their main body that had already crossed the bridge. The commander of the Russian advance guard was himself quite astounded at the success that the fortune of war had thrown into his lap: had not the fog rendered the scouting on both sides illusory, and had not chance allowed him to fall in with this gap in the English columns, the chances would, considering the narrowness of the road, have been much more favourable to the English than for him, and the battle would probably have ended with the defeat of his forces. As it was, General Ivanov, who had crossed the Khyber Pass, came upon the English rearguard, and five thousand men of the Anglo-Indian troops had to surrender after a short struggle. Two thousand English and three thousand Moham-medans fell into the hands of the Russians. As soon as the Mohammedan-Indians were informed by the victors that they were fighting for the true faith against the infidels, they went over without more ado to the Russian side.

The commander at Attock refused to surrender the fortress, and trained his guns upon the Russian columns; but, in consequence of the fog, the batteries did not inflict much damage upon the Russians, who being now in possession of the bridge continued their advance to the south.

But, however, before the march that had thus been so successfully begun was continued, the Russian commander-in-chief collected, not far from Attock, all the troops that had crossed the Hindu-Kush in small detachments, and united them with the army corps advancing from Afghanistan, so that he now disposed of an army of seventy thousand men.

It was a blood-stained road upon which this host travelled behind the retreat-ing English army. This was the road upon which Alexander the Great in days of yore entered India. Here, at the beginning of the sixteenth century, the Afghan sovereign Ibrahim Lodi had fought with the Grand Mogul Baber; here, a few de-cades later, Mohammed Shah Adil, the generallissimo of the Afghans, when at the head of fifty thousand horse, five hundred elephants, and innumerable infantry, was defeated by the youthful Grand Mogul Akbar. Still more bloody was the battle, which about the middle of the eighteenth century the Afghan Sultan Ahmed Shah Durani fought with the great Mahratha princes, Holkar Sindhia, Gaekwar and the Peschwas; and here, once again, all the horrors of war raged, when in the year 1857, the English Generals Havelock, Sir James Outram, Sir Colin Campbell, Sir Hugh Rose, Sir John Lawrence, and Sir Robert Napier, crushed with pitiless severity the dangerous sepoy mutiny. East and West had, in gigantic struggles, fought together on this spot so full of legends, this the cradle of mankind. Hundreds of thousands of human lives had been sacrificed on this blood-drenched soil, and yet again was a decisive battle impending, destined to be engraved with a steel pencil on the tablets of the world's history.

The movements of the Russian army had upset the plan of the English generals. The English corps which had collected at Mooltan were quickly pushed on to Lahore, as soon as the Russians' intention to proceed to the south-east became clear. The time which General Ivanov required for concentrating his troops at Attock rendered it possible for the English to reach Lahore. Here their forces were considerably increased by the strong garrison, and each day new regiments came in from Delhi and Lucknow, which brought the strength of the army commanded by Sir Bindon Blood up to the number of one hundred thousand combatants.

The English prepared for a decisive battle, for already the head of the Russian columns was no further than ten English miles north of the mausoleum of the Emperor Jahangir at Shah Dara, a military station scarcely eight English miles northwest of Lahore.

The English troops advanced in their concentrated formation in single line; their left wing occupied the Shah Dara plantations and the pontoon bridge across the river Ravi that flows close to Lahore. It extended thence five English miles further eastwards to a canal which flows past the Shalimar Park towards the south. This park and a place called Bhogiwal, lying next to it, formed the right wing. Before their front stretched a tributary of the sinuous Ravi with its marshy banks. To the rear of their position lay the fortress of Lahore with its brick wall, fifteen feet in height, pierced by thirteen gates.

The Ravi, a tributary of the Indus, had at this time but little water. The bed of the river was for the most part dry, and only consisted of rapid, irregular rivulets, which here and there exposed between them larger and smaller, but for the most part, muddy islands. The bed of this river formed the chief obstacle to the Russian attack, for they had to pass it before reaching the English front and the city of Lahore.

Heideck occupied a small tent that he had brought with him from Chanidigot. Morar Gopal's horse had carried it on its back during the march from Mooltan to Lahore, for the lancers, whom Heideck had joined as being a friend of their officers, had not covered the distance by railway. They were now encamped in the Shalimar Park, an extensive enclosure surrounded by a wall and full of the most beautiful mango trees, and among them many small fountains and pretty pavilions. As Heideck wore a khaki suit and a cork helmet, he looked, in spite of his having no distinctive military dress, quite like an English officer, the resemblance being increased by his martial bearing.

During the march and during his stay in the camp he had had an opportunity of closely observing the British system of campaigning. But he took good care not to mention it to the English officers, for they were not very favourable conclusions at which he had arrived. He had gained the impression that the troops were neither well led, nor displayed any special knowledge of campaigning. The men both in bivouac and in camp were often in want, and, indeed, frequently suffered real distress, because the necessary material was not always at hand, and their food was not regularly supplied; the greatest confusion reigned in the commissariat department.

Not alone there, but also in the tactical units serious confusion was everywhere apparent, in consequence of the unpractical and heterogeneous composition of the detachments. First of all, the regiments which were to make up the army corps in Peshawar and Quetta were all jumbled up together, because as soon as ever they appeared to be ready to march, they were separately taken away from their garrisons and placed upon the railway. Concentration upon Mooltan and the hurried march to Lahore had resulted in downright inextricable confusion.

Heideck found himself in the middle of an army which had never engaged in a great war and certainly never in one against regular troops. It is true that the English were accustomed to fighting, for they had been constantly obliged to measure themselves with barbarous and semibarbarous peoples. They had made expensive expeditions and gained dearly purchased victories; but it was always the undisciplined, dark-skinned, and black hordes with whom they had had to deal. The experiences of the Boer War had not entered into the flesh and blood of the troops. The personal bravery of the individual had almost always been regarded as the main thing, and it was easy to understand why all the officers should be puffed up with vanity. They looked down with contempt upon all foreigners, because they had, as a matter of fact, almost always gained their victories over superior numbers.

Heideck noticed with astonishment that the tactical rules and instructions in the British army were still often at variance with modern armament, particularly in the case of the infantry; volley firing was habitually employed as the general way of engaging the enemy. The men were drilled at the word of command to open and keep up a steady even fire and then in close ranks to rush with the bayonet on the enemy. This powerful nation was, in fact, too listless to utilise the most modern experiences of the science of war: proud Albion blindly believed everything English to be good and despised everything new and foreign. Or did the English perhaps only avoid advancing in loose order in action because they were afraid that they would otherwise not be able to control their Indian soldiers?

The environs of Lahore, particularly to the north of the city between the wall and the camp, presented a very lively scene. The innumerable camels which had served as baggage animals and formed the major portion of the transports afforded a very peculiar spectacle. They were either lying on the ground closely packed together or solemnly paced along, while the shrill yells of the drivers filled the air. Moreover, there was here congregated a huge crowd of men belonging to the army in one or other capacity without being combatants, and the eye fond of picturesque impressions could feast with delight on the gay, ever-changing kaleidoscopic effects of the wide plain; while the distant scenery was also interesting enough in itself. Between the widely scattered villages and suburbs of the city, which contained 180,000 inhabitants, beautiful parks and gardens shone in fresh green foliage, mostly surrounding the burial-place of a sultan or a famous Mohammedan saint. Towards the south-east there stretched away the great encampments of the cavalry and artillery in which were included many elephant batteries.

The city itself was choked full of military and the families of the officers. Almost all the women and children of the garrisons lying to the north-west of Lahore had fled here at the advance of the troops. Mrs. Baird, too, with her two little daughters and Mrs. Irwin were also in the city, where they were lodged in the Charing Cross Hotel. Although the city was packed to a most alarming degree and the military situation was decidedly critical, Heideck did not anywhere observe any particular excitement.

The English preserved their peculiarly calm demeanour, and the natives kept silence out of fear: upon the latter the fully unexpected and incomprehensible change in the situation had probably had a certain bewildering effect.

When Heideck, shortly before sunset, went from the camp to the city to visit the ladies, he only became more firmly convinced, as he passed through the surging crowd outside the walls, that the position of the army had been very badly selected. Far too large a number of men and animals had been crowded within a comparatively small space. If Russian shrapnel were to fall among this dense mass a terrible panic was inevitable. The proximity of the fortified city was sure to induce the soldiers to take refuge behind its walls. Heideck had hitherto not gained the impression that resolute courage was to be expected of the native soldiers. In the street which led from the Shalimar Park to the railway station in the suburb of Naulakha, Heideck had constantly to go out of his way to allow the long columns of heavily laden camels and ox-waggons which came towards him to pass, and he therefore took nearly two hours to reach his goal. The Charing Cross Hotel was full up to the attics, and the two ladies had, with the children, to be content with a small room on the third floor which had been let to them at an enormous price.

Mrs. Baird, a lady of small, delicate build, but of energetic spirits and genuine English pride, appeared perfectly collected and confident. She did not utter a single word about her own evidently very uncomfortable position and of the privations which, under the existing circumstances, her children had to suffer, but only about the victory of the British arms, that she was convinced would immediately take place. The march from Mooltan to Lahore was, in her eyes, an advance, and she did not entertain the smallest doubt that the Russian insolence would in a short time meet with terrible chastisement.

"It is terrible to think," she said to Heideck, "that a nation that calls itself Christian should dare attack us in India. What was this unhappy land before we took pity on it? England has freed it from the hands of barbarous despots and brought it happiness! The Indian cities have grown in prosperity because our laws have paved the way for free development of commerce and intercourse. It is in the highest sense of the word a mission of civilisation that our nation has here fulfilled. If Heaven gives Russia the victory, this now so happy land will be hurled back into the blackness of barbarism." She appeared to wait for a word of assent from Mrs. Irwin, but the latter sat in serious silence.

"You ought not to be so silent, dearest Edith, and ought not to pull such a melancholy face," said the Colonel's wife, turning to her with a gentle reproach. "I perfectly understand that the sad events of your private life are distressing you. But all personal sorrow should now be merged into the general grief. What is the fate of the individual, when his country is exposed to such danger? I know that you are as good a patriot as any Englishwoman, but it appears to me that it is necessary to prove it in these hours of danger. Anxiety and moroseness have at such times upon one's surroundings the effect of a contagious disease."

"But possibly I am not the good patriot you take me for."

"Ah! What do you mean by that?"

"I cannot look at wars from your point of view, dear Mrs. Baird. It almost seems to me that there is not a very great difference between men and brute beasts, who fight each other out of hunger, or jealousy, and all kinds of low instincts."

"Oh, what a comparison to draw!"

"Well, it is true we know better how to wage war. We invent complicated instruments wherewith to destroy our fellow-beings in enormous numbers, whilst animals are limited to their own natural weapons. But do we, therefore, know better what we are doing than the animals? Don't you think that, when hosts of ants, or bees, or weasels, or fishes in the sea sally forth to destroy other creatures of their species, they may be guided perhaps by the same instincts that govern us also?"

"I cannot follow you there, Mrs. Irwin," the little lady replied, with a shade of irritation in her voice. "Human beings are endowed with reason, and are conscious of their aims and actions."

"Is it really so reasonable when peasants and labourers go to war as soldiers? Are they really led by a conscious purpose within them? None of them has anything to gain. They are compelled by others to allow themselves to be maimed and killed, and to kill their fellow-beings. And the survivors are in no respects better off, after gaining a victory, than they were before. And the leaders themselves? In the morals of Christian faith honours, orders, and endowments are only idle toys. Let us be honest, Mrs. Baird. Did England conquer India in order to propagate the Christian gospel? No! We have shed rivers of blood solely in order to spread our commerce, and in order to increase the wealth of a few, who themselves wisely remained at a safe distance from the fray, in the possession of luxury beyond the dreams of avarice."

"It is sad to hear such words from the mouth of an Englishwoman."

The conversation was in danger of taking a critical turn, as the Colonel's wife felt seriously annoyed and wounded by Edith's words. Heideck turned the discussion into a less dangerous channel. Soon afterwards the Colonel arrived; he occupied a tent further away in the camp, and only rarely found time to look after his family.

He simulated an air of gaiety and composure which he was far from feeling, and he was too indifferent an actor to succeed in his part.

"I am sorry, but I can only stay a very short time," he said, when he had caressed and kissed the little girls, whom he loved so tenderly, with still greater affection than usual. "My chief object in coming was to instruct you, dear Ellen, what you have to do in case we have to retire."

"To retire--? For Heaven's sake--I hope there is no question of retiring!"

The Colonel smiled, though not quite naturally.

"Of course, we cannot reckon with certainty upon victory. He would be a bad general who did not consider the possibility of defeat. During the last few hours all our dispositions have been altered. We are on the point of starting to attack the Russians."

"That is right!" cried Mrs. Baird, with bright eyes. "A British army must not wait for the enemy, but go and meet him."

"We shall march out at early dawn to try and prevent the Russians from crossing the Ravi. The engineers leave to-night in advance to destroy the bridges, if it is not already too late. The army has to execute a considerable movement to the left about, in order to reach the right position. At the same time the front has to be extended and lengthened to the right. The left wing remains at Shah Dara and the pontoon bridge."

"Is it not possible for us to come out also and look on at the battle?" inquired

Mrs. Baird. But her husband shook his head in decided refusal.

"For you, dearest Ellen, our trustworthy Smith will have a cart, with two strong oxen, ready here in the hotel. That is to provide for all eventualities. Should you receive news that the army is retreating upon Lahore--which the Lord forbid--you must lose not a minute, but drive as quick as possible, before the crush at the gates and in the streets begins, through the Akbari gate over the canal bridge leading to the Sadrbazar, and so to Amritsar, where you may be able to take the railway to Goordas. All other lines are closed for other than military purposes. Panic will not extend so far as that, and there, in any small hill station, you will find a safe resting-place for the present. And now, Mr. Heideck, may I trouble you by asking a great favour of you?"

"I am entirely at your disposal, Colonel."

"Stop here in the hotel--try to obtain the latest intelligence as to the course of events, and act as protector to the ladies and children until they are in security. If you will permit me to hand you a cheque--"

"Please leave that for the present, Colonel," Heideck replied. "I am provided with plenty of money and will render you an account later. I promise to protect your family and Mrs. Irwin as well as I can. But I think it would be better for me not to remain in the town, but to accompany the troops. I will return as soon as possible should events take an unfavourable turn. The anxiety of the ladies would be unnecessarily increased, and I myself should be uncertain as to what to do if we received unreliable news here in the hotel as to the position of affairs."

"You are right," said the Colonel, after a moment's hesitation. "Already now the most absurd rumours are flying about. Leaflets have been distributed amongst our Mohammedan troops inciting them with the maddest and most deceitful promises to desert from the British army. A few persons, taken whilst distributing such leaflets, have been already shot without more ado. I leave everything to your circumspection and decision. In any case, it will be best for you to keep as near to the Commander-in-Chief as possible. My permit will open the road to you everywhere. I will thank you later on."

He shook Heideck's hand warmly, and embraced his wife and his children once more, and the two men turned to leave. The dull foreboding that it was a parting for ever lay heavily upon all of them.

XIII
THE BATTLE

As Heideck returned to the camp, the road was lit up by the red glare of innumerable fires. On the wide plain, stretching between the town and river, work was going on in feverish haste. Rations and ammunition were being dealt out, and long lines of beasts of burden were in motion. Thousands of hands were busily employed in trying to facilitate the passage of the troops across the shallow tributary of the Ravi. The boggy places were made firm by a covering of palm branches and leaves; and logs of wood were got ready in hot haste for the artillery. Heideck could not help wondering why it was that the army had not been concentrated from the first at the point the battle was to take place. The approach through the difficult tract of land, in connexion with the contemplated movement to the left, made calls upon the endurance of the troops that could not but have the most detrimental effect upon the issue of the battle.

He met his Indian boy, evidently in great excitement, in front of his tent.

"When we start to-morrow we shall leave the tent with everything in it," said Heideck. "You will ride my horse and I shall take yours."

Morar Gopal was a Hindu from the south, almost as black as a nigger, a small, agile little man, weighing scarcely eight stone. It was in order to save his own horse for the later exertions of the day that Heideck wanted his boy to ride him at first.

Only now he perceived that his servant, contrary to his usual habit, was armed. He carried a sword buckled round his waist, and when asked the reason, the Indian answered, with a certain amount of pathos--

"All Hindus will die to-morrow, but I at least will defend myself bravely."

"What makes you believe that all Hindus must die to-morrow?"

"Oh, sahib! me know it well. The Mohammedans hate the Hindus, and they will kill all of us tomorrow."

"But this is nonsense. Mohammedans and Hindus will unite as one man to fight the Russians to-morrow."

The Indian shook his head.

"No, sahib! The Russians also are Mohammedans."

"Whoever told you so lied. The Russians are Christians, like the English."

But however great his confidence in his master might be in general, this time Morar Gopal evidently did not believe him.

"If they are Christians, why, then, should they wage war against other Christians?"

Heideck saw that it would be impossible to explain these things, that were beyond his own comprehension, to the dark-skinned lad. And only a few hours of the night still remaining for sleep, he despatched him to bed.

The first rays of the sun had begun to quiver over the wide plain when the forward march commenced. Heideck, already before dawn of day, was in the saddle, and found time to exchange a few words with Colonel Baird before setting out.

The Colonel occupied that day a position of great importance and responsibility. He commanded a brigade, consisting of two English and one sepoy regiments, the lancers, and a battery. In addition, he was in command of the auxiliaries sent by the Maharajah of Chanidigot, and led by Prince Tasatat, consisting of one thousand infantry, five hundred cavalry, and one battery. The Prince rode out magnificently attired and armed; the hilt and scabbard of his sword sparkled with precious stones, and a cockade of valuable diamonds flashed from his turban. The bridling and caparison of his mount, a splendid chestnut, represented alone a small fortune. His troops were also splendidly equipped, and displayed great confidence. The horsemen carried long pikes, like the English lancers, and wore red turbans, striped with blue. But many had been obliged to enter the lines of infantry in spite of their heavy boots, since a great number of horses, of the Mohammedan as well as the English cavalry, had died in consequence of bad fodder and over-exertion.

The movement of the British army was rather complicated. The English forces were massed in two divisions between Shah Dara and the park of Shalimar. The first comprised the Indian troops, officered by Englishmen; the second the English regiments. In this way seventy-five thousand Indians were to be prevented from running away. Should the first division be compelled to fall back, it would be checked by the twenty-five thousand English. The advance march was commenced in such fashion that the right half of the line of battle, sweeping far round to the right, executed a left wheel, and in this way lengthened the front by about one-third; this was done in order to fill up the gap caused in the centre. The second division was pushed forward into the first, and now formed the centre of the line of battle. At the same time a new second division was formed by leaving in reserve troops of the advancing divisions and massing them behind the left wing of the entire position; the English considered their left wing to be most threatened. Colonel Baird, with his brigade, occupied the centre of the front line of the main position.

Heideck watched many Indian regiments march past, and he could not help perceiving the difference of mood and carriage of Mohammedans and Hindus. Whilst the first maintained a very energetic and very frequently cheerful attitude, the latter allowed the ends of their turbans to hang loose, as a sign of their despair, and marched dejectedly forward, face and head covered with ashes. Morar Gopal's conception of the fate in store for all Hindus evidently was shared by all.

The wide plain was covered with marching columns of infantry, hosts of cavalry, and heavy, thudding artillery. Whilst the English foot soldiers, in their yellow-brown khaki dress, were hardly distinguishable from the colour of the ground, the cavalry regiments and the troops of the Indian princes looked like gaily coloured islets in the vast and surging sea of the army as it advanced in two divisions.

In obedience to the Colonel's wish, Heideck kept close to the side of the Commander-in-Chief, whose numerous staff and retinue of servants, horses, and carriages allowed him to mix in the crowd without attracting attention. But the General did not remain long with the centre. In order to gain a clearer survey of the entire movement, and to be able to observe the Russian approach, he rode with his staff and a strong cavalry escort towards the Ravi river. Heideck, accompanied by his faithful servant, attached himself to the escort, and thus was soon far in advance of Colonel Baird's brigade.

Nothing was as yet to be seen of the Russians, and about three hours might have passed since the beginning of the advance march, when lo! the dull, rumbling thunder of the first cannon-shot rolled over the wide field.

The General reined in, and directed his field-glasses upon the left wing, where the cannonade increased in violence each minute. Another half-hour and the sharp rattle of infantry fire mixed with the heavy rumbling of big guns. No doubt, on the left wing, by Shah Dara, the battle had commenced. Advancing towards the right bank of the Ravi, the Russians threatened to attack Lahore.

The Commander-in-Chief despatched two orderly officers to the right wing and the centre, with the order to accelerate the march. Then he returned with his suite to his former position.

But Heideck could not at once make up his mind to follow. From the moment the first shot had been fired the battle fever had seized him; he was only a soldier now.

He was irresistibly attracted by a building a short distance away, with a slender minaret, from which he hoped to obtain a better view. It was the half-decayed mausoleum of some saint, and Heideck had some trouble to climb up to the top of the minaret, a height of about twenty feet, whilst his servant waited with the horses down below. But the exertion was fully rewarded. He overlooked the flat plains. The sinuous Ravi river was hardly half an English mile distant. Its banks were covered with high grass and thick jungle growth; on the other side of the river immense thickly-packed masses of troops appeared--the advancing Russian army.

Both armies must soon come into collision by the river, for single English cavalry regiments and horse artillery batteries, advancing in a long line, were already in its immediate neighbourhood.

Heideck had seen sufficient to be able to judge of the position of the battle. He climbed down the minaret and mounted his fresh steed, whilst Morar Gopal sprang into the saddle of his own horse. They quickly arrived amongst the British cavalry, deploying in advance of their main army. The advance march was now executed with greatest rapidity. The English batteries dashed forward at the fastest pace the soft ground would permit, unlimbered, and opened fire. Large masses of infantry marched towards the jungle. But from the other side of the river the lively English fire was but feebly returned. Only from the direction of the left English wing, invisible from this point, did the artillery and infantry fire rage with unabated violence.

In consequence, considerable reinforcements were sent to the apparently hard-pressed left wing, and a distinct weakening of the centre took place, without a clear idea having been formed as to the intention of the Russians. Heideck's conviction was that such probably had been the Russian tactics. He was of opinion that they probably raised a great battle din by Shah Dara, in order to direct the attention of the English to that point, and then deliver their main attack against the centre. He was right; the main forces of the Russians were opposed to Colonel Baird.

Another circumstance he could not explain was the curious fact that the English as well as the Indian infantry regiments halted before the jungle instead of pushing forward to the river. Not even riflemen were sent into it, although the bush was by no means too thick for a chain of riflemen to take cover. The prickly bushes on the river's bank were sparse enough, and the high grass reaching up to the mens' shoulders would have made a splendid hiding-place.

By-and-by the English army had executed the movement to the left, and now stood facing the Russian front. One new regiment after the other was drawn from the second division and placed on the left wing, which was believed to be most threatened. The English guns thundered without interruption, but their position might have been better; many fired without being able to see the enemy at all through the thick jungle, and threw away their ammunition prematurely.

The sun shone brightly in the cloudless sky. A slight north-westerly breeze coming from the far distant hills blew the smoke of the powder in clouds back on the English army.

The enemy being thus completely shrouded from view, the infantry stood motionless. A sullen expectation brooded over the colossal forces, who realised danger, but were yet condemned to a torturing inactivity. Suddenly the wild roar of thousands of voices rose from the river, and hosts of cavalry, which before could have been held back by English infantry, broke through the jungles like immense swarms of locusts. Thousands of wild Afghans and warriors from Bukhara, Samarcand, Khiva, and Semiryechensk, combined in the Turkestan divisions, had crossed the river and, wildly crying "Allah! Allah!" hurled themselves upon the English battalions and batteries. Splendidly trained at firing from the saddle, they were terrible foes indeed.

Although the English returned the unexpected attack with crackling volleys, and did not recoil a hair's breadth from their positions, the Russian lines suffered but small losses in consequence of their open order. One new swarm after the other broke through the jungle, and rushed like an army of devils upon the batteries. A few of these were silenced; the men who served them were killed before they were able to turn their guns against their assailants, so wildly rapid had been this surprise rush of the bold horsemen.

The English cavalry, advancing to a magnificent attack, arrived too late; the weight of the shock was lost, the enemy having already dispersed in all directions. These men understood how to manage their small, rapid horses in a marvellous manner. They seemed like centaurs, and the rapidity with which they broke up their squadron, in order immediately after to close up again at another place in dense masses, rendered a counter attack on the part of the serried ranks of their adversaries almost impossible.

At one time, Heideck, with that part of the staff to which he had attached himself, had been drawn into the shock of battle. He had been obliged to shoot an Afghan, who attacked him, down from his horse, and he would probably, a moment afterwards, have been laid low by the sabre of another, had not the faithful Morar Gopal, who displayed extraordinary courage, just at the right moment made the horseman harmless by a well-directed blow of his sword. The cavalry engagement was still undecided, when lo! in the grass before the jungle were seen a number of glittering sparks. The sharp crack of shots was heard, and their destructive effect showed how admirably the Russian riflemen, who were gradually advancing against the British army, knew how to handle their rifles. The British infantry kept on discharging volleys indefatigably, but no practical result of all this waste of ammunition was apparent. Their targets were too small and too scattered, and the mechanical volleys fired at the word of command had but little effect. Besides this, the Russians had admirable cover, with the variegated jungle as a background, whilst the English stood out sharply against the horizon, and presented an excellent mark. According to their plan, the Russians first of all directed their fire against the men who were serving the batteries. Their well-directed shooting decimated the English artillery to a terrible degree. Scarcely two minutes had elapsed before the order was given to fall back with the guns. As far as was possible, the English harnessed up, and galloped off to take up their position between the infantry battalions, and from there again to open fire. The advance of the English artillery, which had taken place contrary to orders, and which was a result of their over-hasty forward movement, thus showed itself to have been a most disastrous step.

An even stronger and more damaging effect than that of the attack itself, was produced by the ceaseless cries of "Allah! Allah!" which proceeded from the Afghans and the Turkestan cavalry, and penetrated to the Mohammedans who stood in the British lines. Heideck saw quite clearly that, here and there, the Indian soldiers ceased firing as if in obedience to a word of command, and could distinguish how English officers in their excitement struck the men with the flat of the sword and threatened them with the revolver. Obviously, the leaders had lost all influence over the foreign elements under their command. Close to the Commander-in-Chief an English captain was bayoneted by an Indian soldier, and there could be no doubt that similar cases of open mutiny took place amongst the other Indian troops.

The men, who had only followed the orders of the foreign tyrants with the utmost reluctance, evidently believed the moment had come for shaking off the hated yoke, and at the same time the old enmity between the Mohammedans and Hindus, the rivalry between the two religions, which often in times of peace occasioned bloody feuds, burst into open flames. In the midst of the British army duels to the death were fought out between the irreconcilable adversaries. Thus it was unavoidable that the entire discipline became shaken and destroyed.

The battlefield was an awful spectacle. Before the front innumerable wounded, crying out for help, where no help was possible, were writhing in agony, for the retreat of the English artillery had had to be executed without thought of those left behind; wounded horses, wildly kicking to free themselves from their harness, increased the horror of the terrible scene, whilst stray divisions of English cavalry riding amongst them were fired upon by their own infantry out of fear of the advance of the Russian riflemen. Although in war all battlefields present a spectacle of the utmost horror, so that only the excitement of the moment enables human beings to endure it, yet the picture this battle of the advanced lines presented surpassed all imagination. The want of discipline amongst the English lines increased more and more, and the English officers had to fix their whole attention upon their own troops, instead of upon the movements of the enemy. The necessity for this was soon evident.

Prince Tasatat was the first to leave Colonel Baird with his entire force, and openly to march over to the enemy. His example was decisive for the Indians who were still hesitating, and the number of those going over to the enemy increased from minute to minute.

A uniform control of the line of battle had long since become impossible. Colonel Baird gave orders for his guns to open fire upon Prince Tasatat's company, and, like him, many other commanders fought their own individual battle just as their own judgment prompted. Indian regiments dispersed in all directions, because the men cared less for fighting than for getting booty from the prisoners and wounded. There were hand-to-hand fights in many parts of the battlefield, which, owing to the fanatical rage of the combatants, degenerated into horrible butchery. Those falling into the hands of the Afghans were most to be pitied. For these devils in human shape cut off the heads of all their prisoners and all wounded, whether Mohammedans, Hindus, or English, without any further ado, and in their rapacity tore the valuables from the bodies of the dead and wounded.

A line of fugitives, like an immense stream, passed the English regiments, which still stood firm in serried ranks, making for the plain of Lahore, in order to find protection behind the walls of the fortified city.

In Heideck's opinion the day was lost to the English, and he prepared himself to die a soldier's death, together with the brave men surrounding him. With feelings of sincerest admiration he confessed how great was the bravery, and how admirable the discipline that animated the English-born troops. Those regiments and batteries in which no native elements were mingled, stood calm and unshaken amongst all the terrible confusion, and thanks to their bravery, the battle, which opened in such disorder, began to present clear features, like those of the sharp peaks of a chain of mountains appearing above the mist, as it rolls down.

Instead of the semibarbarous horsemen that had opened the attack, new Russian batteries and colossal masses of infantry, with compact companies of riflemen, as well as several regiments of dragoons, now faced the English troops.

The Commander-in-Chief, with about 6,000 men and two batteries, was with the second English division, which had been greatly reduced in numbers. It was evidently his object to retire in good order towards Lahore, and to cover the retreat with his best troops.

He succeeded in withdrawing two smaller bodies from the right and left wing respectively by despatching orderlies. But the first division was so closely engaged with Russian infantry that an orderly retreat was almost impossible.

Notwithstanding this, the Commander was bent on making the attempt to withdraw also the first division of his army. He despatched one of his adjutants to Colonel Baird, who still had perhaps about 2,000 men under his command, with the order to break off the battle and to retire. The young officer saluted with grave face, drew his sword, and galloped away. But he had only traversed a small part of his dangerous journey, a distance of about a mile, when he fell a victim to the call of duty, being attacked and hurled from the saddle by a body of Cossacks mounted on small, rough-haired, but very swift steeds.

The General appeared undecided whether to stake another young life on this hopeless test. Heideck rode up to him and lifted his hand to his helmet.

"Will Your Excellency allow me to ride? I am a friend of Colonel Baird and should be glad of the opportunity of showing him my gratitude for his kindness to me."

The General sharply scrutinised the gentleman who was unknown to him, who looked like an officer, though not wearing the prescribed uniform; but he did not take the time to question him.

"Ride!" he said shortly. "The Colonel is no longer to hold out; he is to march to the right and retreat towards Lahore--if possible."

Heideck saluted and turned his horse. He had replaced his revolver in his belt, and returned his sword to its sheath.

Not by the aid of weapons, but solely by the rapidity of his horse could he hope to reach his goal. He gave his steed its head, and encouraged it by calling to it. The animal did not disappoint the hopes placed upon it. It seemed to fly, rather than run over the trampled ground. The Cossacks, who attempted to intercept this single horseman, were unable to reach him. And of all the shots aimed at the bold rider not one reached its mark.

The volunteer orderly reached the brigade without harm. But he was too late; almost at the same moment the collision with the Russian infantry, which, in spite of their losses, had advanced steadily to the attack, took place. In order to sell his life and those of his brave troops as dearly as possible, Colonel Baird had given orders to form a square, in the midst of which the horsemen and the guns were placed. Many officers, leaving the saddle, had picked up the rifles and cartridge-boxes of those that were killed, and, levelling their bayonets, had taken their places in the front rank of the square. Breathing heavily, and covered with perspiration Heideck stopped before the Colonel and made his report.

But the brave Englishman pointed with his hand towards the Russians.

"Impossible," he said. "We are destined to die upon this spot."

Then he also dismounted and seized a rifle. From a thousand British throats a loud "Hurrah!" broke forth, for the Russians had reached the square, and a hand-to-hand combat took place.

The horror of this terrible struggle at close quarters, the English fighting with the struggle of despair against a foe outnumbering them many times, impressed itself indelibly upon the memory of the young German. He, too, had drawn his sword, but in spite of his personal relations, his political sympathies were not on the English side.

Suddenly he heard, close to him, a hoarse cry of rage, and, on turning round, perceived to his boundless surprise the face of Captain Irwin, terribly distorted by hatred and fury. He had supposed him to be with the depot in Chanidigot, but Irwin must have found an opportunity of getting away from that command. Indeed, under the existing circumstances, it must have seemed equivalent to a severe censure, and Irwin had attached himself to the troops taking the field. He was now fighting in this death-struggle, rifle in hand, like a private soldier. The red blood staining the point of his bayonet bore eloquent testimony to his bravery. But in this supreme moment his country's enemies were forgotten in the sight of the mortal foe, the object of his personal hate, by whose courageous action the dastardly plot against Edith had been frustrated. Here were place and opportunity offered for satisfying the thirst for revenge, which consumed him. What mattered the death of a single unit in the midst of this great holocaust?

Before Heideck could divine the intention of the wretched man he was attacked by his bayonet. It was solely the rearing of a frightened horse that saved the Captain's life; the thrust of the bayonet grazed the animal's neck. At the same moment the terrible sword-cut of a Russian fell upon Irwin's unprotected neck (for he had lost his helmet), and with such force that, with a hollow cry, he fell on his face.

Suddenly the curiously altered, now hoarse voice of the Colonel struck Heideck's ear: "What are you still doing here? Ride, for Heaven's sake! Ride quickly! If you should see them again, take my last loving messages to my poor wife and children! Stay by them!"

The blood from a deep wound on his forehead was pouring over his face, and Heideck saw that only by the greatest exertion of will could he keep himself on his legs. He wanted to reply, but the Colonel had already again hurled himself into the tangled throng of fighters, and a few seconds later fell under the butt-end blows and sabres of the Russians.

Then Hermann Heideck turned his horse and galloped off.

XIV
IN THE PANIC-STRICKEN CITY

As on his ride to Colonel Baird's brigade, so also was Heideck on his return threatened by manifold forms of death. Although he successfully and happily avoided all compact bodies of troops on his way across the bloody battlefield, yet single Russian horsemen came up close to him and more than once he heard the shrill whistle of bullets as they whizzed past his head. But in the battle-fever that had seized him he had no thought of danger: all his thoughts were solely occupied with the question as to how he should contrive to arrive at Lahore, in order to fulfil the last request of the Colonel.

Bleeding from several wounds, his brave stallion put forth his utmost efforts to carry his rider safely away from the turmoil of battle. The wounded animal was still able to travel a considerable distance at full gallop. But suddenly he began to slacken his pace and to stumble, and Heideck perceived that his strength was exhausted. He dismounted in order to examine the injuries the horse had sustained, and at once perceived that he could not expect further exertion from the poor brute. In addition to a bayonet-thrust on the neck, it had also a bullet-hole on the left hind flank, and it was from this wound that the blood was principally streaming. In stertorous panting the poor beast laid his head on his master's shoulder, and Heideck stroked and patted his forehead. "Poor chap--you have done your duty, and I must leave you here behind." And now, for the first time, the anxious dread overcame him that he, too, would not escape with his life from this battlefield, for he perceived a horseman in Indian uniform approaching him, waving a sword. Heideck drew his revolver from his belt in order to protect himself against his assailant. But he immediately recognised in his supposed enemy his faithful boy, Morar Gopal, who beamed with joy at having by chance again found his master, whom he had believed to be dead. He wanted at once to leave Heideck his horse, and to attempt to make his own way on foot. But the German officer would not accept this unselfish sacrifice on the part of his servant; but he was relieved of the necessity of again separating from his faithful henchman by the fortuitous circumstance that, at that very moment, an English officer's riderless charger came in sight. The animal, a beautiful chestnut, was uninjured, and allowed itself to be caught without trouble. They were now in a position to continue their flight together, and Heideck resolved to turn towards the left English wing, because, as it appeared to him, the action was there proceeding with less ill-fortune than at other parts of the now totally defeated British army. This was certainly not the shortest way to reach Lahore, but it would have been a foolhardy enterprise to join the wild throng of fleeing troops and their pursuers which was already pouring along the road towards Lahore.

The far-stretching plantations of Shah Dara, lying on both banks of the Ravi, with the bridge of boats connecting them, were, as a matter of fact, still occupied by English troops, who had until now maintained their positions without any severe loss; but they had been, of course, in superior numbers to the Russians confronting them. For the attack upon Shah Dara, with which the battle had opened, had in the main been only a feint; its object being to force the English centre, against which the main attack was to be directed, to send out reinforcements, and thereby fatally to weaken itself. Heideck had seen with his own eyes how completely this plan had succeeded. Now, however, when the victory they had gained made their forces in other positions available for the work, the Russians commenced to attack this position also in superior numbers. Russian battalions from the reserves were being hurried up at the double, and new batteries made their appearance, ready to open fire upon Shah Dara and the mausoleum of Shah Jahangir, which lay to the south of it.

The English on their side were prudent enough not to engage in a hopeless battle of sheer desperation, but began their retreat, whilst they had still time to carry it out in tolerable order.

When Heideck had reached the southern end of the plantations, a regiment of Bengal cavalry was just crossing the pontoon bridge, and Heideck joined it. A Russian shell, which burst right in the middle of the troop, without, however, despite the severe losses it had caused, interrupting the formation, was a clear proof that the situation was here also quite untenable.

With comparatively few losses and without having once been drawn into an engagement, the regiment drew up close under the citadel, which, in the north of Lahore, lies inside the outer works.

But, with dismay, the hapless lancers perceived that the murderous shot and shell were pursuing them even here. Yet the bullets were not intended for them, but for the treacherous Indian troops and the irregular Russian cavalry, which surged up, in wild panic, against the walls. The effect of the fire was, however, none the less disastrous on that account. The English garrison which had remained in the city had closed all the gates, and appeared to have made up their minds to let no one in, either friend or foe. All the same, the commander of the Bengal regiment drew his men together and with irresistible weight forced his way right through the confused, huddling mass of men engaged in hand-to-hand combat beneath the walls. He made straight for one of the gates, and those within happily understood and anticipated his intentions. Confident that the weighty blows and thrusts of the cavalry would beat off the enemy and prevent them from forcing their way in with them, the garrison opened the gate at the critical moment, and, together with his regiment, Heideck and his faithful companion managed to enter the city. The lancers made their way into the citadel, and Heideck and Morar Gopal, who had followed him like his shadow, turned their steps towards the Charing Cross Hotel. It was, however, far from easy to get there; for the streets were packed with an impenetrable mob of howling and gesticulating natives, who were manifestly in the greatest state of excitement. The news that the English had lost the battle had long since reached the city, and the apprehensions which had long been entertained that such tidings could not fail to have a disastrously disquieting effect upon the Indian population, were only too soon seen to be justified. In all the brown faces which he saw directed towards him Heideck clearly read detestation and menace. They naturally regarded him as an Englishman, and it was only his decided manner and the naked sword in his hand that prevented the rabble from venting in a personal attack their rage against one of the hated race of their oppressors.

The door of the hotel was closed, probably because an attack was feared on the part of the natives; but as soon as a white man, who was at once regarded as an English officer, demanded admittance, it was opened. Heideck found most of the officers' wives and children, who were living in the hotel, assembled in the hall and the dining-room which led from it. The foreboding of a terrible disaster and the fear of coming events, which was perpetually increased by the noise in the streets, did not allow the poor creatures to rest longer in their rooms. Mrs. Baird and Edith Irwin were not, however, among those who thronged round Heideck and, in a hundred confused questions, hoped to obtain from the dust-begrimed man, who had evidently come from the battlefield, news as to how matters stood. Heideck said nothing more than that the army was retreating, bravely fighting the while. It would have been useless cruelty to increase the terror and despair of these unhappy creatures by a detailed account of the whole truth. He had almost to tear himself away by force from this close knot of inquirers, in order to go up to Mrs. Baird's room. It was the first joyous feeling that he had experienced throughout this disastrous day, when in the friendly "Come in," in answer to his knock, he recognised Edith Irwin's voice. The fear that something might have happened to her during his absence had unceasingly tortured him during the last few hours, and for a moment he forgot all the terrors that surrounded her in the rapture which, as he entered, her incomparable beauty awoke in him.

She had risen from the sofa in the middle of the room and stood with a serious, but perfectly composed face, and with bright eyes, which appeared prepared for even the extremest danger. Mrs. Baird was, with her two little girls, in a corner on her knees. So completely was she absorbed in her religious devotions that she had not heard Heideck's entrance into the room. It was only when Edith exclaimed, "Here is Mr. Heideck, dear friend; I knew he would come," that she sprang up in great excitement.

"Thank God! You have come from my husband? How have you left him? Is he alive?"

"I left the Colonel, as he was defending himself at the head of his brave troops against the enemy. He bade me give you his love." He had endeavoured to give a firm tone to his voice. But the sharp feminine instinct of the unhappy woman guessed what was behind his words, intended to give comfort.

"Why don't you tell me the truth? My husband is dead!"

"He was wounded, but you need not give up the hope of seeing him again alive."

"If he is wounded, I will go to him. You will conduct me, Mr. Heideck! There must be a possibility of getting to him."

"I earnestly beseech you, my dear Mrs. Baird, to compose yourself. It is quite natural that your heart should draw you to your husband's side; but it is quite impossible for you to carry out your intention. The night is drawing on, and even if it were broad daylight nobody would be able to get through the confusion of the retiring army to the place where your husband must be sought."

"The battle is then lost? Our army is in full retreat?"

"The treachery of the Indian troops is to blame for this disaster. Your countrymen, Mrs. Baird, have fought like heroes, and as a lost battle does not yet mean a lost campaign, they will perhaps soon retrieve to-day's disaster."

"But what is to become of us? The wounded will be brought in here, won't they? Therefore I shall not think of leaving before I see my husband again."

Her determination to remain in the panic-stricken city would certainly have been impossible to shake by any art of persuasion, but Heideck did not dream of attempting to dissuade Mrs. Baird from her resolve. It was his firm conviction that the flight to Amritsar, which the Colonel had advised in case of a defeat, was, under the present circumstances, quite impracticable. As a matter of fact, there was scarcely anything else possible but to remain in the hotel and patiently await the development of events.

It was now quite impossible for white women and children to trust themselves in the streets in the midst of the excited populace; but Heideck believed that they were, for the present, quite safe in the house, thinking that the fanaticism of the natives would not culminate in an attack upon the hotel so long as any considerable body of English soldiers remained in the town. But only too soon he was compelled to admit that he had under-estimated the seriousness of the situation. A ruddy, flickering flame, which suddenly lit up the room which had been filled by the dying evening glow, caused him to rush to the window, when, to his horror, he perceived that one of the houses on the opposite side of the street was on fire, and that in the adjacent building the tongues of flame had caught the wooden pillars of the verandah. There was no doubt but that the hotel would, within a few minutes, be involved in the conflagration.

Under these circumstances it was impossible to think of remaining longer in the hotel. Its massive walls could, perhaps, withstand the fire for a time, but the biting volumes of smoke, which had already taken Heideck's breath away when he had opened the window for a moment, would soon render it impossible for human beings to stay longer in the heat. All at once came a heavy knocking at the door, and Morar Gopal, who had been looking for Heideck everywhere in the hotel, entreated his master to make his escape as quickly as possible.

The German officer was fully convinced that he had now to exchange one danger for a peril perhaps even greater. But there was no time for delay or consideration.

"We are in the midst of a fire, Mrs. Baird," he said. "No one in the general confusion will attempt to stay the raging element, and if you do not wish to be stifled with your children, you must follow me. I hope to be able to bring you, without harm, into the citadel or into some other place of safety."

Edith Irwin had already taken one of the little girls into her arms; and when the Colonel's wife was looking about her with a wild expression, as if she wished to try and save some of her precious valuables, Edith emphatically insisted upon her hurrying. "There is nothing more precious than the life of your children. Let everything go, in God's name!"

The poor woman, whose senses now began to fail her in the terrors of the moment, quietly obeyed the calm instructions of her young friend. The other residents in the hotel had almost all already fled; only a few unhappy women, who had completely lost their heads, wandered about the lower rooms holding all manner of valueless objects, from which they would not part, in their hands. Heideck called to them to follow him. But they hardly understood him, and he had no more time to trouble about the unfortunate creatures.

With a bare sabre in his hand the faithful Hindu endeavoured to make for his master and those under his protection a path through the crowd which was surging around the burning houses. It was now quite dark, and only the red flames weirdly lit up the hideous nocturnal scene. The raging fanaticism of the crowd appeared during the last half-hour to have increased in vehemence. These men, at other times so modest, submissive, and amiable, had suddenly become metamorphosed into a horde of barbarians. Bare sabres and daggers flashed their menaces on every side, and the air was rent by a deafening din. Never before had Heideck seen human beings in such a state of frenzy. With wild gesticulations these dark-skinned fellows were tossing their arms and legs; they gnashed their teeth like wild beasts, and inflicted wounds on their own breasts and limbs in order to intensify their lust of blood by the sight of it.

The two men, by dint of peremptory commands and vigorous blows with the naked sword, forced their way step by step through the crowd. But after a lapse of ten minutes they had scarcely progressed more than a hundred yards. The surging mob around them became even denser and more threatening in its attitude, and Heideck saw it would be impossible to reach the citadel.

With anxious care for the precious human lives entrusted to his protection, he looked about for another place of safety. But the Europeans had firmly barricaded their houses, and none of them would have opened to admit the poor fugitives. On a sudden the wild cries that had almost terrified the crying children to death rose to appalling shrieks and ravings, and a mob of demons, incited by their fanatic passions almost to frenzy, rushed from a side street straight upon Heideck. They had somewhere on their way been joined by a large number of other female fugitives; and the sight of these unhappy creatures made the German officer's blood run cold in his veins.

The women, among whom were two girls yet on the borders of childhood, had had their clothes torn from their bodies, and they were now being hustled along under such constant ill-usage that they were bleeding from numerous wounds.

Unable further to curb the wrath that rose within him at the sight of this brutality, Heideck took his revolver from his belt, and with a well-aimed shot sent one of the howling, fanatic devils to the ground.

But his action was not well-advised. Although his martial appearance had up till then kept this cowardly crew away from acts of violence against himself and his party, the furious rage of the mob now knew no bounds.

In the next moment the small party found itself hemmed in by a knot of raging black devils, and Heideck was no longer in doubt that it was only a question of bravely fighting to the death. The foremost of the more violent of their assailants he was able to keep off by firing at them the last five shots that remained in his revolver. The last shot snuffed out the light of a black-bearded fellow just at the very moment when he was attacking Edith Irwin with his brutal fists. Then Heideck threw his revolver, useless in that he could not load it afresh, into the face of one of the grinning fiends, and clasping his left arm, which was now free, round Edith, and pressing her tightly to him, carried on a desperate struggle with his sword.

For Mrs. Baird and her children he could do nothing further. Now that he had seen his faithful Morar Gopal fall under the blows of some Mohammedans he felt that they were irretrievably lost. He had seen how the Colonel's wife had had her clothes torn in shreds from her body; he heard the heartrending cry of anguish with which, under the blows and thrusts of her inhuman torturers, she called for her children. But at all events he was spared the agony of seeing with his own eyes the end of the innocent little girls. They disappeared from his view in the terrible confusion, and as they were besides already half dead from terror, Providence would, at all events, have the pity not to let them feel the tortures of the death which their unfeeling butchers had prepared for them.

And what of Edith?

She was not in a faint. In her features one could read nothing of the anguish of horror that overcomes even the bravest in the face of death. One might imagine that all that was going on around her had lost its terrors since Heideck's arm held her fast.

But the moment was not favourable for allowing Heideck to feel the pleasurable bliss of her love. His strength was at an end and, although with the exception of a slight injury on the shoulder he was unwounded, he yet felt it intolerably hard to wield the sword whose heavy blows had hitherto kept their assailants (with the exception of some adventuresome spirits, who had paid dearly for their impudence) at a respectful distance. At the very moment that fatigue compelled him to drop his weapon, Edith and he would be given over helpless to the devilish cruelty of this horde of human beasts. That he knew full well, and, therefore, although before his eyes there floated, as it were, a blood-red mist, he collected the last remnant of his strength to postpone this terrible moment yet for a little--All of a sudden something unexpected, something wonderful, happened--something that in his present condition he could not understand at all; innumerable cries of terror and alarm mingled with the frenzied, triumphant howlings of the rage-intoxicated Indians. With the irresistible force of a wave the whole thickly packed swarm of human beings surged forwards and against the houses on both sides of the street. The trotting of horses, loud words of command, the sound of slashing blows were heard, and the bodies of bearded cavalrymen were visible above the heads of the crowd.

It was a squadron of Cossacks which was mercilessly hewing its way through the crowd. The town was then actually in the hands of the Russians, and orders had evidently been given, the better to prevent further massacre and incendiarism, to clear the street of the fanatic mob.

So the fierce-looking horsemen then swept the way before them clear of all obstacles. And they did their business well; for nothing could withstand the blows from the whips fitted at the end of the lash with thin hard sticks, which in their hands became terrible instruments of punishment.

Heideck suddenly saw himself free of his assailants, and as he with Edith pressed against the wall of a house, they remained happily safe from the horses' hoofs as well as from the blows of the knout which were being dealt out wildly around him.

But the keen eyes of a Cossack officer had perceived the little group amid the great heap of dead and wounded. He rode up to them, and as he thought he recognised in Heideck's khaki dress the English uniform, he gave certain orders to his men, the meaning of which was soon apparent to them both, for they were at once placed between the horses of two Cossacks, and without knowing whither they were being taken, passed through the streets lit up by the flames of the burning houses.

XV
THE COURT-MARTIAL

The mausoleum of Anar Kali, a great octagonal building in the gardens to the south of the town, was the place whither the Russian prisoners were taken. Heideck and Edith Irwin were not the first that had found quarters there; for, besides about a hundred officers, there were already there numberless English ladies and children whose saviours had appeared in time to rescue them from the horrible fate of Mrs. Baird and her children. At the open door of the apartments reserved for the women Heideck and Edith Irwin had to part. They were not allowed a long time to take leave. But even if they had been altogether alone they would at this moment have been scarcely able to find much to say; for after all the exertions and excitements of the terrible day just ended such heavy fatigue and exhaustion had overcome them that they could only mechanically make use of their limbs; and so, instead of the passions, hopes, and fears, with which they had been moved but a short time previously, there was now only a dull void in their brains as in their hearts.

"Au revoir, to-morrow." That was all that passed between them. Then, as soon as they had conducted him into the room assigned to him, Heideck threw himself down, as he was, upon the tiles of the floor, and fell instantaneously into a deep, dreamless sleep.

The glorious Indian sun, which shone through the round opening in the ceiling down upon his face, woke him the next morning.

His limbs were stiff from his uncomfortable couch, but the short sleep had invigorated him, and his nerves had completely regained their old freshness and vigour.

His room-mates must have been taken away early to some other place, for he found himself quite alone in the lofty room which was only lighted by the window in the ceiling. The rays of the sun fell opposite to him upon a tomb of the purest, whitest, marble quite covered with illegible hieroglyphics. Whilst he was still engaged in looking at the apparently ancient memorial tablet, he heard suddenly behind him the light rustling of a woman's dress, and when he turned round he gazed with pleasurable surprise into Edith Irwin's pale, fair face.

"How delighted I am to find you still here," she said with a happy expression. "I was afraid that you had been taken away with the other prisoners."

"As it seems, it was out of consideration for my well-deserved slumber," he replied, with a slight trace of humour. But then, remembering the terrible seriousness of the situation, he continued in altered and hearty tones--

"How have you passed the night, Mrs. Irwin? It appears to me as if all that I have gone through since my return to Lahore has only been a dream."

With a painful quiver of the lips she shook her head.

"Unfortunately, there is no room for doubt that it has been hideous reality. Poor, poor Mrs. Baird! One must almost consider it a happy dispensation of Providence that her husband did not live to see the terrible fate of his family."

"What, have you news from the field of battle? Do you then know that the Colonel is dead?"

Edith nodded.

"The Colonel is dead; my husband is dead; Captain McGregor, and many of my friends from Chanidigot, have been left on the field."

She said it calmly; but he read in her eyes the deep sadness of her soul.

Much affected by her heroic strength of character, he bent his head and kissed her hand. She let him have his way for a moment, but then withdrew her thin, cool fingers with a beseeching look, the meaning of which he full well understood.

"The Commander-in-Chief and his staff reached the railway station," she continued; "they travelled to Delhi with the last train that left Lahore, just at the eleventh hour; for immediately afterwards the Russians entered the town. The wreck of the army is now marching to Delhi, but their pursuers are close at their heels. God alone knows what will be the fate of our poor defeated army."

He did not ask her where she had obtained all this information; but that it was quite correct he was firmly convinced, judging by his own experience. He did not know what to say to her to encourage her, he who never had been able to toy with empty phrases. A short while they remained silent, and their eyes simultaneously fell upon the sunlit marble tomb before them.

"Have you seen this cenotaph before?" the young lady suddenly asked, to Heideck's surprise. On his answering in the negative, she went on--

"This is the famous tomb of Anar Kali, the beloved wife of Sultan Akbar, who, on account of her beauty, was given the name of 'Pomegranate Blossom.' She probably departed this life in the same way that we should have done if the daggers of the murderers yesterday had reached us. She, perhaps, was just as little conscious of what was happening to her, as we should have been in this past night."

"Can you read the inscription?" asked Heideck.

"No, but I have had it interpreted to me; for it is one of the most famous inscriptions in India. The beautiful Anar Kali was once so foolish as to smile when the son of her lord and master entered the harem. And in the selfsame hour the jealous sultan had the unhappy woman executed. But he must have loved her very dearly, for he erected to her this beautiful memorial, which should hand down to generations yet unborn the name of Anar Kali. So full of insoluble riddles is the poor, foolish heart of man."

Jingling footsteps were heard on the flagstones outside, and the next moment an officer appeared at the door accompanied by several soldiers. In abrupt, peremptory tones he ordered Heideck to follow him.

Now, for the first time, the Captain saw in Edith Irwin's face something like an expression of terror.

"What is the meaning of this?" She turned hastily to the Russian. "This gentleman is not an Englishman."

The Russian did not understand the question in English; but when Heideck asked in Russian what they were about to do with him, he replied, shrugging his shoulders--

"I do not know. Follow me."

"They only want me to prove my identity," said Heideck composedly, in order to calm the young lady. "I hope that they will let me free after examining my passports."

"Certainly they must let you go!" she cried, almost passionately. "It would be against all the laws of nations if they were to do you any harm. But how shall I endure the uncertainty as to your fate?"

"I shall come back here at once, as soon as it is possible for me to do so."

"Yes, yes! I beseech you, do not leave me a second longer than you are obliged. I have not as yet had time to thank you."

The Russian officer showed such manifest signs of impatience that Heideck no longer hesitated to follow him.

The way that he had to go was not long. He was taken to a house close by, over whose gate the words "School of Arts" were sculptured in the stone. He had only to wait a short while in the hall, when before him there opened the door of a room on the ground floor, adorned with sculptures, in which a number of officers sat at a long table. To Heideck it was at once clear that he was to be tried before a court-martial. A few very downcast-looking men had just been led out. The officer who presided turned over the papers which lay before him, and then, casting a sharp look at Heideck, spoke a few words with his comrades.

"Who are you?" he asked in English, with a decided Russian accent, which was difficult to understand.

Heideck, who also spoke in English, answered shortly and clearly, and laid his passport, which he always carried in the breast-pocket of his coat as his most valuable possession in ease of emergency, before the Colonel.

As soon as he had read it, the President said in perfect German--

"You are, then, no Englishman, but a German? What are you doing here in India?"

"I am travelling for the firm of Heideck, in Hamburg."

"In business? Really? Is it part of your business to fight against Russia?"

"No! and I have not done so."

"You deny, then, that you took part in yesterday's battle?"

"As a combatant, yes! There were other reasons which led me to the battle-field."

"You only went as a spectator? Didn't it occur to you that, under the circumstances, this might be very dangerous for you?"

"I have personal relations with several gentlemen in the English army, and these relations made it necessary for me to visit them during the battle."

The Colonel turned to a young officer standing a little distance away--

"Lieutenant Osarov, is it true that you recognised in this man, when he was brought in here last night, a person whom you saw in an English square during the progress of the battle?"

"Yes, Colonel, I did!" was the decided reply. "I recognise him now quite clearly. He was riding a black horse, and dashed off when we broke into the square."

Heideck perceived that it would be useless to deny the fact, in the face of this direct evidence, and his military honour would, in any case, not have permitted him to do so.

"What the lieutenant has said is quite correct," he answered, anticipating the Colonel's question; "but I did not take part in the fighting. As a friend of Colonel Baird, who was killed, I kept as long as possible close to him, so as to be able to bring his relations, who were left behind in Lahore, tidings of his fate and of the issue of the battle."

"You, a foreigner, were armed in the English square. Since you confess this much, we need not trouble ourselves with further proceedings. You, gentlemen, will all agree that we should treat him, according to martial law, as a traitor?"

The last words were addressed to the other judges, and, with a silent bow, they declared their assent.

"Since you, a citizen of a nation not at war with us, have fought in the ranks of our enemies, the Court must therefore sentence you to death. The judgment of the Court will be at once carried into effect. Have you anything to say?"

Heideck was as though stunned. It appeared to him as though a black veil was drawn across the world; and a sharp pang of grief shot through him as he reflected that he would never see Edith again, and that she would in vain wait for him for ever.

Then his pride was roused. No one should call him cowardly or timid.

"Is it possible to appeal against the judgment of this court-martial?" he asked, looking firmly at the Colonel.

"No!"

"Then I must, of course, submit to your sentence, but I protest both against the procedure of the Court and against the judgment you have pronounced."

His protest evidently did not make the slightest impression.

"Have you drawn up the execution warrant?" the Colonel said, turning to the secretary. He then appended his signature and handed it to one of the attendant Cossacks.

"Lead the prisoner away."

Two of the soldiers took Heideck between them, and he followed them with a proud, erect bearing, without saying a word more. Amidst the rain of bullets on the battlefield he had not felt the least trace of fear; but the thought of being led like an animal to the slaughter-house, filled him with horror. All the same a power he had hitherto not discovered, sustained him. The new danger awoke in him new vigour of soul and spirit.

The Cossacks conducted him a long way on the road which leads from Anar Kali to the Meean Meer cantonment. Heideck looked about him and observed the changes that had taken place in Lahore, just like a traveller who already in spirit lives in the new world that he intends to visit and who looks upon familiar objects as something strange. Everywhere he saw small detachments of cavalry, who were preserving order. Only faint clouds of smoke still marked the place of the fire in the city, which had evidently been extinguished. The splendid gardens of Donald Town, through which their way led, the agricultural plantations, and Lawrence Park wore the same aspect as in the time of profoundest peace.

Heideck was not chained, but the Cossacks who walked beside him had their carbines presented, ready to fire should he attempt to escape. But how could he escape? Everywhere round and about, outposts of the Russian cavalry were discernible; behind him a body of Cossack horse escorted a whole troop of Indians. Probably they were incendiaries and robbers who were, like him, being led out for execution; and it did not improve his frame of mind to find himself on his last road in the company of such a crew.

After a long march they at length reached the encampment which had been occupied by the English, the barracks and tents of which were now filled with Russian troops. It was only with difficulty that his escort could make their way through the crowd that had assembled; the report that a number of criminals were being brought into camp must have arrived here before them, for soldiers of all arms pressed forward inquisitively from all sides, in order to have a close view of the poor wretches.

Suddenly, Heideck felt the clutch of a small but firm hand upon his arm.

"Oh, master, what is this? Why are they bringing you here like a prisoner?"

At the first word Heideck recognised the soft voice, that in the excitement had assumed its natural feminine tones. In the same fantastic page's livery in which he had last seen him in Chanidigot, the pretended servant of his friend Prince Tchajawadse here stood quite unexpectedly before him, as though he had suddenly sprung from the earth, while the most pained consternation showed itself in his fair, expressive face.

"Is it you, Georgi?" exclaimed Heideck, into whose sadness of heart the sight of the Circassian brought a faint gleam of hope; "and your master--the Prince? Is he also close at hand?"

But the Cossacks did not seem inclined to permit their prisoner any further private conversation.

"Be off with you, young fellow!" one of them exclaimed to the supposed page; "this is a spy, who is to be shot on the spot; and no one is allowed to speak to him."

He made a movement as though with a slight motion of his powerful fist to thrust the slender lithe figure aside, when Georgi fearlessly pushed back his arm and glared at him with flashing eyes.

"Hold your blasphemous tongue, you liar! You are a thousand times more of a spy than this gentleman. If you do not leave go of him at once, you will have a knouting that you will not forget until the end of your life!"

The Cossacks looked at him and laughed. It was only the handsome face and the aristocratic bearing of the bold young fellow that prevented their seizing him.

"Take care, little fellow, that you do not first get the stick," one of them said good-humouredly; "and be off with you, before we, by accident, crush you between our finger and thumb."

"Go now, Georgi," Heideck now said, in his turn, on perceiving that the Circassian was not inclined to obey their orders; "if your master is near by, go and tell him that I am about to be shot against all the rules of international law. But tell him to make haste, if he wants to see me again alive; for it looks as though his comrades intend to make short work of me."

He did not doubt that the beautiful, hot-blooded daughter of the mountains had completely understood him. At all events he saw how she suddenly turned like a flash of lightning, and with the lithe rapidity of a slender lizard threaded her way through the crowd of rough soldiers.

A new hope awoke in Heideck's breast, and he felt himself once more fettered in a thousand bonds to life, which he just before thought he had entirely parted from. He endeavoured to walk more slowly, in order to gain time. But the Cossacks, who had until now treated him with a certain amount of consideration, appeared to have become irritated by the scene with the page, for one of them urged the prisoner in commanding tones to greater haste, while the other raised his fist in his face with a menacing gesture.

Perhaps he would even have struck him; but the German officer looked into his face with such a proud, commanding glance that he let his raised arm sink to his side. The sullen-looking fellow felt at once that he was not here dealing with an ordinary spy, and from this moment neither curses nor abuse passed his lips.

The rattle of a rifle volley struck Heideck's ear, and although he was sufficiently accustomed to the crack of shots, a cold shiver passed over him. The bullets that had just been fired had--he knew it well without anyone telling him--been the portion of some poor devil who had been in the same position as himself. That was why these rifle shots were so full of a significance for him, quite different from that caused yesterday by the rattle and the crash of the raging battle. Truly, one need not be a coward to feel an icy shudder at the thought of ten or twenty rifle barrels directed at one's own breast.

And now they had reached the fatal spot which was to be the goal of all his earthly wanderings. The parade at the rear of the barrack camp had been selected for the place of execution, and so summarily was the punishment being dealt out, that no time had been found to cart away separately the corpses of those who had been shot. They simply left them lying in the trench before which the delinquents were posted, probably because burial in a common grave was more convenient.

An officer was handed the execution warrant, which had been issued by the President of the court-martial, and handed over the prisoner to a non-commissioned officer, who, regarding him with an expression of pity, bade him in an almost apologetic tone to follow him.

Only a few minutes after his arrival on the parade ground, Heideck also was standing before the fatal ditch, and saw a company of infantry, with their arms at attention, drawn up before him.

He had now abandoned all hope. Since the verdict of the court-martial only a miracle could have saved him; and this miracle had not happened. For a few short minutes he had, after the accidental meeting with the Circassian, been foolish enough to entertain new hopes of life, but now even those had vanished. Even had she been animated by the keenest desire to save him, what, after all, could she do to make the impossible possible? He was sorry now that he had not confined himself to begging the Prince through her to allow him decent burial and to send word to the German General Staff. These last wishes would, perhaps, have not been impossible of fulfilment, and he did not doubt that his amiable Russian acquaintance would have gladly rendered him this trifling service.

The word of command rang out, and the soldiers posted opposite to him had already, with clank and rattle, shouldered arms, when from the other side a loud peremptory shout reached Heideck's ear, and he saw a horseman in Russian dragoon's uniform dashing up, in whose dark red face he immediately recognised the Prince Tchajawadse.

Close before Heideck he reined in his dripping charger and sprang from the saddle.

"Little brother! little brother!" he cried, quite breathless from his ride in such hot haste, clasping, with genuine Russian impetuosity, his friend, whom he had found again under such strange circumstances, to his breast. "By all the saints--I should think it was quite time that I came!"

Then, turning to the astonished officer commanding the firing squad--

"There must be a mistake here. No harm must happen to this gentleman, for he is not only a personal friend of my own, but he is also a comrade, an officer of the allied German army."

The lieutenant shrugged his shoulders.

"I have to carry out my orders, Colonel! I can undertake no responsibility for any mistakes on the part of my superior officers or of the court-martial."

"I take, then, all the responsibility on my own shoulders for preventing you from carrying out your instructions, lieutenant! This gentleman will accompany me, and I give my guarantee for him."

He gave his horse to one of the soldiers, linked his arm in that of Heideck, and took him off to the tent he occupied in the camp, giving the while most exuberant expression to his delight at having seen him again. The breakfast, from which Georgi's message had startled him, was still on the table, and Heideck needed not much encouragement to partake of it; for only now he properly realised how much he was in want of bodily sustenance. Prince Tchajawadse would not hear of any thanks for what he had done; but when Heideck asked him if he had really correctly understood that the Prince had spoken of an alliance between the Russian and German armies, the latter was not slow to give all information on this head.

"Yes! yes!--it is the fact! The German Empire is hand-in-hand with us. The first piece of good news that I heard on reaching the army was that William II. had declared war upon England. The world is in flames. Only Austria and Italy are neutral."

"And I had no notion of it! But, after all, that is easy enough to explain. All the telegraph cables are in the hands of the English, and it was easy for them to suppress every unwelcome despatch. The Indian newspapers are only allowed, of course, to publish what is agreeable to the Government; but I am burning with curiosity to learn more. Do you perhaps know how matters have developed as yet, and in what way Germany thinks of carrying on the war?"

"It appears that an invasion of England is contemplated. Germany has mobilised one half of her army, and has occupied Holland. The French troops, on the other hand, have entered Belgium, so that the two Powers control the whole coast opposite England."

"And has any action taken place at sea as yet?"

"No; at least down to the present no news has reached us of a naval battle having been fought. Things are evidently still in the stage of preparation, and nothing has been heard about the movements of the German and French fleets. However, the latest intelligence that I have is now fairly old. We with the army only learn the news that the Cossacks bring us."

Heideck struck his forehead.

"I feel utterly astonished. To comprehend and digest at one time all that you have told me almost passes the capacity of a single brain. But pardon me, Prince, if I trouble you, who have already done so much for me to-day, with a further request. I am in great anxiety about a lady, the widow of an English officer who fell in yesterday's battle, and who was committed to my care. I only left her this morning early, when I was arrested to be taken before the court-martial, at the mausoleum of Anar Kali, where she had been interned with other prisoners. Advise me what to do, in order to send the lady, whose welfare is nearest my heart, a reassuring message as to my fate, and at the same time shield her from annoyance and discomfort."

"That is a very simple matter. Do you object to giving me the name of the lady?"

"Not at all. It is Mrs. Edith Irwin, the widow of Captain Irwin, whom you also perhaps met in Chanidigot."

"I think I have some recollection. There was something about a gambling affair, with which he was not very creditably connected--wasn't it so? Well, then, while you take a good sound sleep in my tent here I will ride over to Anar Kali, visit the lady, and find out how she is situated. Be quite sure that no unpleasantness shall happen to her, if only I succeed in finding her."

"Your kindness puts me quite to shame, Prince. I--"

"You would do precisely the same if fate had happened to have exchanged our roles. Why, then, waste words about it? I cannot, unfortunately, offer you a more comfortable couch than my camp-bed there. But you are a soldier, and I think both of us have, before now, had a worse shakedown. So, then, pleasant dreams, my friend! I will take care that you are not disturbed for the next two hours."

Hurriedly, as though to escape all further expressions of gratitude, the Prince left the tent.

XVI
THE PROFESSOR

Sound though Heideck's sleep was, the confused din that penetrated through the sides of the tent would have recalled an unconscious person to life. Confused and drowsy as he was, he hurried out just in time to prevent a wild-looking, dark-skinned Indian from dealing a heavy blow with a thick staff, which he held in his right hand, upon a thin, black-garbed gentleman, who was surrounded by a whole band of natives. The European, with his emaciated, beardless face, looked like a clergyman, and all the greater was Heideck's surprise that none of the Russian non-commissioned officers and soldiers, who were spectators of the assault, raised a hand to protect him. It was certainly not his duty to act in this place as one in authority, but the danger in which he perceived this perfectly defenceless man to be, made him forget all personal considerations. With a menacing shout he drove off the excited Indians, and, taking the stranger's arm, led him into the tent.

None of the Russian military prevented his doing so. He had been seen in confidential conversation with the Colonel, and his position as a friend of the Prince procured him respect.

The stranger, half dead from fear, gratefully accepted the glass of wine which Heideck poured out for him, and, having recovered somewhat, thanked his protector in simple, but cordial terms. He introduced himself as Professor Proctor, of Acheson College, and explained that he had come to the camp to look after a relation who had probably been seriously wounded. He had on a sudden found himself threatened by a band of excited Indians, who were probably misled by his dress to take him for a cleric.

"You, also, are no Russian, sir. Judging from your accent, I should take you for a German."

Heideck assented, and narrated his history in a few words. Having done so, he could not help expressing his amazement at the attack of which the Professor had been the victim.

"Never during my whole stay in India have I ever before observed any outburst of hatred on the part of the Indian natives against the English clergy," he said.

To this the Professor replied: "Even a few days ago not one of them would, I should think, have had anything to fear; but in the face of such terrible upheavals as are now taking place all ideas are thrown into confusion, all slumbering passions are unfettered. I do not venture to think of the horrors that will take place throughout the whole of India now that the bridle that curbed the people has been rent asunder; and the worst of all is that we have only ourselves to blame."

"Do you mean on account of the carelessness with which the defence of the country was organised?"

"I do not mean that alone. Our fault is that we have ignored an eternal truth, the truth that all political questions are only the external expression, the dress, so to say, of religious questions."

"Pardon me, but I do not quite follow the sense of your words."

"Please consider the slow, steady advance of the Russians in Asia. Every land that they have brought under their sway--all the immense territories of Central Asia have become their assured, undisputed possessions. And why? Because the Russians have known how to win over the hearts of their subject races, and how to humour their religious views. The victors and the vanquished thus better assimilate. The English, on the other hand, have governed India purely from the political side. The hearts of the various races in India have remained strange and hostile to us."

"There may be some truth in what you say. But you must allow that the English have in India substituted a new civilisation in return, that inculcates a spirit of intellectual progress, and I conceive that no nation can for any length of time remain blind in the face of higher ideals. All history forms a continuous chain of evidence for the truth of this statement."

"The word 'civilisation' has various significations. If it is only a question of investigating whether the government and administration of the country have improved, the answer is that the civilisation we brought to India has, beyond all doubt, made enormous strides, in comparison with the conditions that obtained in former centuries. We have broken the despotism of the native princes, and have put an end to the endless sanguinary wars which they waged with each other and with their Asiatic neighbouring despots. We have laid down roads and railways, drained marshes and jungles, constructed harbours, won great tracts of lands from the sea, and built protecting dams and piers. The terrible mortality of the large cities has considerably decreased. We have given them laws assuring personal security and guaranteeing new outlets for trade and commerce. But the aspirations of our English Government have been purely utilitarian, and as regards the deeper-lying current of development no progress is anywhere perceivable."

"And, pray, what do you exactly mean by this?"

"Your views in this matter are possibly divergent. I discern in most of our achievements in India only another manifestation of that materialism which has ever proved the worst obstacle to all real development."

"It appears to me, Mr. Proctor," Heideck interrupted, with a smile, "that you have become a Buddhist, owing to your sojourn in India!"

"Perhaps so, sir, and I should not be ashamed of such a creed. Many a one, who on first coming here regarded India with the eyes of a Christian, has, on nearer acquaintance, become a Buddhist. Greek wise men once expressed the wish that kings should be chosen from among the philosophers. That may possibly be an unrealisable hope, but I do not believe that a ruler who has a contempt for philosophy will ever properly fulfil the high duties of his station. A policy without philosophy is, like an unphilosophical religion, not established on firmer ground than those houses there on the river Ravi, whose existence is not safe for a single day, because the river at times takes it into its head to change its course. A government that does not understand how to honour the religious feelings of its people, does not stand more securely than one of those huts. The fate that has now overtaken the English is the best proof of what I say. We are the only power in Asia that has not founded its political sway upon the religion of the people. In our folly we have destroyed the habitual simplicity of a nation, which, until our coming, had been content with the barest necessities of life, because for thousands of years past it cared more about the life after death than for its earthly existence. We have incited the slumbering passions of this people, and by offering to their eyes the sight of European luxury and European over-civilisation, have aroused in them desires to which they were formerly strangers. Our system of public instruction is calculated to disseminate among all classes of the Indian race the worthless materialistic popular education of our own nation. Of all the governors and inspectors of schools who have been sent hither by England not a single one has taken the trouble to penetrate beneath the surface of the life of the Indian people and to fathom the soul of this religious and transcendentally gifted race. What contrasts are not the result! Here a holy river, priests, ascetics, yogis, fakirs, temples, shrines, mysterious doctrines, a manifold ritual; while side by side, without any transition, are schools wherein homely English elementary instruction is provided, a State-supported university with a medical school and Christian churches of the most varied confessions."

"But how would it have been possible to combine in a school modern scientific education with Indian fanaticism?"

A superior smile flitted across the professor's intellectual face.

"Compare, I pray you, the tiresome trivialities of English missionary tracts with the immortal masterpieces of Indian literature! Then you will understand that the Indian, even when he approves Christianity as a system of morals, demands a deeper and wider basis of these morals, and inquires as to the origin of the Christian doctrine; and then he very soon finds that all light which has come to Europe started from Asia. Ex oriente lux."

"I am not sufficiently well informed to be able to answer you on this point. It may very well be that even Christianity was not the offspring of Judaism alone, but of Buddhism. It may also be the case that the teachings of our missionaries of to-day are too insipid for the Indians. But the metaphysical needs of a people have, after all, little to do with sound policy and good laws. Think of Rome! The Roman state had most excellent laws, and a magnificent political force which for centuries kept it in its predominant position among the nations of the world. But what of religion and philosophy in Rome? There was no state religion whatsoever; there was no priestly hierarchy, no strict theological codex, but only a mythology and worship of gods, which was of an eminently practical character, and it was owing to their practical common sense--or, as you would prefer to call it, materialism--that the Romans were enabled to found an organised society upon purely human needs and aspirations. And why should what they were enabled to achieve be impossible again for other nations who have succeeded them in their world-power? The spirit of the age is ever changing, yet it is only a regularly recurring return of the same conditions, just as the planets in the heavens, ever again in their orbit, come back to their old positions."

"And supposing the 'Zeitgeist,' like many planets, does not move in a circle but in a spiral line? The British world-sovereignty has, as we see, taken a higher flight than did the Roman. Could not this British world-power, by permeating wise diplomacy with the profound idea of Indian philosophy, have attained to a great reformation of the whole of the human race? It would have been a glorious idea, but I have here learnt how far they were from its realisation."

"All the same, I do not think that the English army would have been defeated by the Russian, had they not fought in accordance with the rules of antiquated tactics."

"Oh, sir, if the Indian troops had fought with their whole soul for England we should never have sustained this defeat."

"As a soldier, I am inclined to dispute that. The Indians will never be a match for a well-disciplined European army. The race is wanting in too great a measure in military qualities."

"The Indian people is, by nature, it is true, gentle and good-hearted. In order to render it wild and bloodthirsty it must be wounded in its most sacred feelings."

"Perhaps you judge it rather too mildly. Decided traces of barbarism still linger in this people, even in its highest circles. Here is a case in point that I am able to quote of my own personal knowledge. An Indian prince, before the outbreak of the war, attempted to carry off, by his servants, an English lady from her home, and bribed an assassin to poison the English resident, who rebuked him for his conduct."

The Professor was astounded.

"Is it possible? Can such things be? Have you not perhaps been deceived by an exaggerated report?"

"I myself was close at hand, and observed all that took place, and can give you, the names. The lady upon whom this dastardly attempt was made is Mrs. Edith Irwin, who had followed her husband, a captain in the lancers, to the camp of Chanidigot."

The astonishment of the Professor visibly increased.

"Mrs. Edith Irwin? Is it possible? The daughter of my old friend, the excellent Rector Graham? Yes, beyond doubt, it must be the same, because she was married to a captain in the lancers."

"Since yesterday she is this officer's widow. He fell in the battle of Lahore, and she herself is among the prisoners interned in Anar Kali."

"Then I must endeavour to find her, for she has a claim, for her father's sake, upon my assistance. But, certainly, for the moment," he observed, with a somewhat melancholy smile, "I am myself in the greatest need of protection."

"I believe you may be perfectly easy in your mind as to this lady. My friend, Prince Tchajawadse, has just now ridden over to Anar Kali in order, at my request, to look after the lady."

He had not concluded the sentence when the tall form of the Prince made its appearance at the entrance of the tent. His downcast face presaged no good news. He advanced to Heideck and shook his hand.

"I am not, unfortunately, the bearer of any good news, comrade. I have not discovered the lady whose guardian you are."

"What! Has she left? And you could not learn whither she is gone?"

"All that I have been able to elicit is that she was driven off in an elegant carriage, in the company of several Indians. An English lady who saw the occurrence told me this."

A fearful dread overcame Heideck.

"In the company of Indians? And does nobody know whither she was taken? Did she leave no message for me or anyone else?"

"The lady had no opportunity of speaking to her. She saw the departure at a distance."

"But she must have noticed whether Mrs. Irwin left the mausoleum of her own free will or under compulsion?"

The Prince shrugged his shoulders.

"I cannot, unfortunately, say anything about that. My inquiries were without result. Neither any one of the English prisoners or of the Russian sentries was able to give me further information."

XVII
DOWNING STREET

A meeting of the Cabinet Council was being held at the Foreign Office in London. With gloomy faces the Ministers were all assembled. The foreboding of a catastrophe brooded over England like a black cloud; all manner of rumours of disaster were current in the land, and coming events were awaited with sickening dread.

"A telegram from the general in command," said the Prime Minister, opening the paper he held in his hand. A deadly silence fell upon the room:

"With painful emotion, I communicate to His Majesty's Government the news of a great reverse I suffered the day before yesterday at Lahore. I have only to-day reached Delhi with the remnant of my army, which has been pursued by the Russian advance guard. We had taken up a very favourable position on the left bank of the Ravi and were on the point of preventing the Russian army from crossing the river, when unexpectedly a violent onslaught made upon our left wing at Shah Dara compelled us to send reinforcements to this wing and thus to weaken the centre. Under the cover of jungle on the river-bank, the Russian cavalry and the Mohammedan auxiliaries of the Russian army succeeded in forcing the passage and in throwing our sepoy regiments into disorder. The troops of the Maharajah of Chanidigot traitorously went over to the enemy and that decided the day against us. Had not all the sepoy regiments deserted, I could have maintained my ground, but the English regiments under my command were too weak to resist for long the superior numbers of the enemy. The bravery of these regiments deserves the highest praise, but after a battle lasting several hours I was compelled to give the order to retreat. We fell back upon the city of Lahore, and I contrived to convey a portion of my troops by railway to Delhi. This city I shall defend to the bitter end. Reinforcements are being sent from all military stations in the country. The extent of our losses I am unable to give at the time of writing. I have been able to bring five thousand troops intact to Delhi."

The reading of this terrible report was succeeded by a chilling silence. Then the Minister of War arose and said:--

"This despatch certainly comes upon us as a staggering blow. Our best general and his army, composed of the flower of India's troops, have been defeated. We may rightly say, however, that our power is still established on a firm basis, so long as England, this seagirt isle, is safe from the enemy. No defeat in India or in any one of our colonies can deal us a death-blow. What we lose in one portion of the world, we can recover, and that doubly, in another, so long as we, in our island, are sound in both head and heart. But that is just what makes me anxious. The security of Great Britain is menaced when we have almost the whole world in arms against us. A strong French army is standing ready opposite Dover to invade us, and a German army is in Holland also prepared to make a descent on our coasts. I ask what measures have been taken to meet an attack upon our mother country?"

"The British fleet," replied the First Lord of the Admiralty, "is strong enough to crush the fleets of our enemies should they dare to show themselves on the open seas. But the Russian, French, and German navies are clever enough to remain in harbour under the cover of the fortifications. We have, too, fleets in the Channel, one of ten battleships and eighteen cruisers, and the necessary smaller vessels, told off to engage the German fleet; and a second, a stronger force, of fourteen battleships and twenty-four cruisers, destined to annihilate the French fleet. A third fleet is in the harbour of Copenhagen in order to prevent a union being effected between the Russian and German fleets. The plan of sailing for Cronstadt has been abandoned, from the experiences of the Crimean War and the fear that we should be keeping our naval forces too far apart. Our admirals and captains will, owing to the Russian successes, be convinced that England's honour and England's very existence are now at stake. When in the eighteenth century we swept the sea power of France from all the seas and vanquished the fleet of the Great Napoleon, the rule was laid down that every defeated admiral and captain in our navy should be court-martialled and shot, and that even where the victory of our ships of war was not followed up and taken the utmost advantage of, the court-martial was to remove the commander. The time has now arrived when those old, strict rules must be again enforced."

"According to the last Admiralty reports," said the First Lord of the Treasury, "the fleet consists of twenty-seven new ironclads, the oldest of which is of the year 1895. The ironclads of 1902, the Albemarle, Cornwallis, Duncan, Exmouth, Montagu, and Russell, as well as those of 1899, Bulwark, Formidable, Implacable, Irresistible, London, and Venerable are, as I see from the report, constructed and armed according to the latest technical principles. Are all the most recent twenty-seven battleships with the Channel fleet?"

"No; the Albion, the Ocean, and the Glory are in other waters. The twelve newest ironclads which your lordship mentioned are included in both Channel fleets; in addition, several older battleships, such as the Centurion, Royal Sovereign, and Empress of India are in the Channel. I may say with truth that both the Channel Squadrons are fully suited for the tasks before them. We have, besides, twenty-four ironclads of an older type, all of which are of excellent value in battle."

"Among these older ironclads are there not many which are equipped with muzzle-loaders?"

"Yes, but a naval battle has yet to determine whether the general view that breechloaders are more serviceable in action is correct or not. In the case of quick-firing guns it is certain that the breechloader is alone the right construction; but in our heaviest guns, which have a bore of 30.5 centimetre, and require three to four minutes to load, the advantage of quick-firing is not apparent, for here everything depends upon accurate aim, so that the heavy projectile may hit the right place. For this purpose clever manoeuvring is everything. Moreover, the battles round Port Arthur show us the importance of the torpedo and the mine. The Russian fleet has met with its heaviest losses owing to the clever manoeuvring and the superior torpedo tactics of the Japanese. It looks as if in modern naval battles artillery would prove altogether inferior to mines, and here our superiority in submarines will soon show itself when we attack the fleets of Germany and France in their harbours. Only a naval engagement between our squadrons and those of the French and Germans can teach us the proper use of modern ships of war. And it will be a lesson, a proper lesson for those misguided people who dare expose themselves to the fire of a British broadside and the attack of our torpedo and submarine boats. Let the steel plating of the vessels be as it will, the best cuirass of Great Britain is the firm, true breast of Britons."

"When I hear these explanations," the Colonial Minister interjected, "I cannot suppress the suspicion, that the whole plan of our naval strategy is rotten."

"I beg you to give your reasons for your suspicion," the First Lord of the Admiralty replied, somewhat irritated.

"It has ever been said that England rules the waves. Now the war has been going on for a considerable time and I perceive nothing of our boasted supremacy."

"How can you say so? Our enemies' commerce has been completely paralysed, while our own ships carry on their trade everywhere as freely as ever."

"That may be the case, but by naval supremacy I mean something quite different. No naval victory has as yet been gained. The enemies' fleets are still undamaged: until they are annihilated there is always a danger that the war may take a turn prejudicial to us. Only the struggle on the open sea can decide the issue. If the English fleet is really supreme, she can force the enemies' ships to a decisive action. Why do we not blockade the French and German fleets in their harbours, and compel them to give us battle? Our guns carry three miles, we can attack our enemies in their harbours. What is the meaning of this division of our fleet into three squadrons? Our whole fleet ought to be concentrated in the Channel, in order to deal a crushing blow."

"The right honourable gentleman forgets that a combination of our fleet would also entail the concentration of our enemies' fleets. If we leave our position at Copenhagen, a strong Russian fleet will proceed from Cronstadt and join the German warships in the Baltic. This united fleet could pass through the Kaiser Wilhelm Canal into the North Sea. England in its naval preparations has always adopted the 'two power standard,' and although we have aimed at the 'three power standard,' our resources in money and personnel are not capable of fitting out a naval force superior to the fleets of the now three allied Powers. All the same, our own prestige holds these three Powers so far in check that they dare not attack us on the open seas. Should we not be hazarding this prestige in provoking a naval battle without a definite chance of success? This naval battle will take place, but the favourable moment must be carefully chosen. Considering the present state of the war, it would be in the highest degree frivolous to stake all upon one throw of the dice. Well, that is exactly what we should be doing were we to force on a naval conflict. If the attack failed, if our fleet suffered a defeat, England would be then exposed to the invasion of a Continental army. It is true that our fleet is weakened by being split up, but the same is also true of the fleets of our enemies, so that this apparent disadvantage is equalised. We must keep on the watch for the moment when some alteration of the present situation permits us to attack our enemies' fleets with a superior force."

"There might be a way of enticing the German fleet into the open," maintained the Colonial Minister. "Let us send an ironclad squadron to Heligoland and bombard the island and its fortifications until it crumbles into the sea. The acquisition of Heligoland was the Emperor William's darling idea, and this monarch will take good care that Heligoland does not disappear from the earth's surface. But if, in spite of the bombardment of Heligoland, the Germans do not come out into the open sea, let us send our fleet up the Elbe and lay Hamburg in ashes. Let our warships put to sea from Copenhagen and destroy Kiel harbour and all the German coast towns on the Baltic. Then the German fleet will soon enough put out to meet us!"

"This plan has already been considered, and will perhaps be acted upon. There are, however, two difficulties in the way. First of all, by the destruction of unfortified towns we should be conjuring up odium against us, which--"

"Nonsense! there is no 'odium' for a victor! England would never have attained its present might and grandeur had it allowed itself to be deterred by a too delicate regard for humanity and the law of nations from taking practical steps."

"Well, and then there is, at any rate, the second consideration."

"And that is, my lord?"

"A battle of ships, even though they have the finest possible armour, against land fortifications, is always a hazardous undertaking, and more especially when the coasts are defended by innumerable mines and torpedo boats. Moreover, ironclads are very expensive, and are, in a certain sense, very fragile things."

"Fragile things?"

"The Germans have removed all their light-ships, all their buoys, and, like the French, the German ports are also defended by mines. An ironclad, given calm sea, is strong as against another ship, but the nature of its build makes it weak in a storm and in insecure waters. An ironclad, owing to its enormously heavy armament, goes to the bottom very rapidly, as soon as it gets a heavy list either on the one side or the other. Again, owing to its enormous weight, it can never ram another vessel for fear of breaking to pieces itself; if a torpedo strikes its armour, or if the ship runs upon a mine, the explosion will send it to the bottom with greater ease than it would a wooden ship of a century ago. And then, if it runs on a shallow or a rock it cannot be brought off again. Moreover, its supply of coal requires to be constantly renewed, so that it cannot be sent on long expeditions. Our ironclads have their own specific purpose--they are intended for a naval battle. But they are like giants, are rendered top-heavy by their own weight, and are thus easily capsized, and the loss of an ironclad battleship, apart from the effect it might have upon our chances in the war, entails the loss of more than a million pounds. The cruisers, again, I would not without urgent necessity expose to the steel projectiles of a Krupp's coast battery. Let us take care not to suffer the smallest disaster at sea! It would be as dangerous for our prestige and for our position as a world-power as a steel shot would be for the water-line of one of our ships of war."

The Colonial Minister was silent. He had nothing to urge against these objections.

"Our Indian troops are greatly in need of reinforcements," began the Prime Minister again. "We must put English soldiers into the field, for we cannot rely longer upon the sepoys."

"Certainly," said the Minister of War, "and drafts are constantly being despatched to Bombay. Forty thousand men have been embarked; of these more than twenty thousand have been landed in India; the remainder are still on the sea. A great fleet is on the road, and eight ironclads are stationed in Aden to meet any attack upon our transports. But it is really a question whether we are well advised in still sending more troops to India. My lords! hard as it is for me to say so, we must be prudent. I should be rightly accused of having lost my head if I did more than bare prudence demanded. Great Britain is denuded of troops. Now, I know full well, and England also knows it full well, that an enemy will never plant his foot on these shores; for our fleet assures us the inviolability of our island, but we should not be worthy of our responsible positions were we to neglect any measure for the security of our country. Let us, my lords, be cowards before the battle, provided we are heroes in it! Let us suppose that we had no fleet, but had to defend England's territory on land. We must have an army on English soil ready to take the field; failing this, we are guilty of treason against our country. The mobilisation of our reserve must be further extended. Ten thousand yeomen, whom we have not yet summoned to the ranks, are to-day in a position to bear arms and wave the sword. To-day every capable man must be enlisted. The law provides that every man who does not already belong to a regular army or to a volunteer corps can, from eighteen to fifty years of age, be forced to join the army, and thus a militia can be formed of all men capable of bearing arms. If His Majesty will sanction it, I am ready to form a militia army of 150,000 men. I reckon for India 120,000 men, for Malta 10,000, for Hong Kong 3,500, for Africa 10,000, 3,000 for the Antilles, for Gibraltar 6,000, and 10,000 more for Egypt, apart from the smaller garrisons, which must all remain where they are at present; I shall then hope, after having called up all volunteers and reserves, to be in a position to place an army of 400,000 men in the field for the defence of the mother country."

The First Lord of the Treasury shook his head. "Do not let us be lulled by such figures into false optimism! Great masses without military discipline, unused to firearms, with newly appointed officers (and they chosen, moreover, by the men whom they are to command), troops without any practical intelligence, without any understanding of the requirements of modern warfare, such are the men, as I understand, we are to place in the field against such splendid troops, as are the French and German. Whence should we get our artillery? In 1871 we saw the result, when masses of men with muskets were pitted against regularly disciplined troops. Bourbaki was in command of an army that had been disciplined for months gone by, and yet his host, although they took the field with cavalry and artillery, suffered enormous losses on meeting an army numerically inferior, yet well-organised, and commanded by scientific and experienced officers. They were pushed across the frontier into Switzerland, like a great flock of sheep pursued by a bevy of wolves."

"But they were French, and we are Englishmen!"

"An Englishman can be laid low by a bullet as well as a Frenchman. The days of the Black Prince are past and gone, no Henry V. is to-day victorious at Agincourt, we have to fight with firearms and magazine rifles."

"The Boers, my lord, showed us what a brave militia is capable of doing against regular troops."

"Yes, in the mountains. The Tyrolese held out in the same way against the great Napoleon for a while. But England is a flat country, and in the plain tactical strategy soon proves its superiority. No, England's salvation rests entirely on her fleet."

A despatch from the Viceroy of India was handed to the Prime Minister: "The Viceroy informs His Majesty's Government that the Commander-in-Chief in Delhi has massed an army of 30,000 men, and will defend the city. The sepoys attached to his army are loyal, because they are confined within the fortifications and cannot flee. The Viceroy will take care that the Mohammedan sepoys shall all, as far as possible, be brought south, and that only Hindu troops shall be led against the Russians. Orders have been given that the treacherous Maharajah of Chanidigot, whose troops in the battle of Lahore gave the signal for desertion, shall be shot. The Viceroy is of opinion that the Russian army will have to halt before Delhi in order to collect the reinforcements which, though in smaller numbers, are still coming up through Afghanistan. He does not doubt that the English army, whose numbers are daily increasing by the addition of fresh regiments, will, when massed in the northern provinces, deal the Russians a decisive blow. The Commander-in-Chief will leave to General Egerton the defence of Delhi, and concentrate a new field army at Cawnpore, with which it is his intention to advance to Delhi. All lines of railway are now constantly engaged in forwarding all available troops to Cawnpore."

"This news is, at all events, calculated to inspire new courage," said the Prime Minister after reading the telegram, "and we will not disguise from ourselves the fact, my lords, that we need courage now more than ever. This new man in Germany, whom the Emperor has made Chancellor, is arousing the feelings of the Germans most alarmingly against us. He appears to be a man of the Bismarck stamp, full of insolent inconsiderateness and of a surprising initiative. We stand quite isolated in the world; Russia, France, and Germany are leagued against us. Austria cannot and will not help us, Italy temporises in reply to our advances, says neither 'yes' nor 'no,' and seeks an opportunity of allying herself with France and wresting the remainder of the Italian territories from Austria and of aggrandising herself at the expense of our colonies. Yet, whenever England has stood alone, she has always stood in the halo of glory and power. Let us trust in our own right hand and in the loyalty of our colonies, who are ready to come to our aid with money and men, and whom, after our victory, we will repay with all those good gifts that His Majesty's Government can dispense."

"Our colonies!" the Minister of the Board of Trade intervened. "You are right, they are ready to make sacrifices. Only I am afraid that those sacrifices which the Right Honourable the Minister for the Colonies demands of them will be too great, and that, having regard to the tendency of the modern imperialism of our Government, they will not believe in those rewards that are to be dangled before their eyes."

"My lord," replied the last speaker, "I am considered an agitator, and am accused of being responsible for the present perilous position of England. Well, I will accept that responsibility. Never in the world's history did a statesman entertain great plans without exposing his country to certain risks. I remind you how Bismarck, after the war of 1866 had been fought to a successful issue, said that the old women would have beaten him to death with cudgels had the Prussian army been defeated. But it was not defeated, and he stood before them as a man who had united Germany and made Prussia great. He exposed Prussia to the greatest risks, in that by his agitation he made almost the whole world Prussia's enemy, declared war upon Austria and upon the whole of South Germany, and forced the latter eventually to engage in the war against France. England at that time pursued the luckless policy of observing and waiting for an opportunity, merely because no agitator conducted its policy. Had England in 1866 declared war against Prussia, Germany would not to-day be so powerful as to be able to wage war upon us. Since those days, profound changes have taken place in England itself, and entirely owing to the growth of the German power. Since the fall of Napoleon, we have not troubled ourselves sufficiently about events upon the Continent, but in our proud self-assurance have thought ourselves so powerful, that we only needed to influence the decisions of foreign governments, in order to pursue our own lines of policy. But this self-assurance suffered a severe shock in the events of 1866 and 1870, and England has, and rightly enough, become nervous. The Englishman down to that period despised the forward policy of the Continental powers. This is no longer the case, but, on the other hand patriotic tendencies are at work even in England itself, which are branded by the weak-minded apostles of peace as chauvinistic. Let that pass, I am proud to call myself a chauvinist in the sense that I do not desire peace at any price, but peace only for England's welfare. The patriotic tendencies of our people have been directed into their proper channel by my predecessor Chamberlain. And has not the Government for the last thirty years hearkened to these patriotic feelings, in that, whether led by Disraeli or Gladstone, it has brought about an enormous strengthening of our defensive forces both on land and sea? These military preparations, whilst not only redounding to the advantage of the motherland, but also to that of the colonies (which they shall ever continue to do) have saddled the mother country with the entire burden of expenditure. But how shall the enormous cost of this war be met for the future? How shall the commerce of the English world-empire be increased in the future and protected from competition, if the colonies do not share in the expense? I vote for a just distribution of the burdens, and maintain that not England alone but that the colonies also should share in bearing them. The plan of Imperial Federation, a policy which we are pursuing, is the remedy for our chronic disease, and will strengthen the colonies and the mother country in economic, political, and military respects. Certainly, my lords, such utterances will appear to you to be somewhat impertinent, at a time when a Russian army has invaded India and our army has suffered a severe defeat, but I should wish to remind you that every war that England has yet waged has begun with defeats. But England has never waged other than victorious wars since William the Conqueror infused Romanic blood into England's political life and thus gave it a constitution of such soundness and tenacity that no other body politic has ever been able permanently to resist England. We shall again, as in days of yore, drive the Russians out of India, shall force the fleets of France, Germany, and Russia who are now hiding in their harbours into the open, annihilate them, and thwart all the insolent plans of our enemies, and finally raise the Union Jack as a standard of a world-power that no one will for evermore be able to attack."

XVIII
THE YOUNG RUSSIAN CAPTAIN OF DRAGOONS

The news of Edith's kidnapping--for, in Heideck's opinion, this was the only explanation, because she would otherwise have left a message for him--fell upon Heideck as a crushing blow.

He remembered the terrible cruelties narrated of the period of the Sepoy mutiny. And he only needed to remember his own experiences in Lahore to be convinced that all those horrible stories were no exaggeration, but, rather, well within the actual truth of the facts.

But if it was not a like fate that awaited Edith Irwin, yet perhaps another ignominious lot would be hers, and this could not fail to appear, to the man who loved her, more terrible even than death itself.

His alarm and deep despondency had not escaped the notice of the Prince. He laid his hand sympathetically on Heideck's shoulder, and said--

"I am really quite miserable, comrade! for I now see what you and the lady are to each other. But perhaps you make yourself uneasy without cause; the departure of the lady is capable, perhaps, of a quite simple explanation."

Heideck shook his head.

"I do not entertain any hope in this respect, for everything points to the fact that the Maharajah of Chanidigot is the man who has got the lady into his power. This sensual despot has for months past schemed how to obtain possession of her. What, in Heaven's name, is to be done to free the unhappy creature from his clutches?"

"I will inform the General, and doubt not that he will institute an inquiry. If your supposition is correct, the Maharajah will, of course, be compelled to set the lady free. But I doubt if this is the case. The despot of Chanidigot is at present far away."

"That would not prevent others from acting on his orders. And do you really believe that your General would, for the sake of an English lady, offend an influential Indian prince, whose alliance would at this present moment be very advantageous for Russia?"

"Oh, my dear friend, we are not the barbarians we are held to be in Western Europe. We do not intend to be behind the rest of the world in chivalrous actions, and we certainly should not begin our rule in India by allowing execrable deeds of violence to take place before our very eyes. I am convinced that the General does not in this matter think differently from myself."

"You do not know what a great comfort it is to me to hear that; for I shall myself be unable to do anything more for Mrs. Irwin. Since I know that Germany is engaged in the war, I can have no further interest but to join my army as quickly as possible."

"Of course! A soldier's duty first. But how shall you manage to get to Germany? It will be a devilish hard job."

"I must try all the same. Under no circumstances could I remain quietly here."

"Well, then, let us consider matters. The best plan would be for you to return by sea from Bombay or some other port, like Calcutta, Madras, or Karachi. Karachi is nearest. It has even been given the name of the Entrance Gate to Central Asia. And from Lahore, Quetta, or Mooltan, Karachi can be most readily reached by the railway. Steamship communication between Karachi and Europe is only possible by way of Bombay; there is thence no other direct line of steamers than that plying up the Persian Gulf. You must accordingly go by one of the English steamers of the P. and O. line, which start twice a week. The French Messageries Maritimes, which usually sail between Karachi and Marseilles, will, of course, have long since discontinued their services. You could, therefore, just as well go by railway to Bombay. Via Calcutta or Madras would be a roundabout journey."

"And I should be entirely dependent upon the English steamship lines?"

"I consider it quite out of the question that the ships of the North German Lloyd or the Austrian Lloyd are still running."

"Then I shall have to give up the idea of this route altogether. For if I am not to make use of a forged passport, which, moreover, will be very hard to obtain, no English steamer will take me as a passenger."

"That is certainly very probable," the Prince rejoined, after some thought. "And then--how are you to get to Bombay? The English are, of course, destroying all the railways on their line of retreat."

"Well, so far as that is concerned, I could go on horseback."

"What! right through the English army? and at the risk of being arrested for a spy? Are you not aware that the conquered are, as a rule, smarter at shooting those whom they regard as spies than are the victors?"

Heideck could not suppress a smile.

"In this respect the promptness of the Russian procedure could scarcely be excelled. But I allow, that your fears are quite justified. Accordingly, only the road to the north remains open."

"Yes, you must go to the Khyber Pass on an empty train or with a transport of English prisoners, and then on horseback through Afghanistan to the frontier, and thence again by railway to Kransnovodsk. Your journey would then be across the Caspian to Baku or by railway by way of Tiflis to Poti on the Black Sea and thence by ship to Constantinople. But, my dear comrade, that's a very long and arduous journey."

"I shall have to attempt it all the same. Honour commands; and you yourself say that there is no other route than that you have described."

"Right!--I will take care you are provided with a passport, and will request the General to furnish you with an authority which will enable you to have at any time an escort of Cossacks upon our lines of communication through Afghanistan--But--"

A gleam of pleasure in his face showed that in his view he had hit upon a very happy thought--"Might there not, perhaps, after all be found some solution which would save you all this exertion? The Germans and the Russians are allies. In the ranks of our army you would also be able to serve your fatherland. And an officer who knows India as well as you, would be invaluable to us at the present time. I will, if you like, speak at once with the General; and I am certain that he will not hesitate a moment to attach you to his staff with the rank that you hold in the German army."

Heideck shook his friend's hand with emotion.

"You make it difficult for me to thank you as you deserve. Without your intervention, my existence would have come to an inglorious close, and the proposal you now make to me is a new proof of your amiable sympathy. But you will not be vexed if I decline your offer--will you? It would certainly be a great honour to serve in your splendid army, but you see I cannot dispose of myself as I would, but must, as a soldier, return to my post irrespective of the difficulties I may have to encounter. I beg you--Lord! what's that? in this land of miracles even the dead come to life again."

The astonishment that prompted this question was a very natural one, for the lean, dark-skinned little man who had just appeared at the entrance of the tent was no other than his faithful servant Morar Gopal whom he had believed to be dead. Round his forehead he wore a fresh bandage. For a moment he stood stock-still at the entrance to the tent, and his dark eyes beamed with pleasure at having found his master again unharmed.

Hardly able to restrain his emotion, Morar Gopal advanced towards Heideck, prostrated himself on the ground, Hindu fashion, in order to touch the earth with his forehead, and then sprang to his feet with all the appearance of the greatest joy.

But Heideck was scarcely less moved than the other, and pressed the brown hand of his faithful servant warmly.

"These lunatics did not kill you after all then? But I saw you felled to the ground by their blows."

Morar Gopal grinned cunningly.

"I threw myself down as soon as I saw that further resistance was useless. And, because I was bleeding from a wound in the head, they thought, I suppose, that they had finished me. Directly afterwards the Cossacks came, and in front of their horses, which would otherwise have trampled upon me, I quickly scrambled to my feet."

"You have great presence of mind! But where did you get this fine suit of clothes?"

"I ran back to the hotel--through the back door, where the smoke was not so stifling--because I thought that sahib would perhaps have taken refuge there. I did not find sahib, but I found these clothes, and thought it better to put them on than to leave them to burn."

"Quite right, my brave fellow! you will hardly be brought up for this little theft."

"I looked for sahib everywhere, where English prisoners are; and when I came to Anar Kali just at the moment that Mrs. Irwin was being driven away in a carriage, I knew that I was at length on the track of my master."

Heideck violently clutched his arm.

"You saw it? and you know, too, who it was that took her away?"

"Yes, sir, it was Siwalik, the Master of the Horse to Prince Tasatat; and the lady is now with him on the road to Simla."

"Simla! How do you know that?"

"I was near enough to hear every word that the Indians spoke, and they said that they were going to Simla."

"And Mrs. Irwin? She didn't resist? She didn't cry for help? She allowed herself to be carried off quietly?"

"The lady was very proud. She did not say a word."

An orderly officer stepped into the tent and brought the Prince an order to appear at once before the Commander-in-Chief.

"Do you know what about?" asked the Colonel.

"As far as I know, it concerns a report of Captain Obrutschev, who commanded the file of men told off for the execution. He reported that the Colonel had carried away a spy who was to be shot by order of the court-martial."

Heideck was in consternation.

"Your act of grace is, after all, likely to land you in serious difficulties," he said. "But, as I need now no longer conceal my quality as German officer, I can, in case the field telegraph is working, be able to establish my identity by inquiry at the General Staff of the German Army."

"Certainly! and I entreat you not to be uneasy on my account; I shall soon justify the action I have taken."

He disappeared in company of the orderly officer; and Heideck the while plied the brave Morar Gopal afresh with questions as to the circumstances connected with Edith's kidnapping.

But the Hindu could not tell him anything more, as he had not dared approach Edith. He was only concerned with the endeavour to find his master. He had learnt that Heideck had been carried off by Cossacks and indefatigably pursued his investigations until at last, with the inborn acumen peculiar to his race, he had found out everything. That he, from this time forth, would share the lot of his adored sahib appeared to him a matter of course. And Heideck had not the heart, in this hour of their meeting again, to destroy his illusion.

After the lapse of half an hour Prince Tchajawadse returned. His joyous countenance showed that he was the bearer of good news.

"All is settled. My word was bond enough for the General, and he considered an inquiry in Berlin quite superfluous."

"In truth, you Russians do everything on a grand scale," exclaimed Heideck. "A great Empire, a great army, a wide, far-seeing policy, and a great comprehension for all things."

"I also talked to the General touching my suggestion to include you in the ranks of our army, and he is completely of one mind with me in the matter. He also considers the difficulties of a journey to Germany under the present conditions to be almost unsurmountable. He makes you the offer to enter his staff with the rank of captain. Under the most favourable conditions you would only be able to reach Berlin after the war is over."

"I do not believe that this war will be so soon at an end. Only reflect, half the globe is in flames."

"All the same, you ought not to reject his offer. We could, to ease your mind, make inquiries on your behalf in Berlin. The field telegraph is open as far as Peshawar, and there is consequently connexion with Moscow, St. Petersburg, and Berlin."

"I accept without further consideration. I should be happy, if permission were granted, to fight in your ranks."

"There is no doubt of that whatever. I will at once procure you our white summer uniform and that of a captain of dragoons; and this sword, comrade, I hope you will accept from me as a small gift of friendship."

"I thank you from my heart, Colonel."

"I salute you as one of ours. I might even be in a position to give you at once an order to carry out."

"But not without permission from Berlin, Prince?"

"Well, then, we will wait for it; but it would be a great pity if, contrary to our expectation, it were to be delayed. The commission that I was on the point of procuring for you would certainly have greatly interested you."

"And may I ask--"

"The General has the intention to send a detachment to Simla."

"To Simla, the summer residence of the Viceroy?"

"Yes."

"But this mountain town is at the present moment not within the sphere of hostilities; the Viceroy remains in Calcutta."

"Quite right; but that does not preclude the news of the occupation of Simla having a great effect on the world at large. Moreover, in the Government offices there there might possibly be found interesting documents which it would be worth while to intercept."

"And you consider it possible that His Excellency would despatch me thither?"

"As the detachment to which my dragoons, as well as some infantry and two machine guns, would belong is under my command, I have begged the General to attach you to the expedition."

Heideck understood the high-minded intentions of the Prince, and shook his hands almost impetuously.

"Heaven grant that permission from Berlin comes in time! I desire nothing in the world so earnestly as to accompany you to Simla."

XIX
ON THE ROAD TO SIMLA

Almost quicker than could have been expected, considering the heavy work imposed upon the telegraph wires, the communication arrived from Berlin that Captain Heideck should, for the time being, do duty in the Russian army, and that it should be left to his judgment to take the first favourable opportunity to return to Germany.

He forthwith waited upon the commanding general, was initiated into his new role formally and by handshake, and was in all due form attached as captain to the detachment that was commanded to proceed to Simla.

The next morning the cavalcade set out under the command of Prince Tchajawadse.

Their route led across a part of the battlefield lying east of Lahore, where the battle between the sepoys and the pursuing Russian cavalry had principally taken place.

The sight of this trampled, bloodstained plain was shockingly sad. Although numerous Indian and Russian soldiers under the military police were engaged in picking up the corpses, there still lay everywhere around the horribly mutilated bodies of the fallen in the postures in which they had been overtaken by a more or less painful death. An almost intolerable odour of putrefaction filled the air, and mingled with the biting, stifling smoke of the funeral pyres upon which the corpses were being burnt.

The greater part of the Russian army was in the camp and in the city. Only the advance guard, which had returned from the pursuit of the fleeing English, had taken up a position to the south of the city. The reinforcements which had been despatched from Peshawar, and which had been impatiently expected, had not yet arrived.

Heideck heard that about 4,000 English soldiers and more than 1,000 officers were dead and wounded, while 3,000 men and 85 officers were prisoners in the hands of the Russians. The losses of the sepoy regiment could not at present be approximately determined, as the battle had extended over too wide an area.

Prince Tchajawadse, although showing the same friendly feeling towards Heideck, now adopted more the attitude of his military superior. He narrated during the journey that the Russian army was taking the road through the west provinces, and would leave the valley of the Indus, and the country immediately bordering it, unmolested.

"We shall march to Delhi," he said, "and then probably advance upon Cawnpore and Lucknow."

The detachment was unable to make use of the railway which goes via Amritsar and Ambala to Simla, because it had been to a great extent destroyed by the English. But the rapidity of the march naturally depended upon the marching capabilities of the infantry. And although Heideck could not fail to admire the freshness and endurance of these hardened soldiers, they yet advanced far too slowly for his wishes.

How happy he would have been if, with his squadron, he had been able to make a forced march upon the road which the unhappy Edith must have taken!

On the second day after their start, the blue and violet peaks of the mountains were silhouetted in the distance. It was the mountainous country lying beneath the Himalayas, whose low summer temperature induces the Viceroy and the high officials of the Indian Government every year to take refuge from the intolerably hot and sultry Calcutta in the cool and healthy Simla. Moreover, the families of the rich English merchants and officials living in the Punjab and the west provinces are accustomed to take up their quarters there during the hot season.

The vegetation as they advanced became ever richer and more luxuriant. Their way led through splendid jungles, which in places gave the impression of artificially made parks. Hosts of monkeys sprang about among the palms, and took daring leaps from one branch to the other. The approach of the soldiers did not appear to cause these lively creatures any appreciable fear, for they often remained seated directly over their heads and regarded the unaccustomed military display with as much inquisitiveness as they evidently did with delight. Parrots in gay plumage filled the air with shrill cries, while here and there herds of antelopes were visible, who, however, always dashed away in rapid flight, in which their strange manner of springing from all fours in the air afforded a most strange and delightful spectacle.

On the third day a gay-coloured cavalcade crossed the path of the detachment. They were evidently aristocratic Indians, who in the half-native, half-English dress were seated upon excellent horses, a cross-breed between the Arabian and Gujarat. At their head rode a splendidly dressed, dark-bearded man upon a white horse of special beauty.

He halted to exchange a few words of civil salutation with the Russian colonel. When he had again set himself in motion with his lancers, soon to be lost to view in the thick jungle, the Prince motioned Heideck to his side.

"I have news for you, comrade! The aristocratic Indian with whom I just spoke was the Maharajah of Sabathu who is on the look-out for his guest and friend, the Maharajah of Chanidigot, who is engaged on a hunting expedition."

"The Maharajah of Chanidigot?" Heideck exclaimed with sparkling eyes. "The rogue is then really in our immediate neighbourhood?"

"The hunting-camp that the two Princes have formed lies directly in our line of march, and the Maharajah has invited me to camp this night there with my men. I have really more than half a mind to accept his kind invitation."

"And did you not inquire about Mrs. Irwin, Prince?"

The Colonel's face assumed at Heideck's question a strangely serious, almost repellent expression.

"No."

"But it is more than probable that she is in his camp."

"Possibly, although up to now every proof of that is wanting."

"But you will institute inquiries for her, will you not? You will compel the Maharajah to give us news of her whereabouts?"

"I can, at most, politely ask him for information. But I cannot promise you even that with certainty."

Heideck was extremely surprised. He could not explain in any way the change in the Prince's demeanour. And he would have been inclined to take his strange answers for a not too delicate jest, had not the frigid, impenetrable expression of his face at once excluded any suggestion of the sort.

"But I don't understand, Prince," he said, surprised. "It was only a few days ago that you were kind enough to promise me your active support in this matter."

"I am to my regret compelled to cancel that promise; for I have received strict instructions from His Excellency to avoid everything that can lead to friction with the native Princes, and that my superiors laid great stress upon a good understanding with the Maharajah of Chanidigot was not known to me at the time of our conversation. He was the first who openly declared for Russia and whose troops have come over to our side. The happy issue of the Battle of Lahore is perhaps in no small degree due to him. You understand, Captain, that it would make the worst possible impression were we to come into conflict with a man so needful to us for such a trifling cause."

"Trifling cause?" Heideck asked earnestly, his eyes sparkling with excitement.

"Well, yes, what appears to you of such great importance is, when regarded from a high political point of view, very trifling and insignificant. You cannot possibly expect that the political interests of a world empire should be sacrificed for the interests of a single lady, who, moreover, by nationality belongs to our enemies."

"Shall she then be handed over helpless to the bestiality of this dissolute scoundrel?"

Prince Tchajawadse shrugged his shoulders, while at the same time he cast a strange side-glance at Heideck, who was riding beside him, which seemed to say--

"How dense you are, my dear fellow! And how slow of understanding!"

But the other did not understand this dumb play of the eyes; and, after a short pause, he could not refrain from saying in a tone of painful reproach--

"Why, my Prince, did you so generously procure for me permission to take part in this expedition if I was at once to be doomed to inaction in a matter, which, as you know, is at present nearer my heart than aught else!"

"I do not remember, Captain, to have imposed any such restraint upon you. It was purely my own attitude as regards this matter which I wished to make clear to you. And I hope that you have completely understood me. I will not, and dare not, have anything officially to do with the affair of Mrs. Irwin, and I should like to hear nothing about it. That I, on the other hand, do not interfere with your private concerns, and would not trouble about them, is quite a matter of course. It entirely suffices for me, if you do not bring me into any embarrassment and impossible situation."

That was, at all events, much less than Heideck had expected after the zealous promises of his friend. But after quiet reflection he came to the conclusion that the Prince could, as a matter of fact, scarcely act otherwise, and that he went to the utmost limits of the possible, if he did not absolutely forbid him to undertake anything for the advantage of the unhappy Edith. Heideck's decision to leave not a stone unturned to liberate the woman he loved was not thereby shaken for a moment, but he knew now that he would have to proceed with the greatest circumspection, and that he could not reckon upon anyone's assistance--an admission which was not exactly calculated to fill him with joyous hope.

After a short march the detachment reached the spot lying immediately at the foot of the first hill, a wide space shaded by mighty trees, upon which the Maharajah had erected his improvised hunting-camp. A great number of tents had been pitched under the trees. A gay-coloured throng of men surged amongst them.

It was perfectly clear to Heideck that he could not himself search the camp for Edith Irwin without exciting the attention of the Indians, thereby at once compromising the success of his venture. And he had no one to whom he could entrust the important task, except the faithful Morar Gopal, who, in spite of all the terrors of war, had also followed him on this march to Simla, although Heideck had offered him his discharge, together with the payment of his wages for several months more.

Accordingly, after the signal had been given to halt and dismount, he took him aside and communicated to him his instructions, at the same time handing him a handful of rupees to enable him to give the necessary bribes.

The Hindu listened with keen attention, and the play of his dark, clever face showed what a lively personal interest he took in this affair nearest his master's heart.

"Everything shall be done according to your wishes, sahib," he said, and soon afterwards was lost to view among the innumerable crowd of the two Indian Princes' servants and followers.

XX
A FRIEND IN NEED

Whilst the Russians were digging their cooking trenches somewhat aside from the main camp, and making all necessary arrangements for bivouacking, Heideck had an opportunity of admiring the magnificence with which these Indian Princes organised their hunting excursions.

The tents of the two Maharajahs were almost the size of a one-floor bungalow, and on peering through the open entrance of one of them into the interior, Heideck saw that it was lavishly hung with red, blue, and yellow silk, and furnished with most costly carpets.

About half a hundred smaller tents were destined to receive the retinue and servants. Behind them again was a whole herd of camels and elephants, which had carried the baggage and material for the tents. The bleating of countless sheep mingled with the hundred-voiced din of the Indians as they busily ran hither and thither, and Heideck computed the number of buffaloes and tethered horses which grazed round the camp at more than three hundred.

The Maharajah of Sabathu regarded the Russians, who had here made halt at his invitation, as his guests, and he discharged the duty of hospitality with genuine Indian lavishness. He had so many sheep and other provisions placed at the disposal of the soldiers that they could now amply compensate themselves for many a day's privation in the past. But the officers were solemnly bidden to the banquet that was to take place in the Maharajah's tent.

Heideck's hope of meeting on this occasion the Maharajah of Chanidigot once more, and of perhaps finding an opportunity of conversation with him, was disappointed.

On returning from a walk through the camp, in which he did not discover anywhere a trace of Edith, back to the Russian bivouac, Heideck learnt from the mouth of Prince Tchajawadse that the Maharajah of Chanidigot had met with a slight accident in the hunting excursion that day, and was under surgical treatment in his tent, whither he had been brought.

It was said that the tusks of a wild boar, which had run between his horse's legs, had inflicted a severe wound on the foot, and it was in any case certain that he would not be visible that day.

On this occasion Heideck also learnt the circumstances to which the meeting with the two Indian Princes was due.

The Maharajah of Chanidigot, who knew full well that the English had sentenced him to death for high treason, had fled from his capital. With a hundred horse and many camels, carrying the most precious part of his movable treasures, he had advanced northwards out of the sphere of British territory into the rear of the Russian advancing army. He had visited his friend, the Maharajah of Sabathu, who was likewise a Mohammedan, and both Princes had for their greater safety proceeded hither to the foot of the mountain chain, where, for the present, despite the exciting times, they could pursue the pleasures of sport with all the nonchalance of real gentlemen at large.

The treacherous despot of Chanidigot would probably have preferred to have gone direct to Simla, and it was only the intelligence that had reached the Russians, that English troops were still in Ambala, that probably caused him to stop half-way.

Prince Tchajawadse was also induced by this intelligence to abandon his intended route via Ambala, and to proceed in a direct line through the jungle. In this way he could confidently hope to reach Simla without a battle, and, moreover, should it turn out that the garrison of Ambala was not over strong, he might deliver a surprise attack upon the English from the north. In time of peace Ambala was one of the larger encampments, but now it was to be expected that the main body of the troops stationed there had been ordered to Lahore.

The whole opulence of an Indian Court was unfolded at the Maharajah's banquet. At the table covered with red velvet and luxuriously laid with gold and silver plate, the Russian officers sat in gay-coloured ranks with the chiefs of the Prince's retinue. The viands were excellent, and champagne flowed in inexhaustible streams. The Russians required but few invitations to drink, but the Mohammedan Indians were not in this respect far behind them. It is true that the drinking of wine is forbidden by the tenets of their religion; but in respect of champagne, they understand how to evade this commandment by christening it by the harmless name of "sparkling lemonade," a circumlocution which of course did not in the slightest counteract its exhilarating effects. The Indians who were less proof against the effects of alcohol were much more quickly intoxicated than their new European friends; and under the influence of the potent liquor universal fraternisation inevitably resulted.

The Maharajah himself delivered a suggestive speech in praise of the Russian victors who had at last come as the long-desired saviours of the country from the British yoke. Of course he had to employ the accursed English language, it being the only one that he understood besides his own mother tongue; and Prince Tchajawadse had to translate his words into Russian in order that they should be intelligible to all the Russian heroes.

In spite of this somewhat troublesome procedure, however, his words roused intense enthusiasm, and embracings and brotherly kisses were soon the order of the day.

When the universal jollity had reached its height, two Bayaderes, who belonged to the suite of the Maharajah of Sabathu, made their appearance, Indian beauties, whose voluptuous feminine charms were calculated to make the blood even of the spoilt European run warm. Dressed in gold-glittering petticoats and jackets, which left a hand's breadth of light brown skin visible round the waist, with gold coins upon the blue-black hair, they executed their dances to the monotonous tone of weird musical instruments upon a carpet spread in the middle of the tent. The bare arms, the bones and toes of their little feet were adorned with gold bracelets set with pearls and rings bedizened with jewels. Though their motions had nothing in common with the bacchanalian abandon of other national dances, yet the graceful play of their supple, lithe limbs was seductive enough to enchant the spectators. The Indians threw silver coins to the dancers, but the Russians, according to their native custom, clapped applause and never tired of demanding amid shouts of delight a repetition of the dance.

Amid the general wantonness there was only one who remained morose and anxious, and this was Heideck, the newly-made captain in the Russian army.

He knew that it would be easy for Morar Gopal's shrewdness to find him in case he had something to report. And that the Hindu did not make his appearance was for him a disheartening proof that his servant had not hitherto succeeded in discovering Edith's whereabouts or in obtaining any certain news of her fate.

What did it avail him, that after much thought he had already evolved a plan for her liberation, if there was no possibility of putting himself in communication with her!

Believing her to be kept prisoner in a harem tent, his idea was to send Morar Gopal with a letter to her, fully convinced that the wily Indian would succeed by stratagem and bribery in reaching her. Before the banquet he had negotiated with one of the Indian rajahs for the purchase of an ox-waggon, and if Edith could by his letter be prevailed upon to make an attempt at flight, it would not in his view be very difficult to bring her under Morar Gopal's protection to Ambala, where she would again find herself among her English countrymen.

But this plan was unrealisable so long as he did not even know where Edith was. Incapable of bearing any longer this condition of uncertainty, he was just on the point of leaving the tent in order, at all risks, to hunt for the beloved lady, when a Russian dragoon stepped behind his chair and informed him with a military salute that a lady outside the tent wished to speak to the Captain.

Full of blissful hope that it was Edith he jumped up and hurried out. But his longing eyes sought in vain for Captain Irwin's widow. Instead of her whom he sought he perceived a tall female form in the short jacket and short-cut coloured dress which he had seen on his journeys among the inhabitants of the Georgian mountains. The hair and the face of the girl were almost entirely hidden by a scarf wound round the head. Only when, at his approach, she pushed it back somewhat he perceived who stood before him.

"Georgi--you here!" he exclaimed with surprise. "And in this dress?"

He had indeed reason to be surprised, for he had not again seen the handsome, blonde page, to whom he chiefly owed his life, since their meeting on the way to the place of execution.

When on the evening of that for him so eventful day he asked Prince Tchajawadse about Georgi he had received only a short, evasive reply, and the Prince's knitted brows showed such evident anger that he well perceived that something must have taken place between them, and so it appeared to him to be best to him not to mention again the name of the Circassian girl.

When the detachment started he had in vain looked for the page who had hitherto been inseparable from "his master," and only the anxiety for Edith, which was so much nearer his heart, was the cause that he had not thought much about the inexplicable disappearance of the disguised girl.

He had certainly least of all expected to find her here, so far from the Russian headquarters, and in woman's dress to boot. But the Circassian did not seem inclined to give him detailed information.

"I have begged you to come out to see me, sir," she said, "because I did not want the Prince to see me. I met your Indian servant. And he told me about the English lady whom the Maharajah of Chanidigot has carried off from you."

"He did not carry her off from me, Georgi, for I have no claim upon her. She only placed herself under my protection, and therefore it is my duty to do all that I can to set her free."

The girl looked at him, and there was a glance as of suppressed passion in her beautiful eyes.

"Why do you not speak the truth, sir? Say that you love her! Tell me that you love her and I will bring her back to you--and this very evening."

"You, Georgi, how in all the world will you be able to manage that? Do you know then where the lady is to be found?"

"I know it from your servant, Morar Gopal. She is there, in that tent of the Maharajah of Chanidigot, before whose door the two Indians are standing sentry. Take care and do not attempt to force your way in, for the sentries would cut you to pieces before allowing you to put a foot in the tent."

"It may be that you are right," said Heideck, whose breast was now filled with a blissful feeling at having at last learned with certainty that the adored woman was close by. "But how shall you be able to get to her?"

"I am a woman, and I know how one must treat these miserable Indian rogues; the Maharajah of Chanidigot is ill, and in his pain he has something else to think of than of the joys of love. You must make use of this favourable moment, sir! and in this very night whatever is to happen must happen."

"Certainly! every minute lost means perhaps a terrible danger to Mrs. Irwin. But if you have a plan for saving her please tell me--"

The Circassian shook her head.

"Why talk of things that must be first accomplished? Return to the banquet, sir, that no one may suspect of you. At midnight you will find the English lady in your tent, or you will never set eyes on me again."

She turned as if to go; but after having taken a few steps came back once more to him.

"You will not tell the Prince that I am here, do you understand? It is not time yet for him to learn that."

With these words she disappeared, before Heideck could ask another question. Little as he felt inclined after what he had just experienced to return to the mad riot of the banquet, he perceived that there was scarcely anything else open to him, for any interference with the unknown plans of the Circassian would scarcely be of any advantage to Edith.

But if the minutes had hitherto appeared endless, they now crept on with quite intolerable slowness. He scarcely heard or saw anything that was taking place about him. The rajah who had the next place to him tried in vain to open a conversation in his broken English, and at last, shaking his head, abandoned the silent stranger to his musings, which in the middle of this riotous festivity must certainly have appeared very strange to him.

Shortly before midnight, before Prince Tchajawadse and his other comrades thought of moving, Heideck once more left the state tent of the Maharajah and turned his steps towards the Russian camp, which was far away visible in the red glare of the bivouac fires, around which the loudest merriment was also taking place.

In reality he entertained very little hope that the Circassian would be able to fulfil her bold promise, for what she had taken upon herself appeared to him to be absolutely impracticable. Yet his heart throbbed wildly when he thrust back the linen sheet that covered the entrance of the tent which had been assigned to him.

On the folding-table in the middle of the little room were two lighted candles beside a burning lantern. And in their light Heideck discerned--not Edith Irwin, but instead, the handsomest young rajah who had ever crossed his eyes under the glowing skies of India.

For a moment Heideck was uncertain, for the slender youth, in the silken blouse tied round with a red scarf, English riding-breeches and neat little boots, had turned his back to him, so that he could not see his face, and his hair was completely hidden under the rose-and-yellow striped turban. But the blissful presentiment which told him who was concealed beneath the charming disguise could not deceive him. A few rapid steps and he was by the side of the delicate-limbed Indian youth. Overpowered by a storm of passionate emotions, he forgot all obstacles and scruples, and the next moment clasped him in his arms with an exultant cry of joy.

"Edith! my Edith!"

"My beloved friend!"

In the exceeding delight of this reunion the confession which had never passed her lips in the hours of familiar tete-a-tete, or in the moments of extreme peril which they had endured together, forced its way irresistibly from her heart--the confession of a love which had long absorbed her whole life.

XXI
EDITH'S ADVENTURES

It was a long time before the two lovers were sufficiently composed to explain to each other fully the almost fabulous events that had lately occurred.

Heideck, of course, wanted to know, first of all, how Edith had contrived to escape without making a disturbance and calling for the aid of those about her. What she told him was the most touching proof of her affection for him. The Maharajah's creatures must have heard, somehow or other, of Heideck's imprisonment and condemnation, and they had reckoned correctly on Edith's attachment to the man who had saved her life.

She had been told that a single word from the Maharajah would be sufficient to destroy the foolhardy German, and that her only hope of saving him from death lay in a personal appeal to His Highness's clemency. Although she knew perfectly well the shameful purpose this suggestion concealed, she had not hesitated, in her anxiety for her dear one's safety, to follow the men who promised to conduct her to the Maharajah, full of hypocritical assurances that she would come to no harm. She had had so many proofs of the revengeful cruelty of this Indian despot that she feared the worst for Heideck, and resolved, in the last extremity, to sacrifice her life--if she could not preserve her honour--to save him.

The Maharajah had received her with great courtesy and promised to use his influence in favour of the German who had been seized as a spy and traitor by the Russians. But he had at the same time thrown out fairly broad hints what his price would be, and, from the moment she had delivered herself into his hands, he had treated her as a prisoner, although with great respect. All communication, except with persons of the Maharajah's household, was completely cut off; and she was under no delusion as to the lot which awaited her, as soon as the Prince again felt himself completely secure in some mountain fastness unaffected by the events of the war.

Feeling certain of this, she had continually contemplated the idea of flight; but the fear of sealing the fate of her unhappy friend, even more than the ever-watchful suspicion of her guards, had prevented her from making the attempt.

Her joy had been all the greater when, the same evening, Morar Gopal appeared in the women's tent with the Circassian, to relieve her from the almost unendurable tortures of uncertainty as to Heideck's fate.

The cunning Hindu had managed to gain access to the carefully guarded prisoners for himself and his companion by pretending that the Maharajah had chosen the Circassian girl to be the English lady's servant. He had whispered a few words to Edith, telling her what was necessary for her to know for the moment.

After he had retired, it roused no suspicion when she asked to be left alone for a few moments with the new servant. With her assistance, she made use of the opportunity to put on the light Indian man's clothes which the Circassian had brought with her in a parcel. The guards, who were by this time intoxicated, had allowed the slender young rajah, into whom she had transformed herself, to depart unmolested, and Morar Gopal, who was waiting for her at a place agreed upon close at hand, had conducted her to Heideck's tent, where she might, for the moment at least, consider herself to be safe.

"But Georgi?" asked the Captain with some anxiety. "She remained in the women's tent? What will happen to her when her share in your flight is discovered?"

"The idea also tormented me. But the heroic girl repeatedly assured me that she would find a way to escape, and that in any case she would have nothing to fear, as soon as she appealed to Prince Tchajawadse."

"That may be so; but that hardly agrees with her wish to keep the fact of her presence in the camp a secret from the Prince. The girl's behaviour is a complete riddle to me. I do not understand what can have induced her to sacrifice herself with such wonderful unselfishness for us, who are really only strangers to her, in whom she can feel no interest. Certainly she was not actuated by any thought of a reward. She has the pride of her race, and I am certain that she would consider any offer of one as an insult."

"I think the same. But perhaps I can guess her real motives."

"And won't you tell me what you think?"

Edith hesitated a little; but she was not one of those women who allow any petty emotion to master them.

"I think, my friend, that she loves you," she said, with a slight, enchanting smile. "Some unguarded expressions and the fire that kindled in her eyes as soon as we mentioned your name, made me feel almost certain of it. The fact that, notwithstanding, she helped to set me free, is certainly, in the circumstances, only a stronger proof of her magnanimity. But I understand it perfectly. A woman in love, if of noble character, is capable of any act of self-denial."

Heideck shook his head.

"I think your shrewdness has played you false on this occasion. I am firmly convinced that she is Prince Tchajawadse's mistress, and, from all I have seen of their relations, it seems to me inconceivable that she would be unfaithful to him for the sake of a stranger, with whom she has only interchanged a few casual words."

"Well, perhaps we may have an opportunity of settling whether I am wrong or not. But now, my friend, I should first of all like to know what you have decided about me."

Heideck was in some embarrassment how to answer, and spoke hesitatingly of his intention to send her to Ambala with Morar Gopal. But Edith would not allow him to finish. She interrupted him with a decided gesture of dissent.

"Ask of me what you like--except to leave you again. What shall I do in Ambala without you? I have suffered so unutterably since you were carried off before my eyes at Anar Kali, that I will die a thousand times rather than again expose myself to the torture of such uncertainty."

A noise behind him made Heideck turn his head. He saw the curtain before the door of the tent slightly lifted, and that it was Morar Gopal who had attempted to draw his attention by coughing discreetly.

He called to the loyal fellow to come in, and thanked him, not condescendingly, as a master recognises the cleverness of his servant, but as one friend thanks another.

The Hindu's features showed how delighted he was by the kindness of his idolised master, although there was no alteration in his humble and modest demeanour even for a moment. As respectful as ever, he said: "I bring good news, sahib. One of the Maharajah's retinue, whose tongue I loosened with some of your rupees, has told me that the Maharajah of Sabathu is going to give the Russians forty horsemen to show them the best roads to Simla. The country here is under his rule, and his people know every inch of ground to the top of the mountains. If the lady joins these horsemen to-morrow in the dress of a rajah, she will be sure to get away from here unmolested."

The excellence and practicability of this plan was obvious, and Heideck again recognised what a treasure a lucky accident had bestowed upon him in the shape of this Indian boy. Edith also agreed, since she saw how joyfully Heideck welcomed the proposal, although the prospect of being obliged to show herself in broad daylight before everybody in man's dress was painful to her feelings as a woman.

She asked Morar Gopal whether he had heard anything of Georgi in the meantime. He nodded assent.

"I was talking to her half an hour ago. She had escaped from the women's tent and was on the point of leaving the camp."

"What?" cried Heideck. "Where in the world did she intend to go?"

"I don't know, sahib. She was very sad, but when I asked her to accompany me to the sahib, she said she did not want to see him and the lady again; she sent her respects to the sahib, and begged him to remember his promise that he would say nothing to Prince Tchajawadse of her having been here."

Heideck and Edith exchanged a significant look. This singular girl's behaviour set them riddles which for the moment they were unable to solve. But it was only natural and human that in their own affairs they very soon forgot the Circassian.

Edith had to consent to Heideck leaving his tent at her disposal for the rest of the night, while he himself spent the few hours before daybreak at one of the bivouac fires. But Morar Gopal was to take up his quarters before the entrance to the tent, and Heideck felt confident that he could not entrust his valuable treasure to a more loyal keeper.

. . . .

Fortune, which had reunited the lovers in so wonderful a manner, still continued favourable to them. Very early on the following day, Heideck had purchased a neat little bay horse, already saddled and bridled, for Edith's use. When the troop of Indian horsemen, who were to serve as guides and spies for the Russians, started on their way, the boyish young rajah joined them, and no one made his strange appearance the subject of obtrusive questions. The Indians probably at first thought he was a very youthful Russian officer, who wore the native dress for special reasons, and on that account preserved a most respectful demeanour. Tchajawadse, who accidentally found himself close to Edith before starting, said nothing, although he certainly looked keenly at her for a moment.

The bad reports of the health of the Maharajah of Chanidigot, which spread through the camp, were sufficient explanation why he made no attempt to regain possession of the beautiful fugitive. He was said to be suffering from such violent pain and fever, caused by his wounds, that he had practically lost all interest in the outside world.

Having taken a hearty leave of their Indian hosts, the Russian detachment advanced further into the hilly country, and at noon spies reported to Prince Tchajawadse that the English had completely evacuated Ambala and had set out on the march to Delhi. Probably the strength of the Russian division, whose advance had been reported, had been greatly exaggerated at Ambala, and the English had preferred to avoid a probably hopeless engagement.

With a woman's cleverness, Edith managed, without attracting observation, to keep near Heideck, so that they often had the opportunity of conversing. Her tender, fair skin must have appeared striking amongst all the brown faces, but the will and caprice of Russian officers demanded respect, and so no one appeared to know that there was an English lady in the troop wearing the costume of a rajah. Besides, the march was not a long one. The hunting-camp was only about 150 miles from Simla, situated below Kalka. On the next morning the column arrived before Simla and found that Jutogh, the high-lying British cantonment to the west of the far-extended hill city, had been evacuated.

Prince Tchajawadse quartered his infantry and artillery in the English barracks, and marched with the horsemen into the crescent-shaped bazaar, the town proper, surrounded by numerous villas, scattered over the hills and in the midst of pleasure-gardens. He at once sent off patrols of officers to the town hall, the offices of the Government and Commander-in-Chief, while he himself made his way to Government House, a beautiful palace on Observatory Hill.

Although it was spring, Simla still lay in its winter sleep. It had been deserted by the lively, brilliant society which, when the intolerable, moist heat of summer drove the Viceroy from Calcutta, enlivened the magnificent valleys and heights with its horses and carriages, its games, parties, and elegant dresses. Only the resident population, and the servants who had been left to look after the buildings and keep them in good order, remained, English Society being kept away by the war.

The hills were about a mile and three-quarters above the level of the Indian Ocean, and frequent showers of rain made the climate so raw that Heideck rode with his cloak on, and Edith flung a dragoon's long cloak over her shoulders to protect herself against the cold.

The officers were commissioned to search the Government buildings for important legal documents and papers, which the English Government might have left behind in Simla, and which were of importance to the Russian Government.

Heideck had to examine the seven handsome blocks of Government offices, especially the buildings set apart for the Commander-in-Chief, the Quartermaster-General, the general railway management, and the post and telegraph offices.

He found none but subordinate officials anywhere until he came to the office of the Judge Advocate General. Here he found a dignified old gentleman, sitting so quietly in his armchair that Heideck was involuntarily reminded of Archimedes when the Roman soldiers surprised him at his calculations.

As the officer entered, accompanied by the soldiers, the old gentleman looked at them keenly out of his large, yellowish eyes. But he neither asked what they wanted, nor even attempted to prevent their entrance. Heideck bowed politely, and apologised for the intrusion necessitated by his duty. This courteous behaviour appeared to surprise the old gentleman, who returned his greeting, and said that there was nothing left for him but to submit to the orders of the conqueror.

"As there seems nothing to be found in these rooms but legal books and documents," said Heideck, "I need not make any investigation, for we are simply concerned with military matters. I should be glad if I could meet any personal wishes of yours, for I do not think I am mistaken in assuming that I have the honour of speaking to a higher official, whom special reasons have obliged to remain in Simla."

"As a matter of fact, my physicians were of opinion that it would be beneficial to my health to spend the winter in the mountains. You can imagine how greatly I regret that I took their advice--I am Judge-Advocate-General Kennedy."

"Is your family also in Simla?" asked Heideck.

"My wife and daughter are here."

"Sir, there is an English lady with our column, the widow of an officer who was killed at Lahore. Would you be disposed to let her join your family?"

"An English lady?"

"She is the victim of a series of adventurous experiences, as to which she can best inform you herself. Her name is Mrs. Irwin. Would you be disposed to grant her your protection? If so, I should certainly be the bearer of welcome news to her."

"My protection?" repeated the old gentleman in surprise. "My family and I need protection ourselves, and how can we, in the present circumstances, undertake such a responsibility?"

"You and your family have nothing to fear from us, sir. On the contrary, we intend to maintain quietness and order."

"Well, sir, your behaviour is that of a gentleman, and if the lady wishes to come to us we will offer no objection. Can I speak to her, that we may come to an understanding?"

"I will make haste and fetch her."

In fact, he did not hesitate for a moment. As he expected, Edith was very grateful to him for his friendly proposition.

Mr. Kennedy was extremely astonished to see a young rajah enter the room, and did not seem quite agreeably impressed by the masquerade.

"Is this the lady of whom you spoke?" he asked in surprise. But his serious face visibly cleared when Edith said, in her sweet, gentle voice--

"A countrywoman, who owes her life to this gentleman here, and who has only escaped death and dishonour by the aid of this disguise."

"Mrs. Irwin, if you decide to join Mrs. Kennedy," said Heideck, "I will send your belongings to Mr. Kennedy's house. I must now leave you for the present. I have other official duties to perform, but I will return later."

"In any case I am glad to welcome my countrywoman," protested the old gentleman. "You can see my house from the window here, and I beg you will call upon me when your duties are over."

It was not till after sunset that Heideck called at Mr. Kennedy's house. He stood for a moment at the garden-gate and saw the snow-clad heights glowing in the fire of the evening light. Long chains of blue hills rose higher and higher towards the north, till at last the highest range on the distant horizon, bristling with eternal glaciers, mounted towards the sky in wondrous brilliancy.

Mr. Kennedy lived in a very imposing villa. Heideck was received with such friendliness by the master of the house and the ladies that he recognised only too clearly that Edith must have spoken warmly in his favour. She must also certainly have told them that he was a German. She was dressed as a woman again, and had already won the hearts of all by her frankness. Mrs. Kennedy was a matron with fine, pleasant features, and evidently of high social standing. Her daughter, about the same age as Edith, appeared to have taken a great fancy to the visitor.

Heideck sat with the family by the fire, and all tried to forget that he wore the uniform of the enemy.

"I wish we could manage to leave India and get back to England," said Mrs. Kennedy. "My husband wants to remain in Calcutta to perform his duties, but he cannot stand the climate. Besides, how could we get to Calcutta? Our only chance would be to obtain a Russian passport, enabling us to travel without interference."

"My dearest Beatrice," objected her husband. "I know that you, like myself, no longer care what happens to us, at a time when such misfortune has overtaken our country. Amidst the general misfortune, what matters our own fate?"

"I should think," interposed Heideck politely, "that the individual, however deeply he feels the general misfortune, ought not to give way to despair, but should always be thinking of his family as in time of peace."

"No!" cried Mr. Kennedy. "An Englishmen cannot understand this international wisdom. A German's character is different; he can easily change his country, the Englishman cannot. But you must excuse me," he continued, recollecting himself. "You wounded my national honour, and I forgot the situation in which we are. Of course, I had no intention of insulting you."

"There is some truth in what you say," replied Heideck, seriously, "but allow me to explain. Our German fatherland, in past centuries, was always the theatre of the battles of all the peoples of Europe. At that time few of the German princes were conscious of any German national feeling; they were the representatives of narrow-minded dynastic interests. Thus our German people grew up without the consciousness of a great and common fatherland. Our German self-consciousness is no older than Bismarck. But we have become large-hearted, generous-minded, by having had to submit to foreign peoples and customs. Our religious feeling and our patriotism are of wider scope than those of others. Hence, I believe that, now that we have been for a generation occupied with our material strength and are politically united, our universal culture summons us to undertake the further development of civilisation, which hitherto has been chiefly indebted to the French and English."

The old gentleman did not answer at once. He sat immersed in thought, and a considerable time elapsed before he spoke.

"Anyone can keep raising the standpoint of his view of things. It is like ascending the mountains there. From each higher range the view becomes more comprehensive, while the details of the panorama gradually disappear. Naturally, to one looking down from so lofty a standpoint, all political interests shrivel up to insignificant nothings, and then patriotism no longer exists. But I think that we are first of all bound to work in the sphere in which we have once been placed. A man who neglects his wife and children in the desire to benefit the world by his ideas, neglects the narrowest sphere of his duties. But in that case the welfare of his own people, of his own state, must be for every man the highest objects of his efforts; then only, starting from his own nation, may his wishes have a higher aim. I cannot respect anyone who abandons the soil of patriotism in order to waste his time on visionary schemes in the domain of politics, to wax enthusiastic over universal peace and to call all men brothers."

"And yet," said Edith, "this is the doctrine of Christianity."

"Of theoretical, not practical Christianity," eagerly rejoined the Englishman. "I esteem the old Roman Cato, who took his life when he saw his country's freedom disappearing, and England would never have grown great had not many of her sons been Catos."

"Mr. Kennedy, you are proclaiming the old Greek idea of the state," said Heideck. "But I do not believe that the old Greeks had such a conception of the state as modern professors assert, and as ancient Rome practically carried out. Professors are in the habit of quoting Plato, but Plato was too highly gifted not to understand that the state after all consists merely of men. Plato regarded the state not as an idol on whose altar the citizen was obliged to sacrifice himself, but as an educational institution. He says that really virtuous citizens could only be reared by an intelligently organised state, and for this reason he attached such importance to the state. A state is in its origin only the outer form, which the inner life of the nation has naturally created for itself, and this conception should not be upset. The state should educate the masses, in order that not only justice, but also external and internal prosperity may be realised. The Romans certainly do not appear to have made the rearing of capable citizens, in accordance with Plato's idea, the aim of the state; they were modern, like the great Powers of to-day, whose aim it is to grow as rich and powerful as possible. We Germans also desire this, and that is why we are waging this war; but at the same time I assert that something higher dwells in the German national character--the idea of humanity. With us also our ideals are being destroyed, and therefore we are fighting for our 'place under the sun,' in order to protect and secure our ideals together with our national greatness."

At this point a servant entered and announced dinner.

At table the conversation shifted from philosophy and politics to art. The ladies tried to cheer the old gentleman and banish his despair. Elizabeth talked of the concerts in Simla and Calcutta, mentioning the great technical difficulties which beset music in India, owing to the instruments being so soon injured by the climate. The moist air of the towns on the coast made the wood swell; the dry air of Central India, on the other hand, made it shrink, which was very injurious to pianos, but especially to violins and cellos. Pianos, with metal instead of wood inside, were made for the tropics; but they had a shrill tone and were equally affected by abrupt changes of temperature.

After dinner Elizabeth seated herself at the piano, and it did Heideck good to find that Edith had a pleasant and well-trained alto voice. She sang some melancholy English and Scotch songs.

"I have never sung since I left England," she said, greatly moved.

Heideck had listened to the music with rapture. After the fearful scenes of recent times the melodies affected him so deeply that his eyes filled with tears. It was not only the music that affected him, but Edith's soul, which spoke through it.

"What are you thinking of doing, Mr. Kennedy?" he asked the old gentleman. "Shall you remain in Simla and keep Mrs. Irwin with you?"

"I have thought it over," he replied. "I shall not stay here. I shall go to Calcutta, if I can. It is my duty to be at my post there."

"But how do you intend to travel? The railways still in existence have been seized for the exclusive use of the army. Remember that you would have to pass both armies, the Russian and the English. You would have to go from Kalka to Ambala, and thence to Delhi."

"If I could get a passport, I could travel post to Delhi, where I should be with the English army. Can you get me a passport?"

"I will try. Possibly Prince Tchajawadse may be persuaded to let me have one. I will point out to him that you are civilian officials."

· · · · · · ·

Prince Tchajawadse most emphatically refused to make out the passport for Mr. Kennedy and his family.

"I am very sorry, my friend," said he, "but it is simply impossible. The Judge-Advocate-General is a very high official; I cannot allow him to go to the English headquarters and give information as to what is going on here. The authorities would justly put a very bad construction upon such ill-timed amiability, and I should not like to obliterate the good impression which the success of the expedition to Simla has made upon my superiors by an unpardonable act of folly on my own part."

Heideck saw that any attempt at persuasion would be useless in the face of the Prince's determination. He therefore acquainted Mr. Kennedy with the failure of his efforts, at the same expressing his sincere regret.

"Then I shall try to return to England," said the old gentleman, with a sigh. "Please ask the Prince if he has any objection to my making my way by the shortest road to Karachi? Perhaps he will let me have a passport for this route."

Prince Tchajawadse was quite ready to accede to this request.

"The ladies and gentlemen can travel where they please in the rear of the Russian army, for all I care," he declared. "There is not the least occasion for me to treat the worthy old gentleman as a prisoner."

On the same day Heideck had a serious conversation with Edith about her immediate future. He inquired what her wishes and plans were, but she clung to him tenderly and whispered, "My only wish is to stay with you, my only plan is to make you happy."

Kissing her tender lips, which could utter such entrancing words, he said, deeply moved: "Well, then, I propose that we travel together to Karachi. I am resolved to quit the Russian service and endeavour to return to Germany. But could you induce yourself to follow me to my country, the land of your present enemies?"

"My home is with you. Suppose that we were to make a home here in Simla, I should be ready, and only too glad to live here for the rest of my life. Take me to Germany or Siberia, and I will follow you--it is all the same to me, if only I am not obliged to leave you."

For a moment Heideck was pained to think that she had no word of attachment for her country; but he had already learnt not to measure her by the standard of the other women whom he had hitherto met on his life's journey, and it ill became him to reproach her for this want of patriotism.

"Mr. Kennedy has assured me that he is ready to take you under his protection during the journey," said he. "I will speak to the Prince again to-day, and, as he has no right to detain me, it will be possible for me, as I confidently hope, to start with you for Karachi."

"But I shall only accept the Kennedys' offer if you go with us," declared Edith in a tone of decision, which left no doubt as to her unshakable resolution.

As a matter of fact, Prince Tchajawadse put no difficulties in his way.

"I sincerely regret to lose you again so soon," he declared, "but it is for you alone to decide whether you go or stay. It was arranged beforehand that you could leave the Russian service as soon as it became worth your while. Women are, after all, the controlling spirits of our lives."

Of course the Prince had long since been aware that the Kennedys' visitor was Edith Irwin, but this was the first time he had alluded to his German friend's love affair.

As if he felt bound to defend himself against a humiliating reproach, Heideck hastened to reply.

"You misunderstand my motives. It is my duty as a soldier which summons me first of all. Hitherto I have had no prospect of getting a passage on an English steamer. But, in the company of Mr. Kennedy, and on his recommendation, I have hopes that it will not be refused me."

"Pardon me. I never for a moment doubted your patriotic sense of duty, and I wish you from my heart a happy voyage home. Of course, notwithstanding the alliance of our nations, it is not the same to you, whether you fight in the ranks of the Russian or the German army. And if the prospect of travelling in such pleasant society has finally decided you, you have, in my opinion, no reason at all to be ashamed of it. Certainly, for my own part, I am convinced that it is better, for a soldier to make the female element play as subordinate a role as possible in his life. He ought to do like most of my countrymen, and get a wife who will not resent being thrashed, with or without cause. It may be that I am mistaken on this point, and I have been severely punished for it."

His countenance had suddenly become very grave, and as he could only be alluding to his lost page, Heideck thought he might at last venture to ask a question as to the whereabouts of the Circassian.

But the Prince shook his head deprecatingly.

"Do not ask me about her. It is a painful story, which I do not care to mention, since it recalls one of the worst hours of my life. It is bad enough that we poor, weak creatures cannot atone for the mistakes of a moment."

Then, as if desirous of summarily cutting short an inconvenient discussion, he returned to the original subject of conversation.

"From my point of view, for purely practical reasons I must regard it as a mistake that you should so soon give up your career in the Russian army, which has begun under the most favourable auspices. A brilliant career is open to capable men of your stamp amongst us, for there is more elbow-room in our army than in yours. But I know that it is useless to say anything further about it. One word more! You need not at once take off the uniform to which you do honour before you leave Simla. To-morrow I am returning to Lahore, and during the march I beg you will still remain at the head of your squadron. It will be safest for your English friends to travel with our column. At Lahore you can do as you please. Since the course of the campaign is in a south-easterly direction, the west is free, and you may possibly be able to travel by train for a considerable portion of the journey to Karachi."

In this proposal Heideck recognised a fresh proof of the friendly disposition

ment. Only the actual presence of the Russian troops had disturbed the patient and peaceful people. The travellers even passed through Chanidigot without any interruption of their occupations or meeting with any unexpected delay.

The weather was not too hot; the stormy season had begun, and travelling in the roomy, comfortable railway carriages would have been in other circumstances a real pleasure.

The travellers safely reached Karachi, the seaport town on the mouths of the Indus with its numerous tributaries, where Mr. Kennedy's high position procured them admission to the select Sind Club, where the attendance and lodging were all that could be desired. The club was almost entirely deserted by its regular visitors, since, in addition to the officers, all officials who could be dispensed with had joined the army. But neither the Kennedys nor Edith and Heideck had any taste for interesting society. Their only wish was to leave the country as soon as possible, and to see the end of the present painful condition of affairs. As the result of inquiries at the shipping agency, they had decided to travel to Bombay by one of the steamers of the British India Company, and to proceed thence to Europe by the Caledonia, the best vessel belonging to the P. and O. line.

In the afternoon, before going on board, Heideck hired a comfortable little one-horsed carriage and drove to Napier mole, where an elegant sailing-boat, manned by four lascars, was placed at their disposal at the Sind Club boathouse. They sailed through the harbour protected by three powerful forts, past Manora Point, the furthest extremity of the fortified mole, into the Arabian Sea.

"Really, it is hard to leave this wonderful land," said Heideck seriously. "It is hard to take leave for ever of this brilliant sun, this glittering sea, and these mighty works of men's hands, which have introduced luxury and the comforts of a refined civilisation into a natural paradise. I have never understood Mr. Kennedy's sorrow better than at this moment. And I can sympathise with the feeling of bitterness which makes him shut himself up in his room, to avoid the further sight of all this enchanting and splendid magnificence."

Edith, clinging to his arm and looking up fondly into his face only answered, "I only see the world as it is reflected in your eyes. And there its beauty is always the same to me."

XXII
THE ETHICS OF ESPIONAGE

The steamer from Karachi to Bombay had about twenty officers and a larger number of noncommissioned officers and men on board who had been wounded in the first engagements on the frontier. The sight of them was not calculated to relieve the gloomy feelings of the English travellers, although during the three days of the voyage the weather was magnificent as they proceeded through the bright, blue sea along the west coast of India, so lavishly supplied with the beauties of Nature.

The harbour of Bombay, one of the most beautiful in the world, presented a singularly altered appearance to those who had seen it on previous visits. There was a complete absence of the French, German, and Russian merchantmen, which usually lay at anchor in considerable numbers; besides English steamers there were only a few Italian and Austrian vessels in the roadstead.

The steamer from Karachi cast anchor not far from the Austrian Lloyd steamer Imperatrix, from Trieste, and the passengers were taken from the Apollo Bandar in small boats to the landing-stage.

Heideck took up his quarters with his new English friends at the Esplanade Hotel. The admirably conducted house was well known to him, since he had stayed there a few days on his arrival in India. But the appearance of the hotel had altered during the interval as completely as that of the European quarter of the city, from which all life seemed to have disappeared. The ravages of the plague might have had something to do with it, but the main cause was the war, which made its presence felt in the absence of various elements of life which at other times were especially remarkable.

Formerly the meeting-place of fashionable society, nearly all its guests at the present time were connected with the army; the few ladies were in mourning, and an oppressive silence prevailed during meals.

Mr. Kennedy, immediately on his arrival, had paid a visit to the Governor in Heideck's interest and returned with good news. He had obtained permission for the young German to leave India by the Caledonia, which was starting in a few days with a considerable number of sick and wounded officers. The route to be taken was the usual one by Aden and Port Said. Those passengers who intended to travel further by the railway would be landed at Brindisi, the destination of the steamer being Southampton.

"So we shall have the pleasure of your company as far as Brindisi," said Mr. Kennedy, turning to Heideck. The latter bowed, to show the old gentleman that he had interpreted his intentions correctly.

An expression of violent alarm overspread Edith's face, when the contradiction which she might assuredly have expected did not follow. She got up to go to her room, but, passing close by Heideck, she found an opportunity to whisper, "To-night on the balcony! I must speak to you!"

After dinner Heideck and Mr. Kennedy sat smoking on the terrace in front of the dining-room. A warm sea-breeze rustled through the banyan trees, with their thick, shining arch of foliage. Heideck again thanked the old gentleman for his kindly efforts on his behalf.

"I have only repaid to a very moderate extent all you have done for us," replied Mr. Kennedy. "Besides, there was no difficulty in the matter. I told the Governor that you were a German and a friend of my family, who had rendered most valuable service to an English lady and myself. Certainly, I thought that I might with a good conscience say nothing about your being a soldier, which might easily have caused all kinds of difficulties. With all my patriotism, I do not reproach myself very severely for this reticence. For what military secrets could you disclose in Berlin? Our disasters are plain for all to see, and the papers are filled with news and conjectures."

"Certainly. The real purpose of my journey has been overtaken by events and rendered pointless."

"And this object--if I may speak without mincing words--was espionage. Is not that the case, Mr. Heideck?"

"Espionage in the same sense that the despatch of ambassadors, ministers pleni-potentiary, and military or naval attaches is espionage," replied Heideck, visibly annoyed.

"Oh, I think there is a slight difference in their case. All these gentlemen's names and duties are known beforehand, and they are expressly accredited in their character of diplomatists."

"Mr. Kennedy, I could never think of justifying myself to you, for I have not the least reason to be ashamed of my mission. The military authorities of every country must have information as to the military condition of other powers, even though war is not definitely expected or contemplated. In order to be equipped against all eventualities, it is necessary to know the forces and resources of other powers, no matter whether, in case of war, they would be enemies or allies."

Mr. Kennedy, evidently irritated, replied: "It almost seems as if we English had grossly neglected this precaution. The Russians would hardly have surprised us, if we had known how to calculate with German astuteness."

"Well, I hardly believe that the English method in this respect is different from ours. Your Government, like the German, doubtless sent officers everywhere to obtain information. Just as the General Staff in Berlin collects information about all foreign armies, fortifications, and boundaries, I have no doubt that the same thing happens in London. Besides, it is a purely theoretical procedure, just like the drawing up of schemes of war to suit all cases. In reality, things usually turn out quite differently from what is expected. The present war is the most convincing proof of this. I was sent here to study the Anglo-Indian army and the Russo-Indian frontiers, although we had no presentiment that war was imminent, and had made no plans for attacking India. The folly of such an idea is obvious. Further, if you regard me as a spy, Mr. Kennedy, I beg you will have no scruple about informing the Governor of my real character. I am ready at any time to justify myself before the English authorities."

Mr. Kennedy held out his hand to him.

"You have misunderstood me, my dear Mr. Heideck. Your personal honour is to me so far beyond all doubt, that I should never think for a moment of putting you on a level with those spies who are tried for their lives when caught."

At this moment one of the barefooted waiters, dressed in white, came running and shouting into the saloon, "Great victory near Delhi! total defeat of the Russian army!" at the same time triumphantly waving a printed paper in his hand.

Mr. Kennedy jumped up, tore the paper from the boy's hand, and read the news given out by the Bombay Gazette.

"Yes, it is true," he cried, his face beaming with joy. "A victory, a great, decisive victory! Heaven be thanked--the fortune of war has changed."

He gave the bearer of the joyful news a piece of gold and hastened to inform the ladies. Heideck, however, remained behind, immersed in thought. The hotel soon became lively. The English ran here and there, shouting to one another the contents of the despatch, while a growing excitement gradually showed itself in the streets. In the so-called fort, the European quarter of Bombay, torches were lighted and feux-de-joie fired. Heideck took one of the traps standing in front of the hotel and ordered the driver to drive through the town. Here he observed that the rejoicings were confined to the fort. As soon as the conveyance reached the town proper, he found that it presented the same appearance as on his first visit, and that there was nothing to show or indicate the occurrence of extraordinary events. In spite of the lateness of the hour, the narrow streets were busy and full of traffic. All the houses were lighted up, and all the doors open, affording a view of the interior of the primitive dwellings, of the artisans busy at their work, of the dealers plying their trade, of the housewives occupied with their domestic affairs. Evidently the inhabitants troubled no more about the war than about the terrible scourge of the Indian population--the plague. The despatch announcing the victory, although no doubt it was known in the native quarter, had evidently not made the slightest impression.

About eleven o'clock Heideck returned to the hotel, where he found the Kennedys and Edith still conversing eagerly on the terrace.

"Of course we shall not leave now," he declared. "As soon as the Russians have evacuated the north, we shall return to Simla."

Heideck made no remark, and since the openly expressed and heartfelt joy of the English affected him painfully, he soon took leave of them, and went up to his room, which, like Edith's, was on the second storey.

According to the custom of the country, all the rooms opened on to the broad balcony which ran round the whole floor like an outer corridor. As a look from

Edith had repeated her wish that he should wait for her there, he stepped out on to the balcony. His patience was not put to a severe trial. She must have quickly found an opportunity of escaping from the Kennedys' society, for he saw her coming towards him even sooner than he had expected.

"I thank you for waiting for me," she said, "but we cannot stay here, for we should not be safe from surprise for a moment. Let us go into my room."

Heideck followed her with hesitation. But he knew that Edith would feel insulted if he expressed any scruples at her request, for her firm confidence in his chivalrous honour relieved her of all apprehension. Only the moon, shining faintly, shed a dim light over the room. The clock on the tower of the neighbouring university struck twelve.

"Destiny is playing a strange game with us," said Edith, who had seated herself in one of the little basket chairs, while Heideck remained standing near the door. "I confess that since the arrival of the news of the victory I have spent some terrible hours, for the Kennedys have, in consequence, abandoned their idea of leaving, and seem to take it for granted that I shall remain with them in India."

"And would you not, in fact, be forced to do so, my dearest Edith?"

"So then you have already reckoned with this contingency? You would not, surely, think of travelling without me? But perhaps you would even feel relieved at being freed from me?"

"How can you say such things, Edith, which, I am sure, you do not believe?"

"Who knows? You are ambitious, and we poor women are never worse off than when we have to do with ambitious men."

"But there is probably no necessity for us to torment ourselves with the discussion of such contingencies. I have never for a moment believed in any alteration of our arrangements for the journey."

"That is to say you doubt the trustworthiness of the report of the victory?"

"To speak frankly, I do. I did not wish to mortify the old gentleman and spoil his shortlived joy. That is the reason why I did not express my distrust in his presence. But the despatch does not really convey the impression of being true. It does not even contain a more exact statement of the place where the battle is said to have taken place. It must, at least, strike the unprejudiced observer as being very suspicious."

"But who would take the trouble to obtain the melancholy satisfaction of deceiving the world in such a manner for a short time?"

"Oh, there are many who would be interested in doing so. In the course of every war such false reports are always floating about, in most cases without their origin being known. It may be a money-market manoeuvre."

"So you think it quite impossible that we can beat the Russians?"

"Not exactly impossible, but extremely improbable--at least while the military situation remains what it is. Again, it is the absence of definite information that surprises me. A victorious general always finds time to communicate details, which the vanquished is only too glad to defer. I am convinced that the bad news will soon follow, and that, as far as our plans for the journey are concerned, everything will remain as before."

Edith was silent. Her belief in Heideck was so unbounded that his words had completely convinced her. But they did not restore the joyful confidence of the last few days.

"Everything will remain as before?" she said at length. "That means you will leave us at Brindisi."

"Certainly. There is no other way for me to reach the army."

"And suppose you abandon the idea of returning to the army altogether? Have you never thought that we might find another foundation on which to build our future happiness?"

Heideck looked at her in amazement.

"No, dearest Edith, I have not thought of it. It would have been a useless and foolish idea, so long as my duty and honour prescribe most definitely what I have to do."

"Duty and honour! Of course, I ought to have known that you would at once be ready again with fine words. It is so convenient to be able to take shelter behind so unassailable a rampart, if at the same time it falls in with one's own wishes."

"Edith! How unjust the melancholy events of the last few weeks have made you! If you think it over quietly, you will see that my personal wishes and my heart's desires are not in question at all. And really I do not understand what you think I could possibly do."

"Oh, there would be more than one way of sparing us the pain of a separation, but I will only mention the first that occurs to me. Couldn't we very well remain together in India? If it is the question of money that makes you hesitate, I can soon make your mind easy on that point. I have enough money for both of us, and what is mine is yours. If we retire to a part of the country which the war cannot reach, a hill station such as Poona or Mahabeleshwar, no one will trouble you with questions or think of following you. And if you live there and devote yourself to your love instead of slaying your fellow-men, it will be more acceptable to God."

In spite of the seriousness with which she spoke, Heideck could not help smiling as he answered: "What a wonderful picture of the world and its affairs is sometimes drawn in a pretty woman's little head! It is really fortunate that we sober-minded men do not allow our heart to run away with our head so easily. Otherwise we should come badly off, for you yourselves would certainly be the first to turn away from us with contempt, if we tried to purchase the happiness of your love at any price--even at the price of your respect."

Edith Irwin did not contradict him. Silent and sorrowful, for a long time she looked out upon the bright moonlight Indian night. Then, when Heideck approached her, to take leave of her with tender words, she said in a voice which cut him to the heart: "Whether we understand each other or not, in one thing at least you shall be under no delusion. Whereever you may go--into a paradise of peace or the hell of war--I will not forsake you."

With passionate impetuosity she flung herself into his arms and pressed her burning lips upon his. Then, as if afraid of her own heart's passion, she gently pushed him towards the door.

XXIII
HOMEWARD BOUND

As Heideck had foreseen, the announcement of the victory was followed by disastrous tidings for the English. Up to noon on the following day Bombay had waited in vain for confirmation of the despatch and fuller particulars. Very late in the evening, amidst a general feeling of depression, the Governor published the following despatch from the Commander-in-Chief:--

"The enemy having been reported in great force yesterday to the north of Delhi, our army took up a favourable defensive position, and a battle was fought with great honour to the British arms. The Russians suffered enormous losses. The approach of darkness preventing us from following up the advantages we had gained, I ordered the main body of the army to carry out a strategic retreat on Lucknow, chiefly along the railway. Simpson's brigade remained behind to defend Delhi. The heavy guns of the Sha, Calcutta gate, and north gate bastions were very effective. All arms distinguished themselves, and deserve the highest praise. The bridge over the Jumna is intact and affords direct communication with General Simpson."

While Mr. Kennedy was sitting pondering over this despatch, Heideck came up to him.

"A decisive defeat, isn't it, Mr. Heideck?" said he. "As a military man, you can read between the line, better than I can. But I know Delhi. If the Jumna bridge batteries have been firing, the Russians must be on the point of capturing this passage. The north gate bastion is the head of the bridge."

Heideck was obliged to agree; but he had read more in the despatch, and drew the worst conclusions from the general's retreat on Lucknow.

No more despatches from the theatre of war were published during the day, since the Governor was desirous of concealing the melancholy state of affairs from the people. But Mr. Kennedy, who had been in Government House, knew more. He told Heideck that the English army had fled in complete disorder, having lost 8,000 killed and wounded, twenty guns, and a number of colours and standards. The Government had already abandoned all hope of saving Delhi, for General Simpson could not possibly hold it. "We have lost India," sorrowfully concluded Mr. Kennedy. "It is the grave of my last hopes."

. . . .

The Caledonia was moored in Victoria Dock, which formed part of the magnificent harbour on the east coast of the peninsula. In the midst of a seething crowd the passengers were making their way on board. Many wounded and sick officers and soldiers were returning on the fast steamer to England, and filled the places intended for passengers. No travellers to Europe on business or pleasure were to be seen. All the women on board belonged to the families of the military. The general feeling was one of extreme melancholy.

Before embarking Heideck had discharged his faithful servant. Morar Gopal, with tears in his eyes, had begged him to take him with him, but Heideck was afraid that the European climate would be the death of the poor fellow. Besides, he would have been obliged to part with him on active service. So he gave him a hundred rupees--a fortune for Morar Gopal.

The great steamer moved slowly out of the basin of the harbour, past English merchantmen and the white ships of war, which had brought troops and war material.

As the Caledonia, continually increasing her speed, made her way through the outer harbour, Heideck saw some twenty men-of-war in the roadstead, including several large ironclads. English troops from Malta were being landed in boats from two transports, the decks of which glistened with arms.

The Caledonia proceeded with increasing rapidity into the open sea. The city and its lighthouses disappeared in the distance, the blue mountains of the mainland and of the island were lost in a floating mist. A long, glittering, white furrow followed in the wake of the steamer.

It was a wonderful journey for all whom a load of anxiety had not rendered insensible to the grandeur of Nature. Heideck, happy at being at last on the way home, enjoyed the beauty of sea and sky to the full. The uneasy doubts which sometimes assailed him as to his own and Edith's future were suppressed by the charm of her presence. Her impetuosity caused him perpetual anxiety, but he loved her. Ever since she had declared that she would never leave him she had been all devotion and tenderness, as if tormented by a constant fear that he might nevertheless one day cast her off.

So they sat once again, side by side, on the promenade deck. The azure billows of the sea splashed round the planks of the vessel. The boundless surface of ocean glittered with a marvellous brilliancy, and everything seemed bathed in a flood of light. The double awning over the heads of the young couple kept off the burning heat of the sun, and a refreshing breeze swept across the deck beneath it.

"Then you would land with me at Brindisi?" asked Heideck.

"At Brindisi, or Aden, or Port Said--where you like."

"I think Brindisi will be the most suitable place. Then we can travel together to Berlin."

Edith nodded assent.

"But I don't know how long I shall stay in Berlin," continued Heideck. "I hope I shan't be sent to join my regiment at once."

"If you are I shall go with you, wherever it may be," she said as quietly as if it were a matter of course.

"That would hardly be possible," he rejoined, with a smile. "We Germans make war without women."

"And yet I shall go with you."

Heideck looked at her in amazement. "But don't you understand, dear, that it would be something entirely novel, and bound to create a sensation, for a German officer to take the field with his betrothed?"

"I am not afraid of what people think. I don't care what the Kennedys may say if I leave the ship at Brindisi and go with you. Of course it will be a sad downfall for me. They would look on me as a lost woman from that moment. But I care nothing about that. I have long been cured of the foolish idea that we must sacrifice our happiness to what the world may say."

Of course Heideck refused to take her words seriously. He did not believe she meant to accompany him to the field, and seized the opportunity of making a proposal which he had already carefully considered.

"I should think the best thing for you to do, my dear Edith, would be to go to my uncle at Hamburg and stay there till the war is over. Then--if Heaven spare my life--there will be nothing to prevent our union."

As she made no answer Heideck, who wanted to give her time to think, hastened to turn the conversation.

"Look how beautiful it is!" he said, pointing to the water.

A long succession of white, foaming waves kept pace with the vessel on either side. The keel seemed to be cutting its way through a number of tiny cliffs, over which the sea was breaking. But closer inspection showed that they were no cliffs, but countless shoals of large fish, swimming alongside the ship, as if in order of battle. From time to time they leaped high out of the water, their bright, scaly bodies glistening in the sun.

"I should like to be one of those dolphins," said Edith. "Look, how free they are! how they enjoy life!"

"You believe in the transmigration of souls?" said Heideck jestingly; "perhaps you have once been such a dolphin yourself."

"Then certainly I have made no change for the better. There is no doubt that our higher intellectual development prevents us from properly enjoying our natural existence. But it teaches us to feel more deeply the sorrows, which are far more numerous than the joys of human life."

· · · · · · ·

The journey through the Indian Ocean took six days, and Heideck frequently had an opportunity of hearing the views of English officers and officials on the political situation. All blamed the incapacity of the Government, which had brought England into so perilous a situation.

"The good old principles of English policy have been abandoned," said a Colonel, who had been severely wounded and was returning home invalided. "In former times England made her conquests when the continental Powers were involved in war, or she carried on war with allies, to enlarge her possessions. But she has never allowed herself to be so disgracefully surprised before. Of course we shall beat France and Germany, for it is a question of sea power. But even when they are beaten, we shall still have the worst of it; the loss of India is as bad for England's health and efficiency as the amputation of my left leg for me. I am returning to England a cripple, and my poor country will only be a cripple after she has lost India."

"Quite true," said Mr. Kennedy; "I am afraid it will be difficult--impossible, to recover India. We were able to rob the French, the Dutch, and the Portuguese of their Indian possessions, since their only connexion with India was by sea; but the Russians will annex the peninsula to their Empire and, even in case of a defeat, will be able to send fresh troops without number overland. I can already see them attacking Calcutta, Bombay, and Madras, occupying the harbours built with our money, and building a fleet in our docks with the resources of India."

"We have no right to blame the continental Powers," continued the Colonel, "for using our defeats for their own aggrandisement. There is no Power at whose expense we have not grown great. We took all our possessions by force of arms from the Spaniards, the Dutch, the Portuguese, and the French; we have always opposed Russia, since she began to develop her power. We supported Turkey, we invaded the Crimea and destroyed Sebastopol, we suffocated her fleet in the Black Sea. But this time we are out of our reckoning. We have allowed the Japanese to attack Russia; but if our ministers believed that Japan would fight for any one but herself, they have made a great mistake. Russia is making us pay for her losses in the Far East."

"It is not Russia, but Germany, that is our worst enemy," contradicted Mr. Kennedy. "Russia has only been our enemy since we let Germany grow so powerful. I remember how our ministers exulted when Prussia was at war with France and Austria. The continent of Europe again seemed paralysed for a long time by internal disruption. But our triumph was short-lived! No one had suspected that Prussia would prove so strong. Then the first defects in our policy became apparent. After the first German victories on the Rhine, England ought to have concluded an alliance with France and declared war against Prussia. Great political revolutions require considerable time, and a clever government should always look ahead. Bismarck slowly prepared England's defeat. Thirty years ago we had a presentiment of this; it threatened us like a storm-cloud, but our Government had not the courage to look things in the face and lacked the energy."

A general, who had hitherto said nothing, took up the conversation. He belonged to the engineers, and was on his way to take over the command of Gibraltar.

"We talk about the loss of India," said he; "but who knows whether we have not to fear an invasion of England herself?"

"Impossible!" exclaimed all the gentlemen present; "England will never allow her men-of-war to be driven out of the Channel."

"I hope so too, but I don't know whether you gentlemen remember how close the danger of Napoleon landing an army on English soil once was."

"And if it had made its appearance, it would have been smashed to pieces by British fists!" cried Mr. Kennedy.

"Perhaps. But why have we never consented to the Channel Tunnel being made? All military authorities, especially Wolseley, are absolutely opposed to opening a road so convenient for traffic and trade. They have always declared that England must remain an island, only accessible by sea. This is certainly the first and most essential condition of England's power."

"Well, then," said Mr. Kennedy, "as England is still an island, and we have always adhered to the principle of keeping a fleet superior to that of the two strongest naval powers, where is the danger?"

"Danger? There is always a danger, when one has enemies," replied the General. "I maintain that at the beginning of the nineteenth century, it was a toss up whether Napoleon crossed or not; and I don't believe that we should have been a match for our great opponent, if he had once got a firm footing on our coast."

"His plan was a visionary one and therefore impracticable."

"His plan only failed because it was too complicated. If he had had modern telegraphic communication at his disposal, this would not have been the case. He could have directed the operations of his fleet by cable. If Admiral Villeneuve had sailed to Brest (instead of Cadiz) as he was ordered and joined Admiral Gantaume, he would have had fifty-six ships of the line to cover Napoleon's passage from Boulogne to the English coast. No, gentlemen, you must not think England's strategical position unassailable. I am as confident of the superiority of our naval forces as you are, but in these days of steam and electricity England is no longer as safe as she was when the movement of ships depended on the wind and orders had to be given by mounted messengers and signals."

"So you really think, General, that Napoleon's plan would have been practicable?"

"Most certainly. Napoleon had no luck in this enterprise. In the first place, his greatest misfortune was the death of Admiral Latouche-Treville. If he had been in Villeneuve's place, he would most likely have proved a competent commander. He was the only French naval officer who could have opposed Nelson. But he died too soon for France, and his successor, Villeneuve, was his inferior in ability. But there are other special circumstances, more favourable to a landing in England than in Napoleon's day. For instance--to say nothing of cable and steam--the fact that modern transports can carry an enormously larger number of troops. Napoleon had to fit out 2,293 vessels to transport his army of 150,000 men and to protect the transports, had 1,204 gunboats and 135 other armed vessels at his disposal, in addition to the transports proper. As nearly all his ships were constructed to land men, horses, and guns on the level beach without the aid of boats, they wanted calm weather for crossing the Channel. They would have taken about ten hours, with a calm sea, to reach a point between Dover and Hastings. It is different now. The large French and German companies' steamers are at the disposal of their Admiralties."

"And yet things are just the same as before," said Mr. Kennedy. "Victory on the open sea turns the scale. No hostile fleet will be able to show itself in the Channel without being destroyed by ours."

"Let us hope so!" said the General.

On the way to Aden the Caledonia only met a few ships--all English. Several transports with troops on board and a few men-of-war passed her; as she travelled on the average twenty-two knots an hour, no vessel overtook her. On the morning of the sixth day the reddish brown rocks of Aden appeared, and the Caledonia cast anchor in the roadstead. A number of small vessels darted towards her. Naked, black Arab boys cried for money and showed their skill in diving, fishing up pieces of silver thrown from the ship. As the Caledonia had to coal, those passengers who were able to move went ashore in boats rowed by Arabs.

Heideck joined the Kennedy family.

When the boat reached the deeply indented harbour, which with its numerous bends between fortified heights afforded a safe shelter for a whole fleet, Heideck saw some twenty English men-of-war, and at least three times that number of French and German and a few Russian merchantmen, which had been captured by the English. Several cruisers of the three Powers at war with England also lay in the harbour. They had been captured in the Indian Ocean at the outbreak of war by superior English naval forces.

As the party had the whole day at their disposal, Mr. Kennedy took a conveyance, and Heideck drove with the family to the town, which, invisible from the roadstead, lay embedded between high, peaked mountains. The road went past a large, open space, on which thousands of camels and donkeys were exposed for sale. Here Heideck had the opportunity of admiring, close at hand, the mighty fortifications which the English had constructed on the important corner of the mountain commanding the sea since the capture of Aden by them from the Turks on the 9th of January, 1839. They also inspected the remarkable tanks, those famous cisterns which supply Aden with water, some fifty basins said to hold 30,000,000 gallons of water, whose origin is lost in the hoary mist of antiquity. They are said to have been constructed by the Persians.

About seven o'clock in the evening the passengers were again on board. While the Caledonia continued her journey, they were absorbed in the perusal of the English, French, and German newspapers which they had bought at Aden. The papers were ten days old, certainly, but contained much that was new to the travellers.

It was very hot in the Red Sea, and most of the first-class passengers slept on deck, as they had done just before they reached Aden. Part of the deck, over which a sail had been stretched, was specially reserved for ladies.

The Caledonia, having again coaled at Port Said, where a number of English men-of-war were lying, resumed her journey, with unfavourable weather and a rather rough sea, into the Mediterranean. Passing along the south of Crete, the steamer turned northwest in the direction of Brindisi, where she was due on the eighth day after leaving Aden. On the morning of the seventh day a ship was seen coming from the north side of Crete, whose appearance caused the captain of the Caledonia the liveliest anxiety, which soon communicated itself to the passengers.

All the telescopes and field-glasses were directed towards the vessel, whose course was bound to cut across that of the Caledonia. She soon came near enough to be recognised. She was the small French cruiser Forbin, and was bound to meet the Caledonia if the latter continued her course.

The Forbin was a third-class cruiser, not so fast as the Caledonia (the officers estimated her speed at twenty-one knots), which could have beaten her in a race; but if the Caledonia made for Brindisi, she was bound to meet the Frenchman, and could only expect to be captured. Accordingly, the captain altered his course and turned westwards towards Malta, without heeding the signal to stop or the shots that were fired, one of which only went through the rigging, without doing any damage worth mentioning.

"It is now noon," said Heideck. "We ought to be in Brindisi to-morrow. Instead, we shall be in La Valetta, unless the captain changes his course again and trusts to the speed of the Caledonia to reach Brindisi in spite of the Forbin."

Then a loud shout was heard. The look-out man reported a ship on the port side, and in a few minutes two other vessels suddenly appeared.

One of them afterwards proved to be the French second-class cruiser Arethuse; the others were the protected cruiser Chanzy and a torpedo-destroyer.

The Caledonia could not possibly get past the French in the direction of Malta, for the destroyer was much faster and capable of making, at full speed, twenty-seven knots an hour. The captain had no choice; he accordingly turned round, and began to make for Alexandria again.

While the great vessel was wheeling round, those on board perceived that the French had seen her and had started in pursuit.

Meanwhile the Forbin had approached considerably nearer and was attempting to cut off the Caledonia. The captain accordingly gave orders to steer further south.

Heideck, standing with Edith on the promenade-deck, followed the movements of the vessels.

"What would happen to us if the French overtook us?" asked Edith. "Surely they would not fire on an unarmed ship?"

"Certainly not. But they would call upon us to discontinue our journey, and then they would take the Caledonia to the nearest French port."

"Is that the rule of naval warfare? Is the general law of nations so defective that a passenger steamer can be captured? The Caledonia is not a combatant. She is taking home wounded men and harmless passengers."

"Our captain doesn't seem to have much confidence in the laws of naval warfare or nations in this case," said Heideck. "In fact, nothing is more uncertain than these definitions. Strictly speaking, there is no such thing as international law; the stronger does what he likes with the weaker, and the only check on the arbitrariness of the victor is the fear of public opinion. But this fear does not weigh much with him who has might on his side, especially as he knows that public opinion can be bribed."

"Then," said Edith, with a pitiful smile, "international law is very like the law which is generally practised amongst human beings on land."

"Besides, the French would not make a bad catch if they brought in the Caledonia," continued Heideck. "Of the eight hundred passengers about three hundred belong to the army, and I have heard that there are large sums of money on board."

The promenade-deck was full of first-class passengers, who anxiously followed the movements of the ships. The second-class and steerage passengers were equally anxious. In the most favourable circumstances, if the Caledonia escaped her pursuers, her passage would, of course, be considerably delayed. But it was hardly to be expected that she would reach Alexandria; for though the Chanzy (travelling about twenty-two knots) was obviously outpaced, the destroyer kept creeping up and the Forbin was dangerously near.

Then a fresh surprise was reported. Two steamships were coming towards the Caledonia. All glasses were directed to where the tiny pillars of smoke appeared above the surface of the water, and it was soon seen beyond doubt that they carried the British flag.

The second officer informed the passengers that they were the first-class cruiser Royal Arthur and the gunboat O'Hara. He expressed his hope that the Caledonia would reach their protection before the French overtook her.

The water was fairly calm. Sky and sea had ceased to shine and sparkle since the Caledonia had left the Suez Canal and emerged into the Mediterranean. The grey colouring, peculiar to European latitudes, was seen instead, and streaky clouds scudded over the pale-blue sky. The movements of the ships could be closely followed by this light.

The English vessels approached rapidly. When the distance between the Royal Arthur and the French destroyer was about two knots and a half the cruiser opened fire from her bow-guns upon the destroyer, which only stood out a little above the surface of the water. One of the heavy shot whizzed so closely past the Caledonia, which was now between the two, that the passengers could plainly hear the howling noise of the shell as it cut through the air.

The Frenchman, without returning the fire, slackened speed, to wait till the Chanzy came up. Meanwhile the Forbin advanced from the north and opened fire from its bow-guns upon the British gunboat, and soon afterwards the Chanzy fired its first shot. The position of the vessels was now as follows: the gunboat lay broadside opposite the Forbin, the two cruisers were firing with their bow-guns on each other, while the destroyer kept in the background. In the meantime the Caledonia had advanced so far that she was completely protected by the British guns.

If the captain had now continued his course he would probably have reached Alexandria in safety. But he wished to avoid the delay, which would have been considerable, and the entreaties of the passengers, who, greatly excited, begged him to remain near the scene of action, coincided with his own wishes.

Accordingly the Caledonia slackened speed, and took up a position to the south-east of the field of battle, whence she could make for Brindisi or Alexandria as soon as the result was decided.

For some time neither side gained the advantage. The Chanzy and Royal Arthur had turned broadsides to each other and fired, but the effect was not visible from the Caledonia.

Suddenly the Royal Arthur began to move in a northerly direction, firing upon the enemy from her stern-guns.

"It almost looks as if he meant to help the O'Hara," said Heideck to Edith, who was standing by his side with a field-glass. "The gunboat is clearly no match for the Forbin, and has perhaps been hopelessly damaged."

In fact, the Royal Arthur continued her course northwards, maintaining an incessant fire upon the Chanzy and the destroyer, which still kept on the watch in the rear, and made for the Forbin, on which she immediately opened fire with her bow-guns.

As the scene of action thus shifted further and further north, the captain of the Caledonia resolved to turn westwards again. It did not seem advisable to call at Malta, but assuming that the Royal Arthur could hold the French ships for a considerable time, he might fairly hope to reach Brindisi, his original destination.

But the course of events disappointed his hopes. A ship was reported ahead, which proved to be the Arethuse, bearing down straight on the Caledonia. To avoid meeting her the captain immediately headed northwards. This brought the Caledonia closer to the scene of action than had been intended, so close that a British shell, discharged at the destroyer lying to the east, flew over the low French vessel, and fell into the sea right before the bows of the Caledonia, raising great jets of water.

A few seconds later the French destroyer moved rapidly in the direction of the Royal Arthur, and the passengers of the Caledonia, and all the sailors on the now more restricted field of operations, witnessed a fearful sight. The destroyer had seized the right moment to attack, and from one of its tubes had launched a torpedo with splendid aim against the enemy. In the centre of the Royal Arthur, just above the water-line, a tiny cloud of smoke was seen, and then a large column of water spurting up. At the same time a dull, loud report was heard that shook the air for a considerable distance round and drowned the thunder of the guns.

It looked as if the cruiser was being torn asunder by the hands of giants. The enormous hull split in two. Slowly the prow leaned forwards, the stern backwards. Immediately afterwards both parts righted themselves again, as if they would close up over the gaping breach. But this movement only lasted a few seconds. Then the weight of the water rushing in drew the gigantic hull into the depths. The Royal Arthur sank with awe-inspiring rapidity. Now only her three funnels were seen above the surface of the water; a few minutes later nothing was visible save the top of the mast and the top-pennants hoisted for battle. Then a mighty, foaming billow rose on high, and only the breaking of the waves marked the spot where the proud cruiser lay.

The guns had ceased firing, and deep silence reigned on all the ships. The passengers were paralysed by overwhelming horror. The captain ordered all the boats to be launched to go to the assistance of the crew of the Royal Arthur. The Chanzy also was seen to be letting down boats. The O'Hara fled, to avoid falling into the hands of the superior French forces, and withdrew from the scene of action in an easterly direction, pursued by the Forbin, which sent shot after shot after her. If the captain of the Caledonia had abandoned all idea of flight, he was not only following the dictates of humanity, but obeying the signals of the destroyer, ordering him to bring to. He knew that there was no longer any chance of escape for the steamer entrusted to his care, since the shells of the Royal Arthur had ceased to threaten the enemy.

The struggles of the unhappy men, who had reached the surface from the gloomy depths, and were now making desperate efforts to save themselves, presented an affecting sight. Those who could not swim soon went under, unless they succeeded in getting hold of some floating object. Every second more of the numerous heads, which had been seen above the water immediately after the sinking of the cruiser, disappeared, and there was no doubt that the crews of the boats, though working heroically, would only be able to save a small part of the crew.

Meanwhile the commander of the Chanzy's gig lay to at the gangway of the Caledonia. The first officer, with four marines and a non-commissioned officer, boarded the steamer and saluted the captain with naval politeness.

"I greatly regret, sir, to be compelled to inconvenience you and your passengers. But I am acting under orders, and must ask you to show me your papers and to allow me to search the ship."

"It is yours to command, as things are," replied the Englishman gloomily.

He then went down with the Frenchman into the cabin, while the non-commissioned officer remained with the soldiers on the gangway. The proceedings lasted nearly two hours, during which the work of rescuing the crew of the Royal Arthur was continued unremittingly. A hundred and twenty soldiers and sailors and five officers, besides the commander, were saved. Most of the officers and crew were lost.

Unusual steps were taken to secure the prize. The captain, with the first and second officers, was taken on board the Chanzy. The first officer of the Chanzy took command of the ship, and two lieutenants and fifty men were transferred to the Caledonia. These precautions were sufficiently justified by the great value of the cargo. According to the ship's papers, the Caledonia carried no less than 20,000,000 rupees, some in specie, others in silver bars, consigned from Calcutta to England. The French commander was naturally very anxious to take so valuable a cargo safely to Toulon.

A further triumph fell to the lot of the French. The British gunboat, flying the tricolour in place of the Union Jack, was brought back to the scene of action by the Forbin. All four French ships accompanied the two captive vessels on the voyage to Toulon--full steam ahead.

XXIV
THE ADVENTURES OF THE CALEDONIA

The passengers of the Caledonia were in a state of hopeless dejection and violent exasperation. An attempt was made to throw the blame of their misfortune on the unpardonable carelessness of the responsible military authorities, rather than attribute it to an accident that could not have been reckoned upon.

"Here we have another striking example of English lack of foresight," said Mr. Kennedy. "The idea of allowing the Caledonia to travel without protection! Think of all the men-of-war lying idle at Bombay, Aden, and Port Said! And yet nobody thought there was any occasion to send one or more of them to escort this splendid ship, with nearly a thousand Englishmen on board, and a cargo worth more than a million. Had our commanders no suspicion that the French ships were so near?"

"Our commanders relied upon there being enough English ships cruising in the Mediterranean to prevent such enterprises," said the General.

But this excuse was not accepted, and bitter were the reproaches hurled at the English way of managing the war. When night came on the majority of the passengers, utterly exhausted by the exciting events they had gone through, retired to their cabins. But Heideck remained on deck for some time, cooling his heated forehead in the delightful night breeze. The squadron quickly pursued its course through the gently rushing waves, the position of each ship being clearly defined by the sidelights. On the right was the Chanzy, on the left the Arethuse, in the rear the Forbin and the O'Hara, manned by a French crew. Nothing could be seen of the destroyer. At length Heideck, tired of hearing the regular steps of the French sentries pacing up and down the deck, went down to his cabin. He was soon asleep, but his rest was broken by uneasy dreams. The battle, of which he had been a spectator, was fought again. His dreams must have been very vivid, for he thought he heard, without cessation, the dull roar of the guns. He rubbed his eyes and sat up in his narrow berth. Was it a reality or only a delusion of his excited senses? The dull thunder still smote on his ear; and, having listened intently for a few moments, he jumped up, slipped on his clothes, and hurried on deck. On the way he met several passengers, who had also been woke by the report of the guns. As soon as he reached the deck, he saw that another violent naval engagement was in progress.

The night was rather dark, but the flash from the guns showed fairly the position of the enemy, which became perfectly clear, when a searchlight from the Arethuse played over the surface of the water with dazzlingly clear light. The huge hulks of two battleships, white and glittering, emerged from the darkness. In addition, there were to be seen five smaller warships and several small, low vessels, the torpedo-boats of the British squadron, which was advancing to meet the French. Then, bright as a miniature sun, a searchlight was turned on also by the English. It was an interesting spectacle to notice how the two electric lights, slowly turning round, as it were lugged each ship out of the darkness, showing the guns where to aim.

The French squadron, whose commander was well aware of the enemy's superiority, began to bestir itself rapidly. All the vessels, the Caledonia included, turned round and retreated at full speed. But the heavy English shells from the guns of the battleships were already beginning to fall amongst them, although the distance might have been three knots. Suddenly, when the Caledonia, in the course of a turning manoeuvre, showed a broadside to the British fire, a sharp, violent shock was felt, followed by the report of a violent explosion. The Caledonia stopped dead, and loud cries of agony were heard from the engine-room. The passengers, frightened to death, ran about the deck. It could not be concealed from them that the ship had been struck by a shell, which had exploded.

But it proved that the Caledonia, although badly injured, was in no immediate danger. Only her speed and manoeuvring capacity had suffered considerably owing to a steampipe having been hit.

The French warships retired as rapidly as possible, leaving the Caledonia and the prize crew on board to their fate, since it was impossible to take her with them. They were obliged to abandon the valuable prize and rest content with their great success in the destruction of the Royal Arthur and the capture of the O'Hara. The Caledonia, being recognised by the searchlight thrown upon her, had no fear of being shot at again. She moved slowly northwards, and in the early morning was overtaken by two British cruisers. An officer came on board, declared the French prize crew prisoners of war, and was informed by the third officer, who was now in command, of the events of the last twenty-four hours.

While the British squadron followed the French ships the Caledonia, only travelling eight knots an hour, made for Naples, which was reached without further incidents. The passengers were disembarked, the large sum of money was deposited in the Bank of Naples to the credit of the English Government, and only the cargo of cotton, carpets, and embroidered silkstuffs was left on board.

The Kennedys and Mrs. Irwin went to the Hotel de la Riviera. They were accompanied by Heideck, who intended to stay only one day at Naples, and then to take the through train to Berlin.

Although he had said nothing to her about going to Berlin Edith suspected his intention. A few hours later she spoke to him in the reading-room, where he was eagerly studying the papers.

"Any news of importance?"

"Everything is new to me. Up to the present we have only had a glimpse of what has been going on; these papers have given me a comprehensive view of events for the first time."

"And now, of course, your only desire is to see your colours again? I know that it is only ambition that guides you."

"Can you reproach an officer for that?"

"Yes, if he forgets humanity as well. But make your mind easy, I shall not attempt to hinder you. I will not stand in the way of your ambition, but neither will I sacrifice myself to it."

"Certainly you should not do so. We shall be happy when the war is over. I will be as true to you as to my duty. If I return alive my existence shall be devoted to making you happy."

"Love is like a bird; it must not be allowed too much freedom. Remember, I have always told you I will never leave you."

"But, dearest Edith, that is utterly impossible! Have you any idea what war is like?"

"I should have thought I had seen enough of it."

"Yes, in India and on sea. But in Europe war is carried on somewhat differently. Every seat in the trains is calculated exactly; it is the same in barracks, cantonments, and bivouacs. There is no room for a woman. What would my comrades say of me if I appeared in your company?"

"You can say I am your wife."

"But, Edith, the idea is not to be seriously thought of. As a Prussian officer I need permission before I can marry. How can I join my regiment in the company of a lady? Or how could I now get leave to marry?"

"Quite easily. Many officers marry at the beginning of a war."

"Well, but even if I get leave now, according to the law we could not be married for some months. I have already proposed that you should go to my relatives at Hamburg and wait there till the war is over, and I still think that is the only right thing to do."

"But I will not go to your relatives at Hamburg."

"And why not?"

"Do you think that I, an Englishwoman, would go and live in a German family to be stared at? Do you think I could bear to read all the lies about England in the German newspapers?"

"My uncle and aunt are people of great tact, and my cousins will show you due respect."

"Cousins! No, thank you! I should be out of place in the midst of the domestic felicity of strangers."

"If you won't go there, you might stop at a pension in Berlin."

"No, I won't do that either. I will stay with you."

"But, dearest Edith, how do you think this could be managed?"

"I will have nothing to do with conventionalities; otherwise life in Germany would be intolerable. I should die of anxiety in a pension, thinking every moment of the dangers to which you are exposed. No, I couldn't endure that. I have lived through too much--seen too much that is terrible. My nerves would not be strong enough for me to vegetate in a family or a Berlin pension in the midst of the trivialities of everyday life. Have pity on me, and don't leave me! Your presence is the only effectual medicine for my mind."

"Ah! dearest Edith, my whole heart is full of you, and I would gladly do as you wish. But every step we take must be practical and judicious. If you say you will stay with me, you must have some idea in your mind. How, then, do you think we can manage to be together? Remember that on my return I shall be an officer on service, and shall have to carry out the orders I receive."

"I have already thought of a way. Prince Tchajawadse had a page with him; I will be your page."

"What an absurd idea! Prussian officers don't take pages with them on active service."

"Never mind the name. You must have servants, like English officers; I will be your boy."

"With us soldiers are told off for such duties, my dear Edith."

"Then I will go with you as a soldier. I have already gone as a rajah."

Heideck knitted his brows impatiently. The young woman, whose keen eyes had noticed it, went on impetuously: "Although it seems you are tired of me, I will not leave you. Distance is love's worst enemy, and you are the only tie that binds me to life."

Heideck cast down his eyes, so as not to betray his thoughts. Since he had read the papers, which gave him a clearer idea of the political situation, his mind was fuller than before of warlike visions. He loved Edith, but love did not fill his life so completely as it did hers. The news in the Italian and French papers had put him into a regular fever after his long absence from Europe. The dissolution of the Triple Alliance, and Germany's new alliance with France and Russia, had caused a complete alteration in the political horizon. He heard the stamping of horses, the clash of arms, the thunder of cannon. The war was full of importance and boundless possibilities.

It was a question of Germany's existence! Her losses up to the present were estimated at more than three milliards. All the German colonies had been seized by the English, hundreds of German merchant-men were lost, German foreign trade was completely paralysed, German credit was shaken. Unless Germany were finally victorious, the war meant her extinction as a great Power.

He sprang up.

"It must be, dearest Edith; we must soon part!"

She turned pale. With a look of anguish she caught at his hand and held it fast.

"Do not leave me!"

"I must have perfect freedom--at present. After the war I belong entirely to you."

"No, no, you cannot be so cruel! You must not leave me!"

"We shall meet again! I love you and will be true to you. But now I ask a sacrifice from you. I am a German officer; my life now belongs to my country."

She slid from her chair to the ground and clasped his knees.

"I cannot leave you; it will bring you no happiness, if you destroy me."

"Be strong, Edith. I always used to admire your firm, powerful will. Have you all at once lost all sense, all reason?"

"I have lost everything," she cried, "everything save you. And I will not give you up!"

"Mrs. Irwin!" cried a voice of horror at this moment, "can it be possible?"

Edith got up hurriedly.

Mrs. Kennedy and her daughter had entered unobserved. They had witnessed the singular situation with utter astonishment and heard Edith's last words.

"Good Heavens, can it be possible?" stammered the worthy lady; then, turning to her daughter, she added, "Go, my child."

Edith Irwin had quickly recovered her composure. Standing up, her head proudly raised, she faced the indignant lady.

"I beg you to remember, Mrs. Kennedy, that no one should pass judgment without knowing the real state of things."

"I think what I have seen needs no explanation."

"If there is anything blameworthy in it, I alone am responsible," interposed Heideck. "Spare me a few minutes in private, Mrs. Kennedy, and I will convince you that no blame attaches to Mrs. Irwin."

"I want no one to defend me or intercede for me!" cried Edith passionately. "Why should we any longer conceal our love? This man, Mrs. Kennedy, has saved my life and honour more than once, and it is no humiliation for me to go on my knees before him."

Perhaps there was something in her face and the tone of her voice that touched the Englishwoman's heart, in spite of her outraged sense of propriety. The stern expression disappeared from her features, and she said with friendly, almost motherly gentleness--

"Come, my poor child! I have certainly no right to set up for a judge of your actions. But I am certainly old enough for you to trust in me."

Edith, overcome by this sudden kindness, leaned her head on Mrs. Kennedy's shoulder. Heideck felt it would be best to leave the two ladies to themselves.

"If you will permit me, ladies, I will leave you for the present."

With a rapid movement Edith laid her hand upon his arm.

"You give me your word, Captain Heideck, that you will not leave without saying good-bye to me?"

"I give you my word."

He left the room in a most painful state of mind. It seemed as if, in the fulfilment of his duty, he would have to pass over the body of the being who was dearest to him on earth.

In the evening Mrs. Kennedy's maid brought him a short note from Edith, asking him to come to her at once. He found her in her dimly-lighted room on the couch; but as he entered she got up and went to meet him with apparent calmness.

"You are right, my friend; I have in the meantime come to my senses again. Nothing else is possible--we must part."

"I swear to you, Edith--"

"Swear nothing. The future is in God's hands alone."

She drew from the ring-finger of her left hand the hoop-ring, set in valuable brilliants, which had given rise to their first serious conversation.

"Take this ring, my friend, and think of me whenever you look at it." Tears choked her utterance. "Have no anxiety for me and my future. I am going with the Kennedys to England."

XXV
A SUSPICIOUS FISHING-SMACK

A raw north wind swept over the island of Walcheren and the mouth of the West Schelde, ruffling into tiny waves the water of the broad stream, which in the twilight looked like a shoreless sea. Only those acquainted with the ground knew that the flashing lights of the beacons at Flushing on the right and at Fort Frederik Hendrik on the left marked the limits of the wide mouth of the harbour. Here, in 1809, when Holland was under the rule of Napoleon Bonaparte, a powerful English fleet had entered the Schelde to attack Flushing, and take the fortress. In the centre, between the two lights, which were about three miles apart, the German cruiser Gefion lay tossing at anchor. On the deck stood Heideck, who on his return had been promoted to major and appointed to the intelligence department for the coast district of Holland.

In the afternoon he had seen a vessel entering the Schelde, which the pilot had identified as one of the fishing-smacks plying between the Shetland Islands and the Dutch ports. Heideck had informed the captain of the Gefion of his suspicion that the smack might be intended for another purpose than trading in herrings. The little vessel had put in on the left bank, between the villages of Breskens and Kadzand, and Heideck decided to row across to it.

Six marines and four sailors, under the command of a mate, manned one of the Gefion's boats, and set out for the left bank in the direction of the suspected vessel. It cost the oarsmen, struggling with the tide and wind which came howling from the sea, nearly half an hour's hard work before they saw the dark hull of the smack emerging clearly outlined before them. A hoarse voice from on board asked what they wanted.

"His Majesty's service!" answered Heideck, and, as the boat lay to, he threw off his cloak, so as to spring on deck more easily. Three men, in the dark, woollen smock and tarpaulined hat of coast fishermen, approached him and, in answer to his inquiry for the master, told him, in an unintelligible mixture of Dutch and German, that he had gone ashore.

"His name?"

"Maaning Brandelaar."

"What is the name of this vessel?"

"Bressay."

The answers were given with hesitation and sullenly, and the three men showed such evident signs of irritation that Heideck felt they would have gladly thrown him overboard had it not been for the respect inspired by his uniform.

"Where from?" he asked.

"From Lerwick."

"Where to?"

"We are going to sell our herrings. We are respectable people, Herr major."

"Where are you going to sell your herrings?"

"Where we can. The skipper has gone to Breskens. He intended to be back soon."

Heideck looked round. The smack had put to in a little bay, where the water was quiet. The village of Breskens and the little watering-place, Kadzand, were both so near that the lighted windows could be seen. It was nine o'clock--rather late for the business which Maaning Brandelaar intended to transact at Breskens.

Heideck sent the marines on deck with orders to see that no one left the ship before the captain returned. He then ordered a lantern to be lighted to examine below. It was a long time before the lantern was ready, and it burned so dully that Heideck preferred to use the electric lamp which he always carried with him as well as his revolver. He climbed down the stairs into the hold and found that the smell of pickled herrings, which he had noticed on deck, was sufficiently explained by the cargo. In the little cabin two men were sitting, drinking grog and smoking short clay pipes. Heideck greeted them courteously and took a seat near them. They spoke English with a broad Scotch accent, and used many peculiar expressions which Heideck did not understand. They declared they were natives of the island of Bressay. Heideck gathered from their conversation that the smack belonged to a shipowner of Rotterdam, whose name they appeared not to know or could not pronounce. They were very guarded and reserved in their statements generally. Heideck waited half an hour, an hour--but still no signs of the captain. He began to feel hungry, and throwing a piece of money on the table, asked whether they could give him anything to eat.

The fishermen opened the cupboard in the wall of the cabin and brought out a large piece of ham, half a loaf of black bread, and a knife and fork. Heideck noticed two small white loaves in the cupboard amongst some glasses and bottles. "Give me some white bread," said he. The man who had brought out the eatables murmured something unintelligible to Heideck and shut the cupboard again without complying with his request. His behaviour could not help striking Heideck as curious. He had, as a matter of fact, only asked for white bread because the black was old, dry, and uncommonly coarse; but now the suspicion forced itself upon him that there was some special meaning behind the rude and contemptuous manner in which his request had been received.

"You don't seem to have understood me," he said. "I should like the white bread."

"It belongs to the captain," was the reply; "we mustn't take it."

"I will pay for it. Your captain will certainly have no objection."

The men pretended not to hear.

Heideck repeated his request in a stern and commanding tone. The men looked at each other; then one of them went to the cupboard, took out the white bread, and set it on the table. Heideck cut it and found it very good. He ate heartily of it, wondering at the same time why the men had been so disobliging about it at first. When he took up the bread again to cut himself off a second piece, it occurred to him that it was remarkably heavy. He cut into the middle and, finding that the blade of the knife struck on something hard, he broke the loaf in two. The glitter of gold met his eyes. He investigated further and drew out, one after the other, thirty golden coins with the head of the Queen of England upon them. Thirty pounds sterling had been concealed in the loaf.

"Very nourishing bread of yours," said he, looking keenly at the men, who merely shrugged their shoulders.

"What has it to do with us how the captain keeps his money?" said one of them.

"You are quite right. What has it to do with you? We will wait till the captain comes. There, put the bread and the money back into the cupboard, and then make a nice glass of grog for my men, the poor fellows will be frozen. Here are three marks for you."

The men did as they were asked. One of them went upstairs with the smoking jug, bringing it back empty some time afterwards, with the thanks of the Herr major's men.

A few minutes later one of the soldiers appeared at the cabin door and announced that two men were approaching from land. "Good," said Heideck; "keep quiet, till they are on deck; then don't let them go down again, but tell them to come here."

Almost immediately steps and voices were heard above, and in a few minutes two men entered the cabin. The first, who wore the dress of a skipper, was of unusually powerful build, broad-shouldered, bull-necked, with a square weather-beaten face, from which two crafty little eyes twinkled. The second, considerably younger, was dressed rather foppishly, and wore a beard trimmed in the most modern style.

"Mynheer Brandelaar?" queried Heideck.

"That's me," replied the man with the broad shoulders, in a brusque, almost threatening tone.

"Very glad to see you, mynheer. I want to speak to you on a matter of business; I have been waiting for you more than an hour. May I ask you to introduce me to this gentleman?"

The Dutchman was slow in answering. It was evident that he was in a very bad temper and did not quite know what to do. The officer's quiet, somewhat mocking tone obviously disconcerted him.

He signed to the two sailors to withdraw, then turned to Heideck.

"This gentleman is a business friend. And I should like to know what I and my affairs have got to do with you at all. I am here to sell my herrings. I suppose that isn't forbidden?"

"Certainly not. But if you have your business, mynheer, I have mine. And I think it would be pleasantest for both of us if we could settle the matter here at once without having to row over to the Gefion."

"To the Gefion? What's the meaning of that? What right have you to use force with me? My papers are in order; I can show them to you."

"I should like to see them. But won't you be kind enough to tell me this gentleman's name? It is really of interest to me to make your business friend's acquaintance."

The second visitor now thought it advisable to introduce himself.

"My name is Camille Penurot," said he; "I am a grocer in Breskens. Maaning Brandelaar has offered to sell me his cargo, and I have come with him to inspect the goods."

"And no doubt night is the best time for that," rejoined Heideck in a sarcastic tone, but with an imperturbably serious air. "Now let me see your papers, Mynheer Brandelaar."

Just as he had expected, the papers were in perfect order. The fishing smack Bressay, owner Maximilian van Spranekhuizen of Rotterdam, sailing with a cargo of pickled herrings from Lerwick. Captain, Maaning Brandelaar. Attested by the English harbour officials at Lerwick. Everything perfectly correct.

"Very good," said Heideck. "Rear-Admiral Sir Frederick Hollway of Dover has not endorsed them, but that was not necessary at all."

These words, uttered with perfect calmness, had an astounding effect upon the two men. Penurot's pale face turned almost green; Brandelaar's hard features were frightfully distorted in a grimace of rage. Half choking in the effort to keep down a furious curse, he drew a deep breath, and said--

"I don't know any Admiral Hollway, and I have never been in Dover in my life."

"Well, well! Let us talk about your business--or yours, M. Penurot. Of course the cargo of herrings which you want to buy is not meant to be sold at Breskens, but to some business friend at Antwerp? isn't it so?"

No answer was given. Heideck, as if it were the most natural thing in the world, turned to the cupboard and, before the others had grasped his intention, took out the second white loaf and broke it in two. This time a folded paper came to light. Heideck spread it out and saw that it was covered with a long list of questions written in English.

"Look here," said he, "the gentleman who had this paper baked with your breakfast bread must be confoundedly curious. 'How strong is the garrison of Antwerp? What regiments? What batteries? Who are the commanders of the outer fort? What is the exact plan of the flooded district? How is the population disposed towards the German troops? How many German men-of-war are there in the harbour and in the Schelde? How are they distributed? Exact information as to the number of cannon and crews of all the men-of-war. How many and which ships of the German navigation companies are allotted to the German fleet? How many troops are there on the island of Walcheren? How many in the neighbourhood of Antwerp? How are the troops distributed on both banks of the Schelde? Are troops ready to be put on board the men-of-war and transports? Has a date been settled for that? Is there a plan for employing the German fleet? What is said about the German fleet joining the French?' That is only a small portion of the long list; but it is quite enough for anyone to guess at the nature of the rest of the questions. What the deuce! Admiral Hollway would like to learn everything for his paltry thirty pounds! or were they only a little on account? I cannot believe, M. Penurot, that your Antwerp correspondent would be willing to sell so much for thirty pounds."

The two men were clearly overwhelmed by the weight of the unexpected blow. For a moment, when Heideck drew the paper out of the bread, it looked as if Brandelaar would have thrown himself upon him and attempted to tear it from him by force. But the thought of the soldiers probably restrained him opportunely from such an act of folly. He stood where he was with tightly compressed lips and spitefully glistening eyes.

"I don't understand you, Herr major," exclaimed Penurot with a visible effort. "I know nothing whatever about this paper. I am an honest business man."

"And of course, Herr Brandelaar, you had no suspicion of the important stuffing in your white bread? Now, I am not called upon to investigate the matter further. It will be for the court-martial to throw light on the affair."

The grocer turned as pale as death, and lifted up his hands imploringly.

"Mercy, Herr major, mercy! As true as I live, I am innocent."

Heideck pretended not to have heard his assertion.

"Further, I must tell you, gentlemen, that you are confoundedly bad men of business, to risk your lives for a miserable thirty pounds. That was an inexcusable folly. If ever you wanted to make money in that way, really you would have done better to work for us. We would pay a man five times as much without haggling, if he would furnish us with really trustworthy information of this kind about the English fleet and army."

At these words, spoken almost in a jovial tone, a gleam of hope showed itself in the countenance of the two men. The grocer had opened his mouth to reply, when Heideck signed to him to be silent.

"Be so good as to go on deck for a while, Penurot," said he. "I will call you when I want to continue the conversation. You shall give me your company first, Brandelaar. I should like a few words with you in private."

The man with the fashionably pointed beard obeyed. Then Heideck turned to the Dutchman--

"This Penurot is the guilty party, isn't he? As a skipper you have probably never troubled yourself much about politics during your lifetime: you scarcely had a correct idea of the risk you were running. If the court-martial condemns you, you will only have your friend Penurot to thank for it."

"What you say is quite true, sir," replied Brandelaar with well-acted simplicity. "I have my cargo to sell for the firm of Van Spranekhuizen, and I don't care a damn for war or spying. I beg the Herr major to put in a good word for me. I had no suspicion of what was inside the bread."

"So this Penurot has drawn you into the affair without your knowing it. Did he intend to go with you to Antwerp?"

"I will tell you the whole truth, Herr major! Admiral Hollway at Dover, who is in control of the intelligence department for the Channel and the coast from Cuxhaven to Brest, gave me the two loaves for Camille Penurot. That is all I know of the matter."

"Was it the first time you had to carry out such commissions for Admiral Hollway?"

"So help me God, the first time!"

"But Penurot was not meant to keep these peculiar loaves for himself? He, like yourself, is only an agent? If you want me to speak for you, you must tell me unreservedly everything you know about it."

"Penurot has a business friend in Antwerp, as the Herr major has rightly guessed."

"His name?"

"Eberhard Amelungen."

"What is he?"

"A wholesale merchant. My cargo is intended for him."

"And how is he connected with Penurot?"

"I don't know. Penurot is an agent who does all kinds of business."

"Oh! and what does the owner, Mynheer van Spranekhuizen, say to your having anything to do with such things as the conveyance of these loaves?"

"Mynheer van Spranekhuizen and Mynheer Amelungen are near relations."

"In other words, these two gentlemen have agreed to send the Bressay from the Shetlands to Dover, and from Dover to Antwerp."

"I know nothing about that, Herr major. I have told you everything I know. No vessel can go further up the Schelde than Ternenzen, and I can unload at Breskens just as well as at Ternenzen and send the goods by rail to Antwerp."

"Now, Brandelaar, go upstairs again and send M. Penurot down to me."

With heavy tread the skipper mounted the narrow ladder, and almost at once Penurot entered. Heideck, with a wave of his hand, invited him to sit down opposite and began to speak.

"From what I have seen of Brandelaar I am convinced that he is an arrant rascal. It was very imprudent on your part to have anything to do with a man like that. If you are brought before a court-martial, you have him to thank for it."

"For God's sake, Herr major--my life isn't in danger? I implore you, have pity on me!"

"It will matter little whether personally I have pity on you. You will go with me to the Gefion and be brought before a court-martial at Flushing. The fact that you have been Brandelaar's accomplice cannot be got rid of. He has just now declared definitely that the two loaves were intended for you."

"For me? That is a vile lie. I have never received a penny from the English."

"Well--but, without special reasons, a man doesn't amuse himself by paying a visit to a herring-smack at night. The cargo could have been delivered to Herr Eberhard Amelungen without your inspection."

"Eberhard Amelungen?"

"Don't pretend to be so ignorant. Brandelaar has already confessed so much, that you can easily admit the rest. Amelungen and Van Spranekhuizen are in a conspiracy to carry on a regular system of espionage in the interests of England. You are used as an agent, and Maaning Brandelaar is trying to get out of it by sacrificing you."

"So it seems, really. But I am quite innocent, Herr major. I know nothing of all that. The last time Brandelaar left the Schelde, he came to see me here in Breskens and told me that he would soon be back again and that it would be a good business for me."

"When did that happen?"

"Three weeks ago. I had no reason to distrust Brandelaar, since he had often supplied goods for Amelungen."

"But why did you come on board to-day?"

"Brandelaar wanted it. He said I could look at the cargo and discuss whether it should be unloaded here or at Ternenzen."

"Now, M. Penurot, I will tell you something. You will go with me to Antwerp, where I will call on Herr Amelungen and convince myself whether you are really as innocent as you say, and as I shall be glad to believe you are for the present."

The grocer appeared to be getting still more uneasy.

"But you won't take me before the court-martial?"

"That remains to be seen. I can promise you nothing. Everything will depend on the information which Herr Amelungen gives me about you, and on your future behaviour. I will now have Brandelaar down again, and you will remain silent while I speak to him."

"Of course, I will do everything the Herr major tells me."

Brandelaar having been summoned to the cabin, Heideck addressed him as follows:--

"Listen to me, Maaning Brandelaar. I know everything, and I need not tell you that it is more than enough to put your neck in danger according to martial law. But I will show you a way to save yourself. Go to-morrow to Ternenzen and wait there till you hear from me. I will make it easy for you to execute your commission; I will write the answers to Admiral Hollway's questions myself. You can then take them to Dover to your customer. But at the same time I will give you a number of questions, to which you will bring me trustworthy answers at Flushing. If you carry out this mission to my satisfaction, I will pay you 3,000 marks on your return. As you will also have your fee from the Admiral, you will make a very good thing out of it. But beware of attempting to betray me; it would turn out an extremely bad job for you. I know where I can catch you, and you would be imprisoned as soon as you showed yourself anywhere on the Dutch coast. So you had better think it over carefully."

The skipper's broad countenance had gradually brightened, and at these words a cunning grin overspread his features.

"Three thousand marks! If that's a bargain, Herr major, you can count upon my serving you honourably."

"Perhaps it isn't so much a matter of your honour as of your cleverness. Unless the information you bring me corresponds with my expectations, of course the payment will suffer accordingly. The price depends upon the quality of the goods."

"Oh, you will be satisfied with me. I have connexions over there, and if you want anything else, you shall see what Brandelaar can do."

"Good! It will be to your own interest to serve me well and faithfully."

Suddenly the skipper again looked thoughtful.

"There is still one thing that troubles me, Herr major."

"What is that?"

"My men have seen an officer and soldiers visit my ship. Suppose they talk about it over in England and the Admiral should suspect me?"

"He will have no reason to do so, if he is convinced that your information is correct. He will have other sources of information besides yourself, and if he finds your statements confirmed, he will have complete confidence in you."

These words did not allay Maaning Brandelaar's uneasiness.

"Yes, but--you don't mean to give me correct information?"

"Certainly I do. Everything I write for you will be perfectly correct."

This reply was clearly too much for the skipper to understand. He stared in speechless amazement at Heideck, who proceeded quietly--

"The Admiral wants to know the strength of the German army at Antwerp, and I will tell you the condition of affairs. We have 120,000 men in Holland and the small portion of Belgian territory which we have occupied round Antwerp. In the fortress itself there are 30,000 men; on the island of Walcheren only 5,000, in occupation of Flushing and other important points. These are entirely trustworthy facts."

The Captain shook his head.

"If it were not disrespectful, I should think you were making a fool of me."

"No, my friend, I have no reason to do so; you can go bail for everything I write, and your fee will be honourably earned. It would be somewhat different with the news you might take over to the Admiral on your own responsibility."

Brandelaar nodded.

"I understand, Herr major, and I will act accordingly. But I must certainly get a fresh crew; these men know too much; that is bad, and they might make it unpleasant for me."

"No, no, that would be quite a mistake. Keep your men and make no fuss. When I get to Ternenzen, I will have you and the crew arrested. You will be examined by me and in a few days set at liberty."

The skipper did not seem to relish this prospect.

"But suppose you should change your mind in the meantime, and take me before the court-martial?"

"You may confidently trust my word. It will only be a sham examination to prevent your men getting unprofitable ideas into their heads and betraying anything which might arouse suspicion across the water. On the contrary, it will look as if you had had to endure all kinds of dangers and disappointments; and if my estimate of you is correct, my worthy Brandelaar, you will not lose the opportunity of extracting an extra fee from the Admiral to make up for the anxiety you have suffered."

XXVI
CAMILLE PENUROT

When Heideck and his prisoner, Penurot, reached the Gefion he found the Commander on deck, notwithstanding the lateness of the hour. He reported himself, and asked him to treat Penurot as a guest.

"I was getting anxious about you," said the Captain, "and was on the point of sending the steam pinnace after you. Have you found out anything important?"

"I believe I have. The two rascals whom I caught there don't seem to belong to the ordinary class of spies. They are the skipper Brandelaar and the man I have brought with me."

"Didn't you arrest the skipper as well?"

"I intend to use them in our interest, and hope that Admiral Hollway will find himself caught in his own net."

"Isn't that rather a risky game? If the fellows have betrayed Admiral Hollway, you may rely upon it they will do the same by us."

"I trust to their fears and selfishness more than their honour. To take information about us to the English they must return here again, and so I hold them in my hand."

"But the converse is true. I confess I have very little faith in such double-dealing spies."

"Of course, I feel the same; but I believe I have at last found the way to the headquarters of the English system of espionage. In order to get to the bottom of the matter I cannot do without the aid of the two spies."

"The headquarters?"

"Yes. The underlings who risk their lives are always of subordinate importance.

It is, above all, necessary to find out the persons of higher rank who prudently contrive to keep themselves in the background."

"I wish you success."

"Before going to Antwerp, whither M. Penurot is to accompany me to-morrow, I should like to make a report to the Imperial Chancellor. May I ask you to let me have a boat to-morrow morning to go to Flushing?"

"Certainly. You can have any boat you like."

"Then I should like the steam pinnace."

"Perhaps you know whether the Chancellor intends to stay long at Flushing?"

"I cannot say. In many ways Antwerp would certainly be a better place; but he has gone to Flushing to make a demonstration."

"To make a demonstration?" repeated the Commander in a tone of astonishment.

"The English, of course, know that he is there, and his presence at Flushing is bound to strengthen their belief that our main base of operations will be the mouth of the Schelde."

"Is it not surprising that our Chancellor is always at the centre of operations, though he is neither a general nor an admiral?"

"We have seen the same before in the case of Bismarck. If we follow the history of the wars of 1864, 1866, and 1870-71 we get the impression that Bismarck was in like manner the soul of all the operations, although his military title was only an honorary one."

"That is true; but the circumstances are essentially different. Bismarck was a trained official, diplomatist, ambassador, before he became Chancellor. His authority was great in military matters, independently of the generals; but our new Chancellor comes from quite a different sphere."

"But he has the power of a strong personality, and it is that which turns the scale in all great matters. The fine instinct of the people feels that the Emperor has chosen rightly, and the Chancellor's general popularity insures him powerful support even against the generals. Besides, everyone must admire his practical understanding and his wide range of vision. Is not the occupation of Antwerp a fresh proof of it? The rest of Belgium is occupied by the French army, but the Chancellor has arranged with the French Government for us to hold Antwerp, since our fleet is in the Schelde. And I am sure we shall never give it up again."

The Commander shook his head doubtfully.

"You really think we shall be able to keep Antwerp without further trouble?"

"We must, and shall, have Antwerp. Belgium and the Netherlands may continue to exist, for we cannot with any justification annex them. But the Netherlands and Antwerp will enter into closer political relations with the German Empire for the sake of their own interests. Their Governments are too weak to put down revolutionary movements in their countries for any length of time. We are moving irresistibly towards the formation of larger states. The fact that war in its attendant manifestations is a means of promoting the union of peoples seems to me to some extent to mitigate its cruelty."

"That sounds very fanciful, Herr major," said the Captain, turning the conversation. "But what sort of information do you propose to send by your agents to Dover?"

"I propose to confirm the Admiral in the idea that we intend to leave the Schelde with the fleet and a number of our private companies' steamers, and, with the support of the French fleet, to throw an army across to Dover."

"I am surprised that the English have not even attempted to force our positions. One is almost tempted to believe that the English navy is as inefficient as the English army. If our enemies felt strong enough, they would have appeared long ago before Brest, Cherbourg, Flushing, Wilhelmshaven, or Kiel. Heligoland could not stop a fleet of ironclads from forcing its way into the Elbe; it ought rather to be a welcome object of attack for the English fleet. If I were in command, I should set out against Heligoland with the older ironclads--Albion, Glory, Canopus, Coliath, Ocean, and Vengeance. The little island could hardly resist these six battleships for long, and the German North Sea fleet--supposing one to exist--would be obliged to come out from Wilhelmshaven to save its honour."

"The reason they do nothing of the sort is not so much the consciousness of their own weakness, as the fact that they have no one whose genius would be equal to the situation. Certainly, they have several capable admirals, but there is no Nelson among them. Perhaps our war also would have remained in abeyance, had not the Emperor discovered in our new Chancellor the genius needed by the times. The wars against Denmark, Austria, and France would hardly have taken place without

Bismarck's initiative. Even under a most wretched government which commits the grossest blunders great states can exist for a long time; but advancement, real progress is only possible through the intervention of a strong personality."

"I am not quite of your opinion. I am convinced that it is economic conditions that from time to time force on great revolutions. Do you think, for instance, that the Russians would have conquered India if the economic conditions of the natives had been better?"

"Certainly not. Even a great man must have the soil prepared on which to prove his strength. And I think that our Chancellor has appeared on the scene just at the right moment."

Heideck took leave of the Commander and retired to his cabin to draw up a report and take a well-deserved rest.

When he sent for M. Camille Penurot on the following morning, he found a striking alteration in him. That foppish gentleman no longer showed the dejection of the day before, his dark eyes were bright and full of confidence. By daylight, Heideck saw that his captive was a good-looking man about thirty years of age, more like a Spaniard than a Netherlander.

He bowed politely to Heideck and then asked, with a certain amount of confidence, "Pardon me, Herr major, if I serve the German Empire well, may I count on an adequate reward?"

"I have already told you, M. Penurot, that we are prepared to pay more than the English."

"Oh, that was not what I meant. You mustn't class me with Maaning Brandelaar and people of that sort."

Heideck smiled.

"Will you be good enough to tell me, then, M. Penurot, with whom I am to class you?"

"I am willing from this moment to devote all my energies to the cause of the allies."

"Granted. But what are your wishes in the matter of reward?"

"I should like you to use your influence to obtain me the honour of an order."

Heideck was unable to conceal his astonishment at this strange request.

"Such distinctions are, as a rule, only given in Germany for acts of bravery or for services which cannot be adequately requited in hard cash."

"What I am willing to do requires bravery."

"You are only going to help me to find out the spies in Antwerp."

"But they are dangerous people to make enemies of--people whose tools would be capable of anything."

"Rest assured, M. Penurot, that your reward will correspond with the services rendered. You know that I have no order to bestow, and besides, I do not quite understand of what importance a decoration can be to you."

"You rate my sense of honour too low, Herr major! But in order that you may understand me, I will tell you a secret. I am in love with a lady of very good family, and her people would be more ready to welcome me, if I had an order."

"Then you have fixed your affections very high, I suppose?"

"That's as one takes it. In the matter of birth, I am in that painful situation which is the inheritance of all children born out of wedlock. My mother was a Spanish dancer, my father is the wealthy Amelungen. He is fond of me and provides for me. It was he who bought the business in Breskens for me. But his wife, who is English, has no liking for me."

"I understand you even less than before. If you have such resources at your disposal, why on earth do you mix yourself up in such dangerous undertakings?"

"Herr Amelungen wished it."

"So, then, he really is the guilty party?"

"For God's sake, Herr major, you won't abuse my confidence. I should never forgive myself if anything I said were to harm Herr Amelungen."

"Do not be unnecessarily anxious. Nothing will happen either to you or to Herr Amelungen, if you can induce him to change sides and help us for the future instead of the English."

Penurot hung down his head and remained silent.

"And how about Herr van Spranekhuizen in Rotterdam?" continued Heideck. "Of course he belongs to the league."

"He is my father's brother-in-law. His wife is an Amelungen."

"And what is the real reason why these two gentlemen, who I hear are wealthy merchants, have undertaken to act as spies for England?"

"Oh, there is nothing so wonderful in that, Herr major. France has occupied

Belgium, Germany the Netherlands. Of course they are very bitter about it."

"That may be. But well-to-do merchants are not in the habit of risking their lives out of pure patriotism in such circumstances. As a rule, only those people do that who have little to lose."

"I have already told you that my father's wife is English. For love of her he does a great deal which certainly nothing else would induce him to do."

At this moment Heideck, being informed that the pinnace was ready, requested Penurot to accompany him on board. In the harbour of Flushing he took leave of him for a while, with instructions to call upon him in an hour at his office, having told him exactly where it was. He had no fear that Penurot would attempt flight. He felt absolutely sure of this gentleman.

XXVII
EBERHARD AMELUNGEN

On arriving at his office close to the Duke of Wellington Hotel, Heideck found his staff extremely busy. One lieutenant was looking through the French and German newspapers for important information; another was studying the Russian and English journals. The last were few in number and not of recent date, limited to those which had been smuggled across from England by daring skippers and fishermen. There were several despatches from St. Petersburg, containing news of fresh victories in India.

The Russian army had pushed on to Lucknow without any further engagement worth mentioning having taken place since the battle of Delhi. It seemed as if the English were for the time unwilling to meet the enemy in the open field. They apparently calculated that the heat and the enormous length of their line of communication would prevent the Russians from reaching the southern provinces in sufficient strength to overcome an energetic resistance there. But Heideck no longer believed in the possibility of such a resistance, concluding from the announcement of a stream of reinforcements arriving through the Khyber Pass that all the Russian losses would be speedily made up. In his opinion, practically the only thing left for the English was to embark the remnants of their army at Calcutta, Madras, and Bombay, and to get a portion at least of their beaten forces safely out of India.

While he was in his office, despatches were continually arriving from Wilhelmshaven, Kiel, Brest, and Cherbourg. The intelligence department of the entire north coast was under Heideck's control.

Except for isolated naval engagements, the strategic position had, on the whole, remained unaltered for months. Both sides hesitated to risk a decisive battle. The English fleets did not venture to attack the enemy's harbours; the combined squadrons of the continental Powers seemed no more inclined to try their fortune on the open sea. Each was endeavouring to get in touch with the other, waiting for the favourable moment when his adversary's weakness might offer the prospect of successful action.

"The risks these dwellers on the coast run are astonishing," said one of Heideck's staff. "They cross the Channel in their fishing-boats and slip by the warships. The man who brought the last English papers told me that he passed close by them to give the impression that there was nothing wrong. It needed considerable courage to risk that."

"But the enemy's spies are equally efficient. Yesterday, more by accident than any merit of my own, I caught a herring fisher in the mouth of the Schelde who was in English pay; I think I have hit on an apparently important clue, which I intend to follow up in Antwerp, after reporting myself to the Chancellor."

"He is no longer in Flushing. He has left for Antwerp with the Minister for War and the chief of the General Staff; I am told he has matters of importance to arrange with the chief of the French General Staff."

"Have you heard anything more definite as to the nature of these matters?"

"Only that the question of further mobilisation is to be discussed. Apparently, however, the six army corps, which we now have on a war footing, are thought to be enough on our side. We are not waging war by land; why then should the burden of a further mobilisation be imposed upon the people?"

"Certainly, the sacrifices entailed by this war are enormous without that; trade and industry are completely ruined."

"The only gainer by this universal conflagration is America. Since the war broke out, the United States has supplied England with everything she used to get from the Continent."

"Well, it will all come right in the end. Now, as there seems nothing urgent for me to do here, it is time I went to Antwerp."

· · · · · · ·

Eberhard Amelungen was unable to conceal his confusion, when an officer in the uniform of the Prussian General Staff appeared at the door of his private office.

Amelungen was a man about sixty years of age, a typical specimen of a substantial, respectable merchant.

"I am somewhat surprised, sir," he said in measured tones. "What can I do for you?"

Heideck introduced himself, and without wasting words told him the reason of his visit.

"I have reason to believe, Herr Amelungen, that you hold in your hands some, if not all, of the chief meshes of a widespread net of espionage. And I think it would be to your interest to tell me the whole truth of your own accord. We know so much already that presumably it will be of little use to you to have recourse to lies."

Amelungen played with his penholder, but his hands trembled visibly, and words failed him. His face had turned ashy pale, and Heideck could not help feeling sorry for him.

"I regret that my duty obliges me to proceed against you," he continued. "I can easily understand your motives. You are a Netherlander and a patriot, and, as perhaps you do not quite understand the political situation, the occupation of your country by a foreign power appears to you an act of violence, which fills you with anger and hatred against us. Therefore I think I may promise you that you will be treated as leniently as possible, if you make my task easy by an open confession."

Eberhard Amelungen shook his head.

"I know nothing of what you charge me with," he said feebly. "You have the power, and can do as you please with me. But I have nothing to confess."

"Not if I tell you that my information comes from the mouth of your own son?"

The merchant stared at the speaker with wide-open eyes full of anxiety.

"From the mouth of my own son? But--I have no son."

"Then M. Camille Penurot also was lying when he said you were his father?"

"For God's sake be merciful! Don't torture me! What is the matter with Camille? Where is he?"

"He has been caught spying. What will happen to him depends on your own behaviour."

Eberhard Amelungen sank back in his stool in a state of collapse.

"My God! you don't mean to put him in prison? or to shoot him?"

"As you may imagine, his fate is not in my hands alone. But in this instance my influence may perhaps be considerable, and it would certainly have weight if I threw it into the scale in your favour and his. Therefore I again ask you to consider whether, as things are, it would not be best for you to be perfectly frank with me. Those who are behind you can no longer protect you, and your only hope lies in the leniency of the German authorities. Do not reject the possibility of securing this leniency."

The merchant was evidently carrying on a severe struggle with himself. After a few moments he raised his head, and in an altered, defiant tone replied--

"Do what you like with me, I have nothing to confess."

Heideck then assumed a sterner, official demeanour.

"Then you must not complain if I begin to search your house."

"Do as you think fit. The victor can take what liberties he pleases."

Heideck opened the door and summoned two of the Berlin criminal police, who at his request had been ordered to Antwerp on this affair with a large number of policemen. Certainly he felt sure in advance that they would find nothing, for Eberhard Amelungen would have been very foolish not to have reckoned long ago on the possibility of such a visit, and to have taken precautions accordingly. The Major, in bringing the police with him, had thought more of the moral impression of the whole procedure. His knowledge of men told him that it had its effect.

"One thing more, Herr Amelungen," said he. "About the same time as the search begins here, another will take place in your private house. I expect the report of those entrusted with it at any moment."

Amelungen breathed hard. He looked nervously at Heideck, as if trying to read his thoughts. Then, after a brief struggle with himself, he whispered--

"Send these men out, Herr major! I should like to speak to you privately."

When Heideck had complied with his request, Amelungen continued, speaking hastily, and bringing out his words with difficulty: "In me you see a man who deserves compassion, a man who has been, entirely against his will and inclination, compromised. If anyone is guilty in this matter, it is my brother-in-law Van Spranekhuizen and a lady correspondent of my wife in Brussels. Occasionally I have acted as agent, when it was a matter of forwarding letters, or of handing over sums of money to the Countess--to the lady; but I have never personally taken any part in the matters in question."

"That statement is not enough for me. I do not doubt the truth of what you say, but I must be informed of all the details before I can drop further proceedings against you. Who is the lady you speak of?"

"A former maid of honour to the late Queen."

"Her name?"

"Countess Clementine Arselaarts."

"How did you come to know her?"

"She is a friend of my wife, who made her acquaintance last year when staying in Brussels."

"And your wife is English?"

"Yes; her maiden name was Irwin."

At the sound of this name a flood of painful recollections rushed over Heideck's mind.

"Irwin?" he repeated. "Has the lady by chance any relatives in the British army?"

"I had a brother-in-law, who was a captain in the Indian Lancers. But, according to the news that has reached us, he was killed at the battle of Lahore."

The Major found it hard to control his excitement, but as if he had already allowed himself to be too long diverted from his duty, he hastily returned to the real subject of his examination.

"You said that you have handed over certain sums of money to Countess Arselaarts. By whose order? and on whose account?"

"On account of the English Government and on the order of an English banking house with which I have had business dealings for many years."

"Were the sums large?"

"Latterly, on an average about 10,000 francs a month."

"And how were they paid?"

"Sometimes I sent the amount in cash, often by cheque on Brussels banks."

"Have you any evidence on the point--a receipt signed by the Countess?"

Amelungen hesitated.

"I strongly advise you to keep nothing back from me. So much is at stake for you and your relatives who are involved in this affair that it is of the utmost consequence that you should secure lenient treatment by a frank confession."

"Well, then, I have some receipts."

"Please let me see them."

Amelungen pulled open a drawer in his writing-table, pressed a spring, and a secret compartment at the back flew open.

"There they are!" said he, handing a small bundle of sheets of paper to Heideck. But the Major's keen eye had noticed, as he glanced rapidly at the compartment, that it contained some other papers, which he politely but firmly demanded to see.

"They are private letters of no importance," objected Amelungen, "some of my wife's correspondence, which she accidentally left in my office. I don't know what they are about myself."

"Be assured that harmless private correspondence will not be abused. But I must claim the absolute right to convince myself of the correctness of your assertions by examining them."

The merchant could see that there was no chance of getting out of it, and, visibly excited, handed the little roll over to Heideck.

The Major took it, without examining the contents more closely at once.

"You definitely assure me, Herr Amelungen, that you have nothing else referring to this matter?"

"Nothing! I give you my word, Herr major."

Heideck got up.

"I charge you not to attempt to leave the town or in any other way evade the German authorities. You will guarantee this not only as regards yourself, but also as regards your wife; and you will further promise me to break off at once all relations with the persons involved in this espionage affair, unless at our order, or in agreement with us."

Eberhard Amelungen, whose powers of resistance seemed completely broken in this painful hour, nodded assent.

"I promise both, Herr major!"

Heideck, having left a criminal official with instructions to keep watch, repaired without delay to the office of Lieutenant-Colonel Nollenberg, head of the intelligence department for Antwerp. He informed him of the result of his conversation and examined the confiscated papers in his presence.

A large number were letters from the Countess Clementine Arselaarts to Frau Beatrix Amelungen, and their contents were harmless, with the exception of a few expressions advising watchfulness and despatch.

But in a special envelope, sealed several times, there was a sheet of paper, covered with close writing, which could not be read offhand, since the letters were apparently jumbled together quite arbitrarily and irregularly.

"A cipher!" said Heideck. "But we shall soon get to the bottom of it. You have some capable interpreters at your disposal, and it might be a good thing if they set to work at once."

He continued his examination, and suddenly the blood rushed to his face, for in his hands he held a letter, the handwriting of which he recognised at the first glance as Edith's. Its contents were as follows:--

"DEAR BEATRICE,--As you see, I am again in England. You know that I have returned a widow, and you can believe that my experiences have been terrible. Your brother met an honourable death at Lahore; with the utmost difficulty I myself succeeded in getting away from India under the protection of Attorney-General Kennedy and his family. I should have to fill a book if I were to tell you all the horrors of our journey. But this is not the proper time to complain of the melancholy lot of an individual. We are all strangers and pilgrims on earth, and must bear the cross that is laid upon us.

"The immediate reason of my writing to-day is that I want your opinion on a certain matter. When I arrived at my parents' house, I heard that uncle Godfrey had died on the 16th of April. I do not know whether you have already heard of this, as regular communication with the Continent is interrupted. My uncle Godfrey has left a will, dividing his property equally between you as his niece and my deceased husband. His property was larger than my husband thought. After division, both you and my husband would have had a yearly income of 5,000 pounds. Now your brother has died without having disposed of his property. But my lawyer tells me that, as his sole heiress, I can claim his share of the inheritance. To arrange about this I have come here to Dover; for I found that I could only get the letter forwarded to Antwerp with the assistance of Admiral Hollway, who is charged with the protection of our coast. To my surprise the Admiral informed me that your name was known to him, and he willingly undertook to forward this letter to you. Now please consent to uncle Godfrey's property being divided between you and me. I do not believe you will have any objection, but I consider it a duty to obtain your definite consent. I shall be glad to hear from you that you are well.

"Yours truly,

"EDITH IRWIN.

"P.S.--In India I made the acquaintance of a German officer who rendered me great service during the terrible times of the war and saved my life more than once. He travelled with the Kennedys and myself on the Caledonia to Naples. From there he went on to Berlin, while we continued our voyage on a man-of-war through the Straits of Gibraltar to Southampton. This officer is a Captain Heideck of the Prussian General Staff. I should be thankful to you if you would find out where he is at present. I am very anxious to know his address. For a time I am staying in Dover. Letters addressed to Mrs. Jones, 7, St. Paul's Street, will reach me."

The perusal of this letter revived a crowd of painful recollections in Heideck's mind. He never doubted for a moment that the postscript, in which his name occurred, explained Edith's real object in writing. All the rest was certainly a mere pretext; for he knew how indifferent Edith was in regard to money matters, and was convinced that she was in no such hurry about the settlement of the inheritance as might have been thought from her letter.

The Lieutenant-Colonel approached him at this moment.

"It has taken less time to decipher the document than I had ventured to hope," said he. "I have telegraphed at once to the police at Schleswig to arrest the writer, one Brodersen, without delay. Please convince yourself what sort of friends we have amongst the Danes."

Heideck read as follows:--

"In the harbour of Kiel, the larger warships are the battleships Oldenburg,

Baden, Wurttemberg, Bayern, Sachsen; the large cruisers Kaiser, Deutschland, Konig Wilhelm; the small cruisers Gazelle, Prinzess Wilhelm, Irene, Komet, and Meteor, with the torpedo division boats D 5 and D 6 with their divisions. In addition, there are about 100 large and small steamers of the North-German Lloyd, the Hamburg-America Line, the Stettin Company, and others. All the large steamers are equipped with quick-firing cannon and machine-guns; the small, only with machine-guns. In the neighbourhood of Kiel there are 50,000 infantry and artillery from Hanover, Mecklenburg, Pomerania, and the province of Saxony, with only two regiments of hussars. My friends' opinions differ as to the plans of the German Government. Possibly ships of the line will proceed through the Kaiser Wilhelm Canal and make a combined attack with the Russian fleet on the British near Copenhagen.

"It is most probable that the fleet of transports will take on board the army collected at Kiel and convey it through the Kaiser Wilhelm Canal into the North Sea, where the German battleships now at Antwerp will join the French squadrons from Cherbourg. An attempt would then be made, under cover of the warships, to land the German army and the French troops from Boulogne at Dover, or some place near on the English coast.

"I acknowledge the receipt of 10,000 francs from Mynheer van Spranekhuizen, but must ask you to send a further sum twice that amount. My agents are risking their lives, and will not work for less."

"You, too, my dear Brodersen, have risked your life," said the Lieutenant-Colonel seriously. "I should not like to give much for it at the present moment."

"These notes are very instructive," observed Heideck. "If we strengthen Admiral Hollway in the belief that we intend to land the German troops in England from Antwerp and not from Kiel, our fleet of transports at Kiel will be able to cross the North Sea all the more safely and effect the landing in Scotland."

XXVIII
THE FATE OF A SPY

Colonel Mercier-Milon reported from Brussels that he had arrested Countess Arselaarts and thought he had made a valuable capture. The Countess was deeply in debt and lived very extravagantly. A little time ago she had been assisted financially by an exalted personage, who had left the country. Since then her resources had become exhausted, and it was supposed that she had acted as a spy for the English at a high salary. He added that he was on the point of discovering a widespread network of espionage in France and Belgium.

Herr van Spranekhuizen and Hinnerk Brodersen of Schleswig had also been arrested the same morning.

"I wish we had trustworthy information as to the strength of the British fleet," said the Lieutenant-Colonel, who had communicated the above report to Heideck. "Sometimes I am really inclined to believe that this fleet is not so effective as all the world has hitherto assumed. It is almost impossible for outsiders to get a clear insight into the condition of the English navy. So far as I can remember, false reports are systematically published about the fleet--officially, semi-officially, and privately. From time to time a speaker is put up in Parliament by the Government to deliver a violent attack on the naval administration. He is contradicted by a representative of the Admiralty, and dust is again thrown in the eyes of the world. On one of Queen Victoria's last birthdays a powerful squadron, as it was called, was assembled for review off Spithead. But no foreigner was allowed a close inspection of these imposing fleets, and I am greatly inclined to think that it was another case of the famous movable villages, which Potemkin showed the Russian Empress on her journey to the Crimea. Official statements give the number of English warships as more than four hundred, not including torpedo-boats, but amongst them is a large number of obsolete and inefficient vessels."

Heideck nodded.

"If the English fleet were really so efficient as is believed, it would be difficult to understand why it has not attempted any decisive action up till now."

"That is also my view. The Copenhagen fleet would have attacked Kiel harbour long ago. It was said that it was to hold the Russian fleet in check. But that would be superfluous to start with, as long as the Gulfs of Bothnia and Finland were blocked with ice and the Russian squadrons were unable to move. This way of making war reminds me forcibly of the state of things in the Crimean War, when a powerful English fleet set out with a great flourish of trumpets against Cronstadt and St. Petersburg, but did nothing except bombard Bomarsund, a place nobody cared about. The English Press had great difficulty in excusing the fiasco of its world-renowned fleet."

Returning to the previous subject of conversation, Heideck said to the Lieutenant-Colonel: "I don't think we need trouble ourselves any more about the communications of Countess Arselaarts and Messrs. Amelungen and Co. The court-martial may settle with them. I attach incomparably greater importance to skipper Brandelaar, whom I hold in my hand, and through whom--perhaps with the help of Camille Penurot--I hope to obtain information about the British fleet and its proposed employment. Brandelaar's vessel should now be off Ternenzen. I will ask you, Herr Lieutenant-Colonel, to have the man and his crew arrested to-day."

"But how does that agree with your intention of using him as a spy in our interest?"

"I forgot to tell you that it is an agreement between Brandelaar and myself. He himself thought it necessary for his own safety; he was afraid of the crew. Of course it will only be a sham examination, and the man must be released as soon as possible, on the ground of insufficient evidence, so that he can return to England to-morrow."

The Lieutenant-Colonel promised to do as the Major desired.

The same evening Heideck met Penurot by arrangement at a tavern.

"Our business is somewhat complicated," said Heideck. "There must be some more people working for your father, hitherto unknown to us."

"Why do you think that, Herr major?"

"Your father had some letters from Admiral Hollway, which were not brought by Brandelaar."

"Yes, yes, I know. I can imagine that."

"Do you know who brought them over?"

"I don't know for certain, but I can guess."

"Can't you get me more certain information?"

"I will try."

"How will you set about it?"

"There are some sailors' taverns here, where I hope to get on the track. But they are desperate fellows, and it is dangerous to meddle with them."

"If you will point out the taverns to me, I will have all the customers arrested to-night."

"For Heaven's sake, don't, Herr major! We should ruin everything by that. These men would let themselves be cut to pieces rather than betray anything to you. If anyone can get them to speak, it is myself."

"Wouldn't you be trusting them too much?"

"No, no. I know best how to deal with them, and I know many ways of making them open their mouths."

"Well, do what you can. The matter is important. I am very anxious to find someone to obtain trustworthy information about the British fleet, and you know we don't spare money."

Penurot was ready to attempt his difficult task at once, and took leave of Heideck, promising to meet him soon after midnight at the same tavern. Heideck left the restaurant soon after him, and walked along the quay Van Dyck, to cool his heated brow. In time of war the town presented a strangely altered appearance. There was a swarm of German soldiers in the streets; the usual busy traffic at the harbour had entirely ceased. There had been no trade since the German warships, like floating citadels, had been lying in the Schelde. And yet it was almost incomprehensible, how the change had come about so rapidly. Antwerp was an almost impregnable fortress, if the flooding of the surrounding country was undertaken in time. But the Belgian Government had not even made an attempt at defence, when the vanguard of the seventh and eighth army corps had appeared in the neighbourhood of the town. It had surrendered the fortress at once, with all its strong outer forts, to the German military commanders and had withdrawn its own army. The Imperial Chancellor was certainly right in attaching such importance to the possession of Antwerp by Germany. The population was almost exclusively Flemish, and Antwerp was thus in nationality a German town.

From the general political situation Heideck's thoughts returned to Edith and her letter, and at last he decided to write to her that very evening.

To carry out his intention, he went back to the restaurant where he had met Penurot, and called for ink and paper. When he had finished his letter, he looked over the words he had written, in which, contrary to his usual practice, he had given utterance to his real feelings:--

"MY DEAR EDITH,--In the exercise of my duty, I accidentally came into possession of your letter to Frau Amelungen. I was looking for something quite different at the time, and you can imagine how great was my surprise at the unexpected discovery.

"From the hour when we were obliged to separate and you, possibly not without resentment and reproach, held out your hand at parting, I have felt more and more how indispensable you are to me. I treasure every word you have said to me, every look you have bestowed upon me, and your image is before my mind, ever brighter, ever more beautiful. I have never met a woman whose mind was so beautiful, so refined, so keen as yours. I must confess that your ideas at first sometimes terrified me. Your views are often so far removed from the commonplace, so far above the ordinary, that it needs time to estimate them correctly. If I now recall to mind what formerly seemed strange to me, it is only with feelings of admiration. From day to day the impression you made upon me at our first conversation has sunk deeper into my mind, and the comforting certainty, that love for you will fill my entire life in the future, grows more and more unshakable.

"Nevertheless, I may not regret that I had the strength to leave you at Naples. The beautiful dream of our life together would have been disturbed too soon by the rude reality. My duty calls me from one place to another, and as long as this war lasts I am not my own master for an hour. We must have patience, Edith. Even this campaign cannot last for ever, and if Heaven has decreed that I shall come out of it alive, we shall meet again, never more to part.

"You may not be able to answer this letter, for communication with Frau Amelungen is interrupted. But I know you will answer me if it is possible, and I am happy to think that, by letting you know I am alive, I have given you a pleasure, soon, I hope, to be followed by the still greater happiness of meeting again. Let us wait patiently and confidently for that hour!"

He sealed the letter and put it in his pocket, in order to hand it over to Brandelaar on the following day. He then waited for the reappearance of Penurot, who had promised to be back at midnight. But although he waited nearly an hour over the time in the tavern, he waited in vain. The terms in which Herr Amelungen's natural son had spoken of the people he intended to look for that evening made the Major anxious about his fate. Before returning to his quarters, he paid a visit to the town police office, requesting that a search might be made in the less reputable sailors' taverns near the harbour for M. Camille Penurot, of whose appearance he gave a careful description.

As there was no news of him on the following morning, Heideck felt almost certain that the affair had turned out disastrously for Penurot. However, for the moment, he could not stop to investigate the young man's whereabouts.

He was informed by the Lieutenant-Colonel that Brandelaar, whose vessel actually lay off Ternenzen, had been arrested with his crew, examined, and liberated during the course of the night, as had been agreed between the two officers.

Heideck now set out for Ternenzen to give Brandelaar the information for Admiral Hollway that had been collected at his office, together with the private information that was of such importance to him.

At last, having paid Brandelaar a thousand francs on account, Heideck also gave him the letter to Edith, with careful instructions as to its delivery. The skipper, whose zeal for the cause of Germany was now undoubtedly honourable, repeatedly promised to carry out his orders conscientiously and to the best of his power.

On returning to Antwerp at noon, Heideck found a communication at his office from the police to the effect that Camille Penurot's body had been found in one of the harbour basins, stabbed in several places in the breast and neck. A search for the assassins had been immediately set on foot, but up to the present no trace of them had been discovered.

XXIX
A WOMAN'S TREACHERY

According to the agreement with Heideck, Brandelaar, on his return from Dover, was to put in at Flushing, and the Major had instructed the guardships at the mouth of the West Schelde to allow the smack to pass unmolested without detention. But he waited for the skipper from day to day in vain. The weather could not have been the cause of his delay; certainly it had not been too bad for a man of Brandelaar's daring. A moderate north wind had been blowing nearly the whole time, so that a clever sailor could have easily made the passage from Dover to Flushing in a day.

Consequently, other reasons must have kept him in England. Heideck began to fear that either his knowledge of men, so often tried, had deceived him on this occasion, or that Brandelaar had fallen a victim to some act of imprudence in England.

A whole week having passed since Brandelaar had started, Heideck at least hoped for his return to-day. The north wind had increased towards evening; there was almost a storm, and the blast rattled violently at the windows of the room in the hotel, in which Heideck sat still writing at midnight.

A gentle knock at the door made him look up from his work. Who could have come to see him at this late hour? It was certainly not an orderly from his office, which was open day and night, for soldiers' fingers as a rule knocked harder.

"Come in!" he said. The door opened slowly, and Heideck saw, in the dimly-lighted corridor, a slender form in a long oilskin cape and a large sailor's hat, the brim of which was pressed down over the forehead.

A wild idea flashed through Heideck's mind. He sprang up, and at the same moment the pretended young man tore off his hat and held out his arms with a cry of joy.

"My dear--my beloved friend!"

"Edith!"

At this moment all other thoughts and feelings were forgotten by Heideck in the overpowering joy of seeing her again. He rushed to Edith and drew her to his breast. For a long time they remained silent in a long embrace, looking into each other's eyes and laughing like merry children.

At last, slowly freeing herself from his arms, Edith said--

"You are not angry with me, then, for coming to you, although you forbade it? You will not send me away from you again?"

Her voice penetrated his ear like sweet, soothing music. What man could have resisted that seductive voice?

"I should like to be angry with you, my dear, but I cannot--Heaven knows I cannot!"

"I could not have lived any longer without you," whispered the young woman. "I was obliged to see you again, or I should have died of longing."

"My sweet, my only love! But what is the meaning of this disguise? And how did you manage to cross the Channel?"

"I took the way you showed me. And is my disguise so very displeasing to you?"

She had thrown off the ugly, disfiguring cape and stood before him in a dark blue sailor's dress. Even in her dress as an Indian rajah he had not thought her more enchanting.

"The only thing that displeases me is that other eyes than mine have been allowed to see you in it. But you still owe me an explanation how you got here?"

"With your messenger of love, your postillon d'amour, who was certainly rather uncouth and awkward for so delicate a mission."

"What! did you come with Brandelaar?" cried Heideck, in surprise.

"Yes. The moment I received your letter from his clumsy sailor's fist, my mind was made up. I asked him whether he was returning to Flushing, and when he said yes, I declared he must take me with him, cost what it would. I would have paid him all I possessed, without hesitation, to take me across. But the good fellow did it for much less."

"You foolish girl!" said Heideck reprovingly. But pride in his beautiful, fearless darling shone brightly from his eyes. "I shall have to take Brandelaar seriously to task for playing so reckless a game. But what made him so long in returning?"

"I believe he had all kinds of private business to see after. And he was not the only one--I had my business too. I did not want to come to you empty-handed, my friend."

"Empty-handed? I don't understand."

"I puzzled my brains how I could please you, and appease your anger at my sudden appearance--that terrible anger, of which I felt so afraid. And as I heard from Brandelaar that it is your duty to discover military secrets--"

"The worthy Brandelaar is a chatterer. It seems as if your beautiful eyes have tempted him to open his whole heart to you."

"And if it had been the case," she asked, with a roguish smile, "would you not have every reason to be grateful to him as well as myself? But really--you don't even know what I have brought for you. Aren't you the least curious?"

"No military secret, I suppose?"

He spoke jestingly, but she nodded seriously.

"Yes--a great secret. Chance helped me, or I should hardly have got hold of it. There it is! But be sure I shall claim an adequate reward for it."

She handed him a sealed envelope, which she had kept concealed under her dress. When Heideck, with growing excitement, spread out the paper it contained, he recognised at the first glance the blue stamped paper of the English Admiralty.

No sooner had he read the first lines than he started up in the most violent excitement. His face had become dark red, a deep furrow showed itself between his eyebrows.

"What is this?" he ejaculated. "For God's sake, Edith, how did you come by this paper?"

"How did I come by it? Oh, that's quite a secondary consideration. The chief thing is, whether it is of any value to you or not. But aren't you pleased with it?"

Heideck was still staring like one hypnotised at the paper covered with the regularly formed writing of a practised clerk's hand.

"Incomprehensible!" he murmured. Then, suddenly looking at Edith almost threateningly, he repeated--

"How did you come by it?"

"You are questioning me like a magistrate. But you may know, for all I care. The brother of the lady with whom I was staying in Dover is private secretary to the Admiralty--a poor fellow, suffering from disease of the lungs, whose one desire was to go to Egypt or Madeira, to get relief from his sufferings. By finding him the means for this I have done an act of philanthrophy. I asked him, in return for a further present of money, to give me the copy of an important document connected with his department."

She suddenly broke off, and Heideck burst out into a short, sharp laugh which filled her with surprise and alarm.

"An act of philanthrophy!" he repeated in a tone of unspeakable bitterness. "Did you know what this man was selling to you?"

"He said it was the English fleet's plan of attack, and I thought it would interest you."

"But surely you must have known how far-reaching would be the consequences of your act? Had you no suspicion that irreparable harm might overtake your country, if this plan came to the knowledge of its enemies?"

His voice quivered with fearful anxiety, but Edith did not seem to understand his excitement.

"I understand you less and less," she said impatiently. "It can only be one of two things. Either this paper is of importance to you, and then you ought to feel the more grateful to me, the more important it is. Or the secretary has deceived me as to its value. Then it isn't worth the trouble of saying any more about it."

"Do you look at it in that light, Edith?" he said, mournfully. "Only in that light? Did you only think of yourself and me, when you bribed an unfortunate wretch to commit the most disgraceful of all crimes?"

"Oh, my dearest, what strong language! I was not prepared for such reproaches. Certainly I was only thinking of you and me, and I am not in the least ashamed to confess it, for there is nothing in the world of more importance for me than our love."

"And your country, Edith? is that of no account?"

"My country--what is it? A piece of earth with stones, trees, animals, and men who are nothing to me, to whom I owe nothing and am indebted for nothing. Why should I love them more than the inhabitants of any other region, amongst whom there are just as many good and bad people as amongst them? I am an English-woman: well, but I am also a Christian. And who would have the right to condemn me, if the commandments of Christianity were more sacred to me than all narrow-minded, national considerations? If the possession of this paper really made you the stronger--if it should bring defeat upon England, instead of the hoped-for victory which would only endlessly prolong the war--what would mankind lose thereby? Perhaps peace would be the sooner concluded, and, justly proud of my act, I would then confess before all the world."

Heideck had not interrupted her, but she saw that her words had not convinced him. With gloomy countenance he stood before her, breathing hard, like one whose heart is oppressed by a heavy burden.

"Forgive me, but I cannot follow your train of thought," said he, with a melancholy shake of the head. "There are things which cannot be extenuated however we may try to palliate them."

"Well, then, if you think what I have done so monstrous, what is there to prevent us from undoing it? Give me back the paper; I will tear it up. Then no one will be injured by my treachery."

"It is too late for that. Now that I know what this paper contains, my sense of duty as an officer commands me to make use of it. You have involved me in a fearful struggle with myself."

"Oh, is that your logic? Your sense of honour does not forbid you to reap the fruits of my treachery, but you punish the traitress with the full weight of your contempt."

He avoided meeting her flaming eyes.

"I did not say I despised you, but--"

"Well, what else do you mean?"

"Once again--I do not despise you, but it terrifies me to find what you are capable of."

"Is not that the same thing in other words? A man cannot love a woman if he is terrified at her conduct. Tell me straight out that you can no longer love me."

"It would be a lie if I said so, Edith. You have killed our happiness, but not my love."

She only heard the last words of his answer, and with brightening eyes flung herself on his breast.

"Then scold me as you like, you martinet! I will put up with anything patiently, if only I know that you still love me, and that you will be mine, all mine, as soon as this terrible war no longer stands between us like a frightful spectre."

He did not return her caresses, and gently pushed her from him.

"Forgive me, if I must leave you now," he said in a singularly depressed voice, "but I must be in Antwerp by daybreak."

"Is it really so urgent? May I not go with you?"

"No, that is impossible, for I shall have to travel on an engine."

"And when will you return?"

Heideck turned away his face.

"I don't know. Perhaps I shall be sent on further, so that I shall have no opportunity of saying good-bye to you."

"In other words, you don't mean to see me again? You are silent. You cannot have the heart to deceive me. Must I remind you that you have sworn to belong to me, if you survive this war?"

"If I survive it--yes!"

The tone of his reply struck her like a blow. She had no need to look at him again, to know what was passing in his mind. Now for the first time she understood that there was no further hope for her. Heideck had spoken the truth, when he said he still loved her, and the horror which he felt at her conduct did not, according to his conscience, release him from his word. But as he at the same time felt absolutely certain that he could never make a traitress to her country his wife, his idea of the honour of a man and officer drove him to the only course which could extricate him from this fearful conflict of duties.

He had sworn to marry her, if he survived the war. And since he could no more keep his oath than break it, he had at this moment decided to put an end to the struggle by seeking death, which his calling made it so easy for him to find. With the keen insight of a woman in love Edith read his mind like an open book. She knew him so well that she never for a moment cherished the illusion that she could alter his mind by prayers or tears. She knew that this man was ready to sacrifice everything for her--everything save honour. Her mind had never been fuller of humble admiration than at the moment when the knowledge that she had lost him for ever spread a dark veil over all her sunny hopes of the future.

She did not say a word; and when her silence caused him to turn his face again towards her, she saw an expression of unutterable pain in his features, usually so well controlled. Then she also felt the growing power of a great and courageous resolution. Her mind rose from the low level of selfish passion to the height of self-sacrificing renunciation. But it had never been her way to do by halves what she had once determined to carry out. What was to be done admitted no cowardly delay, no tender leave-taking must allow Heideck to guess that a knowledge of his intentions had decided her course of action.

With that heroic self-command of which, perhaps, only a woman is capable in such circumstances, she forced herself to appear outwardly calm and composed.

"Then I am no longer anxious about our future, my friend," she said after a long silence, smiling painfully. "I will not detain you any longer now; for I know that your duties as a soldier must stand first. I am happy that I have been permitted to see you again. Not to hinder your doing your duty in this serious time of war, I give you your freedom. Perhaps your love will some day bring you back to me of your own accord. And now, farewell."

Her sudden resolution and the calmness with which she resigned herself to this second separation must have seemed almost incomprehensible to Heideck after what had passed. But her beautiful face betrayed so little of the desperate hopelessness she felt, that, after a brief hesitation, he regarded this singular change in the same light as the numerous other surprises to which her mysterious nature had already treated him. She had spoken with such quiet firmness, that he could no longer look upon her resolution as the suggestion of a perverse or angry whim.

"For God's sake, Edith, what do you intend to do?"

"I shall try to return to Dover to-morrow. I should only be in your way here."

"In that case, we should not see each other again before you leave?"

"You said yourself that there was little chance of that."

"I am not my own master, and this information--"

"No excuse is necessary; no regard for me should hinder you in the performance of your official duties. Once again then, good-bye, my dear, my beloved friend! May Heaven protect you!"

She flung herself on his breast and kissed him; but only for a few seconds did her soft arm linger round his neck. She did not wish to give way, and yet she felt that she would not be able to control herself much longer. She hurriedly picked up her oilskin cape from the floor and seized her fisherman's hat. Heideck fervently desired to say something affectionate and tender, but his throat seemed choked as it were by an invisible hand; he could only utter, in a voice that sounded cold and dry, the words, "Farewell, my love! farewell!"

When he heard the door close behind her, he started up impetuously, as if he meant to rush after her and call her back. But after the first step he stood still and pressed his clenched left hand upon his violently beating heart. His face, as if turned to stone, wore an expression of inflexible resolution, and the corners of his mouth were marked by two deep, sharp lines, as if within this single hour he had aged ten years.

XXX
EDITH'S LAST JOURNEY

Skipper Brandelaar had given Edith the name of the inn near the harbour, where he expected a message from Heideck in the course of the night; for he felt certain that the Major would be anxious to speak to him as soon as possible.

But he was considerably surprised when, instead of the messenger he expected, he saw his beautiful disguised passenger enter the low, smoke-begrimed taproom. He went to meet Edith with a certain clumsy gallantry, to shield her from the curiosity and importunities of the men seated with him at the table, whose weather-beaten faces inspired as little confidence as their clothing, which smelt of tar and had suffered badly from wind and weather.

Utterly surprised, he was going to question Edith, but she anticipated him.

"I must get back to Dover to-night," she said hurriedly, in a low tone. "Will you take me across? I will pay you what you ask."

The skipper shook his head slowly, but resolutely.

"Impossible. Even if I could leave again, it couldn't be done in such weather."

"It must be done. The weather is not so bad, and I know you are not the man to be afraid of a storm."

"Afraid--no! Very likely I have weathered a worse storm than this with my smack. But there is a difference between the danger a man has to go through when he cannot escape it, and that to which he foolishly exposes himself. When I am on a journey, then come what pleases God, but--"

"No more, Brandelaar," interrupted Edith impatiently. "If you cannot, or will not go yourself, surely one of your acquaintances here is brave and smart enough to earn a couple of hundred pounds without any difficulty."

The skipper's little eyes twinkled.

"A couple of hundred pounds? Is it really so important for you to leave Flushing to-day? We have hardly landed!"

"Yes, it is very important. And I have already told you that I don't care how much it costs."

The skipper, who had evidently begun to waver, rubbed his chin thoughtfully.

"H'm! Anyhow, I couldn't do it myself. I have important information for the Herr major, and he would have a right to blame me, if I went away without even so much as speaking to him. But perhaps--perhaps I might find out a skipper who would take the risk, provided that I got something out of it for myself."

"Of course, of course! I don't want a favour from you for nothing. You shall have fifty pounds the moment I set foot in the boat."

"Good! And two hundred for the skipper and his men? The men are risking their lives, you mustn't forget that. Besides, they will have to manage confoundedly cleverly to get past the German guardships unnoticed."

"Yes, yes! Why waste so much time over this useless bargaining? Here is the money--now get me a boat."

"Go in there," said Brandelaar, pointing to the door of a little dark side room. "I will see whether my friend Van dem Bosch will do it."

Before complying with Brandelaar's suggestion, Edith glanced at the man whom he had indicated with a movement of his head. Externally this robust old sea-dog was certainly not attractive, but his alarming appearance did not make Edith falter in her resolution for a moment.

"Good--talk to your friend, Brandelaar! And mind that I don't have to wait too long for his consent."

. . . .

The gallant Brandelaar must have found a very effective means of persuasion, for in less than ten minutes he was able to inform Edith that Van dem Bosch was ready to risk the journey on the terms offered. He said nothing more about the danger of the undertaking, as if he were afraid of frightening the young Englishwoman from her plan, so profitable to himself. From this moment nothing more was said about the matter. It was not far to the place where the cutter lay at anchor, and Edith struggled on bravely between the two men, who silently walked along by her side, in the face of the hurricane from the north, roaring in fitful gusts from the sea. They rowed across to the vessel in a yawl, and when Brandelaar returned to the quay he had his fifty pounds all right in his pocket.

"If the Herr major asks after me, you may tell him the whole truth with confidence," Edith had said to him. "And greet him from me--greet him heartily. Don't forget that, Brandelaar."

. . . .

The skipper's two men, who had been lying fast asleep below deck in the cutter, were considerably astonished and certainly far from pleased at the idea of the nocturnal passage. But a few words from the skipper in a language unintelligible to Edith speedily removed their discontent. They now readily set to work to set sail and weigh anchor. The skipper's powerful hands grasped the helm; the small, strongly-built vessel tacked a little and then, heeling over, shot out into the darkness.

It passed close by the Gefion, and had it by accident been shown up by the electric light which from time to time searched the disturbed surface of the water, the nocturnal trip would in any case have experienced a very disagreeable interruption. But chance favoured the rash undertaking. No signal was made, no shout raised from the guardship, and the lights of Flushing were soon lost in the darkness.

Since the start Edith had been standing by the mast, looking fixedly backwards to the place where she was leaving everything which had hitherto given all its value and meaning to her life. The skipper and his two men, whom the varying winds kept fully occupied with their sails, did not seem to trouble about her, and it was not till a suddenly violent squall came on that Van dem Bosch shouted to her that she had better go below, where she would at least be protected against the wind and weather.

But Edith did not stir. For her mind, racked by all the torments of infinite despair, the raging of the storm, the noise of the rain rattling down, and the hissing splash of the waves as they dashed against the planks of the boat, made just the right music. The tumult of the night around her harmonised so exactly with the tumult within her that she almost felt it a relief. The close confinement of a low cabin would have been unbearable. She could only hold out by drinking in deep draughts of air saturated with the briny odour of the sea, and by exposing her face to the storm, the rain, and the foam of the waves. It was a kind of physical struggle with the brute forces of Nature, and its stirring effect upon her nerves acted as a tonic to a mind lacerated with sorrow.

She had no thought for time or space. Only the hurricane-like rising of the storm, the increasingly violent breaking of the waves, and the wilder rocking of the boat, told her that she must be on the open sea. In spite of her oilskin cape, she was completely wet through, and a chill, which gradually spread over her whole body from below, numbed her limbs. Nevertheless, she never for a moment thought of retiring below. She had no idea of danger. She heard the sailors cursing, and twice the skipper's voice struck her ears, uttering what seemed to be an imperious command. But she did not trouble herself about this. As if already set free from everything earthly, she remained completely indifferent to everything that was going on around her. The more insensible her body became, paralysed by the penetrating damp and chill, the more indefinite and dreamlike became all the impressions of her senses. She seemed to have lost all foothold, to be flying on the wings of the storm, free from all restrictions of corporeal gravity, through unlimited space. All the rushing, howling, rattling, and splashing of the unchained elements seemed to her to unite in one monotonous, majestic roar, which had no terrors for her, but a wonderfully soothing influence. As her senses slowly failed, the tumult became a lofty harmony; she felt so entirely one with mighty, all-powerful Nature that the last feeling of which she was conscious was a fervent, ardent longing to dissolve in this mighty Nature, like one of the innumerable waves, whose foam wetted her feet in passing.

. . . .

A loud sound, like the sharp report of a gun, was heard above the confusion of noises--a loud crash--some wild curses from rough sailors' throats! The boat suddenly danced and tossed upon the waves like a piece of cork, while the big sail flapped in the wind as if it would be torn the next minute into a thousand pieces.

The peak-halyard was broken, and the gaff, deprived of its hold, struck with fearful force downwards. With all the might of his arms, strong as those of a giant, the skipper pulled at the helm to bring the vessel to the wind. The two other men worked desperately to make the sail fast.

In these moments of supreme danger none of the three gave a thought to the disguised woman in the oilskin cape, who had stood so long motionless as a statue by the mast. Not till their difficult task was successfully finished did they notice that she had disappeared. They looked at each other with troubled faces. The skipper at the helm said--

"She has gone overboard. The gaff must have hit her on the head. There is no more to be done. Why would she stay on deck?"

He cleared his throat and spat into the sea, after the fashion of sailors.

The other two said nothing. Silently they obeyed the orders of the skipper, who made for the mouth of the Schelde again.

They made no attempt to save her. It would have been a useless task.

XXXI
THE STOLEN DOCUMENT

The last ordinary train to Antwerp had gone long before Heideck reached the station. But a short interview with the railway commissioner sufficed, and an engine was at once placed at the Major's disposal. When he had mounted to the stoker's place the station-master saluted and signalled to the driver to start. For a moment Heideck felt a sharp pain in his heart like a knife when the grinding engine started. It was his life's happiness that he was leaving behind him for ever. A dull, paralysing melancholy possessed his soul. He seemed to himself to be a piece of lifeless mechanism, like the engine puffing ceaselessly onwards, subject and blindly obedient to the will of another. All his actions were decided, no longer by his own resolutions, but by an inexorable, higher law--by the iron law of duty. He was no longer personally free nor personally responsible. The way was marked out for him as clearly and distinctly as the course of the engine by the iron lines of rails. With tightly compressed lips he looked fixedly before him. What lay behind was no longer any concern of his. Only a peremptory "Forward" must henceforth be his watchword.

About six o'clock in the morning he stood before the royal castle on the Place de Meix, where the Prince-Admiral had fixed his quarters, King Leopold having offered him the castle to reside in.

In spite of the early hour Heideck was at once conducted to the Prince's study.

"Your Royal Highness," said Heideck, "I have a report of the utmost importance to make. These orders of the English Admiralty have fallen into my hands."

The Prince motioned him to a seat by his desk. "Be good enough to read the orders to me, Herr major."

Heideck read the important document, which ran as follows:--

"The Lords of the Admiralty think it desirable to attack the German fleet first, as being the weaker. This attack must be carried out before the Russian fleet is in a position to go to its assistance in Kiel harbour. Therefore a simultaneous attack should be made on the two positions of the German fleet on the 15th of July."

"On the 15th of July?" repeated the Prince, who had risen in great excitement. "And it is the 11th to-day! How did you get possession of these orders, Herr major? What proof have you that this document is genuine?"

"I have the most convincing reasons for believing it genuine, your Royal Highness. You can see for yourself that the orders are written on the blue stamped paper of the English Admiralty."

"Very well, Herr major! But that would not exclude the idea of a forgery. How did you come into possession of this paper?"

"Your Royal Highness will excuse my entering into an explanation."

"Then read on."

Heideck continued--

"On the day mentioned the Copenhagen fleet has to attack Kiel harbour. Two battleships will take up a position before the fortress of Friedrichsort and Fort Falkenstein on the west side, two more before the fortifications of Labo and Moltenort on the east side of Kiel inlet; they will keep up so hot a fire on the fortifications that the rest of the fleet will be able to enter the harbour behind them under their protection.

"In the harbour of Kiel there are about a hundred transports and some older ironclads and cruisers, which cannot offer a serious resistance to our fleet. All these ships must be attacked with the greatest rapidity and vigour. It is of the utmost importance to send a battleship to the entrance of the Kaiser Wilhelm Canal, in order to cut off the retreat of the German ships. All the German ships in the harbour are to be destroyed. The attack is to be commenced by some cruisers from the rest of the fleet, which will enter the inlet in advance, without any consideration of the chance of their being blown up by mines. These vessels are to be sacrificed, if necessary, in order to set the entrance free.

"For the attack on the German fleet in the Schelde, which must also take place on the 15th of July, Vice-Admiral Domvile will form a fleet of two divisions from the Channel squadrons and the cruiser fleet.

"The first division will be formed of the following battleships: Bulwark (Vice-Admiral Domvile's flagship), Albemarle, Duncan, Montagu, Formidable, Renown, Irresistible, and Hannibal.

"The cruisers Bacchante (Rear-Admiral Walker), Gladiator, Naiad, Hermione, Minerva, Rainbow, Pegasus, Pandora, Abukir, Vindictive, and Diana.

"The destroyers Dragon, Griffin, Panther, Locust, Boxer, Mallard, Coquette, Cygnet, and Zephyr.

"Two torpedo flotillas.

"Two ammunition ships, two colliers, and a hospital ship are to be allotted to the division.

"The second division will be formed of the following battleships: Majestic (Vice-Admiral Lord Beresford), Magnificent (Rear-Admiral Lambton), Cornwallis, Exmouth, Russell, Mars, Prince George, Victorious, and Caesar.

"The cruisers St. George (Captain Winsloe), Sutlej, Niobe, Brilliant, Doris, Furious, Pactolus, Prometheus, Juno, Pyramus, and Pioneer.

"The destroyers Myrmidon, Chamois, Flying Fish, Kangaroo, Desperate, Fawn, Ardent, Ariel, and Albatross.

"Two torpedo flotillas.

"Two ammunition ships, two colliers, and a hospital ship are to be alloted to the division.

"A squadron under Commodore Prince Louis of Battenberg (flagship, Implacable) will remain in reserve to watch for the possible approach of a French fleet. In case one is seen, the first division is to unite with this reserve squadron under the supreme command of Vice-Admiral Domvile, and to attack the French fleet vigorously, it being left to the second division to give battle to the German fleet. The general orders given to the fleet for the attack will then only apply to the second division. His Majesty's Government expects that the division will be able to defeat the enemy, even without the help of the first division. As soon as the scouts of the second division have driven the German guardships from the mouth of the West Schelde, the left wing of the fighting ships will open fire on Flushing, the right on the land fortifications of the south bank. The wings are not to stop, but to advance with the rest of the fleet, and the entire division will press on to Antwerp or until it meets the German fighting fleet, which must be attacked with the greatest vigour.

"The precise details of the manner of attack are left to Vice-Admiral Domvile.

"If, contrary to expectation, the German fleet, at the beginning of the attack in the mouth of the Schelde, should decide upon an advance, the admiral commanding must act upon his own judgment, according to circumstances; but, above all, it should be remembered that it is of more importance to capture as many German ships as possible than to destroy them, so that the captured ships may be used by us during the further course of the war."

The Prince-Admiral had listened in silence while Heideck was reading. The excitement which what he had heard had caused him was plainly reflected in his features.

"There seems a strong internal probability that these orders are genuine," he said thoughtfully; "but I should like to have further and more positive proof of it; for it is quite possible that it is intentionally designed to mislead us. Where does this document come from, Herr major?"

"I have already most humbly reported to your Royal Highness that I have induced the skipper Brandelaar, whom I arrested as an English spy, to act for the future in our interest. Brandelaar's boat brought this order."

"Where is this man?"

"His boat lies in Flushing harbour."

"And how did Brandelaar get possession of it?"

"I did not get it from Brandelaar himself, but from a lady, an Englishwoman, who crossed with him from Dover. My honour imposes silence upon me. I must not mention this lady's name, but I am firmly convinced and believe that I can guarantee that the document in Admiral Hollway's office has been copied word for word."

"We can soon find means of convincing ourselves whether the British fleet is preparing to carry out these orders. Then at last the time for energetic action would have arrived. His Majesty has foreseen some such advance on the part of the British fleet, and we have now to carry out the plan of the supreme commander. I thank you, Herr major!"

Heideck bowed and turned to go. He felt that he could endure it no longer, and it was only with an effort that he maintained his erect, military bearing.

When he reached the threshold, the Prince turned to him again, and said, "I think I shall be doing you an honour, Herr major, if I give you the opportunity of witnessing, by my side, the events of that great and glorious day in the life of our youthful fleet. Report yourself to me on the morning of the 15th of July on board my flagship. I will see that your present post is provided for."

"Your Royal Highness is very gracious."

"You have a claim on my thanks. Au revoir, then, Herr major."

The Prince immediately summoned the adjutant on duty, and ordered him to have several copies of the English naval plan of attack prepared at once.

One of these was intended for the admiral in command of the French fleet at Cherbourg. The Prince gave the imperial messenger, who was to convey the document to him, an autograph letter in which he urged upon the admiral to do his utmost to reach Flushing on the morning of the 15th with as strong a fighting fleet as possible, so as to assist the German fleet in its engagement with the numerically superior fleet of the English.

XXXII
NEWS OF AN OLD FRIEND

Dear Friend and Comrade,--Although it is still painful for me to write, I cannot deny myself the pleasure of being the first to congratulate you on receiving the Order of St. Vladimir. A friend in the War Office has just informed me that the announcement has appeared in the Gazette. I hope that this decoration, which you so fully earned by your services at the occupation of Simla, will cause you some satisfaction. You are aware that the Vladimir can only be bestowed on Russians or foreigners in the service of Russia, and thus you will be one of the few German officers whose breast is adorned with this mark of distinction so highly prized in this country.

"You will be surprised that my congratulations are sent from St. Petersburg; no doubt you thought of me as still in sunny India, the theatre of our mutual adventures in the war. I should certainly have remained there till the end of the campaign, had not an English bullet temporarily put an end to my military activity--all too soon for my ambition, as you can imagine. Uninjured in two great battles and a number of trifling skirmishes, I was unhappily destined to be incapacitated in quite an unimportant and inglorious encounter. Had I not been saved by an heroic woman, you would have heard no more of your old friend Tchajawadse, except that he was one of those who had remained on the field of honour.

"Can you guess the name of this woman, comrade? I do not think you can have entirely forgotten my supposed page Georgi, and I am telling you nothing new to-day in lifting the veil of the secrecy, with which for obvious reasons I was obliged to shroud his relations to me in India. Georgi was a girl, and for years she has been dearer to me than anyone else. She was of humble birth, and possessed little of what we call culture. But, nevertheless, she was to me the dearest creature that I have ever met on my wanderings through two continents; a wonderful compound of savagery and goodness of heart, of ungovernable pride and unselfish, devoted affection--a child and a heroine. She had given herself to me, and followed me on my journeys from pure inclination, not for the sake of any advantage. It had been her own wish to play the part of a servant. I do not, however, mean to say that she never made use of the power she possessed over me, for she was proud, and knew how to govern.

"Once, at the beginning of our Indian journey, extremely irritated by her obstinate pride, I raised my hand against her. One look from her brought me to my senses before the punishment followed. Afterwards, when my blood had long cooled, she said to me, her eyes still blazing with anger, 'If you had really struck me I should have left you at once, and no entreaties would ever have induced me to return to you.' I laughed at her words, but from that time exercised more control over myself. We lived in perfect harmony till the day when Georgi saved your life in Lahore, my valued comrade. It was she who brought me the terrible news that you were being led away to death. I had never seen the girl so fearfully excited before. Her eyes glistened and her whole frame trembled. It seemed as if she would have driven me forward with the lash, that I might not be too late. I myself was too anxious to worry my head much about the girl's singular excitement. But after you were happily saved, when you were concealed in my tent, and I looked for Georgi to tell her of the result of my intervention, she fell into such a paroxysm of joy that my jealous suspicions were aroused. Carried away by excitement I flung an insult at her, and then, when she answered me defiantly--to her misfortune and mine I had my riding-whip in my hand--I committed a hateful act, which I would rather have recalled than any of my other numerous follies. She received the blow in silence. The next moment she had disappeared, and I waited in vain for her return. Till we left Simla I had her searched for everywhere, but no trace of her could be found. I myself then gave her up for lost. After our return to Lahore, when we were marching on to Delhi, I occasionally heard of a girl wearing Indian dress who had appeared in the neighbourhood of our troop and resembled my lost page Georgi. But as soon as I made inquiries after this girl it seemed as if the earth had swallowed her up, and under the rapidly changing impressions of the war her image gradually faded from my mind.

"During a reconnaissance near Lucknow, which I had undertaken with my regimental staff and a small escort, my own carelessness led us into an ambuscade set by the English, which cost most of my companions their lives. At the beginning of the encounter a shot in the back had unhorsed me. I was taken for dead, and those few of my companions who were able to save themselves by flight had no time to take the fallen with them. After lying for a long time unconscious, I saw, on awaking, a number of armed Indians plundering the dead and wounded. One of the brown devils approached me. When he saw me lifting myself up to grasp my revolver, he rushed upon me brandishing his sword. I parried the first thrust at my head with my right arm. Defenceless as I was, I was already prepared for the worst. But at the moment, when the rascal was lifting up his arm for another thrust, he reeled backwards and collapsed without uttering a sound. It was Georgi, who had saved my life by a well-directed shot.

"She had accompanied the dragoons sent from our camp to recover the dead and wounded, and had got considerably in advance of the horsemen. Hence it had been possible for her to save me.

"I was too weak to ask her many questions, and my memory is a blank as to the few moments of this meeting.

"For a week I lay between life and death. Then my iron constitution triumphed. You can imagine, my dearest friend, how great my desire was to see Georgi again. But she was no longer in the camp, and no one could tell me where she was. She disappeared again as suddenly as she had appeared on that day. This time I must make up my mind to the conviction that I have lost her for ever. While on my sick bed I received a command to repair to St. Petersburg. At the same time I was highly flattered to learn that I had been promoted, and as soon as my condition permitted it, I started on my journey.

"Pardon me, dear friend, for lingering so long over a personal matter, which, after all, can have very little interest for you.

"You are as well informed as myself of the manifold changes of this war, which has already destroyed the value of untold millions, and has cost hundreds of thousands of promising human lives. I could almost envy you for being still spared to be an eyewitness of the great events, while I am condemned to the role of an inactive spectator. But I do not believe the struggle will last much longer. The sacrifices which it imposes on the people are too great to be endured many months longer. Everything is pressing to a speedy and decisive result, and I have no doubt what that result will be. For although the defeats and losses sustained by the English are partly compensated by occasional successes, one great naval victory of the allies would finally decide the issue against Great Britain. Hitherto, both sides have hesitated to bring about this decisive result, but all here are convinced that the next few weeks will at last bring those great events on the water, so long and so eagerly expected.

"To my surprise, I see that our treaty of peace with Japan is still the subject of hostile criticism in the foreign Press. Certainly, in the second phase of the campaign, the fortune of war had turned in our favour, but the struggle for India was so important for Russia that she was unwilling to divide her forces any longer. Hence we were able to build a golden bridge for Japan, and hence the peace of Nagasaki. The German Imperial Chancellor is highly popular in Russia also, owing to the part he took in the conclusion of the peace.

"Have you had the opportunity of approaching the Imperial Chancellor? This Baron Grubenhagen must be a man of strong personality.

"I am sending this letter to you by way of Berlin, for I do not know where you are at this moment. I hope it will reach you, and that you will occasionally find time to gladden your old friend Tchajawadse by letting him know that you are still alive."

Heideck had glanced rapidly through the Prince's letter, written in French, which he had found waiting for him after his return from Antwerp. Not even the news of the honourable distinction conferred by the bestowal of the Russian order had been able to evoke a sign of joy on his grave countenance. The amiable Russian Prince and his beautiful page were to him like figures belonging to a remote past, that lay an endless distance behind him. The events of the last twenty-four hours had shaken him so violently that what might perhaps a few days before have aroused his keenest interest now seemed a matter of indifference and no concern of his.

At this moment the orderly announced a man in sailor's dress, and Heideck knew that it could only be Brandelaar. The skipper had already given the information which he had brought from Dover to the officer on duty who had taken Heideck's place. If they were not exactly military secrets which by that means became known to the German military authorities, some items of the various information might prove of importance as affecting the Prince-Admiral's arrangements.

Heideck assumed that Brandelaar had now come for his promised reward. But as the skipper, after receiving the money, kept turning his hat between his fingers, like a man who does not like to perform a painful errand or make a disagreeable request, Heideck asked in astonishment: "Have you anything else to say to me, Brandelaar?"

Only after considerable hesitation he replied, "Yes, Herr major, I was to bring you a greeting--you will know who sent it."

"I think I can guess. You have seen the lady again since yesterday evening?"

"The lady came to me last night at the inn and demanded to be taken back to Dover at once. But I thought you would not like it."

"So then you refused?"

Brandelaar continued to stare in front of him at the floor.

"The lady would go--in spite of the bad weather. And she would not be satisfied till I had persuaded my friend Van dem Bosch to take her in his cutter to Dover?"

"This was last night?"

"Yes--last night."

"And what more?" persisted Heideck.

"He came back at noon to-day. They had a misfortune on the way."

Heideck's frame shook convulsively. A fearful suspicion occurred to him. He needed all his strength of will to control himself.

"And the lady?"

"Herr major, it was the lady who met with an accident. She fell overboard on the journey."

Heideck clasped the back of the chair before him with both hands. Every drop of blood had left his face.

"Fell--overboard? Good God, man--and she was not saved?"

Brandelaar shook his hand.

"No, Herr major! She would stay on deck in spite of the storm, though Van dem Bosch kept asking her to go below. When a violent squall broke the halyard, she was knocked overboard by the gaff. As the sea was running high, there was no chance of saving her."

Heideck had covered his face with his hand. A dull groan burst from his violently heaving breast and a voice within him exclaimed--

"The guilt is yours. She sought death of her own accord, and it was you who drove her to it!"

His voice sounded dry and harsh when he turned to the skipper and said--

"I thank you for your information, Brandelaar. Now leave me alone."

XXXIII
THE LANDING IN SCOTLAND

The ninth and tenth army corps had collected at the inlet of Kid harbour. The town of Kiel and its environs resounded with the clattering of arms, the stamping of horses and the joyful songs of the soldiers, who, full of hope, were expecting great and decisive events. But no one knew anything for certain about the object of the impending expedition.

From the early hours of the morning of the 13th of July an almost endless stream of men, horses, and guns poured over the landing-bridges, which connected the giant steamers of the shipping companies with the harbour quays. Other divisions of troops were taken on board in boats, and on the evening of the 14th the whole field army, consisting of 60,000 men, was embarked.

Last of all, the general commanding, accompanied by the Imperial Chancellor, proceeded in a launch on board the large cruiser Konig Wilhelm, which lay at anchor in the Bay of Holtenall. Immediately afterwards, three rockets, mounting brightly against the dark sky, went up from the flagship. At this signal, the whole squadron started slowly in the direction of the Kaiser Wilhelm Canal.

The transport fleet consisted of about sixty large steamers, belonging to the North-German Lloyd, the Hamburg-America, and the Stettin companies. They were protected by the battleships Baden, Wurttemberg, Bayern, and Sachsen, the large cruisers Kaiser and Deutschland, the small cruisers Gazelle, Prinzess Wilhelm, Irene, Komet, and Meteor, and the torpedo divisions D 5 and D 6, accompanied by their torpedo-boat divisions.

The last torpedo-boat had long left the harbour, when, about eleven o'clock in the forenoon of the 15th of July, the dull thunder of the English ironclads resounded before the fortifications of the inlet of Kiel, answered by the guns of the

German fortress.

Bright sunshine was breaking through the light clouds when the Konig Wilhelm entered the Elbe at Brunsbuttel. The boats of the torpedo division, hastening forward, reported the mouth of the river free from English warships, and a wireless message was received from Heligoland in confirmation of this.

The squadron proceeded at full speed to the north-west. The torpedo division D 5 reconnoitred in advance, the small, swift boats being followed by the cruisers Prinzess Wilhelm and Irene, which from their high rigging were especially adapted for scouting operations and carried the necessary apparatus for wireless telegraphy. The rest of the fleet, whose speed had to be regulated by that of the Konig Wilhelm, followed at the prescribed intervals.

When the sharp outlines of the red cliffs of Heligoland appeared, the German cruiser Seeadler came from the island to meet the squadron and reported that the coast ironclads Aegir and Odin, the cruisers Hansa, Vineta, Freya, and Hertha, together with the torpedo-boats, had set out from Wilhelmshaven during the night and had seen nothing of the enemy. The sea appeared free. All the available English warships of the North Sea squadron had advanced to attack Antwerp.

Since the transport fleet did not appear to need reinforcements, it proceeded on its way west-north-west with its attendant warships, the Wilhelmshaven fleet remaining at Heligoland.

What was its destination?

Only a few among the many thousands could have given an answer, and they remained silent. The red cliffs of Heligoland had long since disappeared in the distance. Hours passed, but nothing met the eyes of the eagerly gazing warriors, save the boundless, gently rippling sea and the crystal-clear blue vault of heaven, stretched above it like a huge bell.

"What is our destination?"

It could not be the coast of England, which would have been reached long ago. But where was the landing to take place, if not there? To what distant shore was the German army being taken, the largest whose destinies had ever been entrusted to the treacherous waves of the sea?

When daylight again brought a report from the scouts that the enemy's ships were nowhere to be seen, the Commander-in-Chief of the army could not help expressing his surprise to the Admiral that the English had apparently entirely neglected scouting in the North Sea, and further, that they did not even see any merchant vessels.

"The explanation of this apparently surprising fact is not very remote, Your Excellency," replied the Admiral. "We should hardly sight any merchantmen, since maritime trade is now almost entirely at a standstill, owing to the insecurity of the seas. We have not met a flotilla of fishing-boats, since in this part of the North Sea there are no fishing-grounds. We see none of the enemy's ships, since the English have most likely calculated every other possibility except our attempting to land in Scotland."

"Your explanation is obvious, Herr Admiral; nevertheless, it seems to me that our enemy must have neglected to take the necessary precautions in keeping a look-out."

"Your Excellency must not draw an offhand comparison between operations on land and on sea. The conditions in the latter are essentially different. I do not doubt for a moment that there is a sufficient number of English scouts in the North Sea; if we have really escaped their notice, the fortune of war has been favourable to us. I may tell Your Excellency that, even during our manoeuvres in the Baltic, where we know the course as well as the speed and strength of the marked enemy, he has sometimes succeeded in making his way through, unseen by our scouts. Perhaps this will mitigate your judgment of this apparent want of foresight on the part of the English."

At last, on the evening of the 16th of July, land was reported by the Konig Wilhelm. The end of the journey was in sight, and the news spread rapidly that it was the coast of Scotland rising from the waves.

"We are going to enter the Firth of Forth," was the general opinion. Even the brave soldiers, who perhaps heard the name for the first time in their lives, repeated the word with as important an air as if all the secrets of the military staff had been all at once revealed to them.

In the red light of the setting sun both shores appeared tinged with violet from the deep-blue sky and the grey-blue sea, the north shore being further off than the south. Favoured by a calm sea, the squadron, extended in close order to a distance of about five knots, made for the entrance of the Firth of Forth.

Full of expectation, the expeditionary army saw the vast, bold undertaking develop before its eyes. For nine hundred years no hostile army had landed on the coast of England. Certainly, in ancient times Britain had had to fight against invading enemies: Julius Caesar had entered as a conqueror, Canute the Great, King of Denmark, had subdued the country. The Angles and Saxons had come over from Germany, to make themselves masters of the land. Harold the Fairhaired, King of Norway, had landed in England. But since the time of William of Normandy, who defeated the Saxons at Hastings and set up the rule of the Normans in England, not even her most powerful enemies, neither Philip of Spain nor the great Napoleon, had succeeded in landing their troops on the sea-girt soil of England.

Would a German army now succeed?

The outlines of the country became clearer and clearer; some even believed they could see the lofty height of Edinburgh Castle on the horizon. But soon the distant view was obscured and darkness slowly came on.

Hitherto not a single hostile ship had been seen. But now, when the greater part of the squadron had already entered the bay, the searchlights discovered two English cruisers whose presence had already been reported by the advance boats of the torpedo division.

In view of our great superiority, these cruisers declined battle, and by hauling down their flag, signified their readiness to surrender. From the sea, nothing remained to hinder the landing of the troops. The transports approached the south shore of the bay, on which Edinburgh and the harbour town of Leith are situated; and, after casting anchor, landed the troops in boats by the electric light. The infantry immediately occupied the positions favourable to meet any attack that might be made. But nothing happened to prevent the landing. The Scottish population remained perfectly calm, so that the disembarkation was completed without disturbance.

The population of Leith and the inhabitants of Edinburgh, who had hurried up full of curiosity, beheld, to their boundless astonishment, a spectacle almost incomprehensible to them, carried out with admirable precision under the bright electric light from the German ships.

The people had taken the keenest interest in the great war of England against the allied Powers--Germany, France, and Russia--but with a feeling that it was a matter which chiefly concerned the Government, the Army, and the Navy. They were painfully aware that things were going worse and worse for them, but were convinced that the Government would soon overthrow the enemy. Everyone knew that the Russians had penetrated into India, but the great mass of the people did not trouble about that. It could only be a passing misfortune, and trade, which was at present ruined, would soon revive and be all the more flourishing. But the idea that an enemy, a continental army, could land on the coast of Great Britain, that German or French soldiers could ever set foot on British soil, had seemed to Scotsmen so remote a contingency that they now appeared completely overcome by the logic of accomplished facts.

About noon on the following day the two army corps were already south of Leith. A brigade had been pushed forward towards the south; the rest of the troops had bivouacked, that the men might recuperate after their two days' sea journey.

The quartermasters had purchased provisions for ready money in the town, the villages, and the scattered farmhouses. The warships filled their bunkers from the abundant stock of English coal, guardships being detached to ensure the safety of the squadron. The Admiral had ordered that, after coaling, the warships should take up a position at the entrance to the bay, the transports remaining in the harbour. In the possible event of the appearance of a superior English squadron the whole fleet was to leave the Firth of Forth as rapidly as possible and disperse in all directions. Certainly in that case the army would be deprived of the means of returning, but the military authorities were convinced that the appearance of an army of 60,000 German troops on British soil would practically mean the end of the war, especially as an equally strong French corps was to land in the south. The military authorities consequently thought they need not trouble themselves further about the possibility of the troops having to return.

The garrison of Edinburgh had surrendered without resistance, since it would have been far too weak to offer any opposition to the invading army. Accordingly the German officers and soldiers could move about in the town without hindrance. A number of despatches and fresh war bulletins were found which threw some light upon the strategic position, although they were partly obscure, and partly contained obvious falsehoods.

A great naval battle was said to have taken place off Flushing on the 15th of

July, ending in the retreat of the German and French fleets with heavy losses. It was further reported that the British fleet had destroyed Flushing and bombarded several of the Antwerp forts. Lastly, according to the newspapers, the English fleet which had been stationed before Copenhagen had entered Kid harbour and captured all the German ships inside, the loss of the English battleships at the Kieler Fohrde being admitted. The German officers were convinced that only the report of the loss of the two battleships deserved credit, since the English would hardly have invented such bad news. Everything else, from the position of things, bore the stamp of improbability on the face of it.

The trumpets blew, the soldiers grasped their arms, the battalions began their march. The batteries clattered along with a dull rumble. In four columns, by four routes, side by side the four divisions started for the south.

XXXIV
THE BATTLE OF FLUSHING

The strategy of red tape, by which the Commander-in-Chief's hands were tied, was destined, as in so many previous campaigns, to prove on this occasion also a fatal error to the English.

Sir Percy Domvile, the British admiral, had received with silent rage the order of battle communicated to him from London--the same order that had fallen into the hands of the Germans. More than once already he had attempted to show the Lords of the Admiralty what injury might be caused by being tied to strict written orders in situations that could not be foreseen. He now held in his own hands the proof how little the officials, pervaded by the consciousness of their own importance and superior wisdom, were disposed to allow themselves to be taught. But he was too much of a service-man not to acquiesce in the orders of the supreme court with unquestioning obedience. Certainly, if he had been able to gauge in advance the far-reaching consequences of the mistake already committed, he would probably, as a patriot, rather have sacrificed himself than become the instrument for carrying out the fundamentally erroneous tactics of the plan of battle communicated to him. For more was now at stake than the proud British nation had ever risked before in a naval engagement. It was a question of England's prestige as the greatest naval power in the world, perhaps of the final issue of this campaign which had been so disastrous for Great Britain. All-powerful Albion, the dreaded mistress of the seas, was now fighting for honour and existence. A great battle lost might easily mean a blow from which the British lion, wounded to death, would never be able to recover.

. . . .

At the time when the Konig Wilhelm entered the Kaiser Wilhelm Canal at the head of the German transport fleet, the Prince-Admiral, who had hoisted his flag on the Wittelsbach, led the fighting fleet from the harbour of Antwerp into the Zuid Bevelanden Canal, which connects the East and West Schelde, and separates the island of Walcheren from Zuid Bevelanden. Anchor was then cast.

His squadron consisted of the battleships of the Wittelsbach class--Mecklenburg, Schwaben, Zahringen, Wettin, and Wittelsbach (the flagship of the Prince-Admiral), and the battleships of the Kaiser class--Kaiser Wilhelm der Grosse, Barbarossa, Karl der Grosse, Wilhelm II., and Friedrich III.

These ironclads were accompanied by the large cruisers Friedrich Karl, Prinz Adalbert, Prinz Heinrich, Furst Bismarck, Viktoria Luise, Kaiserin Augusta, and the small cruisers Berlin, Hamburg, Bremen, Undine, Arcona, Frauenlob, and Medusa.

The torpedo flotilla at the Prince's disposal consisted of the torpedo-boats S 102 to 107, G 108 to 113, S 114 to 125, with the division boats D 10, D 9, D 7, and D 8, built on the scale of destroyers.

The three fast cruisers Friedrich Karl, Prinz Adalbert and Kaiserin Augusta, with the torpedo-boats S 114 to 120, had been sent on as scouts, to announce the approach of the enemy in good time. The cruisers had been ordered to post themselves thirty knots west-north-west of Flushing at intervals of five knots, while the torpedo-boats patrolled on all sides to keep a look-out. After having reported the approach of the English fleet to the main squadron by wireless telegraphy, the scouts were to retire before the enemy out of range into the West Schelde, and at the same time to keep up such a fire in their boilers that the clouds of thick smoke might deceive the enemy as to the size and number of the retiring ships. When out of sight of the English, they were to wheel round and show themselves, and, if circumstances permitted, take up the positions previously assigned them; otherwise they were to act according to circumstances.

The object of this manoeuvre, calculated to mislead the enemy, was completely attained.

A signal informed the Prince-Admiral that the English were in sight, and a torpedo-boat detached from the scouting squadron brought more exact information as to the number and formation of the enemy's ships--information which exactly corresponded with the instructions given in the order of battle, and was a fresh proof that it was intended to adhere to them.

This provided a sure foundation for the tactical operations of the German fleet. No alteration was necessary in the course of action decided upon at the council of war on the previous day, and no fresh instructions had to be issued to individual commanders.

The order of battle settled at this council of war ran, in the main, as follows:--

"The squadron will lie at anchor off Zuid-Beveland, fires banked, so that they can get up steam in a quarter of an hour. The battleships will anchor in double line, according to their tactical numbers. The cruisers between Nord-Beveland and Zuid-Beveland. The torpedo-boats with their division boats behind.

"At the signal 'weigh anchor' the ships carry out the order according to their tactical number; the battleships through the Roompot; the cruisers will re-enter the West Schelde through the canal and lie off Flushing athwart.

"The two other torpedo-boat divisions will accompany the squadron."

The course of events developed exactly in accordance with these dispositions.

When the approach of the enemy's ships was announced, the Prince-Admiral's flaghip signalled: "Weigh anchor! hoist top pennants! clear for action! follow in the Admiral's wake! cruiser division and torpedo-boats execute orders!"

Keeping close under the coast of Walcheren, the German squadron, full steam up, advanced to meet the enemy.

Meanwhile the approaching English, having left their hospital and munition ships and colliers in the open under the protection of the cruisers and taken up their appointed positions, opened fire at a distance of about 6,000 yards on Flushing and Fort Frederik Hendrik.

The English Admiral adhered so strictly to his instructions that, with an incomprehensible carelessness, he neglected to search the East Schelde with his second squadron, or even with his scouts. The entry of the German ships which had been sent back from the open into the West Schelde, evidently appeared to Sir Percy Domvile a sufficient confirmation of the assumption that the whole German fleet was in this arm of the river's mouth, for the clouds of smoke which they emitted rendered an accurate computation of their strength impossible.

Thus, the Prince-Admiral's squadron was enabled to approach the enemy so far unobserved that it would be able to take the British fleet in the flank, when it had reached the west point of Walcheren.

At the signal: "Full steam ahead!" the German ships in the formation agreed steamed against the surprised English, and opened fire from their bow-guns. Naturally, the English Admiral at once ordered the first squadron to take up its position behind the second, turned left with both, and went to meet the enemy in double line.

This was the opportune moment, foreseen in the Prince's plan of battle, for the advance of the cruisers lying in the West Schelde. In order to deceive the enemy as to their number, they rapidly approached, accompanied by the torpedo-boats which again sent up their clouds of smoke. The English Admiral, completely surprised by the double attack, was obliged to divide his attention.

Certainly this torpedo attack was still a hazardous undertaking, under existing conditions. The English shot well, and two German boats were sunk by the enemy's shells. Three others, however, hit their mark, damaging three of the English ships so severely that they were incapable of manoeuvring.

It was especially disadvantageous to the English that their torpedo-boats, owing to the unforeseen change in the formation of the battleships, were deprived of the necessary protection. The German destroyers were not slow to make full use of this favourable situation, and began to chase them. In this engagement, which the speed of the little vessels rendered especially exciting for those who took part in it, the pursuers succeeded in destroying four English torpedo-boats without themselves suffering any damage worth mentioning. The others escaped, and, for the time, might be regarded as out of action.

The enemy having altered his front, the Prince-Admiral had turned right about, so that he might enter into action with all the guns of one side. The English Admiral also doubled, but the manoeuvre proved the cause of a fatal misfortune. Whether the disturbance of the tactical unity by the loss of the three torpedoed vessels was the cause of it, or whether the first and second divisions were unaccustomed to manoeuvre together, the Formidable carried out orders so clumsily, that she was rammed amidships by her neighbour the Renown, and immediately heeled over and sunk in a few minutes, carrying hundreds of brave English sailors with her into the deep.

The Renown herself, whose ram had caused the fearful disaster, had not escaped without severe injury in the collision, which had shattered the mighty floating fortress in all its joints. The two first fore compartments, as the bulkheads did not hold together, had filled with water. This caused the vessel to heel over; her value as a fighting instrument was thereby sensibly diminished.

Thus the first great catastrophe in the battle was caused, not by the power of the enemy, but by the clumsy manoeuvring of a friendly ship. This naturally caused many of the spectators, deeply affected by the sinking of the magnificent vessel and her gallant crew, to ask themselves whether the great perfection attained in the construction of modern ships of war was not to a great extent counterbalanced by the defects that were combined with the increasing size and fighting strength of these gigantic ironclads. No ship of the line, no frigate, not even the little gun-boat of earlier times could have disappeared from the line of battle so speedily and without leaving a trace behind as the Formidable, built of mighty dimensions and equipped with all the appliances of naval technique. No doubt her armour-plate and steel turrets would have been able successfully to resist a hail of the heaviest projectiles, but a misunderstood steering order had been sufficient to send her to the bottom. Neither the double bottoms nor the division of the bulkheads, which should have prevented the inrush of an excessive amount of water, had been able to avert the fate which threatens every modern ironclad when severely damaged below the water-line. The wooden ship of former times might have been riddled like a sieve without sinking. But the stability of a modern ironclad could be endangered by a single leak, whether caused by a torpedo or a ram, to such an extent that the gigantic mass of iron would be drawn down into the depths by its own weight in a few minutes.

A running fire now went on at a distance of about 2,000 yards, in which the superiority of the Krupp guns was as clearly manifested as the admirable training of the German artillerists, in which the English were far inferior. Certainly, the German ships also suffered various injuries, but no serious damage had as yet occurred.

The three torpedoed and helpless English warships offered especially favourable targets to the German cruisers. The latter, taking up positions at a suitable distance, kept up such a heavy fire upon the vessels, which could scarcely move, that their surrender was inevitable. But before deciding on this, the English offered an heroic resistance, and many of their shots took effect. The conning tower of the

Friedrich Karl was pierced by a shell, and the brave commander with those around him found a glorious soldier's death. Other more or less serious injuries were sustained, and it was almost a miracle that no vital damage was done to any part of the ships' hulls.

After the three English ships had been put out of action, it was unnecessary for the cruiser division to remain any longer in this quarter of the scene of action. They accordingly proceeded with the utmost despatch to where the Prince-Admiral was engaged in the main fight with the battleships. Here, indeed, assistance was needed. For, although four of the enemy's ships were lost, the superiority in numbers still remained with the English, especially as the Mecklenburg had been obliged to sheer off, her steering gear having been shot to pieces.

When the English Admiral saw the cruisers approaching, so that they could bring all their bow-guns to bear at once, he recognised that the decisive moment was at hand.

The cruisers' guns inflicted severe damage on the English, for the crews had practised shooting rapidly at a gradually diminishing distance. The high deck structures of the battleships offered an admirable target, so that in the extended English line of battle nearly every shot took effect.

For Sir Percy Domvile rapid and energetic action now became a necessary condition of self-preservation. In the circumstances, the capture of the German fleet, which according to the order of battle was to be the object aimed at, was no longer to be thought of; the only thing left to the Admiral was to endeavour to destroy as many of the enemy's ships as possible. The British flagship signalled "Right about," and the commandants knew that this was as good as an order to ram the German ironclads.

But this manoeuvre, by which alone Sir Percy Domvile could meet the danger that threatened him in consequence of the attack from two sides, had been provided for by the Prince-Admiral. It had been taken into consideration at the council of war held on the previous evening, and each commander had received instructions as to the tactics to be pursued in such an event. A special signal had been agreed upon, and as soon as the English ironclads were observed wheeling round, it was hoisted on the Admiral's ship. Each of the German battleships immediately took up the position prescribed by the plan of battle. The squadron separated into two halves; the first division, wheeling into line behind the flagship, made "left about" with it, while the second division, also making "left about," took up its position between the left wing ship.

These tactics, quite unknown to him, were completely unexpected by the English Admiral. His purpose was entirely frustrated by the speedy and clever manoeuvre of the German ships, the plan of destruction failed, and his own ironclads, while proceeding athwart, had to stand a terrible fire right and left, which was especially disastrous to the two ships on the wings. Overwhelmed by a hail of light and heavy projectiles, and in addition hit by torpedoes, they were in a few minutes put out of action; one of them, the Victorious, sharing the fate of the unlucky Formidable, sank with its crew of more than 700 men beneath the waves.

But the youthful German fleet had also received its baptism of fire in this decisive battle.

All the means of destruction with which the modern art of war is acquainted were employed by each of the two opponents to snatch victory from his adversary. The shells of the heavy guns were combined with the projectiles of the lighter armament and the machine-guns posted in the fighting-tops, so that in the real sense of the word it was a "hail of projectiles," which came down in passing on the ships wrapped in smoke and steam.

Hermann Heideck had become so thoroughly familiar in India with the horrors of war on land in their various forms, that he believed his nerves were completely proof against the horrible sight of death and devastation. But the scenes which were being enacted around him in the comparatively narrow space of the magnificent flagship during this engagement, far surpassed in their awfulness everything that he had hitherto seen. Heideck was full of admiration for the heroic courage, contempt of death, and discipline of officers and men, not one of whom stirred a foot from the post assigned him.

As he only played the part of an inactive spectator in the drama that had now reached its climax, he was able to move freely over the ship. Wherever he went, the same spectacle of horrible destruction and heroic devotion to duty everywhere met his eye.

The men serving the guns in the turrets and casemates were enduring the pains of hell. In the low, ironclad chambers a fiery heat prevailed, which rendered even breathing difficult. The terrific noise and the superhuman excitement of the nerves seemed to have so dulled the men's senses, that they no longer had any clear idea of what was going on around them. Their faces did not wear that expression of rage and exasperation, which Heideck had seen in so many soldiers in the land battle at Lahore; rather, he observed a certain dull indifference, which could no longer be shaken by the horror of the situation.

A shell struck a battery before Heideck's eyes, exploded, and with its flying splinters struck down nearly all the men serving the guns. Happy were those who found death at once; for the injuries of those who writhed wounded on the ground were of a frightful nature. The red-hot pieces of iron, which tore the unhappy men's flesh and shattered their bones, at the same time inflicted fearful burns upon them. Indeed, Heideck would have regarded it as an act of humanity to have been allowed with a shot from a well-aimed revolver, to put an end to the sufferings of this or that unfortunate, whose skin and flesh hung in shreds from his body, or whose limbs were transformed into shapeless, bloody masses.

But those who had escaped injury, after a few moments' stupefaction, resumed their duty with the same mechanical precision as before. Amidst their dead and dying comrades, about whom nobody could trouble himself for the moment, they stood in the pools of warm, human blood, which made the deck slippery, and quietly served the gun which had not been seriously damaged.

A very young naval cadet, who had been sent down to the engine-room from the Prince-Admiral's conning-tower with an order, met Heideck on the narrow, suffocatingly hot passage. He was a slender, handsome youth with a delicate, boyish face. The blood was streaming over his eyes and cheeks from a wound in the forehead. He was obliged to lean with both hands against the wall for support, while, with a superhuman effort of will, he compelled his tottering knees to carry him forward, his sole thought being that he must keep upright until he had fulfilled his errand. When Heideck inquired sympathetically after the nature of his wound, he even attempted to wreathe his pale lips, quivering with pain, into a smile, for in spite of his seventeen years he felt himself at this moment quite a man and a soldier, to whom it was an honour and a delight to die for his country. But his heroic will was stronger than his body, wounded to death. In the attempt to assume an erect military bearing before the Major, he suddenly collapsed. He had just strength enough to give Heideck the Admiral's order and ask him to carry it out. Then his senses left him.

In another battery the store of ammunition had been exploded by a shell. Not a man had escaped alive. Heideck himself, although since the beginning of the engagement he had recklessly exposed himself to danger, had hitherto, by a miracle, escaped death that threatened him in a hundred different forms. He had been permitted, by express command of the Prince, to stay a considerable time in the upper conning-tower, from which the Imperial Admiral directed the battle, and the deliberate calmness of the supreme commander, steadily pursuing his object, had filled him with unshaken confidence in a victory for the German fleet, in spite of the numerical superiority of the English.

Ever since Heideck had heard the news of Edith Irwin's death from Brandelaar, all purely human feelings and sensations that connected him with life had died in his heart. He was no longer anything but the soldier, whose thoughts and efforts were filled exclusively with anxiety for the victory of his country's arms. All personal experiences were completely forgotten as if they had taken place ten years ago. At this moment, when the existence or extinction of nations was at stake, his own life was of so little importance to him that he was not even conscious of the foolhardy intrepidity with which he risked it at every step.

Majestic and powerful, sending forth death-dealing flashes from her turrets and portholes, the Wittelsbach had hitherto proceeded on her way, not heeding the wounds which the enemy's shot had inflicted in her hull. An almost thankful feeling for the glorious ship which carried him arose in Heideck's breast.

"You do honour to the great name you bear," he thought. Through smoke and steam he looked up at the conning-tower, where he knew the Prince-Admiral was. Then he saw it no more, for suddenly a thick, black cloud overspread his eyes. He had only felt a slight blow in his breast, but no pain. He tried to lift his hand to the place where he had been hit, but it sank powerlessly. It seemed as if he were being turned round in a circle by an invisible hand. Thousands of fiery sparks shot up suddenly from the dark cloud--the night closed completely round him--deep, impenetrable night, and still, solemn silence.

Major Hermann Heideck had found a hero's death.

. . . .

A torpedo-boat that had been summoned by signal hurried up at full speed to the Admiral's flagship which was lying on her side. A broadside torpedo had struck the Wittelsbach; and although there was no fear of her sinking, it was impossible for operations to be directed from her any longer.

Regardless of the danger it involved, the Prince-Admiral had himself and his staff transferred by the torpedo-boat to the Zahringen, on which his flag was at once hoisted.

. . . .

The progress of the engagement had hitherto been favourable to the German fleet to a surprising extent. Its losses were considerably less than those of its numerically far superior enemy, and its ships, with few exceptions, were still able to fight and manoeuvre. But as yet, considering the strength of the ships still at the enemy's disposal, it was too early to speak of a decision in favour of the German fleet. Although the clever manoeuvre of the German squadron had frustrated the intended attack of the English, and inflicted very considerable losses upon them, it might still be possible for Sir Percy Domvile to atone for his mistake and to bind the capricious fortune of war to his flag.

The same frightful scenes which Major Heideck had witnessed on board the Wittelsbach had also taken place on the other German battleships and cruisers. Blood flowed in rivers, and, if the murderous engagement continued much longer, the moment could not be far off when it would no longer be possible to fill the gaps caused by death in the ranks of the brave crews. A few luckily-aimed English torpedoes, and no genius in the supreme command, no heroism on the part of the captains, officers, and crew would have been able to avert disaster from the German arms.

Then, suddenly a fresh, apparently very powerful squadron, was sighted from the south-west, which, if it had proved to be a British reserve fleet, must have decided the victory at once in favour of the English.

The moments that passed until the question was definitely settled were moments of the keenest suspense and excitement for those on board the German vessels. The relief was so much the greater when it was seen to be no fresh hostile force, but Admiral Courtille's squadron, advancing at full speed, just at the right moment to decide the issue.

The state of affairs was now changed at one stroke so completely to the disadvantage of the English, that a British victory had become an impossibility. The intervention of the French squadron, still perfectly intact, consisting of ten battleships, ten large and ten small cruisers, was bound to bring about the annihilation of the English fleet. The English Admiral was quickwitted enough to gauge the situation correctly, as soon as he had recognised the approaching ships as the French fleet and assured himself of the enemy's strength. The orders given to form again for an attack were succeeded by fresh signals from the English flagship, ordering a rapid retreat. The English Admiral, regarding the battle as definitely lost, considered it his duty to save what could still be saved of the fleet under his charge. Before the French could actively intervene the English fleet steamed away at full speed to the north-west.

Thundering hurrahs on all the German ships acclaimed the victory announced by this retreat. The boats of the torpedo division and some swift cruisers were ordered to keep in touch with the fleeing enemy.

The French Admiral in command had gone on board the flagship Zahringen to place himself and his squadron under the command of the Prince-Admiral and to come to an arrangement as to the further joint operations of the combined fleets. For there was no doubt that the victory ought to be utilised at once to the fullest extent, if it were really to be decisive.

Deeply moved, the Prince embraced Admiral Courtille, and thanked him for appearing at the critical moment. The French Admiral, however, excused himself for intervening so late. "I was obliged," said he, "to wait till it was night and steer far out to the south-west before I could turn north; I had to do this, so as to be able to break through Prince Louis of Battenberg's blockading squadron without being seen, under cover of night."

Meanwhile, the scouts sent after the enemy had returned with the information that the English fleet had altered its course and appeared making for the Thames. Further pursuit was impossible, as the English Admiral had detached some ships, for which the German cruisers were not a match.

Previous arrangements had been made for transferring the dead and wounded to the ships signalled to for the purpose, and were carried out without great difficulty, the sea being now calmer. Now that the fearful battle had ceased, for the first time the crews became fully conscious of the horrors they had passed through. The rescue of the wounded showed what cruel sacrifices the battle had demanded. It was a difficult and melancholy task, which made many a sailor's heart beat with sorrow and compassion. The dead were for the most part horribly mangled by the splinters of the shells which had caused their death, and the injuries of the wounded, for whom the surgeons on board had, of course, only been able to provide first aid in the turmoil of battle, were nearly all so severe, that they could only be moved slowly.

After the German ships had signalled that they were again ready for action, those which had the dead and wounded on board, together with the German ships put out of action and the captured English ships, were ordered to make for Antwerp. The combined Franco-German fleet, under the supreme command of the Prince-Admiral, resumed its voyage in the direction of the mouth of the Thames.

XXXV
AT HAMPTON COURT

The long rows of windows in Hampton Court Palace were still a blaze of light, notwithstanding the lateness of the hour. The double post of the royal uhlans before the entrance was still busy, for the unceasing arrival and departure of officers of rank of the three allied nations demanded military honours. Immediately after the naval engagement at Flushing, so disastrous to the English, a large French army and some regiments of the Russian Imperial Guard had landed at Hastings and were now quartered at Aldershot, on the best of terms with the French and the German troops who had marched from Scotland. The Prince-Admiral's headquarters had been removed to Hampton Court, whose silent, venerable, and famous palace became suddenly the centre of stirring military and diplomatic life.

Any further serious military operations were hardly considered, for the supposition that the landing of large hostile armies would practically mean the end of the campaign, had proved correct.

In the resistance which bodies of English troops had attempted to offer to the French advance on London, the volunteers had clearly shown their bravery and patriotic devotion; but had been unable to check the victorious course of their better-led opponents. Accordingly, an armistice had been concluded for the purpose of considering the terms of peace offered by England, even before the German troops advancing from Scotland had had the opportunity of taking part in the land operations.

The conclusion of peace, eagerly desired by all the civilised nations of the world, might be considered assured, although, no doubt, its final ratification would be preceded by long and difficult negotiations. The idea, mooted by the German

Imperial Chancellor, of summoning a general congress at the Hague, at which not only the belligerents, but all other countries should be represented, had met with general approval, since all the states were interested in the reorganisation of the relations of the Powers. But the settlement of the preliminaries of peace was necessarily the business of the belligerents, and it was for this purpose that the German Imperial Chancellor, Freiherr von Grubenhagen, the French Foreign Minister, M. Delcasse, and the Russian Secretary of State, M. de Witte, accompanied by Count Lamsdorff, and a full staff of officials and diplomatic assistants, had met at Hampton Court Palace.

The preliminary negotiations between these statesmen and the English plenipotentiaries, Mr. Balfour, Prime Minister and First Lord of the Treasury, and the Marquis of Londonderry, Lord President of the Privy Council, were carried on with restless eagerness. But the strictest silence in regard to their results up to the present was observed by all who had taken part in them.

The conduct of the Prince-Admiral was an obvious proof that the military leaders were not inactive, in spite of the commencement of peace negotiations. Although he took no part in the diplomatic proceedings and simply occupied himself with military affairs, not only every minute of the day, but a good part of the night, was spent by him in work and discussions with his staff officers, with the chief officers of the land forces, and with the chief commanders of the allied Franco-Russian army. Everyone was full of admiration for the Prince's never-failing vigour and indefatigable power of work; his tall, slender, Teutonic form, and fair-bearded face, with the quiet, clear sailor's eyes, never failed to impress all who came in contact with him. Only his imperial brother, who held in his hand all the threads of political action, could rival the Prince in the traditional Hohenzollern capacity for work at this important time.

It was close on midnight when, after a long and lively consultation, the French general, Jeannerod, left the Prince's study. No sooner had the door closed behind him than the adjutant on duty, with an evident expression of astonishment in the sound of his voice, announced: "His Excellency the Imperial Chancellor, Frieherr von Grubenhagen."

The Prince advanced to the middle of the room to meet his visitor and shook him heartily by the hand.

"I thank Your Excellency for granting me an interview with you to-day, although it is so late and you are overwhelmed with work. I had a special reason for wishing to confer with you, which you will understand when I tell you that all kinds of rumours have reached me as to exaggerated demands on the part of our allies. My previous attitude will have shown you that I have no intention of interfering in diplomatic negotiations, or even exercising my influence in one direction or another. I feel that I am here not as a statesman, but simply as a soldier; and for that very reason I think you can speak the more openly to me. I have been told that the complete annihilation of England is intended as indispensable to the conditions of peace."

The Chancellor, whose manly, determined face showed no signs of exhaustion, notwithstanding his almost superhuman labours, looked frankly at the Prince and shook his head.

"Your Royal Highness has been incorrectly informed. Neither we nor our allies have the intention of annihilating England. Certainly we are all fully agreed that this fearful war must not be waged in vain, and that the reward must correspond with the greatness of the sacrifice at which it has been purchased."

"And to whom is the reward to fall?"

"To all the nations, Your Royal Highness. It would have been a sin to kindle this universal conflagration had it not been taken for granted that its refining flames would prepare the ground for the happiness and peace of the world. For centuries Great Britain has misused her power to increase her own wealth at the cost of others. Unscrupulously she grabbed everything she could lay hands on, and, injuring at every step important and vital interests of other nations, she challenged that resistance which has now shattered her position as a power in the world. The happiness of the peoples can only be restored by a peace assured for years, and only a just division of the dominion of the earth can guarantee the peace of the world. Therefore England must necessarily surrender an essential part of her possessions over sea. Russia wants the way free to the Indian Ocean, for only if she has a sufficient number of harbours open all the year round will the enormous riches of her soil cease to be a lifeless possession. And France--"

"Let us keep to Russia first, Your Excellency. Has the Russian Government already formulated its demands?"

"These demands are the essential outcome of the military situation; they culminate in the cession of British India to Russia. Whatever else our Eastern neighbour may strive to gain, is intended to ensure the peace of Europe more than her own aggrandisement. The standing danger which threatens the peace of Europe from the stormy corner of the old world, the Balkan Peninsula, must be finally removed. A fundamental agreement has been arrived at between the Powers concerned that the Russian and Austrian spheres of influence in the Balkans are to be defined in such a manner that a definite arrangement of affairs in the Balkan States will be the result. There is talk of an independent Kingdom of Macedonia, under the rule of an Austrian archduke. The equivalent to be given to the Russian Empire as a set-off to this increase of the power of Austria will have to be finally settled at the conference at the Hague. But in any case the dangers which threaten the peace of Europe from Bulgaria, Servia, and Montenegro will be effectually obviated for the future."

"But are you not afraid that the Sultan will resist such an agreement, by which Turkey is essentially the sufferer?"

"The Sultan will have to yield to the force of circumstances. We must not forget, Your Royal Highness, that Turkey has hitherto retained her European possessions more from the lack of unanimity among the great Powers than any consecrated rights of the Porte. The unceasing troubles in Macedonia have shown that the Sultan has neither the power nor the intention to give the Balkan countries under his rule a government corresponding to the demands of modern civilisation. If the Porte loses the support it has hitherto received from England, the Sultan is at the same time deprived of all possibility of serious resistance."

"And what is arranged about Egypt?"

"Egypt is the prize of victory for France; but only what she can justly claim on the ground of a glorious history will be restored to her. The sovereignty of the Sultan, which is a mere formality, will remain. But England's present position in Egypt--certainly with a definite limitation--will henceforth fall to France."

"And what is the limitation?"

"It will be administered, not by France alone, but by an international commission, appointed by all the Powers, under the presidency of France, in the place of the present English administration. The first condition is that England must cede all her financial claims and her Suez Canal shares to the allied Powers. These financial sacrifices will at the same time be part of the war indemnity which England will have to pay."

"Does France raise no further claims?"

"France is the more satisfied with the results of this war, since an annexation of Belgium to the French Republic is very probable. Germany, however, claims the harbour of Antwerp, which we have occupied since the beginning of the war."

"If I am correctly informed, was it not suggested that Aden should fall to France or be neutralised?"

"The idea was certainly mooted, but the allied Powers have decided to leave Aden to England. On the other hand, England will have to pledge herself to raise no obstacles which would render the construction and working of the Bagdad railway illusory. The harbour of Koweit on the Persian Gulf, the south-eastern terminus of this railway, must remain the uncontested possession of Turkey."

"And Gibraltar? It raised a storm of indignation in England, when the report suddenly spread that the cession of this fortress would be demanded."

"And yet the English Government will have to submit, for the surrender of Gibraltar is an indispensable condition on the part of the allies."

"It is impossible to rase this natural fortress."

"It would suffice if the English garrison were withdrawn, and all the fortifications dismantled. Gibraltar will cease to exist as a fortress, and will be restored to Spain on definite conditions. However, as it is not the intention of the allies completely to destroy English influence in the Levant, Malta will continue to form part of the British Empire. Thus England retains in the Mediterranean the most important point d'appui for her fleet."

"It will not be easy to get the English Government to accept these conditions. But you have not yet spoken of the demands of Germany--Antwerp does not touch England's interests directly."

"The policy of the German Government will culminate in ensuring settled commercial and political relations with England and her colonies and the rounding off of our own colonial possessions. We therefore demand Walfish Bay for German South-West Africa, the only good harbour, which, at the present time, being English, is closed to our young South African Colony. Besides this, we must insist upon the East African districts, which we gave up in exchange for Heligoland, being restored to us. This serious mistake in German policy must be rectified; for the abandonment of the Protectorate of Zanzibar to England was a blow, which not only paralysed the zeal of our best colonial friends, but also depreciated the value of our East African Colonies."

"If I understand you correctly, Your Excellency, your policy is directed towards setting Germany's colonial efforts on a firmer basis."

"I certainly regard this as one of the most important demands of our time. We must recover what the policy of the last centuries has lost by neglect. At the same time that Your Royal Highness's great ancestor waged war for seven years for a mere strip of land--for tiny Silesia, the far-seeing policy of England succeeded, at a smaller sacrifice, in getting possession of enormous tracts of territory far larger in their whole extent than the entire continent of Europe."

"But for centuries England has been a naval power, and obliged to direct her efforts to the acquisition of colonies over sea."

"And what was there to prevent Prussia, centuries ago, from becoming a naval power that should command respect? It was our misfortune that the mighty ideas and far-seeing plans of the great Elector were frustrated by the inadequate means at his disposal. Had his successors continued what he had begun, Great Britain's power would never have been able to reach such a height. We should have secured in time, in previous centuries, our due share of the parts of the world outside Europe."

The Prince looked thoughtfully before him. After a brief silence the Imperial Chancellor continued--

"Your Royal Highness may have heard that the Netherlands are firmly resolved, in the interest of self-preservation, to be incorporated with the German Empire as a federal state, like Bavaria, Saxony, Wurtemburg, Baden, and the other German states, after the Franco-German War. The rich and extensive Dutch colonies would then also become German colonies; that is to say, they would enter into the political union of the other German colonies while remaining under the administration of Holland. Our intention of repairing the wrong done by England to the Boers has made a very good impression on the Dutch population. The Boer states will enter into the same relation to us in which they stood to England before the Boer War, and their independence will be restored to them."

"Meaning self-government with the recognition of German supremacy. Certainly, they are kinsmen of the Dutch. But, my dear Baron, will not the German people be alarmed at the consequences of an extension of our possessions over sea? Larger colonial possessions necessitate a larger fleet. Think of the struggle which the allied Governments had to carry through Parliament even a modest increase in the German fleet!"

"I am not so much afraid of this difficulty, for the German people have learnt the value of the fleet. We have got beyond the tentative stage, and have paid enough for our experience. We must hold fast what we possess and recover what we have lost during the last decades through the unfortunately unbusiness-like spirit of our foreign policy. Then the German people will have renewed confidence in our colonial policy."

"But how will you raise the sums necessary to make our fleet strong and powerful?"

"Our negotiations with the friendly Governments of France and Russia are a proof that in these states, just as in the German people, there is a desire for a diminution of the land army; there is an equally strong feeling in Italy and Austria. The people would break down under the burden if the expenses for the army were increased, if we diminish our land army we shall have the means to increase our naval forces. Now, after a victorious war, the moment has come when the whole Continent can reduce its enormous standing armies to a footing commensurate with the financial capacities of its people. The external enemy is conquered; we must not think of conjuring up the internal enemy by laying excessive burdens on all classes."

"You spoke just now of the unbusiness-like spirit of our foreign policy. How is this reproach to be understood?"

"Quite literally, Your Royal Highness! The bargain which gave up Zanzibar to get Heligoland would never have been possible if our diplomacy had shown the same far-sightedness and intelligence as the English in economic questions, which I can only designate by the honourable title of a 'business-like spirit.' This business-like spirit is the mainspring of industry and agriculture, of trade and handicrafts, as of all industrial life generally, and it is necessary that this business-like spirit should also be recognised in our ministries as the necessary condition for the qualification to judge of the economic interests of the people. In this respect our statesmen and officials and our industrial classes can learn more from our vanquished enemy than in anything else. England owes her greatness to being 'a nation of shopkeepers,' while our economic development and our external influence has been hindered more than anything else by the contempt with which the industrial classes have been treated amongst us up to the most recent times. In England the merchant has always stood higher in the social scale than the officer and official. Amongst us he is looked upon almost as a second-class citizen compared with the other two. What in England is valued as only a means to an end is regarded by us as an end in itself. The spirit of that rigid bureaucracy, of which Prince Bismarck has already complained, is still unfortunately with few exceptions the prevailing spirit in our Empire, from the highest to the lowest circles; the lack of appreciation of the importance of economic life is the cause of the low esteem in which the industrial classes are held. The sound business-like spirit, which pervades all English state life, cuts the ground from under the feet of Social Democracy in England, while with us it is gaining ground year by year. I am convinced that our German people have no need to fear Social Democracy, for in reforming social cancers those who govern are of more importance than those who are governed."

"There may be much that is true in what you say, Herr Chancellor. But the extension of our colonial possessions will, first and foremost, benefit trade, and the merchant will naturally become of greater importance with us. There is already talk of great plantation societies to be started with enormous capital."

"It is just against the formation of these societies that I intend to exert my whole influence, Your Royal Highness. We could commit no more fatal error than to allow the state-privileged speculation in landed property, which has produced such unwholesome fruits in the old civilised states, to exist in our colonies. Real property must be no object of speculation, it must remain the property of the state. Agriculture belongs to the classes, who at the present time suffer most from economic depression. Nothing but an increase of the protective duties can preserve the agricultural population from the threatening danger of economic ruin. Increase of protective duty will bring with it increased profit, combined with a further increase in the value of land, which is also an article of traffic. Then the increase of land values will at the same time create an increase of the rents to be obtained from landed property, and for this reason I cannot help fearing that, in spite of an increase of protective duties, agriculture will have to suffer in the next generation from the further increase in the value of land and the higher rents that will be the result.

"In our colonies we must not fall into the same error that has produced the socialist question in modern civilised states. The earth belongs to those creatures who live on it and by it in accordance with a higher law than human imperfection has framed. Therefore the soil of our earth must be no object of traffic. Its growth is inseparable from that of the body of the state. I dare not hope that it will be allotted to me or my contemporaries to solve this question, yet I shall never tire of using all my influence to prevent at least a false agrarian policy in our young colonies. Injustice dies from its results, for injustice breeds its own avenger. Mankind committed a fatal wrong in permitting the land that supported them to become an object of speculation. This noxious seed brings noxious fruits to light. It must be the highest task of all governments to carry out land reform--the great problem that decides the destiny of a world--by all possible legislative measures. Now that, in all human probability, peace is assured, now that external dangers no longer threaten the existence of our Empire, there is nothing to exonerate us from the serious and sacred obligation to commence the greatest and most powerful work of reform that humanity can undertake. Then our path will lead us--from the conquest of nations to self-conquests."

At this moment the door of the room opened, and a royal messenger, introduced by the adjutant on duty, handed the Prince a letter decorated with the imperial crown and the initial of the imperial name.

The first glimmer of dawn entered the open window, and through the tops of the venerable trees of Hampton Court Park was heard a mysterious rustling and whispering, as if they were talking of the wonderful changes of fortune, of which they had been the mute witnesses since the remote days of their youth.

The blue eyes of the Hohenzollern Prince were shining proudly, while they scanned the imperial missive. For a few moments a deep silence prevailed. Then the Prince turned to the Imperial Chancellor--

"It will be a great day for us, Your Excellency! His Majesty the Emperor will enter London at the head of the allied armies. Peace is assured. God grant that it may be the last war which we shall have to wage for the future happiness of the German nation!"

The Codes Of Hammurabi And Moses
W. W. Davies

QTY

The discovery of the Hammurabi Code is one of the greatest achievements of archaeology, and is of paramount interest, not only to the student of the Bible, but also to all those interested in ancient history...

Religion   **ISBN:** *1-59462-338-4*   **Pages:132**

MSRP $12.95

The Theory of Moral Sentiments
Adam Smith

QTY

This work from 1749. contains original theories of conscience amd moral judgment and it is the foundation for systemof morals.

Philosophy **ISBN:** *1-59462-777-0*   **Pages:536**

MSRP $19.95

Jessica's First Prayer
Hesba Stretton

QTY

In a screened and secluded corner of one of the many railway-bridges which span the streets of London there could be seen a few years ago, from five o'clock every morning until half past eight, a tidily set-out coffee-stall, consisting of a trestle and board, upon which stood two large tin cans, with a small fire of charcoal burning under each so as to keep the coffee boiling during the early hours of the morning when the work-people were thronging into the city on their way to their daily toil...

Pages:84

Childrens **ISBN:** *1-59462-373-2*   *MSRP $9.95*

My Life and Work
Henry Ford

QTY

Henry Ford revolutionized the world with his implementation of mass production for the Model T automobile. Gain valuable business insight into his life and work with his own auto-biography... "We have only started on our development of our country we have not as yet, with all our talk of wonderful progress, done more than scratch the surface. The progress has been wonderful enough but..."

Pages:300

Biographies/ **ISBN:** *1-59462-198-5*   *MSRP $21.95*

The Art of Cross-Examination
Francis Wellman

QTY

I presume it is the experience of every author, after his first book is published upon an important subject, to be almost overwhelmed with a wealth of ideas and illustrations which could readily have been included in his book, and which to his own mind, at least, seem to make a second edition inevitable. Such certainly was the case with me; and when the first edition had reached its sixth impression in five months, I rejoiced to learn that it seemed to my publishers that the book had met with a sufficiently favorable reception to justify a second and considerably enlarged edition. ..

Reference   ISBN: *1-59462-647-2*

Pages:412

MSRP $19.95

On the Duty of Civil Disobedience
Henry David Thoreau

QTY

Thoreau wrote his famous essay, On the Duty of Civil Disobedience, as a protest against an unjust but popular war and the immoral but popular institution of slave-owning. He did more than write—he declined to pay his taxes, and was hauled off to gaol in consequence. Who can say how much this refusal of his hastened the end of the war and of slavery ?

Law   ISBN: *1-59462-747-9*

Pages:48

MSRP $7.45

Dream Psychology Psychoanalysis for Beginners
Sigmund Freud

QTY

Sigmund Freud, born Sigismund Schlomo Freud (May 6, 1856 - September 23, 1939), was a Jewish-Austrian neurologist and psychiatrist who co-founded the psychoanalytic school of psychology. Freud is best known for his theories of the unconscious mind, especially involving the mechanism of repression; his redefinition of sexual desire as mobile and directed towards a wide variety of objects; and his therapeutic techniques, especially his understanding of transference in the therapeutic relationship and the presumed value of dreams as sources of insight into unconscious desires.

Psychology   ISBN: *1-59462-905-6*

Pages:196

MSRP $15.45

The Miracle of Right Thought
Orison Swett Marden

QTY

Believe with all of your heart that you will do what you were made to do. When the mind has once formed the habit of holding cheerful, happy, prosperous pictures, it will not be easy to form the opposite habit. It does not matter how improbable or how far away this realization may see, or how dark the prospects may be, if we visualize them as best we can, as vividly as possible, hold tenaciously to them and vigorously struggle to attain them, they will gradually become actualized, realized in the life. But a desire, a longing without endeavor, a yearning abandoned or held indifferently will vanish without realization.

Self Help   ISBN: *1-59462-644-8*

Pages:360

MSRP $25.45

QTY

The Rosicrucian Cosmo-Conception Mystic Christianity *by Max Heindel*   ISBN: *1-59462-188-8*   **$38.95**
The Rosicrucian Cosmo-conception is not dogmatic, neither does it appeal to any other authority than the reason of the student. It is: not controversial, but is: sent forth in the, hope that it may help to clear..   New Age/Religion Pages 646

Abandonment To Divine Providence *by Jean-Pierre de Caussade*   ISBN: *1-59462-228-0*   **$25.95**
"The Rev. Jean Pierre de Caussade was one of the most remarkable spiritual writers of the Society of Jesus in France in the 18th Century. His death took place at Toulouse in 1751. His works have gone through many editions and have been republished...   Inspirational/Religion Pages 400

Mental Chemistry *by Charles Haanel*   ISBN: *1-59462-192-6*   **$23.95**
Mental Chemistry allows the change of material conditions by combining and appropriately utilizing the power of the mind. Much like applied chemistry creates something new and unique out of careful combinations of chemicals the mastery of mental chemistry...   New Age Pages 354

The Letters of Robert Browning and Elizabeth Barret Barrett 1845-1846 vol II   ISBN: *1-59462-193-4*   **$35.95**
by Robert Browning and Elizabeth Barrett   Biographies Pages 596

Gleanings In Genesis (volume I) *by Arthur W. Pink*   ISBN: *1-59462-130-6*   **$27.45**
Appropriately has Genesis been termed "the seed plot of the Bible" for in it we have, in germ form, almost all of the great doctrines which are afterwards fully developed in the books of Scripture which follow...   Religion/Inspirational Pages 420

The Master Key *by L. W. de Laurence*   ISBN: *1-59462-001-6*   **$30.95**
In no branch of human knowledge has there been a more lively increase of the spirit of research during the past few years than in the study of Psychology, Concentration and Mental Discipline. The requests for authentic lessons in Thought Control, Mental Discipline and...   New Age/Business Pages 422

The Lesser Key Of Solomon Goetia *by L. W. de Laurence*   ISBN: *1-59462-092-X*   **$9.95**
This translation of the first book of the "Lemegton" which is now for the first time made accessible to students of Talismanic Magic was done, after careful collation and edition, from numerous Ancient Manuscripts in Hebrew, Latin, and French...   New Age/Occult Pages 92

Rubaiyat Of Omar Khayyam *by Edward Fitzgerald*   ISBN:*1-59462-332-5*   **$13.95**
Edward Fitzgerald, whom the world has already learned, in spite of his own efforts to remain within the shadow of anonymity, to look upon as one of the rarest poets of the century, was born at Bredfield, in Suffolk, on the 31st of March, 1809. He was the third son of John Purcell...   Music Pages 172

Ancient Law *by Henry Maine*   ISBN: *1-59462-128-4*   **$29.95**
The chief object of the following pages is to indicate some of the earliest ideas of mankind, as they are reflected in Ancient Law, and to point out the relation of those ideas to modern thought.   Religion/History Pages 452

Far-Away Stories *by William J. Locke*   ISBN: *1-59462-129-2*   **$19.45**
"Good wine needs no bush, but a collection of mixed vintages does. And this book is just such a collection. Some of the stories I do not want to remain buried for ever in the museum files of dead magazine-numbers an author's not unpardonable vanity..."   Fiction Pages 272

Life of David Crockett *by David Crockett*   ISBN: *1-59462-250-7*   **$27.45**
"Colonel David Crockett was one of the most remarkable men of the times in which he lived. Born in humble life, but gifted with a strong will, an indomitable courage, and unremitting perseverance...   Biographies/New Age Pages 424

Lip-Reading *by Edward Nitchie*   ISBN: *1-59462-206-X*   **$25.95**
Edward B. Nitchie, founder of the New York School for the Hard of Hearing, now the Nitchie School of Lip-Reading, Inc, wrote "LIP-READING Principles and Practice". The development and perfecting of this meritorious work on lip-reading was an undertaking...   How-to Pages 400

A Handbook of Suggestive Therapeutics, Applied Hypnotism, Psychic Science   ISBN: *1-59462-214-0*   **$24.95**
by Henry Munro   Health/New Age/Health/Self-help Pages 376

A Doll's House: and Two Other Plays *by Henrik Ibsen*   ISBN: *1-59462-112-8*   **$19.95**
Henrik Ibsen created this classic when in revolutionary 1848 Rome. Introducing some striking concepts in playwriting for the realist genre, this play has been studied the world over.   Fiction/Classics/Plays 308

The Light of Asia *by sir Edwin Arnold*   ISBN: *1-59462-204-3*   **$13.95**
In this poetic masterpiece, Edwin Arnold describes the life and teachings of Buddha. The man who was to become known as Buddha to the world was born as Prince Gautama of India but he rejected the worldly riches and abandoned the reigns of power when...   Religion/History/Biographies Pages 170

The Complete Works of Guy de Maupassant *by Guy de Maupassant*   ISBN: *1-59462-157-8*   **$16.95**
"For days and days, nights and nights, I had dreamed of that first kiss which was to consecrate our engagement, and I knew not on what spot I should put my lips..."   Fiction/Classics Pages 240

The Art of Cross-Examination *by Francis L. Wellman*   ISBN: *1-59462-309-0*   **$26.95**
Written by a renowned trial lawyer, Wellman imparts his experience and uses case studies to explain how to use psychology to extract desired information through questioning.   How-to/Science/Reference Pages 408

Answered or Unanswered? *by Louisa Vaughan*   ISBN: *1-59462-248-5*   **$10.95**
Miracles of Faith in China   Religion Pages 112

The Edinburgh Lectures on Mental Science (1909) *by Thomas*   ISBN: *1-59462-008-3*   **$11.95**
This book contains the substance of a course of lectures recently given by the writer in the Queen Street Hall, Edinburgh. Its purpose is to indicate the Natural Principles governing the relation between Mental Action and Material Conditions...   New Age/Psychology Pages 148

Ayesha *by H. Rider Haggard*   ISBN: *1-59462-301-5*   **$24.95**
Verily and indeed it is the unexpected that happens! Probably if there was one person upon the earth from whom the Editor of this, and of a certain previous history, did not expect to hear again...   Classics Pages 380

Ayala's Angel *by Anthony Trollope*   ISBN: *1-59462-352-X*   **$29.95**
The two girls were both pretty, but Lucy who was twenty-one who supposed to be simple and comparatively unattractive, whereas Ayala was credited, as her Bombwhat romantic name might show, with poetic charm and a taste for romance. Ayala when her father died was nineteen...   Fiction Pages 484

The American Commonwealth *by James Bryce*   ISBN: *1-59462-286-8*   **$34.45**
An interpretation of American democratic political theory. It examines political mechanics and society from the perspective of Scotsman James Bryce   Politics Pages 572

Stories of the Pilgrims *by Margaret P. Pumphrey*   ISBN: *1-59462-116-0*   **$17.95**
This book explores pilgrims religious oppression in England as well as their escape to Holland and eventual crossing to America on the Mayflower, and their early days in New England...   History Pages 268

QTY

The Fasting Cure *by Sinclair Upton*   ISBN: *1-59462-222-1* **$13.95**
In the Cosmopolitan Magazine for May, 1910, and in the Contemporary Review (London) for April, 1910, I published an article dealing with my experiences in fasting. I have written a great many magazine articles, but never one which attracted so much attention... New Age/Self Help/Health Pages 164

Hebrew Astrology *by Sepharial*   ISBN: *1-59462-308-2* **$13.45**
In these days of advanced thinking it is a matter of common observation that we have left many of the old landmarks behind and that we are now pressing forward to greater heights and to a wider horizon than that which represented the mind-content of our progenitors... Astrology Pages 144

Thought Vibration or The Law of Attraction in the Thought World   ISBN: *1-59462-127-6* **$12.95**
by William Walker Atkinson   *Psychology/Religion Pages 144*

Optimism *by Helen Keller*   ISBN: *1-59462-108-X* **$15.95**
Helen Keller was blind, deaf, and mute since 19 months old, yet famously learned how to overcome these handicaps, communicate with the world, and spread her lectures promoting optimism. An inspiring read for everyone... Biographies/Inspirational Pages 84

Sara Crewe *by Frances Burnett*   ISBN: *1-59462-360-0* **$9.45**
In the first place, Miss Minchin lived in London. Her home was a large, dull, tall one, in a large, dull square, where all the houses were alike, and all the sparrows were alike, and where all the door-knockers made the same heavy sound... Childrens/Classic Pages 88

The Autobiography of Benjamin Franklin *by Benjamin Franklin*   ISBN: *1-59462-135-7* **$24.95**
The Autobiography of Benjamin Franklin has probably been more extensively read than any other American historical work, and no other book of its kind has had such ups and downs of fortune. Franklin lived for many years in England, where he was agent... Biographies/History Pages 332

Name	
Email	
Telephone	
Address	
City, State ZIP	

☐ **Credit Card**   ☐ **Check / Money Order**

Credit Card Number	
Expiration Date	
Signature	

Please Mail to: Book Jungle
                    PO Box 2226
                    Champaign, IL 61825
or Fax to: *630-214-0564*

ORDERING INFORMATION

web: *www.bookjungle.com*
email: *sales@bookjungle.com*
fax: *630-214-0564*
mail: *Book Jungle PO Box 2226 Champaign, IL 61825*
or PayPal *to sales@bookjungle.com*

Please contact us for bulk discounts

DIRECT-ORDER TERMS

**20% Discount if You Order
Two or More Books**
Free Domestic Shipping!
Accepted: Master Card, Visa,
Discover, American Express

www.ingramcontent.com/pod-product-compliance
Lightning Source LLC
Chambersburg PA
CBHW080953020726

47505CB00009B/2187